A Short Story Collection by Leo Tolstoy

Count Lev Nikolayevich Tolstoy was born on September 9th 1828 into Russian nobility but abandoned his title and through his interpretation of the ethical teachings of Jesus became a fervent Christian anarchist and pacifist. His writings on non-violence were to have a profound impact on Gandhi and Martin Luther King. His reputation for many people is based on the epic, in length and scope, of his novel 'War & Peace'. For that alone Tolstoy would be widely considered to be one of the greatest novelists of all time. But such was the breadth of his talents that he was consummate at short stories, essays and plays. Here we publish a collection of his brilliant short stories includ ng such gems as God Sees The Truth, But Waits, Ivan The Fool, Master and Man, What Men Live By and The Young Tsar.

Leo Tolstoy died acclaimed and admired throughout the world on November 20th 1910.

Index Of Stories

After the Dance

"And you say that a man cannot, of himself, understand what is good and evil; that it is all environment, that the environment swamps the man. But I believe it is all chance. Take my own case . . ."

Thus spoke our excellent friend, Ivan Vasilievich, after a conversation between us on the impossibility of improving individual character without a change of the conditions under which men live. Nobody had actually said that one could not of oneself understand good and evil; but it was a habit of Ivan Vasilievich to answer in this way the thoughts aroused in his own mind by conversation, and to illustrate those thoughts by relating incidents in his own life. He often quite forgot the reason for his story in telling it; but he always told it with great sincerity and feeling.
He did so now.

"Take my own case. My whole life was moulded, not by environment, but by something quite different."

"By what, then?" we asked.

"Oh, that is a long story. I should have to tell you about a great many things to make you understand."

"Well, tell us then."

Ivan Vasilievich thought a little, and shook his head.

"My whole life," he said, "was changed in one night, or, rather, morning."

"Why, what happened?" one of us asked.

"What happened was that I was very much in love. I have been in love many times, but this was the most serious of all. It is a thing of the past; she has married daughters now. It was Varinka B----." Ivan Vasilievich mentioned her surname. "Even at fifty she is remarkably handsome; but in her youth, at eighteen, she was exquisite, tall, slender, graceful, and stately. Yes, stately is the word; she held herself very erect, by instinct as it were; and carried her head high, and that together with her beauty and height gave her a queenly air in spite of being thin, even bony one might say. It might indeed have been deterring had it not been for her smile, which was always gay and cordial, and for the charming light in her eyes and for her youthful sweetness."

"What an entrancing description you give, Ivan Vasilievich!"

"Description, indeed! I could not possibly describe her so that you could appreciate her. But that does not matter; what I am going to tell you happened in the forties. I was at that time a student in a provincial university. I don't know whether it was a good thing or no, but we had no political clubs, no theories in our universities then. We were simply young and spent our time as young men do, studying and amusing ourselves. I was a very gay, lively, careless fellow, and had plenty of money too. I had a fine horse, and used to go tobogganing with the young ladies. Skating had not yet come into fashion. I went to drinking parties with my comrades, in those days we drank nothing but champagne, if we had no champagne we drank nothing at all. We never drank vodka, as they do now. Evening parties and balls were my favourite amusements. I danced well, and was not an ugly fellow."

"Come, there is no need to be modest," interrupted a lady near him. "We have seen your photograph. Not ugly, indeed! You were a handsome fellow."

"Handsome, if you like. That does not matter. When my love for her was at its strongest, on the last day of the carnival, I was at a ball at the provincial marshal's, a good-natured old man, rich and hospitable, and a court chamberlain. The guests were welcomed by his wife, who was as good-natured as himself. She was dressed in puce-coloured velvet, and had a diamond diadem on her forehead, and her plump, old white shoulders and bosom were bare like the portraits of Empress Elizabeth, the daughter of Peter the Great.

"It was a delightful ball. It was a splendid room, with a gallery for the orchestra, which was famous at the time, and consisted of serfs belonging to a musical landowner. The refreshments were magnificent, and the champagne flowed in rivers. Though I was fond of champagne I did not drink that night, because without it I was drunk with love. But I made up for it by dancing waltzes and polkas till I was ready to drop of course, whenever possible, with Varinka. She wore a white dress with a pink sash, white shoes, and white kid gloves, which did not quite reach to her thin pointed elbows. A disgusting engineer named Anisimov robbed me of the mazurka with her, to this day I cannot forgive him. He asked her for the dance the minute she arrived, while I had driven to the hair-dresser's to get a pair of gloves, and was late. So I did not dance the mazurka with her, but with a German girl to whom I had previously paid a little attention; but I am afraid I did not behave very politely to her that evening. I hardly spoke or looked at her, and saw nothing but the tall, slender figure in a white dress, with a pink sash, a flushed, beaming, dimpled face, and sweet, kind eyes. I was not alone; they were all looking at her with admiration, the men and women alike, although she outshone all of them. They could not help admiring her.

"Although I was not nominally her partner for the mazurka, I did as a matter of fact dance nearly the whole time with her. She always came forward boldly the whole length of the room to pick me out. I flew to meet her without waiting to be chosen, and she thanked me with a smile for my intuition. When I was brought up to her with somebody else, and she guessed wrongly, she took the other man's hand with a shrug of her slim shoulders, and smiled at me regretfully.

"Whenever there was a waltz figure in the mazurka, I waltzed with her for a long time, and breathing fast and smiling, she would say, 'Encore'; and I went on waltzing and waltzing, as though unconscious of any bodily existence."

"Come now, how could you be unconscious of it with your arm round her waist? You must have been conscious, not only of your own existence, but of hers," said one of the party.

Ivan Vasilievich cried out, almost shouting in anger: "There you are, moderns all over! Nowadays you think of nothing but the body. It was different in our day. The more I was in love the less corporeal was she in my eyes. Nowadays you think of nothing but the body. It was different in our day. The more I was in love the less corporeal was she in my eyes. Nowadays you set legs, ankles, and I don't know what. You undress the women you are in love with. In my eyes, as Alphonse Karr said and he was a good writer' the one I loved was always draped in robes of bronze.' We never thought of doing so; we tried to veil her nakedness, like Noah's good-natured son. Oh, well, you can't understand."

"Don't pay any attention to him. Go on," said one of them.

"Well, I danced for the most part with her, and did not notice how time was passing. The musicians kept playing the same mazurka tunes over and over again in desperate exhaustion, you know what it is towards the end of a ball. Papas and mammas were already getting up from the card-tables in the drawing-room in expectation of supper, the men-servants were running to and fro bringing in things. It was nearly three o'clock. I had to make the most of the last minutes. I chose her again for the mazurka, and for the hundredth time we danced across the room.

"'The quadrille after supper is mine,' I said, taking her to her place.

"'Of course, if I am not carried off home,' she said, with a smile.

"'I won't give you up,' I said.

"'Give me my fan, anyhow,' she answered.

"'I am so sorry to part with it,' I said, handing her a cheap white fan.

"'Well, here's something to console you,' she said, plucking a feather out of the fan, and giving it to me.

"I took the feather, and could only express my rapture and gratitude with my eyes. I was not only pleased and gay, I was happy, delighted; I was good, I was not myself but some being not of this earth, knowing nothing of evil. I hid the feather in my glove, and stood there unable to tear myself away from her.

"'Look, they are urging father to dance,' she said to me, pointing to the tall, stately figure of her father, a colonel with silver epaulettes, who was standing in the doorway with some ladies.

"'Varinka, come here!' exclaimed our hostess, the lady with the diamond ferronniere and with shoulders like Elizabeth, in a loud voice.

"'Varinka went to the door, and I followed her.

"'Persuade your father to dance the mazurka with you, ma chere. Do, please, Peter Valdislavovich,' she said, turning to the colonel.

"Varinka's father was a very handsome, well-preserved old man. He had a good colour, moustaches curled in the style of Nicolas I., and white whiskers which met the moustaches. His hair was combed on to his forehead, and a bright smile, like his daughter's, was on his lips and in his eyes. He was splendidly set up, with a broad military chest, on which he wore some decorations, and he had powerful shoulders and long slim legs. He was that ultra-military type produced by the discipline of Emperor Nicolas I.

"When we approached the door the colonel was just refusing to dance, saying that he had quite forgotten how; but at that instant he smiled, swung his arm gracefully around to the left, drew his sword from its sheath, handed it to an obliging young man who stood near, and smoothed his suede glove on his right hand.

"'Everything must be done according to rule,' he said with a smile. He took the hand of his daughter, and stood one-quarter turned, waiting for the music.

"At the first sound of the mazurka, he stamped one foot smartly, threw the other forward, and, at first slowly and smoothly, then buoyantly and impetuously, with stamping of feet and clicking of boots, his tall, imposing figure moved the length of the room. Varinka swayed gracefully beside him, rhythmically and easily, making her steps short or long, with her little feet in their white satin slippers.
"All the people in the room followed every movement of the couple. As for me I not only admired, I regarded them with enraptured sympathy. I was particularly impressed with the old gentleman's boots. They were not the modern pointed affairs, but were made of cheap leather, squared-toed, and evidently built by the regimental cobbler. In order that his daughter might dress and go out in society, he did not buy fashionable boots, but wore home-made ones, I thought, and his square toes seemed to me most touching. It was obvious that in his time he had been a good dancer; but now he was too heavy, and his legs had not spring enough for all the beautiful steps he tried to take. Still, he contrived to go twice round the room. When at the end, standing with legs apart, he suddenly clicked his feet together and fell on one knee, a bit heavily, and she danced gracefully around him, smiling and adjusting her skirt, the whole room applauded.

"Rising with an effort, he tenderly took his daughter's face between his hands. He kissed her on the forehead, and brought her to me, under the impression that I was her partner for the mazurka.   said I was not. 'Well, never mind. just go around the room once with her,' he said, smiling kindly, as he replaced his sword in the sheath.

"As the contents of a bottle flow readily when the first drop has been poured, so my love for Varinka seemed to set free the whole force of loving within me. In surrounding her it embraced the world. I loved the hostess with her diadem and her shoulders like Elizabeth, and her husband and her guests and her footmen, and even the engineer Anisimov who felt peevish towards me. As for Varinka's father, with his home-made boots and his kind smile, so like her own, I felt a sort of tenderness for him that was almost rapture.
"After supper I danced the promised quadrille with her, and though I had been infinitely happy before, I grew still happier every moment.

"We did not speak of love. I neither asked myself nor her whether she loved me. It was quite enough to know that I loved her. And I had only one fear, that something might come to interfere with my great joy.

"When I went home, and began to undress for the night, I found it quite out of the question. held the little feather out of her fan in my hand, and one of her gloves which she gave me when I helped her into the carriage after her mother. Looking at these things, and without closing my eyes I could see her before me as she was for an instant when she had to choose between two partners. She tried to guess what kind of person was represented in me, and I could hear her sweet voice as she said, 'Pride, am I right?' and merrily gave me her hand. At supper she took the first sip from my glass of champagne, looking at me over the rim with her caressing glance. But, plainest of all, I could see her as she danced with her father, gliding along beside him, and looking at the admiring observers with pride and happiness.

"He and she were united in my mind in one rush of pathetic tenderness.

"I was living then with my brother, who has since died. He disliked going out, and never went to dances; and besides, he was busy preparing for his last university examinations, and was leading a very regular life. He was asleep. I looked at him, his head buried in the pillow and half covered with the quilt; and I affectionately pitied him, pitied him for his ignorance of the bliss I was experiencing. Our serf Petrusha had met me with a candle, ready to undress me, but I sent him away. His sleepy face and tousled hair seemed to me so touching. Trying not to make a noise, I went to my room on tiptoe and sat down on my bed. No, I was too happy; I could not sleep. Besides, it was too hot in the rooms. Without taking off my uniform, I went quietly into the hall, put on my overcoat, opened the front door and stepped out into the street.
"It was after four when I had left the ball; going home and stopping there a while had occupied two hours, so by the time I went out it was dawn. It was regular carnival weather, foggy, and the road full of water-soaked snow just melting, and water dripping from the eaves. Varinka's family lived on the edge of town near a large field, one end of which was a parade ground: at the other end was a boarding-school for young ladies. I passed through our empty little street and came to the main thoroughfare, where I met pedestrians and sledges laden with wood, the runners grating the road. The horses swung with regular paces beneath their shining yokes, their backs covered with straw mats and their heads wet with rain; while the drivers, in enormous boots, splashed through the mud beside the sledges. All this, the very horses themselves, seemed to me stimulating and fascinating, full of suggestion.

"When I approached the field near their house, I saw at one end of it, in the direction of the parade ground, something very huge and black, and I heard sounds of fife and drum proceeding from it. My heart had been full of song, and I had heard in imagination the tune of the mazurka, but this was very harsh music. It was not pleasant.

"'What can that be?' I thought, and went towards the sound by a slippery path through the centre of the field. Walking about a hundred paces, I began to distinguish many black objects through the mist. They were evidently soldiers. 'It is probably a drill,' I thought.

"So I went along in that direction in company with a blacksmith, who wore a dirty coat and an apron, and was carrying something. He walked ahead of me as we approached the place. The soldiers in black uniforms stood in two rows, facing each other motionless, their guns at rest. Behind them stood the fifes and drums, incessantly repeating the same unpleasant tune.

"'What are they doing?' I asked the blacksmith, who halted at my side.

"'A Tartar is being beaten through the ranks for his attempt to desert,' said the blacksmith in an angry tone, as he looked intently at the far end of the line.

"I looked in the same direction, and saw between the files something horrid approaching me. The thing that approached was a man, stripped to the waist, fastened with cords to the guns of two soldiers who were leading him. At his side an officer in overcoat and cap was walking, whose figure had a familiar look. The victim advanced under the blows that rained upon him from both sides, his whole body plunging, his feet dragging through the snow. Now he threw himself backward, and the subalterns who led him thrust him forward. Now he fell forward, and they pulled him up short; while ever at his side marched the tall officer, with firm and nervous pace. It was Varinka's father, with his rosy face and white moustache.

"At each stroke the man, as if amazed, turned his face, grimacing with pain, towards the side whence the blow came, and showing his white teeth repeated the same words over and over. But I could only hear what the words were when he came quite near. He did not speak them, he sobbed them out, "'Brothers, have mercy on me! Brothers, have mercy on me!' But the brothers had, no mercy, and when the procession came close to me, I saw how a soldier who stood opposite me took a firm step forward and lifting his stick with a whirr, brought it down upon the man's back. The man plunged forward, but the subalterns pulled him back, and another blow came down from the other side, then from this side and then from the other. The colonel marched beside him, and looking now at his feet and now at the man, inhaled the air, puffed out his cheeks, and breathed it out between his protruded lips. When they passed the place where I stood, I caught a glimpse between the two files of the back of the man that was being punished. It was something so many-coloured, wet, red, unnatural, that I could hardly believe it was a human body.

"'My God!'" muttered the blacksmith.

The procession moved farther away. The blows continued to rain upon the writhing, falling creature; the fifes shrilled and the drums beat, and the tall imposing figure of the colonel moved along-side the man, just as before. Then, suddenly, the colonel stopped, and rapidly approached a man in the ranks.

"'I'll teach you to hit him gently,' I heard his furious voice say. 'Will you pat him like that? Will you?' and I saw how his strong hand in the suede glove struck the weak, bloodless, terrified soldier for not bringing down his stick with sufficient strength on the red neck of the Tartar.

"'Bring new sticks!' he cried, and looking round, he saw me. Assuming an air of not knowing me, and with a ferocious, angry frown, he hastily turned away. I felt so utterly ashamed that I didn't know where to look. It was as if I had been detected in a disgraceful act. I dropped my eyes, and quickly hurried home. All the way I had the drums beating and the fifes whistling in my ears. And I heard the words, 'Brothers, have mercy on me!' or 'Will you pat him? Will you?' My heart was full of physical disgust that was almost sickness. So much so that I halted several times on my way, for I had the feeling that I was going to be really sick from all the horrors that possessed me at that sight. I do not remember how I got home and got to bed. But the moment I was about to fall asleep I heard and saw again all that had happened, and I sprang up.

"'Evidently he knows something I do not know,' I thought about the colonel. 'If I knew what he knows I should certainly grasp, understand, what I have just seen, and it would not cause me such suffering.'

"But however much I thought about it, I could not understand the thing that the colonel knew. It was evening before I could get to sleep, and then only after calling on a friend and drinking till I; was quite drunk.

"Do you think I had come to the conclusion that the deed I had witnessed was wicked? Oh, no. Since it was done with such assurance, and was recognised by every one as indispensable, they doubtless knew something which I did not know. So thought, and tried to understand. But no matter, I could never understand it, then or afterwards. And not being able to grasp it, I could not enter the service as I had intended. I don't mean only the military service: I did not enter the Civil Service either. And so I have been of no use whatever, as you can see."

"Yes, we know how useless you've been," said one of us. "Tell us, rather, how many people would be of any use at all if it hadn't been for you."

"Oh, that's utter nonsense," said Ivan Vasilievich, with genuine annoyance.

"Well; and what about the love affair?

"My love? It decreased from that day. When, as often happened, she looked dreamy and meditative, I instantly recollected the colonel on the parade ground, and I felt so awkward and uncomfortable that I began to see her less frequently. So my love came to naught. Yes; such chances arise, and they alter and direct a man's whole life," he said in summing up. "And you say . . ."

Alyosha the Pot

Alyosha was the younger brother. He was called the Pot, because his mother had once sent him with a pot of milk to the deacon's wife, and he had stumbled against something and broken it. His mother had beaten him, and the children had teased him. Since then he was nicknamed the Pot. Alyosha was a tiny, thin little fellow, with ears like wings, and a huge nose. "Alyosha has a nose that looks like a dog on a hill!" the children used to call after him. Alyosha went to the village school, but was not good at lessons; besides, there was so little time to learn. His elder brother was in town, working for a merchant, so Alyosha had to help his father from a very early age. When he was no more than six he used to go out with the girls to watch the cows and sheep in the pasture, and a little later he looked after the horses by day and by night. And at twelve years of age he had already begun to plough and to drive the cart. The skill was there though the strength was not. He was always cheerful. Whenever the children made fun of him, he would either laugh or be silent. When his father scolded him he would stand mute and listen attentively, and as soon as the scolding was over would smile and go on with his work. Alyosha was nineteen when his brother was taken as a soldier. So his father placed him with the merchant as a yard-porter. He was given his brother's old boots, his father's old coat and cap, and was taken to town. Alyosha was delighted with his clothes, but the merchant was not impressed by his appearance.

"I thought you would bring me a man in Simeon's place," he said, scanning Alyosha; "and you've brought me THIS! What's the good of him?"

"He can do everything; look after horses and drive. He's a good one to work. He looks rather thin, but he's tough enough. And he's very willing."

"He looks it. All right; we'll see what we can do with him."

So Alyosha remained at the merchant's.

The family was not a large one. It consisted of the merchant's wife: her old mother: a married son poorly educated who was in his father's business: another son, a learned one who had finished school and entered the University, but having been expelled, was living at home: and a daughter who still went to school.

They did not take to Alyosha at first. He was uncouth, badly dressed, and had no manner, but they soon got used to him. Alyosha worked even better than his brother had done; he was really very willing. They sent him on all sorts of errands, but he did everything quickly and readily, going from one task to another without stopping. And so here, just as at home, all the work was put upon his shoulders. The more he did, the more he was given to do. His mistress, her old mother, the son, the daughter, the clerk, and the cook, all ordered him about, and sent him from one place to another.

"Alyosha, do this! Alyosha, do that! What! have you forgotten, Alyosha? Mind you don't forget, Alyosha!" was heard from morning till night. And Alyosha ran here, looked after this and that, forgot nothing, found time for everything, and was always cheerful.

His brother's old boots were soon worn out, and his master scolded him for going about in tatters with his toes sticking out. He ordered another pair to be bought for him in the market. Alyosha was delighted with his new boots, but was angry with his feet when they ached at the end of the day after so much running about. And then he was afraid that his father would be annoyed when he came to town for his wages, to find that his master had deducted the cost of the boots.

In the winter Alyosha used to get up before daybreak. He would chop the wood, sweep the yard, feed the cows and horses, light the stoves, clean the boots, prepare the samovars and polish them afterwards; or the clerk would get him to bring up the goods; or the cook would set him to knead the bread and clean the saucepans. Then he was sent to town on various errands, to bring the daughter home from school, or to get some olive oil for the old mother. "Why the devil have you been so long?" first one, then another, would say to him. Why should they go? Alyosha can go. "Alyosha! Alyosha!" And Alyosha ran here and there. He breakfasted in snatches while he was working, and rarely managed to get his dinner at the proper hour. The cook used to scold him for being late, but she was sorry for him all the same, and would keep something hot for his dinner and supper.

At holiday times there was more work than ever, but Alyosha liked holidays because everybody gave him a tip. Not much certainly, but it would amount up to about sixty kopeks [1s 2d] his very own money. For Alyosha never set eyes on his wages. His father used to come and take them from the merchant, and only scold Alyosha for wearing out his boots.

When he had saved up two roubles [4s], by the advice of the cook he bought himself a red knitted jacket, and was so happy when he put it on, that he couldn't close his mouth for joy. Alyosha was not talkative; when he spoke at all, he spoke abruptly, with his head turned away. When told to do anything, or asked if he could do it, he would say yes without the smallest hesitation, and set to work at once.

Alyosha did not know any prayer; and had forgotten what his mother had taught him. But he prayed just the same, every morning and every evening, prayed with his hands, crossing himself.

He lived like this for about a year and a half, and towards the end of the second year a most startling thing happened to him. He discovered one day, to his great surprise, that, in addition to the relation of usefulness existing between people, there was also another, a peculiar relation of quite a different character. Instead of a man being wanted to clean boots, and go on errands and harness horses, he is not wanted to be of any service at all, but another human being wants to serve him and pet him. Suddenly Alyosha felt he was such a man.

He made this discovery through the cook Ustinia. She was young, had no parents, and worked as hard as Alyosha. He felt for the first time in his life that he, not his services, but he himself, was necessary to another human being. When his mother used to be sorry for him, he had taken no notice of her. It had seemed to him quite natural, as though he were feeling sorry for himself. But here was Ustinia, a perfect stranger, and sorry for him. She would save him some hot porridge, and sit watching him, her chin propped on her bare arm, with the sleeve rolled up, while he was eating it. When he looked at her she would begin to laugh, and he would laugh too.

This was such a new, strange thing to him that it frightened Alyosha. He feared that it might interfere with his work. But he was pleased, nevertheless, and when he glanced at the trousers that Ustinia had mended for him, he would shake his head and smile. He would often think of her while at work, or when running on errands. "A fine girl, Ustinia!" he sometimes exclaimed.

Ustinia used to help him whenever she could, and he helped her. She told him all about her life; how she had lost her parents; how her aunt had taken her in and found a place for her in the town; how the merchant's son had tried to take liberties with her, and how she had rebuffed him. She liked to talk, and Alyosha liked to listen to her. He had heard that peasants who came up to work in the towns frequently got married to servant girls. On one occasion she asked him if his parents intended marrying him soon. He said that he did not know; that he did not want to marry any of the village girls.

"Have you taken a fancy to some one, then?"

"I would marry you, if you'd be willing."

"Get along with you, Alyosha the Pot; but you've found your tongue, haven't you?" she exclaimed, slapping him on the back with a towel she held in her hand. "Why shouldn't I?"

At Shrovetide Alyosha's father came to town for his wages. It had come to the ears of the merchant's wife that Alyosha wanted to marry Ustinia, and she disapproved of it. "What will be the use of her with a baby?" she thought, and informed her husband.

The merchant gave the old man Alyosha's wages.

"How is my lad getting on?" he asked. "I told you he was willing."

"That's all right, as far as it goes, but he's taken some sort of nonsense into his head. He wants to marry our cook. Now I don't approve of married servants. We won't have them in the house."

"Well, now, who would have thought the fool would think of such a thing?" the old man exclaimed. "But don't you worry. I'll soon settle that."

He went into the kitchen, and sat down at the table waiting for his son. Alyosha was out on an errand, and came back breathless.

"I thought you had some sense in you; but what's this you've taken into your head?" his father began.

"I? Nothing."

"How, nothing? They tell me you want to get married. You shall get married when the time comes. I'll find you a decent wife, not some town hussy."

His father talked and talked, while Alyosha stood still and sighed. When his father had quite finished, Alyosha smiled.

"All right. I'll drop it."

"Now that's what I call sense."

When he was left alone with Ustinia he told her what his father had said. (She had listened at the door.)

"It's no good; it can't come off. Did you hear? He was angry, won't have it at any price."

Ustinia cried into her apron.

Alyosha shook his head.

"What's to be done? We must do as we're told."

"Well, are you going to give up that nonsense, as your father told you?" his mistress asked, as he was putting up the shutters in the evening.

"To be sure we are," Alyosha replied with a smile, and then burst into tears.

From that day Alyosha went about his work as usual, and no longer talked to Ustinia about their getting married. One day in Lent the clerk told him to clear the snow from the roof. Alyosha climbed on to the roof and swept away all the snow; and, while he was still raking out some frozen lumps from the gutter, his foot slipped and he fell over. Unfortunately he did not fall on the snow, but on a piece of iron over the door. Ustinia came running up, together with the merchant's daughter.

"Have you hurt yourself, Alyosha?"

"Ah! no, it's nothing."

But he could not raise himself when he tried to, and began to smile.

He was taken into the lodge. The doctor arrived, examined him, and asked where he felt the pain.

"I feel it all over," he said. "But it doesn't matter. I'm only afraid master will be annoyed. Father ought to be told."

Alyosha lay in bed for two days, and on the third day they sent for the priest.

"Are you really going to die?" Ustinia asked.

"Of course I am. You can't go on living for ever. You must go when the time comes." Alyosha spoke rapidly as usual. "Thank you, Ustinia. You've been very good to me. What a lucky thing they didn t let us marry! Where should we have been now? It's much better as it is."

When the priest came, he prayed with his bands and with his heart. "As it is good here when you obey and do no harm to others, so it will be there," was the thought within it.

He spoke very little; he only said he was thirsty, and he seemed full of wonder at something.

He lay in wonderment, then stretched himself, and died.

The Bird

It was Serozha's birthday, and he received many different gifts; peg tops, and hobby horses, and pictures. But Serozha's uncle gave him a gift that he prized above all the rest; it was a trap for snaring birds.

The trap was constructed in such a way that a board was fitted on the frame and shut down upon the top. If seed was scattered on the board, and the trap was put out in the yard, the little bird would fly down, hop upon the board, the board would give way, and the trap would shut with a clap.

Serozha was delighted, and he ran into the house to show his mother the trap.

His mother said:

"It is not a good plaything. What do you want to do with birds? Why do you want to torture them?"

"I am going to put them in a cage," Serozha said. "They will sing, and I will feed them."

He got some seed, scattered it on the board, and set the trap in the garden. And he stood by and expected the birds to fly down. But the birds were afraid of him and would not come near the cage. Serozha ran in to get something to eat, and left the cage.

After dinner he went to look at it. The cage had shut, and in it a little bird was beating against the bars.

Serozha took up the bird, and carried it into the house.

"Mother, I have caught a bird!" he cried. "I think it is a nightingale; and how its heart beats!"

His mother said it was a wild canary. "Be careful! Don't hurt it; you would better let it go."

"No," he said. "I am going to give it something to eat and drink."

Serozha put the bird in a cage, and for two days gave it seed and water, and cleaned the cage. But on the third day he forgot all about it, and did not change the water.

And his mother said, "See here, you have forgotten your bird. You would better let it go."

Serozha thrust his hand in the cage and began to clean it, but the little bird was frightened and fluttered. After Serozha had cleaned the cage, he went to get some water. His mother saw that he had forgotten to shut the cage door, and she called after him.

"Serozha, shut up your cage, else your bird will fly out and hurt itself."

She had hardly spoken the words when the bird found the door, was delighted, spread its wings, and flew around the room toward the window. Serozha came running in, picked up the bird, and put it back in the cage. The bird was still alive, but it lay on its breast, with its wings spread out, and breathed heavily. Serozha looked and looked at it, and began to cry.

"Mother, what can I do now?" he asked.

"You can do nothing now," she replied.

Serozha stayed by the cage all day. He did nothing but look at the bird. And all the time the bird lay on its breast and breathed hard and fast.

When Serozha went to bed, the bird was dead. Serozha could not get to sleep for a long time; every time that he shut his eyes he seemed to see the bird still lying and sighing.

In the morning when Serozha went to his cage, he saw the bird lying on its back, with its legs crossed, and all stiff.

After that Serozha never again snared birds.

The Candle

"Ye have heard that it hath been said, an eye for an eye and a tooth for a tooth: but I say unto you, That ye resist not evil." ST. MATTHEW V. 38, 39.

It was in the time of serfdom, many years before Alexander II.'s liberation of the sixty million serfs in 1862. In those days the people were ruled by different kinds of lords. There were not a few who, remembering God, treated their slaves in a humane manner, and not as beasts of burden, while there were others who were seldom known to perform a kind or generous action; but the most barbarous and tyrannical of all were those former serfs who arose from the dirt and became princes.

It was this latter class who made life literally a burden to those who were unfortunate enough to come under their rule. Many of them had arisen from the ranks of the peasantry to become superintendents of noblemen's estates.

The peasants were obliged to work for their master a certain number of days each week. There was plenty of land and water and the soil was rich and fertile, while the meadows and forests were sufficient to supply the needs of both the peasants and their lord.

There was a certain nobleman who had chosen a superintendent from the peasantry on one of his other estates. No sooner had the power to govern been vested in this newly-made official than he began to practice the most outrageous cruelties upon the poor serfs who had been placed under his control. Although this man had a wife and two married daughters, and was making so much money that he could have lived happily without transgressing in any way against either God or man, yet he was filled with envy and jealousy and deeply sunk in sin.

Michael Simeonovitch began his persecutions by compelling the peasants to perform more days of service on the estate every week than the laws obliged them to work. He established a brick-yard, in which he forced the men and women to do excessive labor, selling the bricks for his own profit.

On one occasion the overworked serfs sent a delegation to Moscow to complain of their treatment to their lord, but they obtained no satisfaction. When the poor peasants returned disconsolate from the nobleman their superintendent determined to have revenge for their boldness in going above him for redress, and their life and that of their fellow-victims became worse than before.

It happened that among the serfs there were some very treacherous people who would falsely accuse their fellows of wrong-doing and sow seeds of discord among the peasantry, whereupon Michael would become greatly enraged, while his poor subjects began to live in fear of their lives. When the superintendent passed through the village the people would run and hide themselves as from a wild beast. Seeing thus the terror which he had struck to the hearts of the moujiks, Michael's treatment of them became still more vindictive, so that from over-work and ill-usage the lot of the poor serfs was indeed a hard one.

There was a time when it was possible for the peasants, when driven to despair, to devise means whereby they could rid themselves of an inhuman monster such as Simeonovitch, and so these unfortunate people began to consider whether something could not be done to relieve THEM of their intolerable yoke. They would hold little meetings in secret places to bewail their misery and to confer with one another as to which would be the best way to act. Now and then the boldest of the gathering would rise and address his companions in this strain: "How much longer can we tolerate such a villain to rule over us? Let us make an end of it at once, for it were better for us to perish than to suffer. It is surely not a sin to kill such a devil in human form."

It happened once, before the Easter holidays, that one of these meetings was held in the woods, where Michael had sent the serfs to make a clearance for their master. At noon they assembled to eat their dinner and to hold a consultation. "Why can't we leave now?" said one. "Very soon we shall be reduced to nothing. Already we are almost worked to death, there being no rest, night or day, either for us or our poor women. If anything should be done in a way not exactly to please him he will find fault and perhaps flog some of us to death, as was the case with poor Simeon, whom he killed not long ago. Only recently Anisim was tortured in irons till he died. We certainly cannot stand this much longer." "Yes," said another, "what is the use of waiting? Let us act at once. Michael will be here this evening, and will be certain to abuse us shamefully. Let us, then, thrust him from his horse and with one blow of an axe give him what he deserves, and thus end our misery. We can then dig a big hole and bury him like a dog, and no one will know what became of him. Now let us come to an agreement to stand together as one man and not to betray one another."

The last speaker was Vasili Minayeff, who, if possible, had more cause to complain of Michael's cruelty than any of his fellow-serfs. The superintendent was in the habit of flogging him severely every week, and he took also Vasili's wife to serve him as cook.

Accordingly, during the evening that followed this meeting in the woods Michael arrived on the scene on horseback. He began at once to find fault with the manner in which the work had been done, and to complain because some lime-trees had been cut down.

"I told you not to cut down any lime-trees!" shouted the enraged superintendent. "Who did this thing? Tell me at once, or I shall flog every one of you!"

On investigation, a peasant named Sidor was pointed out as the guilty one, and his face was roundly slapped. Michael also severely punished Vasili, because he had not done sufficient work, after which the master rode safely home.

In the evening the serfs again assembled, and poor Vasili said: "Oh, what kind of people ARE we, anyway? We are only sparrows, and not men at all! We agree to stand by each other, but as soon as the time for action comes we all run and hide. Once a lot of sparrows conspired against a hawk, but no sooner did the bird of prey appear than they sneaked off in the grass. Selecting one of the choicest sparrows, the hawk took it away to eat, after which the others came out crying, 'Twee-twee!' and found that one was missing. 'Who is killed?' they asked. 'Vanka! Well, he deserved it.' You, my friends, are acting in just the same manner. When Michael attacked Sidor you should have stood by your promise. Why didn't you arise, and with one stroke put an end to him and to our misery?"

The effect of this speech was to make the peasants more firm in their determination to kill their superintendent. The latter had already given orders that they should be ready to plough during the Easter holidays, and to sow the field with oats, whereupon the serfs became stricken with grief, and gathered in Vasili's house to hold another indignation meeting. "If he has really forgotten God," they said, "and shall continue to commit such crimes against us, it is truly necessary that we should kill him. If not, let us perish, for it can make no difference to us now."

This despairing programme, however, met with considerable opposition from a peaceably-inclined man named Peter Mikhayeff. "Brethren," said he, "you are contemplating a grievous sin. The taking of human life is a very serious matter. Of course it is easy to end the mortal existence of a man, but what will become of the souls of those who commit the deed? If Michael continues to act toward us unjustly God will surely punish him. But, my friends, we must have patience."

This pacific utterance only served to intensify the anger of Vasili. Said he: "Peter is forever repeating the same old story, 'It is a sin to kill any one.' Certainly it is sinful to murder; but we should consider the kind of man we are dealing with. We all know it is wrong to kill a good man, but even God would take away the life of such a dog as he is. It is our duty, if we have any love for mankind, to shoot a dog that is mad. It is a sin to let him live. If, therefore, we are to suffer at all, let it be in the interests of the people and they will thank us for it. If we remain quiet any longer a flogging will be our only reward. You are talking nonsense, Mikhayeff. Why don't you think of the sin we shall be committing if we work during the Easter holidays, for you will refuse to work then yourself?"

"Well, then," replied Peter, "if they shall send me to plough, I will go. But I shall not be going of my own free will, and God will know whose sin it is, and shall punish the offender accordingly. Yet we must not forget him. Brethren, I am not giving you my own views only. The law of God is not to return evil for evil; indeed, if you try in this way to stamp out wickedness it will come upon you all the stronger. It is not difficult for you to kill the man, but his blood will surely stain your own soul. You may think you have killed a bad man, that you have gotten rid of evil but you will soon find out that the seeds of still greater wickedness have been planted within you. If you yield to misfortune it will surely come to you."

As Peter was not without sympathizers among the peasants, the poor serfs were consequently divided into two groups: the followers of Vasili and those who held the views of Mikhayeff.

On Easter Sunday no work was done. Toward the evening an elder came to the peasants from the nobleman's court and said: "Our superintendent, Michael Simeonovitch, orders you to go to-morrow to plough the field for the oats." Thus the official went through the village and directed the men to prepare for work the next day, some by the river and others by the roadway. The poor people were almost overcome with grief, many of them shedding tears, but none dared to disobey the orders of their master.

On the morning of Easter Monday, while the church bells were calling the inhabitants to religious services, and while every one else was about to enjoy a holiday, the unfortunate serfs started for the field to plough. Michael arose rather late and took a walk about the farm. The domestic servants were through with their work and had dressed themselves for the day, while Michael's wife and their widowed daughter (who was visiting them, as was her custom on holidays) had been to church and returned. A steaming samovar awaited them, and they began to drink tea with Michael, who, after lighting his pipe, called the elder to him.

"Well," said the superintendent, "have you ordered the moujiks to plough to-day?"

"Yes, sir, I did," was the reply.

"Have they all gone to the field?"

"Yes, sir; all of them. I directed them myself where to begin."

"That is all very well. You gave the orders, but are they ploughing? Go at once and see, and you may tell them that I shall be there after dinner. I shall expect to find one and a half acres done for every two ploughs, and the work must be well done; otherwise they shall be severely punished, notwithstanding the holiday."

"I hear, sir, and obey."

The elder started to go, but Michael called him back. After hesitating for some time, as if he felt very uneasy, he said:

"By the way, listen to what those scoundrels say about me. Doubtless some of them will curse me, and I want you to report the exact words. I know what villains they are. They don't find work at all pleasant. They would rather lie down all day and do nothing. They would like to eat and drink and make merry on holidays, but they forget that if the ploughing is not done it will soon be too late. So you go and listen to what is said, and tell it to me in detail. Go at once."

"I hear, sir, and obey."

Turning his back and mounting his horse, the elder was soon at the field where the serfs were hard at work.

It happened that Michael's wife, a very good-hearted woman, overheard the conversation which her husband had just been holding with the elder. Approaching him, she said:

"My good friend, Mishinka [diminutive of Michael], I beg of you to consider the importance and solemnity of this holy-day. Do not sin, for Christ's sake. Let the poor moujiks go home."

Michael laughed, but made no reply to his wife's humane request. Finally he said to her:

"You've not been whipped for a very long time, and now you have become bold enough to interfere in affairs that are not your own."

"Mishinka," she persisted, "I have had a frightful dream concerning you. You had better let the moujiks go."

"Yes," said he; "I perceive that you have gained so much flesh of late that you think you would not feel the whip. Lookout!"

Rudely thrusting his hot pipe against her cheek, Michael chased his wife from the room, after which he ordered his dinner. After eating a hearty meal consisting of cabbage-soup, roast pig, meat-cake, pastry with milk, jelly, sweet cakes, and vodki, he called his woman cook to him and ordered her to be seated and sing songs, Simeonovitch accompanying her on the guitar.

While the superintendent was thus enjoying himself to the fullest satisfaction in the musical society of his cook the elder returned, and, making a low bow to his superior, proceeded to give the desired information concerning the serfs.

"Well," asked Michael, "did they plough?"

"Yes," replied the elder; "they have accomplished about half the field."

"Is there no fault to be found?"

"Not that I could discover. The work seems to be well done. They are evidently afraid of you."

"How is the soil?"

"Very good. It appears to be quite soft."

"Well," said Simeonovitch, after a pause, "what did they say about me? Cursed me, I suppose?"

As the elder hesitated somewhat, Michael commanded him to speak and tell him the whole truth. "Tell me all," said he; "I want to know their exact words. If you tell me the truth I shall reward you; but if you conceal anything from me you will be punished. See here, Catherine, pour out a glass of vodki to give him courage!"

After drinking to the health of his superior, the elder said to himself: "It is not my fault if they do not praise him. I shall tell him the truth." Then turning suddenly to the superintendent he said:

"They complain, Michael Simeonovitch! They complain bitterly."

"But what did they say?" demanded Michael. "Tell me!"

"Well, one thing they said was, 'He does not believe in God.'"

Michael laughed. "Who said that?" he asked.

"It seemed to be their unanimous opinion. 'He has been overcome by the Evil One,' they said."

"Very good," laughed the superintendent; "but tell me what each of them said. What did Vasili say?"

The elder did not wish to betray his people, but he had a certain grudge against Vasili, and he said:

"He cursed you more than did any of the others."

"But what did he say?"

"It is awful to repeat it, sir. Vasili said, 'He shall die like a dog, having no chance to repent!'"

"Oh, the villain!" exclaimed Michael. "He would kill me if he were not afraid. All right, Vasili; we shall have an accounting with you. And Tishka, he called me a dog, I suppose?"

"Well," said the elder, "they all spoke of you in anything but complimentary terms; but it is mean in me to repeat what they said."

"Mean or not you must tell me. I say!"

"Some of them declared that your back should be broken."

Simeonovitch appeared to enjoy this immensely, for he laughed outright. "We shall see whose back will be the first to be broken," said he. "Was that Tishka's opinion? While I did not suppose they would say anything good about me, I did not expect such curses and threats. And Peter Mikhayeff, was that fool cursing me too?"

"No; he did not curse you at all. He appeared to be the only silent one among them. Mikhayeff is a very wise moujik, and he surprises me very much. At his actions all the other peasants seemed amazed."

"What did he do?"

"He did something remarkable. He was diligently ploughing, and as I approached him I heard some one singing very sweetly. Looking between the ploughshares, I observed a bright object shining."

"Well, what was it? Hurry up!"

"It was a small, five-kopeck wax candle, burning brightly, and the wind was unable to blow it out. Peter, wearing a new shirt, sang beautiful hymns as he ploughed, and no matter how he handled the implement the candle continued to burn. In my presence he fixed the plough, shaking it violently, but the bright little object between the colters remained undisturbed."

"And what did Mikhayeff say?"

"He said nothing, except when, on seeing me, he gave me the holy-day salutation, after which he went on his way singing and ploughing as before. I did not say anything to him, but, on approaching the other moujiks, I found that they were laughing and making sport of their silent companion. 'It is a great sin to plough on Easter Monday,' they said. 'You could not get absolution from your sin if you were to pray all your life.'"

"And did Mikhayeff make no reply?"

"He stood long enough to say: 'There should be peace on earth and good-will to men,' after which he resumed his ploughing and singing, the candle burning even more brightly than before."

Simeonovitch had now ceased to ridicule, and, putting aside his guitar, his head dropped on his breast and he became lost in thought. Presently he ordered the elder and cook to depart, after which Michael went behind a screen and threw himself upon the bed. He was sighing and moaning, as if in great distress, when his wife came in and spoke kindly to him. He refused to listen to her, exclaiming:

"He has conquered me, and my end is near!"

"Mishinka," said the woman, "arise and go to the moujiks in the field. Let them go home, and everything will be all right. Heretofore you have run far greater risks without any fear, but now you appear to be very much alarmed."

"He has conquered me!" he repeated. "I am lost!"

"What do you mean?" demanded his wife, angrily. "If you will go and do as I tell you there will be no danger. Come, Mishinka," she added, tenderly; "I shall have the saddle-horse brought for you at once."

When the horse arrived the woman persuaded her husband to mount the animal, and to fulfil her request concerning the serfs. When he reached the village a woman opened the gate for him to enter, and as he did so the inhabitants, seeing the brutal superintendent whom everybody feared, ran to hide themselves in their houses, gardens, and other secluded places.

At length Michael reached the other gate, which he found closed also, and, being unable to open it himself while seated on his horse, he called loudly for assistance. As no one responded to his shouts he dismounted and opened the gate, but as he was about to remount, and had one foot in the stirrup, the horse became frightened at some pigs and sprang suddenly to one side. The superintendent fell across the fence and a very sharp picket pierced his stomach, when Michael fell unconscious to the ground.

Toward the evening, when the serfs arrived at the village gate, their horses refused to enter. On looking around, the peasants discovered the dead body of their superintendent lying face downward in a pool of blood, where he had fallen from the fence. Peter Mikhayeff alone had sufficient courage to dismount and approach the prostrate form, his companions riding around the village and entering by way of the back yards. Peter closed the dead man's eyes, after which he put the body in a wagon and took it home.

When the nobleman learned of the fatal accident which had befallen his superintendent, and of the brutal treatment which he had meted out to those under him, he freed the serfs, exacting a smal rent for the use of his land and the other agricultural opportunities.

And thus the peasants clearly understood that the power of God is manifested not in evil, but in goodness.

The Coffee-house Of Surat

In the town of Surat, in India, was a coffee-house where many travellers and foreigners from all parts of the world met and conversed.

One day a learned Persian theologian visited this coffee-house. He was a man who had spent his ife studying the nature of the Deity, and reading and writing books upon the subject. He had though:, read, and written so much about God, that eventually he lost his wits, became quite confused, and ceased even to believe in the existence of a God. The Shah, hearing of this, had banished him from Persia.

After having argued all his life about the First Cause, this unfortunate theologian had ended by quite perplexing himself, and instead of understanding that he had lost his own reason, he began to think that there was no higher Reason controlling the universe.

This man had an African slave who followed him everywhere. When the theologian entered the coffee-house, the slave remained outside, near the door, sitting on a stone in the glare of the sun, and driving away the flies that buzzed around him. The Persian having settled down on a divan in the coffee-house, ordered himself a cup of opium. When he had drunk it and the opium had begun to quicken the workings of his brain, he addressed his slave through the open door:

"Tell me, wretched slave," said he, "do you think there is a God, or not?"

"Of course there is," said the slave, and immediately drew from under his girdle a small idol of wood.

"There," said he, "that is the God who has guarded me from the day of my birth. Every one in our country worships the fetish tree, from the wood of which this God was made."

This conversation between the theologian and his slave was listened to with surprise by the other guests in the coffee-house. They were astonished at the master's question, and yet more so at the slave's reply.

One of them, a Brahmin, on hearing the words spoken by the slave, turned to him and said:

"Miserable fool! Is it possible you believe that God can be carried under a man's girdle? There is one God, Brahma, and he is greater than the whole world, for he created it. Brahma is the One, the mighty God, and in His honour are built the temples on the Ganges' banks, where his true priests the Brahmins, worship him. They know the true God, and none but they. A thousand score of years have passed, and yet through revolution after revolution these priests have held their sway, because Brahma, the one true God, has protected them."

So spoke the Brahmin, thinking to convince every one; but a Jewish broker who was present replied to him, and said:

"No! the temple of the true God is not in India. Neither does God protect the Brahmin caste. The true God is not the God of the Brahmins, but of Abraham, Isaac, and Jacob. None does He protect but His chosen people, the Israelites. From the commencement of the world, our nation has been beloved of Him, and ours alone. If we are now scattered over the whole earth, it is but to try us; for God has promised that He will one day gather His people together in Jerusalem. Then, with the Temple of Jerusalem, the wonder of the ancient world, restored to its splendor, shall Israel be established a ruler over all nations."

So spoke the Jew, and burst into tears. He wished to say more, but an Italian missionary who was there interrupted him.

"What you are saying is untrue," said he to the Jew. "You attribute injustice to God. He cannot love your nation above the rest. Nay rather, even if it be true that of old He favored the Israelites, it is now nineteen hundred years since they angered Him, and caused Him to destroy their nation and scatter them over the earth, so that their faith makes no converts and has died out except here and there. God shows preference to no nation, but calls all who wish to be saved to the bosom of the Catholic Church of Rome, the one outside whose borders no salvation can be found."

So spoke the Italian. But a Protestant minister, who happened to be present, growing pale, turned to the Catholic missionary and exclaimed:

"How can you say that salvation belongs to your religion? Those only will be saved, who serve God according to the Gospel, in spirit and in truth, as bidden by the word of Christ."

Then a Turk, an office-holder in the custom-house at Surat, who was sitting in the coffee-house smoking a pipe, turned with an air of superiority to both the Christians.

"Your belief in your Roman religion is vain," said he. "It was superseded twelve hundred years ago by the true faith: that of Mohammed! You cannot but observe how the true Mohammed faith continues to spread both in Europe and Asia, and even in the enlightened country of China. You say yourselves that God has rejected the Jews; and, as a proof, you quote the fact that the Jews are humiliated and their faith does not spread. Confess then the truth of Mohammedanism, for it is triumphant and spreads far and wide. None will be saved but the followers of Mohammed, God's latest prophet; and of them, only the followers of Omar, and not of Ali, for the latter are false to the faith."

To this the Persian theologian, who was of the sect of Ali, wished to reply; but by this time a great dispute had arisen among all the strangers of different faiths and creeds present. There were Abyssinian Christians, Llamas from Thibet, Ismailians and Fireworshippers. They all argued about the nature of God, and how He should be worshipped. Each of them asserted that in his country alone was the true God known and rightly worshipped.

Every one argued and shouted, except a Chinaman, a student of Confucius, who sat quietly in one corner of the coffee-house, not joining in the dispute. He sat there drinking tea and listening to what the others said, but did not speak himself.

The Turk noticed him sitting there, and appealed to him, saying:

"You can confirm what I say, my good Chinaman. You hold your peace, but if you spoke I know you would uphold my opinion. Traders from your country, who come to me for assistance, tell me that though many religions have been introduced into China, you Chinese consider Mohammedanism the best of all, and adopt it willingly. Confirm, then, my words, and tell us your opinion of the true God and of His prophet."

"Yes, yes," said the rest, turning to the Chinaman, "let us hear what you think on the subject."

The Chinaman, the student of Confucius, closed his eyes, and thought a while. Then he opened them again, and drawing his hands out of the wide sleeves of his garment, and folding them on his breast, he spoke as follows, in a calm and quiet voice.

Sirs, it seems to me that it is chiefly pride that prevents men agreeing with one another on matters of faith. If you care to listen to me, I will tell you a story which will explain this by an example.

I came here from China on an English steamer which had been round the world. We stopped for fresh water, and landed on the east coast of the island of Sumatra. It was midday, and some of us, having landed, sat in the shade of some cocoanut palms by the seashore, not far from a native village. We were a party of men of different nationalities.

As we sat there, a blind man approached us. We learned afterwards that he had gone blind from gazing too long and too persistently at the sun, trying to find out what it is, in order to seize its light.

He strove a long time to accomplish this, constantly looking at the sun; but the only result was that his eyes were injured by its brightness, and he became blind.

Then he said to himself:

"The light of the sun is not a liquid; for if it were a liquid it would be possible to pour it from one vessel into another, and it would be moved, like water, by the wind. Neither is it fire; for if it were fire, water would extinguish it. Neither is light a spirit, for it is seen by the eye; nor is it matter, for it cannot be moved. Therefore, as the light of the sun is neither liquid, nor fire, nor spirit, nor matter, it is nothing!"

So he argued, and, as a result of always looking at the sun and always thinking about it, he lost both his sight and his reason. And when he went quite blind, he became fully convinced that the sun did not exist.

With this blind man came a slave, who after placing his master in the shade of a cocoanut tree, picked up a cocoanut from the ground, and began making it into a night-light. He twisted a wick from the fibre of the cocoanut: squeezed oil from the nut in the shell, and soaked the wick in it.

As the slave sat doing this, the blind man sighed and said to him:

"Well, slave, was I not right when I told you there is no sun? Do you not see how dark it is? Yet people say there is a sun. . . . But if so, what is it?"

"I do not know what the sun is," said the slave. "That is no business of mine. But I know what light is. Here I have made a night-light, by the help of which I can serve you and find anything I want in the hut."

And the slave picked up the cocoanut shell, saying:

"This is my sun."

A lame man with crutches, who was sitting near by, heard these words, and laughed:

"You have evidently been blind all your life," said he to the blind man, "not to know what the sun is. I will tell you what it is. The sun is a ball of fire, which rises every morning out of the sea and goes down again among the mountains of our island each evening. We have all seen this, and if you had had your eyesight you too would have seen it."

A fisherman, who had been listening to the conversation said:

"It is plain enough that you have never been beyond your own island. If you were not lame, and if you had been out as I have in a fishing-boat, you would know that the sun does not set among the mountains of our island, but as it rises from the ocean every morning so it sets again in the sea every night. What I am telling you is true, for I see it every day with my own eyes."

Then an Indian who was of our party, interrupted him by saying:

"I am astonished that a reasonable man should talk such nonsense. How can a ball of fire possibly descend into the water and not be extinguished? The sun is not a ball of fire at all, it is the Deity named Deva, who rides for ever in a chariot round the golden mountain, Meru. Sometimes the evil serpents Ragu and Ketu attack Deva and swallow him: and then the earth is dark. But our priests pray that the Deity may be released, and then he is set free. Only such ignorant men as you, who have never been beyond their own island, can imagine that the sun shines for their country alone."

Then the master of an Egyptian vessel, who was present, spoke in his turn.

"No," said he, "you also are wrong. The sun is not a Deity, and does not move only round India and its golden mountain. I have sailed much on the Black Sea, and along the coasts of Arabia, and have been to Madagascar and to the Philippines. The sun lights the whole earth, and not India alone. It does not circle round one mountain, but rises far in the East, beyond the Isles of Japan, and sets far, far away in the West, beyond the islands of England. That is why the Japanese call their country 'Nippon,' that is, 'the birth of the sun.' I know this well, for I have myself seen much, and heard more from my grandfather, who sailed to the very ends of the sea."

He would have gone on, but an English sailor from our ship interrupted him.

"There is no country," he said "where people know so much about the sun's movements as in England. The sun, as every one in England knows, rises nowhere and sets nowhere. It is always moving round the earth. We can be sure of this for we have just been round the world ourselves, and nowhere knocked up against the sun. Wherever we went, the sun showed itself in the morning and hid itself at night, just as it does here."

And the Englishman took a stick and, drawing circles on the sand, tried to explain how the sun moves in the heavens and goes round the world. But he was unable to explain it clearly, and pointing to the ship's pilot said:

"This man knows more about it than I do. He can explain it properly."

The pilot, who was an intelligent man, had listened in silence to the talk till he was asked to speak. Now every one turned to him, and he said:

"You are all misleading one another, and are yourselves deceived. The sun does not go round the earth, but the earth goes round the sun, revolving as it goes, and turning towards the sun in the course of each twenty-four hours, not only Japan, and the Philippines, and Sumatra where we now are, but Africa, and Europe, and America, and many lands besides. The sun does not shine for some one mountain, or for some one island, or for some one sea, nor even for one earth alone, but for other planets as well as our earth. If you would only look up at the heavens, instead of at the ground beneath your own feet, you might all understand this, and would then no longer suppose that the sun shines for you, or for your country alone."

Thus spoke the wise pilot, who had voyaged much about the world, and had gazed much upon the heavens above.

"So on matters of faith," continued the Chinaman, the student of Confucius, "it is pride that causes error and discord among men. As with the sun, so it is with God. Each man wants to have a special God of his own, or at least a special God for his native land. Each nation wishes to confine in its own temples Him, whom the world cannot contain.

"Can any temple compare with that which God Himself has built to unite all men in one faith and one religion?

"All human temples are built on the model of this temple, which is God's own world. Every temple has its fonts, its vaulted roof, its lamps, its pictures or sculptures, its inscriptions, its books of the law, its offerings, its altars and its priests. But in what temple is there such a font as the ocean; such a vault as that of the heavens; such lamps as the sun, moon, and stars; or any figures to be compared with living, loving, mutually-helpful men? Where are there any records of God's goodness so easy to understand as the blessings which God has strewn abroad for man's happiness? Where is there any book of the law so clear to each man as that written in his heart? What sacrifices equal the self-denials which loving men and women make for one another? And what altar can be compared with the heart of a good man, on which God Himself accepts the sacrifice?

"The higher a man's conception of God, the better will he know Him. And the better he knows God, the nearer will he draw to Him, imitating His goodness, His mercy, and His love of man.

"Therefore, let him who sees the sun's whole light filling the world, refrain from blaming or despising the superstitious man, who in his own idol sees one ray of that same light. Let him not despise even the unbeliever who is blind and cannot see the sun at all."

So spoke the Chinaman, the student of Confucius; and all who were present in the coffee-house were silent, and disputed no more as to whose faith was the best.

God Sees The Truth, But Waits

In the town of Vladimir lived a young merchant named Ivan Dmitrich Aksionov. He had two shops and a house of his own.

Aksionov was a handsome, fair-haired, curly-headed fellow, full of fun, and very fond of singing. When quite a young man he had been given to drink, and was riotous when he had had too much; but after he married he gave up drinking, except now and then.

One summer Aksionov was going to the Nizhny Fair, and as he bade good-bye to his family, his wife said to him, "Ivan Dmitrich, do not start to-day; I have had a bad dream about you."

Aksionov laughed, and said, "You are afraid that when I get to the fair I shall go on a spree."

His wife replied: "I do not know what I am afraid of; all I know is that I had a bad dream. I dreamt you returned from the town, and when you took off your cap I saw that your hair was quite grey."

Aksionov laughed. "That's a lucky sign," said he. "See if I don't sell out all my goods, and bring you some presents from the fair."

So he said good-bye to his family, and drove away.

When he had travelled half-way, he met a merchant whom he knew, and they put up at the same inn for the night. They had some tea together, and then went to bed in adjoining rooms.

It was not Aksionov's habit to sleep late, and, wishing to travel while it was still cool, he aroused his driver before dawn, and told him to put in the horses.

Then he made his way across to the landlord of the inn (who lived in a cottage at the back), paid his bill, and continued his journey.

When he had gone about twenty-five miles, he stopped for the horses to be fed. Aksionov rested awhile in the passage of the inn, then he stepped out into the porch, and, ordering a samovar to be heated, got out his guitar and began to play.

Suddenly a troika drove up with tinkling bells and an official alighted, followed by two soldiers. He came to Aksionov and began to question him, asking him who he was and whence he came. Aksionov answered him fully, and said, "Won't you have some tea with me?" But the official went on cross-questioning him and asking him. "Where did you spend last night? Were you alone, or with a fellow-merchant? Did you see the other merchant this morning? Why did you leave the inn before dawn?"

Aksionov wondered why he was asked all these questions, but he described all that had happened, and then added, "Why do you cross-question me as if I were a thief or a robber? I am travelling on business of my own, and there is no need to question me."

Then the official, calling the soldiers, said, "I am the police-officer of this district, and I question you because the merchant with whom you spent last night has been found with his throat cut. We must search your things."

They entered the house. The soldiers and the police-officer unstrapped Aksionov's luggage and searched it. Suddenly the officer drew a knife out of a bag, crying, "Whose knife is this?"

Aksionov looked, and seeing a blood-stained knife taken from his bag, he was frightened.

"How is it there is blood on this knife?"

Aksionov tried to answer, but could hardly utter a word, and only stammered: "I don't know, not mine." Then the police-officer said: "This morning the merchant was found in bed with his throat cut. You are the only person who could have done it. The house was locked from inside, and no one else was there. Here is this blood-stained knife in your bag and your face and manner betray you Tell me how you killed him, and how much money you stole?"

Aksionov swore he had not done it; that he had not seen the merchant after they had had tea together; that he had no money except eight thousand rubles of his own, and that the knife was not his. But his voice was broken, h s face pale and he trembled with fear as though he went guilty.

The police-officer ordered the soldiers to bind Aksionov and to put him in the cart. As they tied his feet together and flung him into the cart, Aksionov crossed himself and wept. His money and goods were taken from him, and he was sent to the nearest town and imprisoned there. Enquiries as to his character were made in Vladim r. The merchants and other inhabitants of that town said that in former days he used to drink ard waste his time, but that he was a good man. Then the trial came on: he was charged with murdering a merchant from Ryazan, and robbing him of twenty thousand rubles.

His wife was in despair, and did not know what to believe. Her children were all quite small; one was a baby at her breast. Taking them all with her, she went to the town where her husband was in jail. At first she was not allowed to see him; but after much begging, she obtained permission from the officials, and was taken to him. When she saw her husband in prison-dress and in chains, shut up with thieves and criminals, she fell down, and did not come to her senses for a long time. Then she drew her children to her, and sat down near him. She told him of things at home, and asked about what had happened to him. He told her all, and she asked, "What can we do now?"

"We must petition the Czar not to let an innocent man perish."

His wife told him that she had sent a petition to the Czar, but it had not been accepted.

Aksionov did not reply, but only looked downcast.

Then his wife said, "It was not for nothing I dreamt your hair had turned grey. You remember? You should not have started that day." And passing her fingers through his hair, she said: "Vanya dearest, tell your wife the truth; was it not you who did it?"

"So you, too, suspect me!" said Aksionov, and, hiding his face in his hands, he began to weep. Then a soldier came to say that the wife and children must go away; and Aksionov said good-bye to his family for the last time.

When they were gone, Aksionov recalled what had been said, and when he remembered that his wife also had suspected him, he said to himself, "It seems that only God can know the truth; it is to Him alone we must appeal, and from Him alone expect mercy."

And Aksionov wrote no more petitions; gave up all hope, and only prayed to God.

Aksionov was condemned to be flogged and sent to the mines. So he was flogged with a knot, and when the wounds made by the knot were healed, he was driven to Siberia with other convicts.

For twenty-six years Aksionov lived as a convict in Siberia. His hair turned white as snow, and his beard grew long, thin, and grey. All his mirth went; he stooped; he walked slowly, spoke little, and never laughed, but he often prayed.

In prison Aksionov learnt to make boots, and earned a little money, with which he bought The Lives of the Saints. He read this book when there was light enough in the prison; and on Sundays in the prison-church he read the lessons and sang in the choir; for his voice was still good.

The prison authorities liked Aksionov for his meekness, and his fellow-prisoners respected him: they called him "Grandfather," and "The Saint." When they wanted to petition the prison authorities about anything, they always made Aksionov their spokesman, and when there were quarrels among the prisoners they came to him to put things right, and to judge the matter.

No news reached Aksionov from his home, and he did not even know if his wife and children were still alive.

One day a fresh gang of convicts came to the prison. In the evening the old prisoners collected round the new ones and asked them what towns or villages they came from, and what they were sentenced for. Among the rest Aksionov sat down near the newcomers, and listened with downcast air to what was said.

One of the new convicts, a tall, strong man of sixty, with a closely-cropped grey beard, was telling the others what be had been arrested for.

"Well, friends," he said, "I only took a horse that was tied to a sledge, and I was arrested and accused of stealing. I said I had only taken it to get home quicker, and had then let it go; besides, the driver was a personal friend of mine. So I said, 'It's all right.' 'No,' said they, 'you stole it.' But how or where I stole it they could not say. I once really did something wrong, and ought by rights to have come here long ago, but that time I was not found out. Now I have been sent here for nothing at all... Eh, but it's lies I'm telling you; I've been to Siberia before, but I did not stay long."

"Where are you from?" asked some one.

"From Vladimir. My family are of that town. My name is Makar, and they also call me Semyonich."

Aksionov raised his head and said: "Tell me, Semyonich, do you know anything of the merchants Aksionov of Vladimir? Are they still alive?"

"Know them? Of course I do. The Aksionovs are rich, though their father is in Siberia: a sinner like ourselves, it seems! As for you, Gran'dad, how did you come here?"

Aksionov did not like to speak of his misfortune. He only sighed, and said, "For my sins I have been in prison these twenty-six years."

"What sins?" asked Makar Semyonich.

But Aksionov only said, "Well, well, I must have deserved it!" He would have said no more, but his companions told the newcomers how Aksionov came to be in Siberia; how some one had killed a merchant, and had put the knife among Aksionov's things, and Aksionov had been unjustly condemned.

When Makar Semyonich heard this, he looked at Aksionov, slapped his own knee, and exclaimed, "Well, this is wonderful! Really wonderful! But how old you've grown, Gran'dad!"

The others asked him why he was so surprised, and where he had seen Aksionov before; but Makar Semyonich did not reply. He only said: "It's wonderful that we should meet here, lads!"

These words made Aksionov wonder whether this man knew who had killed the merchant; so he said, "Perhaps, Semyonich, you have heard of that affair, or maybe you've seen me before?"

"How could I help hearing? The world's full of rumours. But it's a long time ago, and I've forgotten what I heard."

"Perhaps you heard who killed the merchant?" asked Aksionov.

Makar Semyonich laughed, and replied: "It must have been him in whose bag the knife was found! If some one else hid the knife there, 'He's not a thief till he's caught,' as the saying is. How could any one put a knife into your bag while it was under your head? It would surely have woke you up."

When Aksionov heard these words, he felt sure this was the man who had killed the merchant. He rose and went away. All that night Aksionov lay awake. He felt terribly unhappy, and all sorts of images rose in his mind. There was the image of his wife as she was when he parted from her to go to the fair. He saw her as if she were present; her face and her eyes rose before him; he heard her speak and laugh. Then he saw his children, quite little, as they: were at that time: one with a little cloak on, another at his mother's breast. And then he remembered himself as he used to be-young and merry. He remembered how he sat playing the guitar in the porch of the inn where he was arrested, and how free from care he had been. He saw, in his mind, the place where he was flogged, the executioner, and the people standing around; the chains, the convicts, all the twenty-six years of his prison life, and his premature old age. The thought of it all made him so wretched that he was ready to kill himself.

"And it's all that villain's doing!" thought Aksionov. And his anger was so great against Makar Semyonich that he longed for vengeance, even if he himself should perish for it. He kept repeating prayers all night, but could get no peace. During the day he did not go near Makar Semyonich, nor even look at him.

A fortnight passed in this way. Aksionov could not sleep at night, and was so miserable that he did not know what to do.

One night as he was walking about the prison he noticed some earth that came rolling out from under one of the shelves on which the prisoners slept. He stopped to see what it was. Suddenly Makar Semyonich crept out from under the shelf, and looked up at Aksionov with frightened face. Aksionov tried to pass without looking at him, but Makar seized his hand and told him that he had dug a hole under the wall, getting rid of the earth by putting it into his high-boots, and emptying it out every day on the road when the prisoners were driven to their work.

"Just you keep quiet, old man, and you shall get out too. If you blab, they'll flog the life out of me, but I will kill you first."

Aksionov trembled with anger as he looked at his enemy. He drew his hand away, saying, "I have no wish to escape, and you have no need to kill me; you killed me long ago! As to telling of you, I may do so or not, as God shall direct."

Next day, when the convicts were led out to work, the convoy soldiers noticed that one or other of the prisoners emptied some earth out of his boots. The prison was searched and the tunnel found. The Governor came and questioned all the prisoners to find out who had dug the hole. They all denied any knowledge of it. Those who knew would not betray Makar Semyonich, knowing he would be flogged almost to death. At last the Governor turned to Aksionov whom he knew to be a just man, and said:

"You are a truthful old man; tell me, before God, who dug the hole?"

Makar Semyonich stood as if he were quite unconcerned, looking at the Governor and not so much as glancing at Aksionov. Aksionov's lips and hands trembled, and for a long time he could not utter a word. He thought, "Why should I screen him who ruined my life? Let him pay for what I have suffered. But if I tell, they will probably flog the life out of him, and maybe I suspect him wrongly. And, after all, what good would it be to me?"

"Well, old man," repeated the Governor, "tell me the truth: who has been digging under the wall?"

Aksionov glanced at Makar Semyonich, and said, "I cannot say, your honour. It is not God's will that I should tell! Do what you like with me; I am your hands."

However much the Governor! tried, Aksionov would say no more, and so the matter had to be left.

That night, when Aksionov was lying on his bed and just beginning to doze, some one came quietly and sat down on his bed. He peered through the darkness and recognised Makar.

"What more do you want of me?" asked Aksionov. "Why have you come here?"

Makar Semyonich was silent. So Aksionov sat up and said, "What do you want? Go away, or I will call the guard!"

Makar Semyonich bent close over Aksionov, and whispered, "Ivan Dmitrich, forgive me!"

"What for?" asked Aksionov.

"It was I who killed the merchant and hid the knife among your things. I meant to kill you too, but I heard a noise outside, so I hid the knife in your bag and escaped out of the window."

Aksionov was silent, and did not know what to say. Makar Semyonich slid off the bed-shelf and knelt upon the ground. "Ivan Dmitrich," said he, "forgive me! For the love of God, forgive me! I will confess that it was I who killed the merchant, and you will be released and can go to your home."

"It is easy for you to talk," said Aksionov, "but I have suffered for you these twenty-six years. Where could I go to now?... My wife is dead, and my children have forgotten me. I have nowhere to go..."

Makar Semyonich did not rise, but beat his head on the floor. "Ivan Dmitrich, forgive me!" he cried. "When they flogged me with the knot it was not so hard to bear as it is to see you now ... yet you had pity on me, and did not tell. For Christ's sake forgive me, wretch that I am!" And he began to sob.

When Aksionov heard him sobbing he, too, began to weep. "God will forgive you!" said he. "Maybe I am a hundred times worse than you." And at these words his heart grew light, and the longing for home left him. He no longer had any desire to leave the prison, but only hoped for his last hour to come.

In spite of what Aksionov had said, Makar Semyonich confessed, his guilt. But when the order for his release came, Aksionov was already dead.

The Gray Hare

A gray hare lived during the winter near a village. When night came, he would prick up one ear and listen, then he would prick up the other, jerk his whiskers, snuff, and sit up on his hind legs.

Then he would give one leap, two leaps, through the snow, and sit up again on his hind legs and look all around.

On all sides nothing was to be seen except snow. The snow lay in billows and glittered like silver. Above the hare was frosty vapor, and through this vapor glistened the big white stars.

The hare was obliged to make a long circuit across the highway to reach his favorite granary. On the highway he could hear the creaking of the sledges, the whinnying of horses, the groaning of the seats in the sledges.

Once more the hare paused near the road. The peasants were walking alongside of their sledges, with their coat collars turned up. Their faces were scarcely visible. Their beards, their eyebrows were white. Steam came from their mouths and noses.

Their horses were covered with sweat, and the sweat grew white with hoar frost. The horses strained on their collars, plunged into the hollows, and came up out of them again. Two old men were walking side by side, and one was telling the other how a horse had been stolen from him.

As soon as the teams had passed, the hare crossed the road, and leaped unconcernedly toward the threshing-floor. A little dog belonging to the teams caught sight of the hare and began to bark, and darted after him.

The hare made for the threshing-floor across the snowdrifts. But the depth of the snow impeded the hare, and even the dog, after a dozen leaps, sank deep in the snow and gave up the chase.

The hare also stopped, sat on his hind legs, and then proceeded at his leisure toward the threshing-floor.

On the way across the field he fell in with two other hares. They were nibbling and playing. The gray hare joined his mates, helped them clear away the icy snow, ate a few seeds of winter wheat, and then went on his way.

In the village it was all quiet; the fires were out; the only sound on the street was a baby crying in a cottage, and the framework of the houses creaking under the frost.

The hare hastened to the threshing-floor, and there he found some of his mates. He played with them on the well-swept floor, ate some oats from the tub on which they had already begun, mounted the snow-covered roof into the granary, and then went through the hedge toward his hole.

In the east the dawn was already beginning to redden, the stars dwindled, and the frosty vapor grew thicker over the face of the earth. In the neighboring village the women woke up and went out after water; the peasants began carrying fodder from the granaries; the children were shouting. Along the highway more and more teams passed by, and the peasants talked in louder tones.

The hare leaped across the road, went to his old hole, selected a place a little higher up, dug away the snow, curled into the depths of his new hole, stretched his ears along his back, and went to sleep with his eyes wide open

How Much Land Does A Man Need?

I

An elder sister came to visit her younger sister in the country. The elder was married to a tradesman in town, the younger to a peasant in the village. As the sisters sat over their tea talking, the elder began to boast of the advantages of town life: saying how comfortably they lived there, how well they dressed, what fine clothes her children wore, what good things they ate and drank, and how she went to the theatre, promenades, and entertainments.

The younger sister was piqued, and in turn disparaged the life of a tradesman, and stood up for that of a peasant.

"I would not change my way of life for yours," said she. "We may live roughly, but at least we are free from anxiety. You live in better style than we do, but though you often earn more than you need, you are very likely to lose all you have. You know the proverb, 'Loss and gain are brothers twain.' It often happens that people who are wealthy one day are begging their bread the next. Our way is safer. Though a peasant's life is not a fat one, it is a long one. We shall never grow rich, but we shall always have enough to eat."

The elder sister said sneeringly:

"Enough? Yes, if you like to share with the pigs and the calves! What do you know of elegance or manners! However much your good man may slave, you will die as you are living-on a dung heap-and your children the same."

"Well, what of that?" replied the younger. "Of course our work is rough and coarse. But, on the other hand, it is sure; and we need not bow to any one. But you, in your towns, are surrounded by temptations; today all may be right, but tomorrow the Evil One may tempt your husband with cards, wine, or women, and all will go to ruin. Don't such things happen often enough?"

Pahom, the master of the house, was lying on the top of the oven, and he listened to the women's chatter.

"It is perfectly true," thought he. "Busy as we are from childhood tilling Mother Earth, we peasants have no time to let any nonsense settle in our heads. Our only trouble is that we haven't land enough. If I had plenty of land, I shouldn't fear the Devil himself!"

The women finished their tea, chatted a while about dress, and then cleared away the tea-things and lay down to sleep.

But the Devil had been sitting behind the oven, and had heard all that was said. He was pleased that the peasant's wife had led her husband into boasting, and that he had said that if he had plenty of land he would not fear the Devil himself.

"All right," thought the Devil. "We will have a tussle. I'll give you land enough; and by means of that land I will get you into my power."

II

Close to the village there lived a lady, a small landowner, who had an estate of about three hundred acres. She had always lived on good terms with the peasants, until she engaged as her steward an old soldier, who took to burdening the people with fines. However careful Pahom tried to be, it happened again and again that now a horse of his got among the lady's oats, now a cow strayed into her garden, now his calves found their way into her meadows-and he always had to pay a fine.

Pahom paid, but grumbled, and, going home in a temper, was rough with his family. All through that summer Pahom had much trouble because of this steward; and he was even glad when winter came and the cattle had to be stabled. Though he grudged the fodder when they could no longer graze on the pasture-land, at least he was free from anxiety about them.

In the winter the news got about that the lady was going to sell her land, and that the keeper of the inn on the high road was bargaining for it. When the peasants heard this they were very much alarmed.

"Well," thought they, "if the innkeeper gets the land he will worry us with fines worse than the lady's steward. We all depend on that estate."

So the peasants went on behalf of their Commune, and asked the lady not to sell the land to the innkeeper; offering her a better price for it themselves. The lady agreed to let them have it. Then the peasants tried to arrange for the Commune to buy the whole estate, so that it might be held by all in common. They met twice to discuss it, but could not settle the matter; the Evil One sowed discord among them, and they could not agree. So they decided to buy the land individually, each according to his means; and the lady agreed to this plan as she had to the other.

Presently Pahom heard that a neighbor of his was buying fifty acres, and that the lady had consented to accept one half in cash and to wait a year for the other half. Pahom felt envious.

"Look at that," thought he, "the land is all being sold, and I shall get none of it." So he spoke to his wife.

"Other people are buying," said he, "and we must also buy twenty acres or so. Life is becoming impossible. That steward is simply crushing us with his fines."

So they put their heads together and considered how they could manage to buy it. They had one hundred roubles laid by. They sold a colt, and one half of their bees; hired out one of their sons as a laborer, and took his wages in advance; borrowed the rest from a brother-in-law, and so scraped together half the purchase money.

Having done this, Pahom chose out a farm of forty acres, some of it wooded, and went to the lady to bargain for it. They came to an agreement, and he shook hands with her upon it, and paid her a deposit in advance. Then they went to town and signed the deeds; he paying half the price down, and undertaking to pay the remainder within two years.

So now Pahom had land of his own. He borrowed seed, and sowed it on the land he had bought. The harvest was a good one, and within a year he had managed to pay off his debts both to the lady and to his brother-in-law. So he became a landowner, ploughing and sowing his own land, making hay on his own land, cutting his own trees, and feeding his cattle on his own pasture. When he went out to plough his fields, or to look at his growing corn, or at his grass meadows, his heart would fill with joy. The grass that grew and the flowers that bloomed there, seemed to him unlike any that grew elsewhere. Formerly, when he had passed by that land, it had appeared the same as any other land, but now it seemed quite different.

III

So Pahom was well contented, and everything would have been right if the neighboring peasants would only not have trespassed on his corn- fields and meadows. He appealed to them most civilly, but they still went on: now the Communal herdsmen would let the village cows stray into his meadows; then horses from the night pasture would get among his corn. Pahom turned them out again and again, and forgave their owners, and for a long time he forbore from prosecuting any one. But at last he lost patience and complained to the District Court. He knew it was the peasants' want of land, and no evil intent on their part, that caused the trouble; but he thought:

"I cannot go on overlooking it, or they will destroy all I have. They must be taught a lesson."

So he had them up, gave them one lesson, and then another, and two or three of the peasants were fined. After a time Pahom's neighbours began to bear him a grudge for this, and would now and then let their cattle on his land on purpose. One peasant even got into Pahom's wood at night and cut down five young lime trees for their bark. Pahom passing through the wood one day noticed something white. He came nearer, and saw the stripped trunks lying on the ground, and close by stood the stumps, where the tree had been. Pahom was furious.

"If he had only cut one here and there it would have been bad enough," thought Pahom, "but the rascal has actually cut down a whole clump. If I could only find out who did this, I would pay him out."

He racked his brains as to who it could be. Finally he decided: "It must be Simon-no one else could have done it." Se he went to Simon's homestead to have a look around, but he found nothing, and only had an angry scene. However' he now felt more certain than ever that Simon had done it, and he lodged a complaint. Simon was summoned. The case was tried, and re-tried, and at the end of it all Simon was acquitted, there being no evidence against him. Pahom felt still more aggrieved, and let his anger loose upon the Elder and the Judges.

"You let thieves grease your palms," said he. "If you were honest folk yourselves, you would not let a thief go free."

So Pahom quarrelled with the Judges and with his neighbors. Threats to burn his building began to be uttered. So though Pahom had more land, his place in the Commune was much worse than before.

About this time a rumor got about that many people were moving to new parts.

"There's no need for me to leave my land," thought Pahom. "But some of the others might leave our village, and then there would be more room for us. I would take over their land myself, and make my estate a bit bigger. I could then live more at ease. As it is, I am still too cramped to be comfortable."

One day Pahom was sitting at home, when a peasant passing through the village, happened to call in. He was allowed to stay the night, and supper was given him. Pahom had a talk with this peasant and asked him where he came from. The stranger answered that he came from beyond the Volga, where he had been working. One word led to another, and the man went on to say that many people were settling in those parts. He told how some people from his village had settled there. They had joined the Commune, and had had twenty-five acres per man granted them. The land was so good, he said, that the rye sown on it grew as high as a horse, and so thick that five cuts of a sickle made a sheaf. One peasant, he said, had brought nothing with him but his bare hands, and now he had six horses and two cows of his own.

Pahom's heart kindled with desire. He thought:

"Why should I suffer in this narrow hole, if one can live so well elsewhere? I will sell my land and my homestead here, and with the money I will start afresh over there and get everything new. In this crowded place one is always having trouble. But I must first go and find out all about it myself."

Towards summer he got ready and started. He went down the Volga on a steamer to Samara, then walked another three hundred miles on foot, and at last reached the place. It was just as the stranger had said. The peasants had plenty of land: every man had twenty- five acres of Communal land given him for his use, and any one who had money could buy, besides, at fifty-cents an acre as much good freehold land as he wanted.

Having found out all he wished to know, Pahom returned home as autumn came on, and began selling off his belongings. He sold his land at a profit, sold his homestead and all his cattle, and withdrew from membership of the Commune. He only waited till the spring, and then started with his family for the new settlement.

IV

As soon as Pahom and his family arrived at their new abode, he applied for admission into the Commune of a large village. He stood treat to the Elders, and obtained the necessary documents. Five shares of Communal land were given him for his own and his sons' use: that is to say 125 acres (not altogether, but in different fields) besides the use of the Communal pasture. Pahom put up the buildings he needed, and bought cattle. Of the Communal land alone he had three times as much as at his former home, and the land was good corn-land. He was ten times better off than he had been. He had plenty of arable land and pasturage, and could keep as many head of cattle as he liked.

At first, in the bustle of building and settling down, Pahom was pleased with it all, but when he got used to it he began to think that even here he had not enough land. The first year, he sowed wheat on his share of the Communal land, and had a good crop. He wanted to go on sowing wheat, but had not enough Communal land for the purpose, and what he had already used was not available; for in those parts wheat is only sown on virgin soil or on fallow land. It is sown for one or two years, and then the land lies fallow till it is again overgrown with prairie grass. There were many who wanted such land, and there was not enough for all; so that people quarrelled about it. Those who were better off, wanted it for growing wheat, and those who were poor, wanted it to let to dealers, so that they might raise money to pay their taxes. Pahom wanted to sow more wheat; so he rented land from a dealer for a year. He sowed much wheat and had a fine crop, but the land was too far from the village, the wheat had to be carted more than ten miles. After a time Pahom noticed that some peasant-dealers were living on separate farms, and were growing wealthy; and he thought:

"If I were to buy some freehold land, and have a homestead on it, it would be a different thing, altogether. Then it would all be nice and compact."

The question of buying freehold land recurred to him again and again.

He went on in the same way for three years; renting land and sowing wheat. The seasons turned out well and the crops were good, so that he began to lay money by. He might have gone on living contentedly, but he grew tired of having to rent other people's land every year, and having to scramble for it. Wherever there was good land to be had, the peasants would rush for it and it was taken up at once, so that unless you were sharp about it you got none. It happened in the third year that he and a dealer together rented a piece of pasture land from some peasants; and they had already ploughed it up, when there was some dispute, and the peasants went to law about it, and things fell out so that the labor was all lost. "If it were my own land," thought Pahom, "I should be independent, and there would not be all this unpleasantness."

So Pahom began looking out for land which he could buy; and he came across a peasant who had bought thirteen hundred acres, but having got into difficulties was willing to sell again cheap. Pahom bargained and haggled with him, and at last they settled the price at 1,500 roubles, part in cash and part to be paid later. They had all but clinched the matter, when a passing dealer happened to stop at Pahom's one day to get a feed for his horse. He drank tea with Pahom, and they had a talk. The dealer said that he was just returning from the land of the Bashkirs, far away, where he had bought thirteen thousand acres of land all for 1,000 roubles. Pahom questioned him further, and the tradesman said:

"All one need do is to make friends with the chiefs. I gave away about one hundred roubles' worth of dressing-gowns and carpets, besides a case of tea, and I gave wine to those who would drink it; and I got the land for less than two cents an acre. And he showed Pahom the title-deeds, saying:

"The land lies near a river, and the whole prairie is virgin soil."

Pahom plied him with questions, and the tradesman said:

"There is more land there than you could cover if you walked a year, and it all belongs to the Bashkirs. They are as simple as sheep, and land can be got almost for nothing."

"There now," thought Pahom, "with my one thousand roubles, why should I get only thirteen hundred acres, and saddle myself with a debt besides. If I take it out there, I can get more than ten times as much for the money."

V

Pahom inquired how to get to the place, and as soon as the tradesman had left him, he prepared to go there himself. He left his wife to look after the homestead, and started on his journey taking his man with him. They stopped at a town on their way, and bought a case of tea, some wine, and other presents, as the tradesman had advised. On and on they went until they had gone more than three hundred miles, and on the seventh day they came to a place where the Bashkirs had pitched their tents. It was all just as the tradesman had said. The people lived on the steppes, by a river, in felt-covered tents. They neither tilled the ground, nor ate bread. Their cattle and horses grazed in herds on the steppe. The colts were tethered behind the tents, and the mares were driven to them twice a day. The mares were milked, and from the milk kumiss was made. It was the women who prepared kumiss, and they also made cheese. As far as the men were concerned, drinking kumiss and tea, eating mutton, and playing on their pipes, was all they cared about. They were all stout and merry, and all the summer long they never thought of doing any work. They were quite ignorant, and knew no Russian, but were good-natured enough.

As soon as they saw Pahom, they came out of their tents and gathered round their visitor. An interpreter was found, and Pahom told them he had come about some land. The Bashkirs seemed very glad; they took Pahom and led him into one of the best tents, where they made him sit on some down cushions placed on a carpet, while they sat round him. They gave him tea and kumiss, and had a sheep killed, and gave him mutton to eat. Pahom took presents out of his cart and distributed them among the Bashkirs, and divided amongst them the tea. The Bashkirs were delighted. They talked a great deal among themselves, and then told the interpreter to translate.

"They wish to tell you," said the interpreter, "that they like you, and that it is our custom to do all we can to please a guest and to repay him for his gifts. You have given us presents, now tell us which of the things we possess please you best, that we may present them to you."

"What pleases me best here," answered Pahom, "is your land. Our land is crowded, and the soil s exhausted; but you have plenty of land and it is good land. I never saw the like of it."

The interpreter translated. The Bashkirs talked among themselves for a while. Pahom could not understand what they were saying, but saw that they were much amused, and that they shouted and laughed. Then they were silent and looked at Pahom while the interpreter said:

"They wish me to tell you that in return for your presents they will gladly give you as much land as you want. You have only to point it out with your hand and it is yours."

The Bashkirs talked again for a while and began to dispute. Pahom asked what they were disputing about, and the interpreter told him that some of them thought they ought to ask their Chief about the land and not act in his absence, while others thought there was no need to wait for his return.

VI
While the Bashkirs were disputing, a man in a large fox-fur cap appeared on the scene. They all became silent and rose to their feet. The interpreter said, "This is our Chief himself."

Pahom immediately fetched the best dressing-gown and five pounds of tea, and offered these to the Chief. The Chief accepted them, and seated himself in the place of honour. The Bashkirs at once began telling him something. The Chief listened for a while, then made a sign with his head for them to be silent, and addressing himself to Pahom, said in Russian:

"Well, let it be so. Choose whatever piece of land you like; we have plenty of it."

"How can I take as much as I like?" thought Pahom. "I must get a deed to make it secure, or else they may say, 'It is yours,' and afterwards may take it away again."

"Thank you for your kind words," he said aloud. "You have much land, and I only want a little. But I should like to be sure which bit is mine. Could it not be measured and made over to me? Life and death are in God's hands. You good people give it to me, but your children might wish to take it away again."

"You are quite right," said the Chief. "We will make it over to you."

"I heard that a dealer had been here," continued Pahom, "and that you gave him a little land, too, and signed title-deeds to that effect. I should like to have it done in the same way."

The Chief understood.

"Yes," replied he, "that can be done quite easily. We have a scribe, and we will go to town with you and have the deed properly sealed."

"And what will be the price?" asked Pahom.

"Our price is always the same: one thousand roubles a day."

Pahom did not understand.

"A day? What measure is that? How many acres would that be?"

"We do not know how to reckon it out," said the Chief. "We sell it by the day. As much as you can go round on your feet in a day is yours, and the price is one thousand roubles a day."

Pahom was surprised.

"But in a day you can get round a large tract of land," he said.

The Chief laughed.

"It will all be yours!" said he. "But there is one condition: If you don't return on the same day to the spot whence you started, your money is lost."

"But how am I to mark the way that I have gone?"

"Why, we shall go to any spot you like, and stay there. You must start from that spot and make your round, taking a spade with you. Wherever you think necessary, make a mark. At every turning, dig a hole and pile up the turf; then afterwards we will go round with a plough from hole to hole. You may make as large a circuit as you please, but before the sun sets you must return to the place you started from. All the land you cover will be yours."

Pahom was delighted. It-was decided to start early next morning. They talked a while, and after drinking some more kumiss and eating some more mutton, they had tea again, and then the night came on. They gave Pahom a feather-bed to sleep on, and the Bashkirs dispersed for the night, promising to assemble the next morning at daybreak and ride out before sunrise to the appointed spot.

VII

Pahom lay on the feather-bed, but could not sleep. He kept thinking about the land.

"What a large tract I will mark off!" thought he. "I can easily go thirty-five miles in a day. The days are long now, and within a circuit of thirty-five miles what a lot of land there will be! I will sell the poorer land, or let it to peasants, but I'll pick out the best and farm it. I will buy two ox-teams, and hire two more laborers. About a hundred and fifty acres shall be plough-land, and I will pasture cattle on the rest."

Pahom lay awake all night, and dozed off only just before dawn. Hardly were his eyes closed when he had a dream. He thought he was lying in that same tent, and heard somebody chuckling outside. He wondered who it could be, and rose and went out, and he saw the Bashkir Chief sitting in front of the tent holding his side and rolling about with laughter. Going nearer to the Chief, Pahom asked: "What are you laughing at?" But he saw that it was no longer the Chief, but the dealer who had recently stopped at his house and had told him about the land. Just as Pahom was going to ask, "Have you been here long?" he saw that it was not the dealer, but the peasant who had come up from the Volga, long ago, to Pahom's old home. Then he saw that it was not the peasant either, but the Devil himself with hoofs and horns, sitting there and chuckling, and before him lay a man barefoot, prostrate on the ground, with only trousers and a shirt on. And Pahom dreamt that he looked more attentively to see what sort of a man it was lying there, and he saw that the man was dead, and that it was himself! He awoke horror-struck.

"What things one does dream," thought he.

Looking round he saw through the open door that the dawn was breaking.

"It's time to wake them up," thought he. "We ought to be starting."

He got up, roused his man (who was sleeping in his cart), bade him harness; and went to call the Bashkirs.

"It's time to go to the steppe to measure the land," he said.

The Bashkirs rose and assembled, and the Chief came, too. Then they began drinking kumiss again, and offered Pahom some tea, but he would not wait.

"If we are to go, let us go. It is high time," said he.

VIII

The Bashkirs got ready and they all started: some mounted on horses, and some in carts. Pahom drove in his own small cart with his servant, and took a spade with him. When they reached the steppe, the morning red was beginning to kindle. They ascended a hillock (called by the Bashkirs a shikhan) and dismounting from their carts and their horses, gathered in one spot. The Chief came up to Pahom and stretched out his arm towards the plain:

"See," said he, "all this, as far as your eye can reach, is ours. You may have any part of it you like."

Pahom's eyes glistened: it was all virgin soil, as flat as the palm of your hand, as black as the seed of a poppy, and in the hollows different kinds of grasses grew breast high.

The Chief took off his fox-fur cap, placed it on the ground and said:

"This will be the mark. Start from here, and return here again. All the land you go round shall be yours."

Pahom took out his money and put it on the cap. Then he took off his outer coat, remaining in his sleeveless under coat. He unfastened his girdle and tied it tight below his stomach, put a little bag of bread into the breast of his coat, and tying a flask of water to his girdle, he drew up the tops of his boots, took the spade from his man, and stood ready to start. He considered for some moments which way he had better go, it was tempting everywhere.

"No matter," he concluded, "I will go towards the rising sun."

He turned his face to the east, stretched himself, and waited for the sun to appear above the rim.

"I must lose no time," he thought, "and it is easier walking while it is still cool."

The sun's rays had hardly flashed above the horizon, before Pahom, carrying the spade over his shoulder, went down into the steppe.

Pahom started walking neither slowly nor quickly. After having gone a thousand yards he stopped, dug a hole and placed pieces of turf one on another to make it more visible. Then he went on; and now that he had walked off his stiffness he quickened his pace. After a while he dug another hole.

Pahom looked back. The hillock could be distinctly seen in the sunlight, with the people on it, and the glittering tires of the cartwheels. At a rough guess Pahom concluded that he had walked three miles. It was growing warmer; he took off his under-coat, flung it across his shoulder, and went on again. It had grown quite warm now; he looked at the sun, it was time to think of breakfast.

"The first shift is done, but there are four in a day, and it is too soon yet to turn. But I will just take off my boots," said he to himself.

He sat down, took off his boots, stuck them into his girdle, and went on. It was easy walking now.

"I will go on for another three miles," thought he, "and then turn to the left. The spot is so fine, that it would be a pity to lose it. The further one goes, the better the land seems."

He went straight on a for a while, and when he looked round, the hillock was scarcely visible and the people on it looked like black ants, and he could just see something glistening there in the sun.

"Ah," thought Pahom, "I have gone far enough in this direction, it is time to turn. Besides I am in a regular sweat, and very thirsty."

He stopped, dug a large hole, and heaped up pieces of turf. Next he untied his flask, had a drink, and then turned sharply to the left. He went on and on; the grass was high, and it was very hot.

Pahom began to grow tired: he looked at the sun and saw that it was noon.

"Well," he thought, "I must have a rest."

He sat down, and ate some bread and drank some water; but he did not lie down, thinking that if he did he might fall asleep. After sitting a little while, he went on again. At first he walked easily: the food had strengthened him; but it had become terribly hot, and he felt sleepy; still he went on, thinking: "An hour to suffer, a life-time to live."

He went a long way in this direction also, and was about to turn to the left again, when he perceived a damp hollow: "It would be a pity to leave that out," he thought. "Flax would do well there." So he went on past the hollow, and dug a hole on the other side of it before he turned the corner. Pahom looked towards the hillock. The heat made the air hazy: it seemed to be quivering, and through the haze the people on the hillock could scarcely be seen.

"Ah!" thought Pahom, "I have made the sides too long; I must make this one shorter." And he went along the third side, stepping faster. He looked at the sun: it was nearly half way to the horizon, and he had not yet done two miles of the third side of the square. He was still ten miles from the goal.

"No," he thought, "though it will make my land lopsided, I must hurry back in a straight line now. I might go too far, and as it is I have a great deal of land."

So Pahom hurriedly dug a hole, and turned straight towards the hillock.

IX

Pahom went straight towards the hillock, but he now walked with difficulty. He was done up with the heat, his bare feet were cut and bruised, and his legs began to fail. He longed to rest, but it was impossible if he meant to get back before sunset. The sun waits for no man, and it was sinking lower and lower.

"Oh dear," he thought, "if only I have not blundered trying for too much! What if I am too late?"

He looked towards the hillock and at the sun. He was still far from his goal, and the sun was already near the rim. Pahom walked on and on; it was very hard walking, but he went quicker and quicker. He pressed on, but was still far from the place. He began running, threw away his coat, his boots, his flask, and his cap, and kept only the spade which he used as a support.

"What shall I do," he thought again, "I have grasped too much, and ruined the whole affair. I can't get there before the sun sets."

And this fear made him still more breathless. Pahom went on running, his soaking shirt and trousers stuck to him, and his mouth was parched. His breast was working like a blacksmith's bellows, his heart was beating like a hammer, and his legs were giving way as if they did not belong to him. Pahom was seized with terror lest he should die of the strain.

Though afraid of death, he could not stop. "After having run all that way they will call me a fool if I stop now," thought he. And he ran on and on, and drew near and heard the Bashkirs yelling and shouting to him, and their cries inflamed his heart still more. He gathered his last strength and ran on.

The sun was close to the rim, and cloaked in mist looked large, and red as blood. Now, yes now, it was about to set! The sun was quite low, but he was also quite near his aim. Pahom could already see the people on the hillock waving their arms to hurry him up. He could see the fox-fur cap on the ground, and the money on it, and the Chief sitting on the ground holding his sides. And Pahom remembered his dream.

"There is plenty of land," thought he, "but will God let me live on it? I have lost my life, I have lost my life! I shall never reach that spot!"

Pahom looked at the sun, which had reached the earth: one side of it had already disappeared. With all his remaining strength he rushed on, bending his body forward so that his legs could hardly follow fast enough to keep him from falling. Just as he reached the hillock it suddenly grew dark. He looked up, the sun had already set. He gave a cry: "All my labor has been in vain," thought he, and was about to stop, but he heard the Bashkirs still shouting, and remembered that though to him, from below, the sun seemed to have set, they on the hillock could still see it. He took a long breath and ran up the hillock. It was still light there. He reached the top and saw the cap. Before it sat the Chief laughing and holding his sides. Again Pahom remembered his dream, and he uttered a cry: his legs gave way beneath him, he fell forward and reached the cap with his hands.

"Ah, what a fine fellow!" exclaimed the Chief. "He has gained much land!"

Pahom's servant came running up and tried to raise him, but he saw that blood was flowing from his mouth. Pahom was dead!

The Bashkirs clicked their tongues to show their pity.

His servant picked up the spade and dug a grave long enough for Pahom to lie in, and buried him in it. Six feet from his head to his heels was all he needed.

Footnotes:
1. One hundred kopeks make a rouble. The kopek is worth about half a cent.
2. A non-intoxicating drink usually made from rye-malt and rye-flour.
3. The brick oven in a Russian peasant's hut is usually built so as to leave a flat top, large enough to lie on, for those who want to sleep in a warm place.
4. 120 "desyatins." The "desyatina" is properly 2.7 acres; but in this story round numbers are used.
5. Three roubles per "desyatina."
6. Five "kopeks" for a "desyatina."

Ivan The Fool

CHAPTER I
In a certain kingdom there lived a rich peasant, who had three sons, Simeon (a soldier), Tarras-Briukhan (fat man), and Ivan (a fool) and one daughter, Milania, born dumb. Simeon went to war, to serve the Czar; Tarras went to a city and became a merchant; and Ivan, with his sister, remained at home to work on the farm.

For his valiant service in the army, Simeon received an estate with high rank, and married a noble's daughter. Besides his large pay, he was in receipt of a handsome income from his estate; yet he was unable to make ends meet. What the husband saved, the wife wasted in extravagance. One day Simeon went to the estate to collect his income, when the steward informed him that there was no income, saying:

"We have neither horses, cows, fishing-nets, nor implements; it is necessary first to buy everything, and then to look for income."

Simeon thereupon went to his father and said:

"You are rich, batiushka [little father], but you have given nothing to me. Give me one-third of what you possess as my share, and I will transfer it to my estate."

The old man replied: "You did not help to bring prosperity to our household. For what reason, then, should you now demand the third part of everything? It would be unjust to Ivan and his sister."

"Yes," said Simeon; "but he is a fool, and she was born dumb. What need have they of anything?"

"See what Ivan will say."

Ivan's reply was: "Well, let him take his share."

Simeon took the portion allotted to him, and went again to serve in the army.

Tarras also met with success. He became rich and married a merchant's daughter, but even this failed to satisfy his desires, and he also went to his father and said, "Give me my share."

The old man, however, refused to comply with his request, saying: "You had no hand in the accumulation of our property, and what our household contains is the result of Ivan's hard work It would be unjust," he repeated, "to Ivan and his sister."

Tarras replied: "But he does not need it. He is a fool, and cannot marry, for no one will have him; and sister does not require anything, for she was born dumb." Turning then to Ivan he continued: "Give me half the grain you have, and I will not touch the implements or fishing-nets; and from the cattle I will take only the dark mare, as she is not fit to plow."

Ivan laughed and said: "Well, I will go and arrange matters so that Tarras may have his share," whereupon Tarras took the brown mare with the grain to town, leaving Ivan with one old horse to work on as before and support his father, mother, and sister.

CHAPTER II.
It was disappointing to the Stary Tchert (Old Devil) that the brothers did not quarrel over the division of the property, and that they separated peacefully; and he cried out, calling his three small devils (Tchertionki).

"See here," said he, "there are living three brothers, Simeon the soldier, Tarras-Briukhan, and Ivan the Fool. It is necessary that they should quarrel. Now they live peacefully, and enjoy each other's hospitality. The Fool spoiled all my plans. Now you three go and work with them in such a manner that they will be ready to tear each other's eyes out. Can you do this?"

"We can," they replied.

"How will you accomplish it?"

"In this way: We will first ruin them to such an extent that they will have nothing to eat, and we will then gather them together in one place where we are sure that they will fight."

"Very well; I see you understand your business. Go, and do not return to me until you have created a feud between the three brothers or I will skin you alive."

The three small devils went to a swamp to consult as to the best means of accomplishing their mission. They disputed for a long time, each one wanting the easiest part of the work and not being able to agree, concluded to draw lots; by which it was decided that the one who was first finished had to come and help the others. This agreement being entered into, they appointed a time when they were again to meet in the swamp, to find out who was through and who needed assistance.

The time having arrived, the young devils met in the swamp as agreed, when each related his experience. The first, who went to Simeon, said: "I have succeeded in my undertaking, and to-morrow Simeon returns to his father."

His comrades, eager for particulars, inquired how he had done it.

"Well," he began, "the first thing I did was to blow some courage into his veins, and, on the strength of it, Simeon went to the Czar and offered to conquer the whole world for him. The Emperor made him commander-in-chief of the forces, and sent him with an army to fight the Viceroy of India. Having started on their mission of conquest, they were unaware that I, following in their wake, had wet all their powder. I also went to the Indian ruler and showed him how I could create numberless soldiers from straw.

Simeon's army, seeing that they were surrounded by such a vast number of Indian warriors of my creation, became frightened, and Simeon commanded to fire from cannons and rifles, which of course they were unable to do. The soldiers, discouraged, retreated in great disorder. Thus Simeon brought upon himself the terrible disgrace of defeat. His estate was confiscated, and to-morrow he is to be executed. All that remains for me to do, therefore," concluded the young devil, "is to release him to-morrow morning. Now, then, who wants my assistance?"

The second small devil (from Tarras) then related his story.

"I do not need any help," he began. "My business is also all right. My work with Tarras will be finished in one week. In the first place I made him grow thin. He afterward became so covetous that he wanted to possess everything he saw, and he spent all the money he had in the purchase of immense quantities of goods. When his capital was gone he still continued to buy with borrowed money, and has become involved in such difficulties that he cannot free himself. At the end of one week the date for the payment of his notes will have expired, and, his goods being seized upon, he will become a bankrupt; and he also will return to his father."

At the conclusion of this narrative they inquired of the third devil how things had fared between him and Ivan.

"Well," said he, "my report is not so encouraging. The first thing I did was to spit into his jug of quass [a sour drink made from rye], which made him sick at his stomach. He afterward went to plow his summer-fallow, but I made the soil so hard that the plow could scarcely penetrate it. I thought the Fool would not succeed, but he started to work nevertheless. Moaning with pain, he still continued to labor. I broke one plow, but he replaced it with another, fixing it securely, and resumed work. Going beneath the surface of the ground I took hold of the plowshares, but did not succeed in stopping Ivan. He pressed so hard, and the colter was so sharp, that my hands were cut; and despite my utmost efforts, he went over all but a small portion of the field."

He concluded with: "Come, brothers, and help me, for if we do not conquer him our whole enterprise will be a failure. If the Fool is permitted successfully to conduct his farming, they will have no need, for he will support his brothers."

CHAPTER III.

Ivan having succeeded in plowing all but a small portion of his land, he returned the next day to finish it. The pain in his stomach continued, but he felt that he must go on with his work. He tried to start his plow, but it would not move; it seemed to have struck a hard root. It was the small devil in the ground who had wound his feet around the plowshares and held them.

"This is strange," thought Ivan. "There were never any roots here before, and this is surely one."

Ivan put his hand in the ground, and, feeling something soft, grasped and pulled it out. It was like a root in appearance, but seemed to possess life. Holding it up he saw that it was a little devil. Disgusted, he exclaimed, "See the nasty thing," and he proceeded to strike it a blow, intending to kill it, when the young devil cried out:

"Do not kill me, and I will grant your every wish."

"What can you do for me?"

"Tell me what it is you most wish for," the little devil replied.

Ivan, peasant-fashion, scratched the back of his head as he thought, and finally he said:

"I am dreadfully sick at my stomach. Can you cure me?"

"I can," the little devil said.

"Then do so."

The little devil bent toward the earth and began searching for roots, and when he found them he gave them to Ivan, saying: "If you will swallow some of these you will be immediately cured of whatsoever disease you are afflicted with. '

Ivan did as directed, and obtained instant relief.

"I beg of you to let me go now," the little devil pleaded; "I will pass into the earth, never to return."

"Very well; you may go, and God bless you;" and as Ivan pronounced the name of God, the small devil disappeared into the earth like a flash, and only a slight opening in the ground remained.

Ivan placed in his hat what roots he had left, and proceeded to plow. Soon finishing his work, he turned his plow over and returned home.

When he reached the house he found his brother Simeon and his wife seated at the supper-table. His estate had been confiscated, and he himself had barely escaped execution by making his way out of prison, and having nothing to live upon had come back to his father for support.

Turning to Ivan he said: "I came to ask you to care for us until I can find something to do."

"Very well," Ivan replied; "you may remain with us."

Just as Ivan was about to sit down to the table Simeon's wife made a wry face, indicating that she did not like the smell of Ivan's sheep-skin coat; and turning to her husband she said, "I shall not sit at the table with a moujik [peasant] who smells like that."

Simeon the soldier turned to his brother and said: "My lady objects to the smell of your clothes. You may eat in the porch."

Ivan said: "Very well, it is all the same to me. I will soon have to go and feed my horse any way."

Ivan took some bread in one hand, and his kaftan (coat) in the other, and left the room.

CHAPTER IV.

The small devil finished with Simeon that night, and according to agreement went to the assistance of his comrade who had charge of Ivan, that he might help to conquer the Fool. He went to the field and searched everywhere, but could find nothing but the hole through which the small devil had disappeared.

"Well, this is strange," he said; "something must have happened to my companion, and I will have to take his place and continue the work he began. The Fool is through with his plowing, so I must look about me for some other means of compassing his destruction. I must overflow his meadow and prevent him from cutting the grass."

The little devil accordingly overflowed the meadow with muddy water, and, when Ivan went at dawn next morning with his scythe set and sharpened and tried to mow the grass, he found that it resisted all his efforts and would not yield to the implement as usual.

Many times Ivan tried to cut the grass, but always without success. At last, becoming weary of the effort, he decided to return home and have his scythe again sharpened, and also to procure a quantity of bread, saying: "I will come back here and will not leave until I have mown all the meadow, even if it should take a whole week."

Hearing this, the little devil became thoughtful, saying: "That Ivan is a koolak [hard case], and I must think of some other way of conquering him."

Ivan soon returned with his sharpened scythe and started to mow.

The small devil hid himself in the grass, and as the point of the scythe came down he buried it in the earth and made it almost impossible for Ivan to move the implement. He, however, succeeded in mowing all but one small spot in the swamp, where again the small devil hid himself, saying: "Even if he should cut my hands I will prevent him from accomplishing his work."

When Ivan came to the swamp he found that the grass was not very thick. Still, the scythe would not work, which made him so angry that he worked with all his might, and one blow more powerful than the others cut off a portion of the small devil's tail, who had hidden himself there.

Despite the little devil's efforts he succeeded in finishing his work, when he returned home and ordered his sister to gather up the grass while he went to another field to cut rye. But the devil preceded him there, and fixed the rye in such a manner that it was almost impossible for Ivan to cut it; however, after continuous hard labor he succeeded, and when he was through with the rye he said to himself: "Now I will start to mow cats."

On hearing this, the little devil thought to himself: "I could not prevent him from mowing the rye, but I will surely stop him from mowing the oats when the morning comes."

Early next day, when the devil came to the field, he found that the oats had been already mowed. Ivan did it during the night, so as to avoid the loss that might have resulted from the grain being too ripe and dry. Seeing that Ivan again had escaped him, the little devil became greatly enraged, saving:

"He cut me all over and made me tired, that fool. I did not meet such misfortune even on the battle-field. He does not even sleep;" and the devil began to swear. "I cannot follow him," he continued. "I will go now to the heaps and make everything rotten."

Accordingly he went to a heap of the new-mown grain and began his fiendish work. After wetting it he built a fire and warmed himself, and soon was fast asleep.

Ivan harnessed his horse, and, with his sister, went to bring the rye home from the field.

After lifting a couple of sheaves from the first heap his pitchfork came into contact with the little devil's back, which caused the latter to howl with pain and to jump around in every direction. Ivan exclaimed:

"See here! What nastiness! You again here?"

"I am another one!" said the little devil. "That was my brother. I am the one who was sent to your brother Simeon."

"Well," said Ivan, "it matters not who you are. I will fix you all the same."

As Ivan was about to strike the first blow the devil pleaded: "Let me go and I will do you no more harm. I will do whatever you wish."

"What can you do for me?" asked Ivan.

"I can make soldiers from almost anything."

"And what will they be good for?"

"Oh, they will do everything for you!"

"Can they sing?"

"They can."

"Well, make them."

"Take a bunch of straw and scatter it on the ground, and see if each straw will not turn into a soldier."

Ivan shook the straws on the ground, and, as he expected, each straw turned into a soldier, and they began marching with a band at their head.

"Ishty [look you], that was well done! How it will delight the village maidens!" he exclaimed.

The small devil now said: "Let me go; you do not need me any longer."

But Ivan said: "No, I will not let you go just yet. You have converted the straw into soldiers, and now I want you to turn them again into straw, as I cannot afford to lose it, but I want it with the grain on."

The devil replied: "Say: 'So many soldiers, so much straw.'"

Ivan did as directed, and got back his rye with the straw.

The small devil again begged for his release.

Ivan, taking him from the pitchfork, said: "With God's blessing you may depart"; and, as before at the mention of God's name, the little devil was hurled into the earth like a flash, and nothing was left but the hole to show where he had gone.

Soon afterward Ivan returned home, to find his brother Tarras and his wife there. Tarras-Briukhan could not pay his debts, and was forced to flee from his creditors and seek refuge under his father's roof. Seeing Ivan, he said: "Well, Ivan, may we remain here until I start in some new business?"

Ivan replied as he had before to Simeon: "Yes, you are perfectly welcome to remain here as long as it suits you."

With that announcement he removed his coat and seated himself at the supper-table with the others. But Tarras-Briukhan's wife objected to the smell of his clothes, saying: "I cannot eat with a fool; neither can I stand the smell."

Then Tarras-Briukhan said: "Ivan, from your clothes there comes a bad smell; go and eat by yourself in the porch."

"Very well," said Ivan; and he took some bread and went out as ordered, saying, "It is time for me to feed my mare."

CHAPTER V.
The small devil who had charge of Tarras finished with him that night, and according to agreement proceeded to the assistance of the other two to help them conquer Ivan. Arriving at the plowed field he looked around for his comrades, but found only the hole through which one had disappeared; and on going to the meadow he discovered the severed tail of the other, and in the rye-field he found yet another hole.

"Well," he thought, "it is quite clear that my comrades have met with some great misfortune, and that I will have to take their places and arrange the feud between the brothers."

The small devil then went in search of Ivan. But he, having finished with the field, was nowhere to be found. He had gone to the forest to cut logs to build homes for his brothers, as they found it inconvenient for so many to live under the same roof.

The small devil at last discovered his whereabouts, and going to the forest climbed into the branches of the trees and began to interfere with Ivan's work. Ivan cut down a tree, which failed, however, to fall to the ground, becoming entangled in the branches of other trees; yet he succeeded in getting it down after a hard struggle. In chopping down the next tree he met with the same difficulties, and also with the third. Ivan had supposed he could cut down fifty trees in a day, but he succeeded in chopping but ten before darkness put an end to his labors for a time. He was now exhausted, and, perspiring profusely, he sat down alone in the woods to rest. He soon after resumed his work, cutting down one more tree; but the effort gave him a pain in his back, and he was obliged to rest again. Seeing this, the small devil was full of joy.

"Well," he thought, "now he is exhausted and will stop work, and I will rest also." He then seated himself on some branches and rejoiced.

Ivan again arose, however, and, taking his axe, gave the tree a terrific blow from the opposite side, which felled it instantly to the ground, carrying the little devil with it; and Ivan, proceeding to cut the branches, found the devil alive. Very much astonished, Ivan exclaimed:

"Look you! Such nastiness! Are you again here?"

"I am another one," replied the devil. "I was with your brother Tarras."

"Well," said Ivan, "that makes no difference; I will fix you." And he was about to strike him a blow with the axe when the devil pleaded:

"Do not kill me, and whatever you wish you shall have."

Ivan asked, "What can you do?"

"I can make for you all the money you wish."

Ivan then told the devil he might proceed, whereupon the latter began to explain to him how he might become rich.

"Take," said he to Ivan, "the leaves of this oak tree and rub them in your hands, and the gold will fall to the ground."

Ivan did as he was directed, and immediately the gold began to drop about his feet; and he remarked:

"This will be a fine trick to amuse the village boys with."

"Can I now take my departure?" asked the devil, to which Ivan replied, "With God's blessing you may go."

At the mention of the name of God, the devil disappeared into the earth.

CHAPTER VI.
The brothers, having finished their houses. moved into them and lived apart from their father and brother. Ivan, when he had completed his plowing, made a great feast, to which he invited his brothers, telling them that he had plenty of beer for them to drink. The brothers, however, declined Ivan's hospitality, saying, "We have seen the beer moujiks drink, and want none of it."

Ivan then gathered around him all the peasants in the village and with them drank beer until he became intoxicated, when he joined the Khorovody (a street gathering of the village boys and girls, who sing songs), and told them they must sing his praises, saying that in return he would show them such sights as they had never before seen in their lives. The little girls laughed and began to sing songs praising Ivan, and when they had finished they said: "Very well; now give us what you said you would."

Ivan replied, "I will soon show you," and, taking an empty bag in his hand, he started for the woods. The little girls laughed as they said, "What a fool he is!" and resuming their play they forgot all about him.

Some time after Ivan suddenly appeared among them carrying in his hand the bag, which was now filled.

"Shall I divide this with you?" he said.

"Yes; divide!" they sang in chorus.

So Ivan put his hand into the bag and drew it out full of gold coins, which he scattered among them.

"Batiushka," they cried as they ran to gather up the precious pieces.

The moujiks then appeared on the scene and began to fight among themselves for the possession of the yellow objects. In the melee one old woman was nearly crushed to death.

Ivan laughed and was greatly amused at the sight of so many persons quarrelling over a few pieces of gold.

"Oh! you duratchki" (little fools), he said, "why did you almost crush the life out of the old grandmother? Be more gentle. I have plenty more, and I will give them to you;" whereupon he began throwing about more of the coins.

The people gathered around him, and Ivan continued throwing until he emptied his bag. They clamored for more, but Ivan replied: "The gold is all gone. Another time I will give you more. Now we will resume our singing and dancing."

The little children sang, but Ivan said to them, "Your songs are no good."

The children said, "Then show us how to sing better."

To this Ivan replied, "I will show you people who can sing better than you." With that remark Ivan went to the barn and, securing a bundle of straw, did as the little devil had directed him; and presently a regiment of soldiers appeared in the village street, and he ordered them to sing and dance.

The people were astonished and could not understand how Ivan had produced the strangers.

The soldiers sang for some time, to the great delight of the villagers; and when Ivan commanded them to stop they instantly ceased.

Ivan then ordered them off to the barn, telling the astonished and mystified moujiks that they must not follow him. Reaching the barn, he turned the soldiers again into straw and went home to sleep off the effects of his debauch.

CHAPTER VII.

The next morning Ivan's exploits were the talk of the village, and news of the wonderful things he had done reached the ears of his brother Simeon, who immediately went to Ivan to learn all about it.

"Explain to me," he said; "from whence did you bring the soldiers, and where did you take them?"

"And what do you wish to know for?" asked Ivan.

"Why, with soldiers we can do almost anything we wish, whole kingdoms can be conquered," replied Simeon.

This information greatly surprised Ivan, who said: "Well, why did you not tell me about this before? I can make as many as you want "

Ivan then took his brother to the barn, but he said: "While I am willing to create the soldiers, you must take them away from here; for if it should become necessary to feed them, all the food in the village would last them only one day."

Simeon promised to do as Ivan wished, whereupon Ivan proceeded to convert the straw into soldiers. Out of one bundle of straw he made an entire regiment; in fact, so many soldiers appeared as if by magic that there was not a vacant spot in the field.

Turning to Simeon Ivan said, "Well, is there a sufficient number?"

Beaming with joy, Simeon replied: "Enough! enough! Thank you, Ivan!"

"Glad you are satisfied," said Ivan, "and if you wish more I will make them for you. I have plenty of straw now."

Simeon divided his soldiers into battalions and regiments, and after having drilled them he went forth to fight and to conquer.

Simeon had just gotten safely out of the village with his soldiers when Tarras, the other brother, appeared before Ivan, he also having heard of the previous day's performance and wanting to learn the secret of his power. He sought Ivan, saying: "Tell me the secret of your supply of gold, for if I had plenty of money I could with its assistance gather in all the wealth in the world."

Ivan was greatly surprised on hearing this statement, and said: "You might have told me this before, for I can obtain for you as much money as you wish."

Tarras was delighted, and he said, "You might get me about three bushels."

"Well," said Ivan, "we will go to the woods. or, better still, we will harness the horse, as we could not possibly carry so much money ourselves."

The brothers went to the woods and Ivan proceeded to gather the oak leaves, which he rubbed between his hands, the dust falling to the ground and turning into gold pieces as quickly as it fell.

When quite a pile had accumulated Ivan turned to Tarras and asked if he had rubbed enough leaves into money, whereupon Tarras replied: "Thank you, Ivan; that will be sufficient for this time."

Ivan then said: "If you wish more, come to me and I will rub as much as you want, for there are plenty of leaves."

Tarras, with his tarantas (wagon) filled with gold, rode away to the city to engage in trade and increase his wealth; and thus both brothers went their way, Simeon to fight and Tarras to trade.

Simeon's soldiers conquered a kingdom for him and Tarras-Briukhan made plenty of money.

Some time afterward the two brothers met and confessed to each other the source from whence sprang their prosperity, but they were not yet satisfied.

Simeon said: "I have conquered a kingdom and enjoy a very pleasant life, but I have not sufficient money to procure food for my soldiers;" while Tarras confessed that he was the possessor of enormous wealth, but the care of it caused him much uneasiness.

"Let us go again to our brother," said Simeon; "I will order him to make more soldiers and will give them to you, and you may then tell him that he must make more money so that we can buy food for them."

They went again to Ivan, and Simeon said: "I have not sufficient soldiers; I want you to make me at least two divisions more." But Ivan shook his head as he said: "I will not create soldiers for nothing; you must pay me for doing it."

"Well, but you promised," said Simeon.

"I know I did," replied Ivan; "but I have changed my mind since that time."

"But, fool, why will you not do as you promised?"

"For the reason that your soldiers kill men, and I will not make any more for such a cruel purpose." With this reply Ivan remained stubborn and would not create any more soldiers.

Tarras-Briukhan next approached Ivan and ordered him to make more money; but, as in the case of Tarras, Ivan only shook his head, as he said: "I will not make you any money unless you pay me for doing it. I cannot work without pay."

Tarras then reminded him of his promise.

"I know I promised," replied Ivan; "but still I must refuse to do as you wish."

"But why, fool, will you not fulfill your promise?" asked Tarras.

"For the reason that your gold was the means of depriving Mikhailovna of her cow."

"But how did that happen?" inquired Tarras.

"It happened in this way," said Ivan. "Mikhailovna always kept a cow, and her children had plenty of milk to drink; but some time ago one of her boys came to me to beg for some milk, and I asked, 'Where is your cow?' when he replied, 'A clerk of Tarras-Briukhan came to our home and offered three gold pieces for her. Our mother could not resist the temptation, and now we have no milk to drink. I gave you the gold pieces for your pleasure, and you put them to such poor use that I will not give you any more.'"

The brothers, on hearing this, took their departure to discuss as to the best plan to pursue in regard to a settlement of their troubles.

Simeon said: "Let us arrange it in this way: I will give you the half of my kingdom, and soldiers to keep guard over your wealth; and you give me money to feed the soldiers in my half of the kingdom."

To this arrangement Tarras agreed, and both the brothers became rulers and very happy.

CHAPTER VIII.
Ivan remained on the farm and worked to support his father, mother, and dumb sister. Once it happened that the old dog, which had grown up on the farm, was taken sick, when Ivan thought he was dying, and, taking pity on the animal, placed some bread in his hat and carried it to him. It happened that when he turned out the bread the root which the little devil had given him fell out also. The old dog swallowed it with the bread and was almost instantly cured, when he jumped up and began to wag his tail as an expression of joy. Ivan's father and mother, seeing the dog cured so quickly, asked by what means he had performed such a miracle.

Ivan replied: "I had some roots which would cure any disease, and the dog swallowed one of them."

It happened about that time that the Czar's daughter became ill, and her father had it announced in every city, town, and village that whosoever would cure her would be richly rewarded; and if the lucky person should prove to be a single man he would give her in marriage to him.

This announcement, of course, appeared in Ivan's village.

Ivan's father and mother called him and said: "If you have any of those wonderful roots, go and cure the Czar's daughter. You will be much happier for having performed such a kind act, indeed, you will be made happy for all your after life."

"Very well," said Ivan; and he immediately made ready for the journey. As he reached the porch on his way out he saw a poor woman standing directly in his path and holding a broken arm. The woman accosted him, saying:

"I was told that you could cure me, and will you not please do so, as I am powerless to do anything for myself?"

Ivan replied: "Very well, my poor woman; I will relieve you if I can."

He produced a root which he handed to the poor woman and told her to swallow it.

She did as Ivan told her and was instantly cured, and went away rejoicing that she had recovered the use of her arm.

Ivan's father and mother came out to wish him good luck on his journey, and to them he told the story of the poor woman, saying that he had given her his last root. On hearing this his parents were much distressed, as they now believed him to be without the means of curing the Czar's daughter, and began to scold him.

"You had pity for a beggar and gave no thought to the Czar's daughter," they said.

"I have pity for the Czar's daughter also," replied Ivan, after which he harnessed his horse to his wagon and took his seat ready for his departure; whereupon his parents said: "Where are you going, you fool, to cure the Czar's daughter, and without anything to do it with?"

"Very well," replied Ivan, as he drove away.

In due time he arrived at the palace, and the moment he appeared on the balcony the Czar's daughter was cured. The Czar was overjoyed and ordered Ivan to be brought into his presence. He dressed him in the richest robes and addressed him as his son-in-law. Ivan was married to the Czarevna, and, the Czar dying soon after, Ivan became ruler. Thus the three brothers became rulers in different kingdoms.

CHAPTER IX.

The brothers lived and reigned. Simeon, the eldest brother, with his straw soldiers took captive the genuine soldiers and trained all alike. He was feared by every one.

Tarras-Briukhan, the other brother, did not squander the gold he obtained from Ivan, but instead greatly increased his wealth, and at the same time lived well. He kept his money in large trunks, and, while having more than he knew what to do with, still continued to collect money from his subjects. The people had to work for the money to pay the taxes which Tarras levied on them, and life was made burdensome to them.

Ivan the Fool did not enjoy his wealth and power to the same extent as did his brothers. As soon as his father-in-law, the late Czar, was buried, he discarded the Imperial robes which had fallen to him and told his wife to put them away, as he had no further use for them. Having cast aside the insignia of his rank, he once more donned his peasant garb and started to work as of old.

"I felt lonesome," he said, "and began to grow enormously stout, and yet I had no appetite, and neither could I sleep."

Ivan sent for his father, mother, and dumb sister, and brought them to live with him, and they worked with him at whatever he chose to do.

The people soon learned that Ivan was a fool. His wife one day said to him, "The people say you are a fool, Ivan."

"Well, let them think so if they wish," he replied.

His wife pondered this reply for some time, and at last decided that if Ivan was a fool she also was one, and that it would be useless to go contrary to her husband, thinking affectionately of the old proverb that "where the needle goes there goes the thread also." She therefore cast aside her magnificent robes, and, putting them into the trunk with Ivan's, dressed herself in cheap clothing and joined her dumb sister-in-law, with the intention of learning to work. She succeeded so well that she soon became a great help to Ivan.

Seeing that Ivan was a fool, all the wise men left the kingdom and only the fools remained. They had no money, their wealth consisting only of the products of their labor. But they lived peacefully together, supported themselves in comfort, and had plenty to spare for the needy and afflicted.

CHAPTER X.

The old devil grew tired of waiting for the good news which he expected the little devils to bring him. He waited in vain to hear of the ruin of the brothers, so he went in search of the emissaries which he had sent to perform that work for him. After looking around for some time, and seeing nothing but the three holes in the ground, he decided that they had not succeeded in their work and that he would have to do it himself.

The old devil next went in search of the brothers, but he could learn nothing of their whereabouts. After some time he found them in their different kingdoms, contented and happy. This greatly incensed the old devil, and he said, "I will now have to accomplish their mission myself."

He first visited Simeon the soldier, and appeared before him as a voyevoda (general), saying: "You, Simeon, are a great warrior, and I also have had considerable experience in warfare, and am desirous of serving you."

Simeon questioned the disguised devil, and seeing that he was an intelligent man took him into his service.

The new General taught Simeon how to strengthen his army until it became very powerful. New implements of warfare were introduced.

Cannons capable of throwing one hundred balls a minute were also constructed, and these, it was expected, would be of deadly effect in battle.

Simeon, on the advice of his new General, ordered all young men above a certain age to report for drill. On the same advice Simeon established gun-shops, where immense numbers of cannons and rifles were made.

The next move of the new General was to have Simeon declare war against the neighboring kingdom. This he did, and with his immense army marched into the adjoining territory, which he pillaged and burned, destroying more than half the enemy's soldiers. This so frightened the ruler of that country that he willingly gave up half of his kingdom to save the other half.

Simeon, overjoyed at his success, declared his intention of marching into Indian territory and subduing the Viceroy of that country.

But Simeon's intentions reached the ears of the Indian ruler, who prepared to do battle with him. In addition to having secured all the latest implements of warfare, he added still others of his own invention. He ordered all boys over fourteen and all single women to be drafted into the army, until its proportions became much larger than Simeon's. His cannons and rifles were of the same pattern as Simeon's, and he invented a flying-machine from which bombs could be thrown into the enemy's camp.

Simeon went forth to conquer the Viceroy with full confidence in his own powers to succeed. This time luck forsook him, and instead of being the conqueror he was himself conquered.

The Indian ruler had so arranged his army that Simeon could not even get within shooting distance, while the bombs from the flying-machine carried destruction and terror in their path, completely routing his army, so that Simeon was left alone.

The Viceroy took possession of his kingdom and Simeon had to fly for his life.

Having finished with Simeon, the old devil next approached Tarras. He appeared before him disguised as one of the merchants of his kingdom, and established factories and began to make money. The "merchant" paid the highest price for everything he purchased, and the people ran after him to sell their goods. Through this "merchant" they were enabled to make plenty of money, paying up all their arrears of taxes as well as the others when they came due.

Tarras was overjoyed at this condition of affairs and said: "Thanks to this merchant, now I will have more money than before, and life will be much pleasanter for me."

He wished to erect new buildings, and advertised for workmen, offering the highest prices for all kinds of labor. Tarras thought the people would be as anxious to work as formerly, but instead he was much surprised to learn that they were working for the "merchant." Thinking to induce them to leave the "merchant," he increased his offers, but the former, equal to the emergency, also raised the wages of his workmen. Tarras, having plenty of money, increased the offers still more; but the "merchant" raised them still higher and got the better of him. Thus, defeated at every point, Tarras was compelled to abandon the idea of building.

Tarras next announced that he intended laying out gardens and erecting fountains, and the work was to be commenced in the fall, but no one came to offer his services, and again he was obliged to forego his intentions. Winter set in, and Tarras wanted some sable fur with which to line his great-coat, and he sent his man to procure it for him; but the servant returned without it, saying: "There are no sables to be had. The 'merchant' has bought them all, paying a very high price for them."

Tarras needed horses and sent a messenger to purchase them, but he returned with the same story as on former occasions, that none were to be found, the "merchant" having bought them all to carry water for an artificial pond he was constructing. Tarras was at last compelled to suspend business, as he could not find any one willing to work for him. They had all gone over to the "merchant's" side. The only dealings the people had with Tarras were when they went to pay their taxes. His money accumulated so fast that he could not find a place to put it, and his life became miserable. He abandoned all idea of entering upon the new venture, and only thought of how to exist peaceably. This he found it difficult to do, for, turn which way he would, fresh obstacles confronted him. Even his cooks, coachmen, and all his other servants forsook him and joined the "merchant." With all his wealth he had nothing to eat, and when he went to market he found the "merchant" had been there before him and had bought up all the provisions. Still, the people continued to bring him money.

Tarras at last became so indignant that he ordered the "merchant" out of his kingdom. He left, but settled just outside the boundary line, and continued his business with the same result as before, and Tarras was frequently forced to go without food for days. It was rumored that the "merchant" wanted to buy even Tarras himself. On hearing this the latter became very much alarmed and could not decide as to the best course to pursue.

About this time his brother Simeon arrived in the kingdom, and said: "Help me, for I have been defeated and ruined by the Indian Viceroy."

Tarras replied: "How can I help you, when I have had no food myself for two days?"

CHAPTER XI.

The old devil, having finished with the second brother, went to Ivan the Fool. This time he disguised himself as a General, the same as in the case of Simeon, and, appearing before Ivan, said: "Get an army together. It is disgraceful for the ruler of a kingdom to be without an army. You call your people to assemble, and I will form them into a fine large army."

Ivan took the supposed General's advice, and said: "Well, you may form my people into an army, but you must also teach them to sing the songs I like."

The old devil then went through Ivan's kingdom to secure recruits for the army, saying: "Come, shave your heads [the heads of recruits are always shaved in Russia] and I will give each of you a red hat and plenty of vodki" (whiskey).

At this the fools only laughed, and said: "We can have all the vodki we want, for we distill it ourselves; and of hats, our little girls make all we want, of any color we please, and with handsome fringes."

Thus was the devil foiled in securing recruits for his army; so he returned to Ivan and said: "Your fools will not volunteer to be soldiers. It will therefore be necessary to force them."

"Very well," replied Ivan, "you may use force if you want to."

The old devil then announced that all the fools must become soldiers, and those who refused, Ivan would punish with death.

The fools went to the General; and said: "You tell us that Ivan will punish with death all those who refuse to become soldiers, but you have omitted to state what will be done with us soldiers.

We have been told that we are only to be killed."

"Yes, that is true," was the reply.

The fools on hearing this became stubborn and refused to go.

"Better kill us now if we cannot avoid death, but we will not become soldiers," they declared.

"Oh! you fools," said the old devil, "soldiers may and may not be killed; but if you disobey Ivan's orders you will find certain death at his hands."

The fools remained absorbed in thought for some time and finally went to Ivan to question him in regard to the matter.

On arriving at his house they said: "A General came to us with an order from you that we were al to become soldiers, and if we refused you were to punish us with death. Is it true?"

Ivan began to laugh heartily on hearing this, and said: "Well, how I alone can punish you with death is something I cannot understand. If I was not a fool myself I would be able to explain it to you, but as it is I cannot."

"Well, then, we will not go," they said.

"Very well," replied Ivan, "you need not become soldiers unless you wish to."

The old devil, seeing his schemes about to prove failures, went to the ruler of Tarakania and became his friend, saying: "Let us go and conquer Ivan's kingdom. He has no money, but he has plenty of cattle, provisions, and various other things that would be useful to us."

The Tarakanian ruler gathered his large army together, and equipping it with cannons and rifles, crossed the boundary line into Ivan's kingdom. The people went to Ivan and said: "The ruler of Tarakania is here with a large army to fight us."

"Let them come," replied Ivan.

The Tarakanian ruler, after crossing the line into Ivan's kingdom, looked in vain for soldiers to fight against; and waiting some time and none appearing, he sent his own warriors to attack the villages.

They soon reached the first village, which they began to plunder.

The fools of both sexes looked calmly on, offering not the least resistance when their cattle and provisions were being taken from them. On the contrary, they invited the soldiers to come and live with them, saying: "If you, dear friends, find it is difficult to earn a living in your own land, come and live with us, where everything is plentiful."

The soldiers decided to remain, finding the people happy and prosperous, with enough surplus food to supply many of their neighbors. They were surprised at the cordial greetings which they everywhere received, and, returning to the ruler of Tarakania, they said: "We cannot fight with these people, take us to another place. We would much prefer the dangers of actual warfare to this unsoldierly method of subduing the village."

The Tarakanian ruler, becoming enraged, ordered the soldiers to destroy the whole kingdom, plunder the villages, burn the houses and provisions, and slaughter the cattle.

"Should you disobey my orders," said he, "I will have every one of you executed."

The soldiers, becoming frightened, started to do as they were ordered, but the fools wept bitterly, offering no resistance, men, women, and children all joining in the general lamentation.

"Why do you treat us so cruelly?" they cried to the invading soldiers. "Why do you wish to destroy everything we have? If you have more need of these things than we have, why not take them with you and leave us in peace?"

The soldiers, becoming saddened with remorse, refused further to pursue their path of destruction, the entire army scattering in many directions.

CHAPTER XII.
The old devil, failing to ruin Ivan's kingdom with soldiers, transformed himself into a nobleman, dressed exquisitely, and became one of Ivan's subjects, with the intention of compassing the downfall of his kingdom as he had done with that of Tarras.

The "nobleman" said to Ivan: "I desire to teach you wisdom and to render you other service. I will build you a palace and factories."

"Very well," said Ivan; "you may live with us."

The next day the "nobleman" appeared on the Square with a sack of gold in his hand and a plan for building a house, saying to the people: "You are living like pigs, and I am going to teach you how to live decently. You are to build a house for me according to this plan. I will superintend the work myself, and will pay you for your services in gold," showing them at the same time the contents of his sack.

The fools were amused. They had never before seen any money. Their business was conducted entirely by exchange of farm products or by hiring themselves out to work by the day in return for whatever they most needed. They therefore glanced at the gold pieces with amazement, and said, "What nice toys they would be to play with!" In return for the gold they gave their services and brought the "nobleman" the produce of their farms.

The old devil was overjoyed as he thought, "Now my enterprise is on a fair road and I will be able to ruin the Fool as I did his brothers."

The fools obtained sufficient gold to distribute among the entire community, the women and young girls of the village wearing much of it as ornaments, while to the children they gave some pieces to play with on the streets.

When they had secured all they wanted they stopped working and the "noblemen" did not get his house more than half finished. He had neither provisions nor cattle for the year, and ordered the people to bring him both. He directed them also to go on with the building of the palace and factories. He promised to pay them liberally in gold for everything they did. No one responded to his call, only once in awhile a little boy or girl would call to exchange eggs for his gold.

Thus was the "nobleman" deserted, and, having nothing to eat, he went to the village to procure some provisions for his dinner. He went to one house and offered gold in return for a chicken, but was refused, the owner saying: "We have enough of that already and do not want any more."

He next went to a fish-woman to buy some herring, when she, too, refused to accept his gold in return for fish, saying: "I do not wish it, my dear man; I have no children to whom I can give it to play with. I have three pieces which I keep as curiosities only."

He then went to a peasant to buy bread, but he also refused to accept the gold. "I have no use for it," said he, "unless you wish to give it for Christ's sake; then it will be a different matter, and I will tell my baba [old woman] to cut a piece of bread for you."

The old devil was so angry that he ran away from the peasant, spitting and cursing as he went.

Not only did the offer to accept in the name of Christ anger him, but the very mention of the name was like the thrust of a knife in his throat.

The old devil did not succeed in getting any bread, and in his efforts to secure other articles of food he met with the same failure. The people had all the gold they wanted and what pieces they had they regarded as curiosities. They said to the old devil: "If you bring us something else in exchange for food, or come to ask for Christ's sake, we will give you all you want."

But the old devil had nothing but gold, and was too lazy to work; and being unable to accept anything for Christ's sake, he was greatly enraged.

"What else do you want?" he said. "I will give you gold with which you can buy everything you want, and you need labor no longer."

But the fools would not accept his gold, nor listen to him. Thus the old devil was obliged to go to sleep hungry.

Tidings of this condition of affairs soon reached the ears of Ivan. The people went to him and said: "What shell we do? This nobleman appeared among us; he is well dressed; he wishes to eat and drink of the best, but is unwilling to work, and does not beg for food for Christ's sake. He only offers every one gold pieces. At first we gave him everything he wanted, taking the gold pieces in exchange just as curiosities; but now we have enough of them and refuse to accept any more from him. What shallwe do with him? he may die of hunger!"

Ivan heard all they had to say, and told them to employ him as a shepherd, taking turns in doing so.

The old devil saw no other way out of the difficulty and was obliged to submit.

It soon came the old devil's turn to go to Ivan's house. He went there to dinner and found Ivan's dumb sister preparing the meal. She was often cheated by the lazy people, who while they did not work, yet ate up all the gruel. But she learned to know the lazy people from the condition of their hands. Those with great welts on their hands she invited first to the table, and those having smooth white hands had to take what was left.

The old devil took a seat at the table, but the dumb girl, taking his hands, looked at them, and seeing them white and clean, and with long nails, swore at him and put him from the table.

Ivan's wife said to the old devil: "You must excuse my sister-in-law; she will not allow any one to sit at the table whose hands have not been hardened by toil, so you will have to wait until the dinner is over and then you can have what is left.

With it you must be satisfied."

The old devil was very much offended that he was made to eat with "pigs," as he expressed it, and complained to Ivan, saying: "The foolish law you have in your kingdom, that all persons must work, is surely the invention of fools. People who work for a living are not always forced to labor with their hands. Do you think wise men labor so?"

Ivan replied: "Well, what do fools know about it? We all work with our hands."

"And for that reason you are fools," replied the devil. "I can teach you how to use your brains, and you will find such labor more beneficial."

Ivan was surprised at hearing this, and said:

"Well, it is perhaps not without good reason that we are called fools."

"It is not so easy to work with the brain," the old devil said. "You will not give me anything to eat because my hands have not the appearance of being toil-hardened, but you must understand that it is much harder to do brain-work, and sometimes the head feels like bursting with the effort it is forced to make."

"Then why do you not select some light work that you can perform with your hands?" Ivan asked.

The devil said: "I torment myself with brain-work because I have pity for you fools, for, if I did not torture myself, people like you would remain fools for all eternity. I have exercised my brain a great deal during my life, and now I am able to teach you."

Ivan was greatly surprised and said: "Very well; teach us, so that when our hands are tired we can use our heads to replace them."

The devil promised to instruct the people, and Ivan announced the fact throughout his kingdom.

The devil was willing to teach all those who came to him how to use the head instead of the hands, so as to produce more with the former than with the latter.

In Ivan's kingdom there was a high tower, which was reached by a long, narrow ladder leading up to the balcony, and Ivan told the old devil that from the top of the tower every one could see him.

So the old devil went up to the balcony and addressed the people.

The fools came in great crowds to hear what the old devil had to say, thinking that he really meant to tell them how to work with the head. But the old devil only told them in words what to do, and did not give them any practical instruction. He said that men working only with their hands could not make a living. The fools did not understand what he said to them and looked at him in amazement, and then departed for their daily work.

The old devil addressed them for two days from the balcony, and at the end of that time, feeling hungry, he asked the people to bring him some bread. But they only laughed at him and told him if he could work better with his head than with his hands he could also find bread for himself. He addressed the people for yet another day, and they went to hear him from curiosity, but soon left him to return to their work.

Ivan asked, "Well, did the nobleman work with his head?"

"Not yet," they said; "so far he has only talked."

One day, while the old devil was standing on the balcony, he became weak, and, falling down, hurt his head against a pole.

Seeing this, one of the fools ran to Ivan's wife and said, "The gentleman has at last commenced to work with his head."

She ran to the field to tell Ivan, who was much surprised, and said, "Let us go and see him."

He turned his horses' heads in the direction of the tower, where the old devil remained weak from hunger and was still suspended from the pole, with his body swaying back and forth and his head striking the lower part of the pole each time it came in contact with it. While Ivan was looking, the old devil started down the steps head-first, as they supposed, to count them.

"Well," said Ivan, "he told the truth after all, that sometimes from this kind of work the head bursts. This is far worse than welts on the hands."

The old devil fell to the ground head-foremost. Ivan approached him, but at that instant the ground opened and the devil disappeared, leaving only a hole to show where he had gone.

Ivan scratched his head and said: "See here; such nastiness! This is yet another devil. He looks like the father of the little ones."

Ivan still lives, and people flock to his kingdom. His brothers come to him and he feeds them.

To every one who comes to him and says, "Give us food," he replies: "Very well; you are welcome. We have plenty of everything."

There is only one unchangeable custom observed in Ivan's kingdom: The man with toil-hardened hands is always given a seat at the table, while the possessor of soft white hands must be contented with what is left.

A Lost Opportunity

Then came Peter to Him, and said, Lord, how oft shall my brother sin against me, and I forgive him? till seven times?" . . . . "So likewise shall My heavenly Father do also unto you, if ye from your hearts forgive not every one his brother their trespasses." ST. MATTHEW xviii., 21-35.

In a certain village there lived a peasant by the name of Ivan Scherbakoff. He was prosperous, strong, and vigorous, and was considered the hardest worker in the whole village. He had three sons, who supported themselves by their own labor. The eldest was married, the second about to be married, and the youngest took care of the horses and occasionally attended to the plowing.

The peasant's wife, Ivanovna, was intelligent and industrious, while her daughter-in-law was a simple, quiet soul, but a hard worker.

There was only one idle person in the household, and that was Ivan's father, a very old man who for seven years had suffered from asthma, and who spent the greater part of his time lying on the brick oven.

Ivan had plenty of everything, three horses, with one colt, a cow with calf, and fifteen sheep. The women made the men's clothes, and in addition to performing all the necessary household labor, also worked in the field; while the men's industry was confined altogether to the farm.

What was left of the previous year's supply of provisions was ample for their needs, and they sold a quantity of oats sufficient to pay their taxes and other expenses.

Thus life went smoothly for Ivan.

The peasant's next-door neighbor was a son of Gordey Ivanoff, called "Gavryl the Lame." It once happened that Ivan had a quarrel with him; but while old man Gordey was yet alive, and Ivan's father was the head of the household, the two peasants lived as good neighbors should. If the women of one house required the use of a sieve or pail, they borrowed it from the inmates of the other house. The same condition of affairs existed between the men. They lived more like one family, the one dividing his possessions w th the other, and perfect harmony reigned between the two families.

If a stray calf or cow invaded the garden of one of the farmers, the other willingly drove it away, saying: "Be careful, neighbor, that your stock does not again stray into my garden; we should put a fence up." In the same way they had no secrets from each other. The doors of their houses and barns had neither bolts nor locks, so sure were they of each other's honesty. Not a shadow of suspicion darkened their daily ntercourse.

Thus lived the old people.

In time the younger members of the two households started farming. It soon became apparent that they would not get along as peacefully as the old people had done, for they began quarrelling without the slightest provocation.

A hen belonging to Ivan's daugnter-in-law commenced laying eggs, which the young woman collected each morning, intending to keep them for the Easter holidays. She made daily visits to the barn, where, under an old wagon, she was sure to find the precious egg.

One day the children frightened the hen and she flew over their neighbor's fence and laid her egg in their garden.

Ivan's daughter-in-law heard the hen cackling, but said: "I am very busy just at present, for this is the eve of a holy day, and I must clean and arrange this room. I will go for the egg later on."

When evening came, and she had finished her task, she went to the barn, and as usual looked ur der the old wagon, expecting to find an egg. But, alas! no egg was visible in the accustomed place.

Greatly disappointed, she returned to the house and inquired of her mother-in-law and the other members of the family if they had taken it. "No," they said, "we know nothing of it."

Taraska, the youngest brother-in-law, coming in soon after, she also inquired of him if he knew anything about the missing egg. "Yes," he replied; "your pretty, crested hen laid her egg in our neighbors' garden, and after she had finished cackling she flew back again over the fence."

The young woman, greatly surprised on hearing this, turned and looked long and seriously at the hen, which was sitting with closed eyes beside the rooster in the chimney-corner. She asked the hen where it laid the egg. At the sound of her voice it simply opened and closed its eyes, but could make no answer.

She then went to the neighbors' house, where she was met by an old woman, who said: "What do you want, young woman?"

Ivan's daughter-in-law replied: "You see, babushka [grandmother], my hen flew into your yard this morning. Did she not lay an egg there?"

"We did not see any," the old woman repl ed; "we have our own hens. God be praised! and they have been laying for this long time. We hunt only for the eggs our own hens lay, and have no use for the eggs other people's hens lay. Another thing I want to tell you, young woman: we do not go irto other people's yards to look for eggs."

Now this speech greatly angered the young woman, and she replied in the same spirit in which she had been spoken to, only using much stronger language and speaking at greater length.

The neighbor replied in the same angry manner, and finally the women began to abuse each other and call vile names. It happened that old Ivan's wife, on her way to the well for water, heard the dispute, and joined the others, taking her daughter-in-law's part.

Gavryl's housekeeper, hearing the noise, could not resist the temptation to join the rest and to make her voice heard. As soon as she appeared on the scene, she, too, began to abuse her neighbor, reminding her of many disagreeable things which had happened (and many which had not happened) between them. She became so infuriated during her denunciations that she lost all control of herself, and ran around like some mad creature.

Then all the women began to shout at the same time, each trying to say two words to another's one, and using the vilest language in the quarreller's vocabulary.

"You are such and such," shouted one of the women. "You are a thief, a schlukha [a mean, dirty, low creature]; your father-in-law is even now starving, and you have no shame. You beggar, you borrowed my sieve and broke it. You made a large hole in it, and did not buy me another."

"You have our scale-beam," cried another woman, "and must give it back to me;" whereupon she seized the scale-beam and tried to remove it from the shoulders of Ivan's wife.

In the melee which followed they upset the pails of water. They tore the covering from each other's head, and a general fight ensued.

Gavryl's wife had by this time joined in the fracas, and he, crossing the field and seeing the trouble, came to her rescue.

Ivan and his son, seeing that their womenfolk were being badly used, jumped into the midst of the fray, and a fearful fight followed.

Ivan was the most powerful peasant in all the country round, and it did not take him long to disperse the crowd, for they flew in all directions. During the progress of the fight Ivan tore out a large quantity of Gavryl's beard.

By this time a large crowd of peasants had collected, and it was with the greatest difficulty that they persuaded the two families to stop quarrelling.

This was the beginning.

Gavryl took the portion of his beard which Ivan had torn out, and, wrapping it in a paper, went to the volostnoye (moujiks' court) and entered a complaint against Ivan.

Holding up the hair, he said, "I did not grow this for that bear Ivan to tear out!"

Gavryl's wife went round among the neighbors, telling them that they must not repeat what she told them, but that she and her husband were going to get the best of Ivan, and that he was to be sent to Siberia.

And so the quarrelling went on.

The poor old grandfather, sick with asthma and lying on the brick oven all the time, tried from the first to dissuade them from quarrelling, and begged of them to live in peace; but they would not listen to his good advice. He said to them: "You children are making a great fuss and much trouble about nothing. I beg of you to stop and think of what a little thing has caused all this trouble. It has arisen from only one egg. If our neighbors' children picked it up, it is all right. God bless them! One egg is of but little value, and without it God will supply sufficient for all our needs."

Ivan's daughter-in-law here interposed and said, "But they called us vile names."

The old grandfather again spoke, saying: "Well, even if they did call you bad names, it would have been better to return good for evil, and by your example show them how to speak better. Such conduct on your part would have been best for all concerned." He continued: "Well, you had a fight, you wicked people. Such things sometimes happen, but it would be better if you went afterward and asked forgiveness and buried your grievances out of sight. Scatter them to the four winds of heaven, for if you do not do so it will be the worse for you in the end."

The younger members of the family, still obstinate, refused to profit by the old man's advice, and declared he was not right, and that he only liked to grumble in his old-fashioned way.

Ivan refused to go to his neighbor, as the grandfather wished, saying: "I did not tear out Gavryl's beard. He did it himself, and his son tore my shirt and trousers into shreds."

Ivan entered suit against Gavryl. He first went to the village justice, and not getting satisfaction from him he carried his case to the village court.

While the neighbors were wrangling over the affair, each suing the other, it happened that a perch-bolt from Gavryl's wagon was lost; and the women of Gavryl's household accused Ivan's son of stealing it.

They said: "We saw him in the night-time pass by our window, on his way to where the wagon was standing." "And my kumushka [sponsor],' said one of them, "told me that Ivan's son had offered it for sale at the kabak [tavern]."

This accusation caused them again to go into court for a settlement of their grievances.

While the heads of the families were trying to have their troubles settled in court, their home quarrels were constant, and frequently resulted in hand-to-hand encounters. Even the little children followed the example of their elders and quarrelled incessantly.

The women, when they met on the riverbank to do the family washing, instead of attending to their work passed the time in abusing each other, and not infrequently they came to blows.

At first the male members of the families were content with accusing each other of various crimes, such as stealing and like meannesses. But the trouble in this mild form did not last long.

They soon resorted to other measures. They began to appropriate one another's things without asking permission, while various articles disappeared from both houses and could not be found. This was done out of revenge.

This example being set by the men, the women and children also followed, and life soon became a burden to all who took part in the strife.

Ivan Scherbakoff and "Gavryl the Lame" at last laid their trouble before the mir (village meeting), in addition to having been in court and calling on the justice of the peace. Both of the latter had grown tired of them and their incessant wrangling. One time Gavryl would succeed in having Ivan fined, and if he was not able to pay it he would be locked up in the cold dreary prison for days. Then it would be Ivan's turn to get Gavryl punished in like manner, and the greater the injury the one could do the other the more delight he took in it.

The success of either in having the other punished only served to increase their rage against each other, until they were like mad dogs in their warfare.

If anything went wrong with one of them he immediately accused his adversary of conspiring to ruin him, and sought revenge without stopping to inquire into the rights of the case.

When the peasants went into court, and had each other fined and imprisoned, it did not soften their hearts in the least. They would only taunt one another on such occasions, saying: "Never mind; I will repay you for all this."

This state of affairs lasted for six years.

Ivan's father, the sick old man, constantly repeated his good advice. He would try to arouse their conscience by saying: "What are you doing, my children? Can you not throw off all these troubles, pay more attention to your business, and suppress your anger against your neighbors? There is no use in your continuing to live in this way, for the more enraged you become against each other the worse it is for you."

Again was the wise advice of the old man rejected.

At the beginning of the seventh year of the existence of the feud it happened that a daughter-in-law of Ivan's was present at a marriage. At the wedding feast she openly accused Gavryl of stealing a horse. Gavryl was intoxicated at the time and was in no mood to stand the insult, so in retaliation he struck the woman a terrific blow, which confined her to her bed for more than a week. The woman being in delicate health, the worst results were feared.

Ivan, glad of a fresh opportunity to harass his neighbor, lodged a formal complaint before the district-attorney, hoping to rid himself forever of Gavryl by having him sent to Siberia.

On examining the complaint the district-attorney would not consider it, as by that time the injured woman was walking about and as well as ever.

Thus again Ivan was disappointed in obtaining his revenge, and, not being satisfied with the district-attorney's decision, had the case transferred to the court, where he used all possible means to push his suit. To secure the favor of the starshina (village mayor) he made him a present of half a gallon of sweet vodki; and to the mayor's pisar (secretary) also he gave presents. By this means he succeeded in securing a verdict against Gavryl. The sentence was that Gavryl was to receive twenty lashes on his bare back, and the punishment was to be administered in the yard which surrounded the court-house.

When Ivan heard the sentence read he looked triumphantly at Gavryl to see what effect it would produce on him. Gavryl turned very white on hearing that he was to be treated with such indignity, and turning his back on the assembly left the room without uttering a word.

Ivan followed him out, and as he reached his horse he heard Gavryl saying: "Very well; my spine will burn from the lashes, but something will burn with greater fierceness in Ivan's household before long."

Ivan, on hearing these words, instantly returned to the court, and going up to the judges said: "Oh! just judges, he threatens to burn my house and all it contains."

A messenger was immediately sent in search of Gavryl, who was soon found and again brought into the presence of the judges.

"Is it true," they asked, "that you said you would burn Ivan's house and all it contained?"

Gavryl replied: "I did not say anything of the kind. You may give me as many lashes as you please, that is, if you have the power to do so. It seems to me that I alone have to suffer for the truth, while he," pointing to Ivan, "is allowed to do and say what he pleases." Gavryl wished to say something more, but his lips trembled, and the words refused to come; so in silence he turned his face toward the wall.

The sight of so much suffering moved even the judges to pity, and, becoming alarmed at Gavryl's continued silence, they said, "He may do both his neighbor and himself some frightful injury."

"See here, my brothers," said one feeble old judge, looking at Ivan and Gavryl as he spoke, "I think you had better try to arrange this matter peaceably. You, brother Gavryl, did wrong to strike a woman who was in delicate health. It was a lucky thing for you that God had mercy on you and that the woman did not die, for if she had I know not what dire misfortune might have overtaken you! It will not do either of you any good to go on living as you are at present. Go, Gavryl, and make friends with Ivan; I am sure he will forgive you, and we will set aside the verdict just given."

The secretary on hearing this said: "It is impossible to do this on the present case. According to Article 117 this matter has gone too far to be settled peaceably now, as the verdict has been rendered and must be enforced."

But the judges would not listen to the secretary, saying to him: "You talk altogether too much. You must remember that the first thing is to fulfill God's command to 'Love thy neighbor as thyself,' and all will be well with you."

Thus with kind words the judges tried to reconcile the two peasants. Their words fell on stony ground, however, for Gavryl would not listen to them.

"I am fifty years old," said Gavryl, "and have a son married, and never from my birth has the lash been applied to my back; but now this bear Ivan has secured a verdict against me which condemns me to receive twenty lashes, and I am forced to bow to this decision and suffer the shame of a public beating. Well, he will have cause to remember this."

At this Gavryl's voice trembled and he stopped speaking, and turning his back on the judges took his departure.

It was about ten versts' distance from the court to the homes of the neighbors, and this Ivan travelled late. The women had already gone out for the cattle. He unharnessed his horse and put everything in its place, and then went into the izba (room), but found no one there.

The men had not yet returned from their work in the field and the women had gone to look for the cattle, so that all about the place was quiet. Going into the room, Ivan seated himself on a wooden bench and soon became lost in thought. He remembered how, when Gavryl first heard the sentence which had been passed upon him, he grew very pale, and turned his face to the wall, all the while remaining silent.

Ivan's heart ached when he thought of the disgrace which he had been the means of bring- ing upon Gavryl, and he wondered how he would feel if the same sentence had been passed upon him. His thoughts were interrupted by the coughing of his father, who was lying on the oven.

The old man, on seeing Ivan, came down off the oven, and slowly approaching his son seated himself on the bench beside him, looking at him as though ashamed. He continued to cough as he leaned on the table and said, "Well, did they sentence him?"

"Yes, they sentenced him to receive twenty lashes," replied Ivan.

On hearing this the old man sorrowfully shook his head, and said: "This is very bad, Ivan, and what is the meaning of it all? It is indeed very bad, but not so bad for Gavryl as for yourself. Well, suppose his sentence IS carried out, and he gets the twenty lashes, what will it benefit you?"

"He will not again strike a woman," Ivan replied.

"What is it he will not do? He does not do anything worse than what you are constantly doing!"

This conversation enraged Ivan, and he shouted: "Well, what did he do? He beat a woman nearly to death, and even now he threatens to burn my house! Must I bow to him for all this?"

The old man sighed deeply as he said: "You, Ivan, are strong and free to go wherever you please, while I have been lying for years on the oven. You think that you know everything and that I do not know anything. No! you are still a child, and as such you cannot see that a kind of madness controls your actions and blinds your sight. The sins of others are ever before you, while you resolutely keep your own behind your back. I know that what Gavryl did was wrong, but if he alone should do wrong there would be no evil in the world. Do you think that all the evil in the world is the work of one man alone? No! it requires two persons to work much evil in the world. You see only the bad in Gavryl's character, but you are blind to the evil that is in your own nature. If he alone were bad and you good, then there would be no wrong."

The old man, after a pause, continued: "Who tore Gavryl's beard? Who destroyed his heaps of rye? Who dragged him into court? and yet you try to put all the blame on his shoulders. You are behaving very badly yourself, and for that reason you are wrong. I did not act in such a manner, and certainly I never taught you to do so. I lived in peace with Gavryl's father all the time we were neighbors. We were always the best of friends. If he was without flour his wife would come to me and say, 'Diadia Frol [Grandfather], we need flour.' I would then say: 'My good woman, go to the warehouse and take as much as you want.' If he had no one to care for his horses I would say, 'Go, Ivanushka [diminutive of Ivan], and help him to care for them.' If I required anything I would go to him and say, 'Grandfather Gordey, I need this or that,' and he would always reply, 'Take just whatever you want.' By this means we passed an easy and peaceful life. But what is your life compared with it? As the soldiers fought at Plevna, so are you and Gavryl fighting all the time, only that your battles are far more disgraceful than that fought at Plevna."

The old man went on: "And you call this living! and what a sin it all is! You are a peasant, and the head of the house; therefore, the responsibility of the trouble rests with you. What an example you set your wife and children by constantly quarrelling with your neighbor! Only a short time since your little boy, Taraska, was cursing his aunt Arina, and his mother only laughed at it, saying, 'What a bright child he is!' Is that right? You are to blame for all this. You should think of the salvation of your soul. Is that the way to do it? You say one unkind word to me and I will reply with two. You will give me one slap in the face, and I will retaliate with two slaps. No, my son; Christ did not teach us foolish people to act in such a way. If any one should say an unkind word to you it is better not to answer at all; but if you do reply do it kindly, and his conscience will accuse him, and he will regret his unkindness to you. This is the way Christ taught us to live. He tells us that if a person smite us on the one cheek we should offer unto him the other. That is Christ's command to us, and we should follow it. You should therefore subdue your pride. Am I not right?"

Ivan remained silent, but his father's words had sunk deep into his heart.

The old man coughed and continued: "Do you think Christ thought us wicked? Did he not die that we might be saved? Now you think only of this earthly life. Are you better or worse for thinking alone of it? Are you better or worse for having begun that Plevna battle? Think of your expense at court and the time lost in going back and forth, and what have you gained? Your sons have reached manhood, and are able now to work for you. You are therefore at liberty to enjoy life and be happy. With the assistance of your children you could reach a high state of prosperity. But now your property instead of increasing is gradually growing less, and why? It is the result of your pride. When it becomes necessary for you and your boys to go to the field to work, your enemy instead summons you to appear at court or before some kind of judicial person. If you do not plow at the proper time and sow at the proper time mother earth will not yield up her products, and you and your children will be left destitute. Why did your oats fail this year? When did you sow them? Were you not quarrelling with your neighbor instead of attending to your work? You have just now returned from the town, where you have been the means of having your neighbor humiliated. You have succeeded in getting him sentenced, but in the end the punishment will fall on your own shoulders. Oh! my child, it would be better for you to attend to your work on the farm and train your boys to become good farmers and honest men. If any one offend you forgive him for Christ's sake, and then prosperity will smile on your work and a light and happy feeling will fill your heart."

Ivan still remained silent.

The old father in a pleading voice continued: "Take an old man's advice. Go and harness your horse, drive back to the court, and withdraw all these complaints against your neighbor. To-morrow go to him, offer to make peace in Christ's name, and invite him to your house. It will be a holy day (the birth of the Virgin Mary). Get out the samovar and have some vodki, and over both forgive and forget each other's sins, promising not to transgress in the future, and advise your women and children to do the same."

Ivan heaved a deep sigh but felt easier in his heart, as he thought: "The old man speaks the truth." yet he was in doubt as to how he would put his father's advice into practice.

The old man, surmising his uncertainty, said to Ivan: "Go, Ivanushka; do not delay. Extinguish the fire in the beginning, before it grows large, for then it may be impossible."

Ivan's father wished to say more to him, but was prevented by the arrival of the women, who came into the room chattering like so many magpies. They had already heard of Gavryl's sentence, and of how he threatened to set fire to Ivan's house. They found out all about it, and in telling it to their neighbors added their own versions of the story, with the usual exaggeration. Meeting in the pasture-ground, they proceeded to quarrel with Gavryl's women. They related how the latter's daughter-in-law had threatened to secure the influence of the manager of a certain noble's estate in behalf of his friend Gavryl; also that the school-teacher was writing a petition to the Czar himself against Ivan, explaining in detail his theft of the perchbolt and partial destruction of Gavryl's garden, declaring that half of Ivan's land was to be given to them.

Ivan listened calmly to their stories, but his anger was soon aroused once more, when he abandoned his intention of making peace with Gavryl.

As Ivan was always busy about the household, he did not stop to speak to the wrangling women, but immediately left the room, directing his steps toward the barn. Before getting through with his work the sun had set and the boys had returned from their plowing. Ivan met them and asked about their work, helping them to put things in order and leaving the broken horse-collar aside to be repaired. He intended to perform some other duties, but it became too dark and he was obliged to leave them till the next day. He fed the cattle, however, and opened the gate that Taraska might take his horses to pasture for the night, after which he closed it again and went into the house for his supper.

By this time he had forgotten all about Gavryl and what his father had said to him. Yet, just as he touched the door-knob, he heard sounds of quarrelling proceeding from his neighbor's house.

"What do I want with that devil?" shouted Gavryl to some one. "He deserves to be killed!"

Ivan stopped and listened for a moment, when he shook his head threateningly and entered the room. When he came in, the apartment was already lighted. His daughter-in-law was working with her loom, while the old woman was preparing the supper. The eldest son was twining strings for his lapti (peasant's shoes made of strips of bark from the linden-tree). The other son was sitting by the table reading a book. The room presented a pleasant appearance, everything being in order and the inmates apparently gay and happy, the only dark shadow being that cast over the household by Ivan's trouble with his neighbor.

Ivan came in very cross, and, angrily throwing aside a cat which lay sleeping on the bench, cursed the women for having misplaced a pail. He looked very sad and serious, and, seating himself in a corner of the room, proceeded to repair the horse-collar. He could not forget Gavryl, however, the threatening words he had used in the court-room and those which Ivan had just heard.

Presently Taraska came in, and after having his supper, put on his sheepskin coat, and, taking some bread with him, returned to watch over his horses for the night. His eldest brother wished to accompany him, but Ivan himself arose and went with him as far as the porch. The night was dark and cloudy and a strong wind was blowing, which produced a peculiar whistling sound that was most unpleasant to the ear. Ivan helped his son to mount his horse, which, followed by a colt, started off on a gallop.

Ivan stood for a few moments looking around him and listening to the clatter of the horse's hoofs as Taraska rode down the village street. He heard him meet other boys on horseback, who rode quite as well as Taraska, and soon all were lost in the darkness.

Ivan remained standing by the gate in a gloomy mood, as he was unable to banish from his mind the harassing thoughts of Gavryl, which the latter's menacing words had inspired: "Something will burn with greater fierceness in Ivan's household before long."

"He is so desperate," thought Ivan, "that he may set fire to my house regardless of the danger to his own. At present everything is dry, and as the wind is so high he may sneak from the back of his own building, start a fire, and get away unseen by any of us.

He may burn and steal without being found out, and thus go unpunished. I wish I could catch him."

This thought so worried Ivan that he decided not to return to his house, but went out and stood on the street-corner.

"I guess," thought Ivan to himself, "I will take a walk around the premises and examine everything carefully, for who knows what he may be tempted to do?"

Ivan moved very cautiously round to the back of his buildings, not making the slightest noise, and scarcely daring to breathe. Just as he reached a corner of the house he looked toward the fence, and it seemed to him that he saw something moving, and that it was slowly creeping toward the corner of the house opposite to where he was standing. He stepped back quickly and hid himself in the shadow of the building. Ivan stood and listened, but all was quiet. Not a sound could be heard but the moaning of the wind through the branches of the trees, and the rustling of the leaves as it caught them up and whirled them in all directions. So dense was the darkness that it was at first impossible for Ivan to see more than a few feet beyond where he stood.

After a time, however, his sight becoming accustomed to the gloom, he was enabled to see for a considerable distance. The plow and his other farming implements stood just where he had placed them. He could see also the opposite corner of the house.

He looked in every direction, but no one was in sight, and he thought to himself that his imagination must have played him some trick, leading him to believe that some one was moving when there really was no one there.

Still, Ivan was not satisfied, and decided to make a further examination of the premises. As on the previous occasion, he moved so very cautiously that he could not hear even the sound of his own footsteps. He had taken the precaution to remove his shoes, that he might step the more noiselessly. When he reached the corner of the barn it again seemed to him that he saw something moving, this time near the plow; but it quickly disappeared. By this time Ivan's heart was beating very fast, and he was standing in a listening attitude when a sudden flash of light illumined the spot, and he could distinctly see the figure of a man seated on his haunches with his back turned toward him, and in the act of lighting a bunch of straw which he held in his hand! Ivan's heart began to beat yet faster, and he became terribly excited, walking up and down with rapid strides, but without making a noise.

Ivan said: "Well, now, he cannot get away, for he will be caught in the very act."

Ivan had taken a few more steps when suddenly a bright light flamed up, but not in the same spot in which he had seen the figure of the man sitting. Gavryl had lighted the straw, and running to the barn held it under the edge of the roof, which began to burn fiercely; and by the light of the fire he could distinctly see his neighbor standing.

As an eagle springs at a skylark, so sprang Ivan at Gavryl, saying: "I will tear you into pieces! You shall not get away from me this time!"

But "Gavryl the Lame," hearing footsteps, wrenched himself free from Ivan's grasp and ran like a hare past the buildings.

Ivan, now terribly excited, shouted, "You shall not escape me!" and started in pursuit; but just as he reached him and was about to grasp the collar of his coat, Gavryl succeeded in jumping to one side, and Ivan's coat became entangled in something and he was thrown violently to the ground. Jumping quickly to his feet he shouted, "Karaool! derji!"(watch! catch!)

While Ivan was regaining his feet Gavryl succeeded in reaching his house, but Ivan followed so quickly that he caught up with him before he could enter. Just as he was about to grasp him he was struck on the head with some hard substance. He had been hit on the temple as with a stone. The blow was struck by Gavryl, who had picked up an oaken stave, and with it gave Ivan a terrible blow on the head.

Ivan was stunned, and bright sparks danced before his eyes, while he swayed from side to side like a drunken man, until finally all became dark and he sank to the ground unconscious.

When he recovered his senses, Gavryl was nowhere to be seen, but all around him was as light as day. Strange sounds proceeded from the direction of his house, and turning his face that way he saw that his barns were on fire. The rear parts of both were already destroyed, and the flames were leaping toward the front. Fire, smoke, and bits of burning straw were being rapidly whirled by the high wind over to where his house stood, and he expected every moment to see it burst into flames.

"What is this, brother?" Ivan cried out, as he beat his thighs with his hands. "I should have stopped to snatch the bunch of burning straw, and, throwing it on the ground, should have extinguished it with my feet!"

Ivan tried to cry out and arouse his people, but his lips refused to utter a word. He next tried to run, but he could not move his feet, and his legs seemed to twist themselves around each other. After several attempts he succeeded in taking one or two steps, when he again began to stagger and gasp for breath. It was some moments before he made another attempt to move, but after considerable exertion he finally reached the barn, the rear of which was by this time entirely consumed; and the corner of his house had already caught fire. Dense volumes of smoke began to pour out of the room, which made it difficult to approach.

A crowd of peasants had by this time gathered, but they found it impossible to save their homes, so they carried everything which they could to a place of safety. The cattle they drove into neighboring pastures and left some one to care for them.

The wind carried the sparks from Ivan's house to Gavryl's, and it, too, took fire and was consumed. The wind continued to increase with great fury, and the flames spread to both sides of the street, until in a very short time more than half the village was burned.

The members of Ivan's household had great difficulty in getting out of the burning building, but the neighbors rescued the old man and carried him to a place of safety, while the women escaped in only their night-clothes. Everything was burned, including the cattle and all the farm implements. The women lost their trunks, which were filled with quantities of clothing, the accumulation of years. The storehouse and all the provisions perished in the flames, not even the chickens being saved.

Gavryl, however, more fortunate than Ivan, saved his cattle and a few other things.

The village was burning all night.

Ivan stood near his home, gazing sadly at the burning building, and he kept constantly repeating to himself: "I should have taken away the bunch of burning straw, and have stamped out the fire with my feet."

But when he saw his home fall in a smouldering heap, in spite of the terrible heat he sprang into the midst of it and carried out a charred log. The women seeing him, and fearing that he would lose his life, called to him to come back, but he would not pay any attention to them and went a second time to get a log. Still weak from the terrible blow which Gavryl had given him, he was overcome by the heat, and fell into the midst of the burning mass. Fortunately, his eldest son saw him fall, and rushing into the fire succeeded in getting hold of him and carrying him out of it. Ivan's hair, beard, and clothing were burned entirely off. His hands were also frightfully injured, but he seemed indifferent to pain.

"Grief drove him crazy," the people said.

The fire was growing less, but Ivan still stood where he could see it, and kept repeating to himself, "I should have taken," etc.

The morning after the fire the starosta (village elder) sent his son to Ivan to tell him that the old man, his father, was dying, and wanted to see him to bid him good-bye.

In his grief Ivan had forgotten all about his father, and could not understand what was being said to him. In a dazed way he asked: "What father? Whom does he want?"

The elder's son again repeated his father's message to Ivan. "Your aged parent is at our house dying, and he wants to see you and bid you good-bye. Won't you go now, uncle Ivan?" the boy said.

Finally Ivan understood, and followed the elder's son.

When Ivan's father was carried from the oven, he was slightly injured by a big bunch of burning straw falling on him just as he reached the street. To insure his safety he was removed to the elder's house, which stood a considerable distance from his late home, and where it was not likely that the fire would reach it.

When Ivan arrived at the elder's home he found only the latter's wife and children, who were all seated on the brick oven. The old man was lying on a bench holding a lighted candle in his hand (a Russian custom when a person is dying). Hearing a noise, he turned his face toward the door, and when he saw it was his son he tried to move. He motioned for Ivan to come nearer, and when he did so he whispered in a trembling voice: "Well, Ivanushka, did I not tell you before what would be the result of this sad affair? Who set the village on fire?"

"He, he, batiushka [little father]; he did it. I caught him. He placed the bunch of burning straw to the barn in my presence. Instead of running after him, I should have snatched the bunch of burning straw and throwing it on the ground have stamped it out with my feet; and then there would have been no fire."

"Ivan," said the old man, "death is fast approaching me, and remember that you also will have to die. Who did this dreadful thing? Whose is the sin?"

Ivan gazed at the noble face of his dying father and was silent. His heart was too full for utterance.

"In the presence of God," the old man continued, "whose is the sin?"

It was only now that the truth began to dawn upon Ivan's mind, and that he realized how foolish he had acted. He sobbed bitterly, and fell on his knees before his father, and, crying like a child, said:

"My dear father, forgive me, for Christ's sake, for I am guilty before God and before you!"

The old man transferred the lighted candle from his right hand to the left, and, raising the former to his forehead, tried to make the sign of the cross, but owing to weakness was unable to do so.

"Glory to Thee, O Lord! Glory to Thee!" he exclaimed; and turning his dim eyes toward his son, he said: "See here, Ivanushka! Ivanushka, my dear son!"

"What, my dear father?" Ivan asked.

"What are you going to do," replied the old man, "now that you have no home?"

Ivan cried and said: "I do not know how we shall live now."

The old man closed his eyes and made a movement with his lips, as if gathering his feeble strength for a final effort. Slowly opening his eyes, he whispered:

"Should you live according to God's commands you will be happy and prosperous again."

The old man was now silent for awhile and then, smiling sadly, he continued:

"See here, Ivanushka, keep silent concerning this trouble, and do not tell who set the village on fire. Forgive one sin of your neighbor's, and God will forgive two of yours."

Grasping the candle with both hands, Ivan's father heaved a deep sigh, and, stretching himself out on his back, yielded up the ghost.

* * * * * * *

Ivan for once accepted his father's advice. He did not betray Gavryl, and no one ever learned the origin of the fire.

Ivan's heart became more kindly disposed toward his old enemy, feeling that much of the fault in connection with this sad affair rested with himself.

Gavryl was greatly surprised that Ivan did not denounce him before all the villagers, and at first he stood in much fear of him, but he soon afterward overcame this feeling.

The two peasants ceased to quarrel, and their families followed their example. While they were building new houses, both families lived beneath the same roof, and when they moved into their respective homes, Ivan and Gavryl lived on as good terms as their fathers had done before them.

Ivan remembered his dying father's command, and took deeply to heart the evident warning of God that A FIRE SHOULD BE EXTINGUISHED IN THE BEGINNING. If any one wronged him he did not seek revenge, but instead made every effort to settle the matter peaceably. If any one spoke to him unkindly, he did not answer in the same way, but replied softly, and tried to persuade the person not to speak evil. He taught the women and children of his household to do the same.

Ivan Scherbakoff was now a reformed man.

He lived well and peacefully, and again became prosperous.

Let us, therefore, have peace, live in brotherly love and kindness, and we will be happy.

Master and Man

I

It happened in the 'seventies in winter, on the day after St. Nicholas's Day. There was a fete in the parish and the innkeeper, Vasili Andreevich Brekhunov, a Second Guild merchant, being a church elder had to go to church, and had also to entertain his relatives and friends at home.

But when the last of them had gone he at once began to prepare to drive over to see a neighbouring proprietor about a grove which he had been bargaining over for a long time. He was now in a hurry to start, lest buyers from the town might forestall him in making a profitable purchase.

The youthful landowner was asking ten thousand rubles for the grove simply because Vasili Andreevich was offering seven thousand. Seven thousand was, however, only a third of its real value. Vasili Andreevich might perhaps have got it down to his own price, for the woods were in his district and he had a long-standing agreement with the other village dealers that no one should run up the price in another's district, but he had now learnt that some timber-dealers from town meant to bid for the Goryachkin grove, and he resolved to go at once and get the matter settled. So as soon as the feast was over, he took seven hundred rubles from his strong box, added to them two thousand three hundred rubles of church money he had in his keeping, so as to make up the sum to three thousand; carefully counted the notes, and having put them into his pocket-book made haste to start.

Nikita, the only one of Vasili Andreevich's labourers who was not drunk that day, ran to harness the horse. Nikita, though an habitual drunkard, was not drunk that day because since the last day before the fast, when he had drunk his coat and leather boots, he had sworn off drink and had kept his vow for two months, and was still keeping it despite the temptation of the vodka that had been drunk everywhere during the first two days of the feast.

Nikita was a peasant of about fifty from a neighbouring village, 'not a manager' as the peasants said of him, meaning that he was not the thrifty head of a household but lived most of his time away from home as a labourer. He was valued everywhere for his industry, dexterity, and strength at work, and still more for his kindly and pleasant temper. But he never settled down anywhere for long because about twice a year, or even oftener, he had a drinking bout, and then besides spending all his clothes on drink he became turbulent and quarrelsome. Vasili Andreevich himself had turned him away several times, but had afterwards taken him back again, valuing his honesty, his kindness to animals, and especially his cheapness. Vasili Andreevich did not pay Nikita the eighty rubles a year such a man was worth, but only about forty, which he gave him haphazard, in small sums, and even that mostly not in cash but in goods from his own shop and at high prices.

Nikita's wife Martha, who had once been a handsome vigorous woman, managed the homestead with the help of her son and two daughters, and did not urge Nikita to live at home: first because she had been living for some twenty years already with a cooper, a peasant from another village who lodged in their house; and secondly because though she managed her husband as she pleased when he was sober, she feared him like fire when he was drunk. Once when he had got drunk at home, Nikita, probably to make up for his submissiveness when sober, broke open her box, took out her best clothes, snatched up an axe, and chopped all her undergarments and dresses to bits. All the wages Nikita earned went to his wife, and he raised no objection to that. So now, two days before the holiday, Martha had been twice to see Vasili Andreevich and had got from him wheat flour, tea, sugar, and a quart of vodka, the lot costing three rubles, and also five rubles in cash, for which she thanked him as for a special favour, though he owed Nikita at least twenty rubles.

'What agreement did we ever draw up with you?' said Vasili Andreevich to Nikita. 'If you need anything, take it; you will work it off. I'm not like others to keep you waiting, and making up accounts and reckoning fines. We deal straight-forwardly. You serve me and I don't neglect you.'

And when saying this Vasili Andreevich was honestly convinced that he was Nikita's benefactor, and he knew how to put it so plausibly that all those who depended on him for their money, beginning with Nikita, confirmed him in the conviction that he was their benefactor and did not overreach them.

'Yes, I understand, Vasili Andreevich. You know that I serve you and take as much pains as I would for my own father. I understand very well!' Nikita would reply. He was quite aware that Vasili Andreevich was cheating him, but at the same time he felt that it was useless to try to clear up his accounts with him or explain his side of the matter, and that as long as he had nowhere to go he must accept what he could get.

Now, having heard his master's order to harness, he went as usual cheerfully and willingly to the shed, stepping briskly and easily on his rather turned-in feet; took down from a nail the heavy tasselled leather bridle, and jingling the rings of the bit went to the closed stable where the horse he was to harness was standing by himself.

'What, feeling lonely, feeling lonely, little silly?' said Nikita in answer to the low whinny with which he was greeted by the good-tempered, medium-sized bay stallion, with a rather slanting crupper, who stood alone in the shed. 'Now then, now then, there's time enough. Let me water you first,' he went on, speaking to the horse just as to someone who understood the words he was using, and having whisked the dusty, grooved back of the well-fed young stallion with the skirt of his coat, he put a bridle on his handsome head, straightened his ears and forelock, and having taken off his halter led him out to water.

Picking his way out of the dung-strewn stable, Mukhorty frisked, and making play with his hind leg pretended that he meant to kick Nikita, who was running at a trot beside him to the pump.

'Now then, now then, you rascal!' Nikita called out, well knowing how carefully Mukhorty threw out his hind leg just to touch his greasy sheepskin coat but not to strike him, a trick Nikita much appreciated.

After a drink of the cold water the horse sighed, moving his strong wet lips, from the hairs of which transparent drops fell into the trough; then standing still as if in thought, he suddenly gave a loud snort.

'If you don't want any more, you needn't. But don't go asking for any later,' said Nikita quite seriously and fully explaining his conduct to Mukhorty. Then he ran back to the shed pulling the playful young horse, who wanted to gambol all over the yard, by the rein.

There was no one else in the yard except a stranger, the cook's husband, who had come for the holiday.

'Go and ask which sledge is to be harnessed, the wide one or the small one, there's a good fellow!'

The cook's husband went into the house, which stood on an iron foundation and was iron-roofed, and soon returned saying that the little one was to be harnessed. By that time Nikita had put the collar and brass-studded belly-band on Mukhorty and, carrying a light, painted shaft-bow in one hand, was leading the horse with the other up to two sledges that stood in the shed.

'All right, let it be the little one!' he said, backing the intelligent horse, which all the time kept pretending to bite him, into the shafts, and with the aid of the cook's husband he proceeded to harness. When everything was nearly ready and only the reins had to be adjusted, Nikita sent the other man to the shed for some straw and to the barn for a drugget.

'There, that's all right! Now, now, don't bristle up!' said Nikita, pressing down into the sledge the freshly threshed oat straw the cook's husband had brought. 'And now let's spread the sacking like this, and the drugget over it. There, like that it will be comfortable sitting,' he went on, suiting the action to the words and tucking the drugget all round over the straw to make a seat.

'Thank you, dear man. Things always go quicker with two working at it!' he added. And gathering up the leather reins fastened together by a brass ring, Nikita took the driver's seat and started the impatient horse over the frozen manure which lay in the yard, towards the gate.

'Uncle Nikita! I say, Uncle, Uncle!' a high-pitched voice shouted, and a seven-year-old boy in a black sheepskin coat, new white felt boots, and a warm cap, ran hurriedly out of the house into the yard. 'Take me with you!' he cried, fastening up his coat as he ran.

'All right, come along, darling!' said Nikita, and stopping the sledge he picked up the master's pale thin little son, radiant with joy, and drove out into the road.

It was past two o'clock and the day was windy, dull, and cold, with more than twenty degrees Fahrenheit of frost. Half the sky was hidden by a lowering dark cloud. In the yard it was quiet, but in the street the wind was felt more keenly. The snow swept down from a neighbouring shed and whirled about in the corner near the bath-house.

Hardly had Nikita driven out of the yard and turned the horse's head to the house, before Vasili Andreevich emerged from the high porch in front of the house with a cigarette in his mouth and wearing a cloth-covered sheep-skin coat tightly girdled low at his waist, and stepped onto the hard-trodden snow which squeaked under the leather soles of his felt boots, and stopped. Taking a last whiff of his cigarette he threw it down, stepped on it, and letting the smoke escape through his moustache and looking askance at the horse that was coming up, began to tuck in his sheepskin collar on both sides of his ruddy face, clean-shaven except for the moustache, so that his breath should not moisten the collar.

'See now! The young scamp is there already!' he exclaimed when he saw his little son in the sledge. Vasili Andreevich was excited by the vodka he had drunk with his visitors, and so he was even more pleased than usual with everything that was his and all that he did. The sight of his son, whom he always thought of as his heir, now gave him great satisfaction. He looked at him, screwing up his eyes and showing his long teeth.

His wife, pregnant, thin and pale, with her head and shoulders wrapped in a shawl so that nothing of her face could be seen but her eyes, stood behind him in the vestibule to see him off.

'Now really, you ought to take Nikita with you,' she said timidly, stepping out from the doorway.

Vasili Andreevich did not answer. Her words evidently annoyed him and he frowned angrily and spat.

'You have money on you,' she continued in the same plaintive voice. 'What if the weather gets worse! Do take him, for goodness' sake!'

'Why? Don't I know the road that I must needs take a guide?' exclaimed Vasili Andreevich, uttering every word very distinctly and compressing his lips unnaturally, as he usually did when speaking to buyers and sellers.

'Really you ought to take him. I beg you in God's name!' his wife repeated, wrapping her shawl more closely round her head.

'There, she sticks to it like a leech! . . . Where am I to take him?'

'I'm quite ready to go with you, Vasili Andreevich,' said Nikita cheerfully. 'But they must feed the horses while I am away,' he added, turning to his master's wife.

'I'll look after them, Nikita dear. I'll tell Simon,' replied the mistress.

'Well, Vasili Andreevich, am I to come with you?' said Nikita, awaiting a decision.

'It seems I must humour my old woman. But if you're coming you'd better put on a warmer cloak,' said Vasili Andreevich, smiling again as he winked at Nikita's short sheepskin coat, which was torn under the arms and at the back, was greasy and out of shape, frayed to a fringe round the skirt, and had endured many things in its lifetime.

'Hey, dear man, come and hold the horse!' shouted Nikita to the cook's husband, who was still in the yard.

'No, I will myself, I will myself!' shrieked the little boy, pulling his hands, red with cold, out of his pockets, and seizing the cold leather reins.

'Only don't be too long dressing yourself up. Look alive!' shouted Vasili Andreevich, grinning at Nikita.

'Only a moment, Father, Vasili Andreevich!' replied Nikita, and running quickly with his inturned toes in his felt boots with their soles patched with felt, he hurried across the yard and into the workmen's hut.

'Arinushka! Get my coat down from the stove. I'm going with the master,' he said, as he ran into the hut and took down his girdle from the nail on which it hung.

The workmen's cook, who had had a sleep after dinner and was now getting the samovar ready for her husband, turned cheerfully to Nikita, and infected by his hurry began to move as quickly as he did, got down his miserable worn-out cloth coat from the stove where it was drying, and began hurriedly shaking it out and smoothing it down.

'There now, you'll have a chance of a holiday with your good man,' said Nikita, who from kindhearted politeness always said something to anyone he was alone with.

Then, drawing his worn narrow girdle round him, he drew in his breath, pulling in his lean stomach still more, and girdled himself as tightly as he could over his sheepskin.

'There now,' he said addressing himself no longer to the cook but the girdle, as he tucked the ends in at the waist, 'now you won't come undone!' And working his shoulders up and down to free his arms, he put the coat over his sheepskin, arched his back more strongly to ease his arms, poked himself under the armpits, and took down his leather-covered mittens from the shelf. 'Now we're all right!'

'You ought to wrap your feet up, Nikita. Your boots are very bad.'

Nikita stopped as if he had suddenly realized this.

'Yes, I ought to. . . . But they'll do like this. It isn't far!' and he ran out into the yard.

'Won't you be cold, Nikita?' said the mistress as he came up to the sledge.

'Cold? No, I'm quite warm,' answered Nikita as he pushed some straw up to the forepart of the sledge so that it should cover his feet, and stowed away the whip, which the good horse would not need, at the bottom of the sledge.

Vasili Andreevich, who was wearing two fur-lined coats one over the other, was already in the sledge, his broad back filling nearly its whole rounded width, and taking the reins he immediately touched the horse. Nikita jumped in just as the sledge started, and seated himself in front on the left side, with one leg hanging over the edge.

II
The good stallion took the sledge along at a brisk pace over the smooth-frozen road through the village, the runners squeaking slightly as they went.

'Look at him hanging on there! Hand me the whip, Nikita!' shouted Vasili Andreevich, evidently enjoying the sight of his 'heir,' who standing on the runners was hanging on at the back of the sledge. 'I'll give it you! Be off to mamma, you dog!'

The boy jumped down. The horse increased his amble and, suddenly changing foot, broke into a fast trot.

The Crosses, the village where Vasili Andreevich lived, consisted of six houses. As soon as they had passed the blacksmith's hut, the last in the village, they realized that the wind was much stronger than they had thought. The road could hardly be seen. The tracks left by the sledge-runners were immediately covered by snow and the road was only distinguished by the fact that it was higher than the rest of the ground. There was a swirl of snow over the fields and the line where sky and earth met could not be seen. The Telyatin forest, usually clearly visible, now only loomed up occasionally and dimly through the driving snowy dust. The wind came from the left, insistently blowing over to one side the mane on Mukhorty's sleek neck and carrying aside even his fluffy tail, which was tied in a simple knot. Nikita's wide coat-collar, as he sat on the windy side, pressed close to his cheek and nose.

'This road doesn't give him a chance, it's too snowy,' said Vasili Andreevich, who prided himself on his good horse. 'I once drove to Pashutino with him in half an hour.'

'What?' asked Nikita, who could not hear on account of his collar.

'I say I once went to Pashutino in half an hour,' shouted Vasili Andreevich.

'It goes without saying that he's a good horse,' replied Nikita.

They were silent for a while. But Vasili Andreevich wished to talk.

'Well, did you tell your wife not to give the cooper any vodka?' he began in the same loud tone, quite convinced that Nikita must feel flattered to be talking with so clever and important a person as himself, and he was so pleased with his jest that it did not enter his head that the remark might be unpleasant to Nikita.

The wind again prevented Nikita's hearing his master's words.

Vasili Andreevich repeated the jest about the cooper in his loud, clear voice.

'That's their business, Vasili Andreevich. I don't pry into their affairs. As long as she doesn't ill-treat our boy, God be with them.'

'That's so,' said Vasili Andreevich. 'Well, and will you be buying a horse in spring?' he went on, changing the subject.

'Yes, I can't avoid it,' answered Nikita, turning down his collar and leaning back towards his master.

The conversation now became interesting to him and he did not wish to lose a word.

'The lad's growing up. He must begin to plough for himself, but till now we've always had to hire someone,' he said.

'Well, why not have the lean-cruppered one. I won't charge much for it,' shouted Vasili Andreevich, feeling animated, and consequently starting on his favourite occupation, that of horse-dealing, which absorbed all his mental powers.

'Or you might let me have fifteen rubles and I'll buy one at the horse-market,' said Nikita, who knew that the horse Vasili Andreevich wanted to sell him would be dear at seven rubles, but that if he took it from him it would be charged at twenty-five, and then he would be unable to draw any money for half a year.

'It's a good horse. I think of your interest as of my own, according to conscience. Brekhunov isn't a man to wrong anyone. Let the loss be mine. I'm not like others. Honestly!' he shouted in the voice in which he hypnotized his customers and dealers. 'It's a real good horse.'

'Quite so!' said Nikita with a sigh, and convinced that there was nothing more to listen to, he again released his collar, which immediately covered his ear and face.

They drove on in silence for about half an hour. The wind blew sharply onto Nikita's side and arm where his sheepskin was torn.

He huddled up and breathed into the collar which covered his mouth, and was not wholly cold.

'What do you think, shall we go through Karamyshevo or by the straight road?' asked Vasili Andreevich.

The road through Karamyshevo was more frequented and was well marked with a double row of high stakes. The straight road was nearer but little used and had no stakes, or only poor ones covered with snow.

Nikita thought awhile.

'Though Karamyshevo is farther, it is better going,' he said.

'But by the straight road, when once we get through the hollow by the forest, it's good going, sheltered,' said Vasili Andreevich, who wished to go the nearest way.

'Just as you please,' said Nikita, and again let go of his collar.

Vasili Andreevich did as he had said, and having gone about half a verst came to a tall oak stake which had a few dry leaves still dangling on it, and there he turned to the left.

On turning they faced directly against the wind, and snow was beginning to fall. Vasili Andreevich, who was driving, inflated his cheeks, blowing the breath out through his moustache. Nikita dozed.

So they went on in silence for about ten minutes. Suddenly Vasili Andreevich began saying something.

'Eh, what?' asked Nikita, opening his eyes.

Vasili Andreevich did not answer, but bent over, looking behind them and then ahead of the horse. The sweat had curled Mukhorty's coat between his legs and on his neck. He went at a walk.

'What is it?' Nikita asked again.

'What is it? What is it?' Vasili Andreevich mimicked him angrily. 'There are no stakes to be seen! We must have got off the road!'

'Well, pull up then, and I'll look for it,' said Nikita, and jumping down lightly from the sledge and taking the whip from under the straw, he went off to the left from his own side of the sledge.

The snow was not deep that year, so that it was possible to walk anywhere, but still in places it was knee-deep and got into Nikita's boots. He went about feeling the ground with his feet and the whip, but could not find the road anywhere.

'Well, how is it?' asked Vasili Andreevich when Nikita came back to the sledge.

'There is no road this side. I must go to the other side and try there,' said Nikita.

'There's something there in front. Go and have a look.'

Nikita went to what had appeared dark, but found that it was earth which the wind had blown from the bare fields of winter oats and had strewn over the snow, colouring it. Having searched to the right also, he returned to the sledge, brushed the snow from his coat, shook it out of his boots, and seated himself once more.

'We must go to the right,' he said decidedly. 'The wind was blowing on our left before, but now it is straight in my face. Drive to the right,' he repeated with decision.

Vasili Andreevich took his advice and turned to the right, but still there was no road. They went on in that direction for some time. The wind was as fierce as ever and it was snowing lightly.

'It seems, Vasili Andreevich, that we have gone quite astray,' Nikita suddenly remarked, as if it were a pleasant thing. 'What is that?' he added, pointing to some potato vines that showed up from under the snow.

Vasili Andreevich stopped the perspiring horse, whose deep sides were heaving heavily.

'What is it?'

'Why, we are on the Zakharov lands. See where we've got to!'

'Nonsense!' retorted Vasili Andreevich.

'It's not nonsense, Vasili Andreevich. It's the truth,' replied Nikita. 'You can feel that the sledge is going over a potato-field, and there are the heaps of vines which have been carted here. It's the Zakharov factory land.'

'Dear me, how we have gone astray!' said Vasili Andreevich. 'What are we to do now?'

'We must go straight on, that's all. We shall come out somewhere, if not at Zakharova, then at the proprietor's farm,' said Nikita.

Vasili Andreevich agreed, and drove as Nikita had indicated. So they went on for a considerable time. At times they came onto bare fields and the sledge-runners rattled over frozen lumps of earth. Sometimes they got onto a winter-rye field, or a fallow field on which they could see stalks of wormwood, and straws sticking up through the snow and swaying in the wind; sometimes they came onto deep and even white snow, above which nothing was to be seen.

The snow was falling from above and sometimes rose from below. The horse was evidently exhausted, his hair had all curled up from sweat and was covered with hoar-frost, and he went at a walk. Suddenly he stumbled and sat down in a ditch or water-course. Vasili Andreevich wanted to stop, but Nikita cried to him:

'Why stop? We've got in and must get out. Hey, pet! Hey, darling! Gee up, old fellow!' he shouted in a cheerful tone to the horse, jumping out of the sledge and himself getting stuck in the ditch.

The horse gave a start and quickly climbed out onto the frozen bank. It was evidently a ditch that had been dug there.

'Where are we now?' asked Vasili Andreevich.

'We'll soon find out!' Nikita replied. 'Go on, we'll get somewhere.'

'Why, this must be the Goryachkin forest!' said Vasili Andreevich, pointing to something dark that appeared amid the snow in front of them

'We'll see what forest it is when we get there,' said Nikita.

He saw that beside the black thing they had noticed, dry, oblong willow-leaves were fluttering, and so he knew it was not a forest but a settlement, but he did not wish to say so. And in fact they had not gone twenty-five yards beyond the ditch before something in front of them, evidently trees, showed up black, and they heard a new and melancholy sound. Nikita had guessed right: it was not a wood, but a row of tall willows with a few leaves still fluttering on them here and there. They had evidently been planted along the ditch round a threshing-floor. Coming up to the willows, which moaned sadly in the wind, the horse suddenly planted his forelegs above the height of the sledge, drew up his hind legs also, pulling the sledge onto higher ground, and turned to the left, no longer sinking up to his knees in snow. They were back on a road.

'Well, here we are, but heaven only knows where!' said Nikita.

The horse kept straight along the road through the drifted snow, and before they had gone another hundred yards the straight line of the dark wattle wall of a barn showed up black before them, its roof heavily covered with snow which poured down from it. After passing the barn the road turned to the wind and they drove into a snow-drift. But ahead of them was a lane with houses on either side, so evidently the snow had been blown across the road and they had to drive through the drift. And so in fact it was. Having driven through the snow they came out into a street. At the end house of the village some frozen clothes hanging on a line, shirts, one red and one white, trousers, leg-bands, and a petticoat, fluttered wildly in the wind. The white shirt in particular struggled desperately, waving its sleeves about.

'There now, either a lazy woman or a dead one has not taken her clothes down before the holiday,' remarked Nikita, looking at the fluttering shirts.

III
At the entrance to the street the wind still raged and the road was thickly covered with snow, but well within the village it was calm, warm, and cheerful. At one house a dog was barking, at another a woman, covering her head with her coat, came running from somewhere and entered the door of a

hut, stopping on the threshold to have a look at the passing sledge. In the middle of the village girls could be heard singing.

Here in the village there seemed to be less wind and snow, and the frost was less keen.

'Why, this is Grishkino,' said Vasili Andreevich.

'So it is,' responded Nikita.

It really was Grishkino, which meant that they had gone too far to the left and had travelled some six miles, not quite in the direction they aimed at, but towards their destination for all that.

From Grishkino to Goryachkin was about another four miles.

In the middle of the village they almost ran into a tall man walking down the middle of the street.

'Who are you?' shouted the man, stopping the horse, and recognizing Vasili Anereevich he immediately took hold of the shaft, went along it hand over hand till he reached the sledge, and placed himself on the driver's seat.

He was Isay, a peasant of Vasili Andreevich's acquaintance, and well known as the principal horse-thief in the district.

'Ah, Vasili Andreevich! Where are you off to?' said Isay, enveloping Nikita in the odour of the vodka he had drunk.

'We were going to Goryachkin.'

'And look where you've got to! You should have gone through Molchanovka.'

'Should have, but didn't manage it,' said Vasili Andreevich, holding in the horse.

'That's a good horse,' said Isay, with a shrewd glance at Mukhorty, and with a practised hand he tightened the loosened knot high in the horse's bushy tail.

'Are you going to stay the night?'

'No, friend. I must get on.'

'Your business must be pressing. And who is this? Ah, Nikita Stepanych!'

'Who else?' replied Nikita. 'But I say, good friend, how are we to avoid going astray again?'

'Where can you go astray here? Turn back straight down the street and then when you come out keep straight on. Don't take to the left. You will come out onto the high road, and then turn to the right.'

'And where do we turn off the high road? As in summer, or the winter way?' asked Nikita.

'The winter way. As soon as you turn off you'll see some bushes, and opposite them there is a way-mark, a large oak, one with branches, and that's the way.'

Vasili Andreevich turned the horse back and drove through the outskirts of the village.

'Why not stay the night?' Isay shouted after them.

But Vasili Andreevich did not answer and touched up the horse. Four miles of good road, two of which lay through the forest, seemed easy to manage, especially as the wind was apparently quieter and the snow had stopped.

Having driven along the trodden village street, darkened here and there by fresh manure, past the yard where the clothes hung out and where the white shirt had broken loose and was now attached only by one frozen sleeve, they again came within sound of the weird moan of the willows, and again emerged on the open fields. The storm, far from ceasing, seemed to have grown yet stronger. The road was completely covered with drifting snow, and only the stakes showed that they had not lost their way. But even the stakes ahead of them were not easy to see, since the wind blew in their faces.

Vasili Andreevich screwed up his eyes, bent down his head, and looked out for the way-marks, but trusted mainly to the horse's sagacity, letting it take its own way. And the horse really did not lose the road but followed its windings, turning now to the right and now to the left and sensing it under his feet, so that though the snow fell thicker and the wind strengthened they still continued to see way-marks now to the left and now to the right of them.

So they travelled on for about ten minutes, when suddenly, through the slanting screen of wind-driven snow, something black showed up which moved in front of the horse.

This was another sledge with fellow-travellers. Mukhorty overtook them, and struck his hoofs against the back of the sledge in front of them.

'Pass on . . . hey there . . . get in front!' cried voices from the sledge.

Vasili Andreevich swerved aside to pass the other sledge.

In it sat three men and a woman, evidently visitors returning from a feast. One peasant was whacking the snow-covered croup of their little horse with a long switch, and the other two sitting in front waved their arms and shouted something. The woman, completely wrapped up and covered with snow, sat drowsing and bumping at the back.

'Who are you?' shouted Vasili Andreevich.

'From A-a-a . . .' was all that could be heard.

'I say, where are you from?'

'From A-a-a-a!' one of the peasants shouted with all his might, but still it was impossible to make out who they were.

'Get along! Keep up!' shouted another, ceaselessly beating his horse with the switch.

'So you're from a feast, it seems?'

'Go on, go on! Faster, Simon! Get in front! Faster!'

The wings of the sledges bumped against one another, almost got jammed but managed to separate, and the peasants' sledge began to fall behind.

Their shaggy, big-bellied horse, all covered with snow, breathed heavily under the low shaft-bow and, evidently using the last of its strength, vainly endeavoured to escape from the switch, hobbling with its short legs through the deep snow which it threw up under itself.

Its muzzle, young-looking, with the nether lip drawn up like that of a fish, nostrils distended and ears pressed back from fear, kept up for a few seconds near Nikita's shoulder and then began to fall behind.

'Just see what liquor does!' said Nikita. 'They've tired that little horse to death. What pagans!'

For a few minutes they heard the panting of the tired little horse and the drunken shouting of the peasants. Then the panting and the shouts died away, and around them nothing could be heard but the whistling of the wind in their ears and now and then the squeak of their sledge-runners over a windswept part of the road.

This encounter cheered and enlivened Vasili Andreevich, and he drove on more boldly without examining the way-marks, urging on the horse and trusting to him.

Nikita had nothing to do, and as usual in such circumstances he drowsed, making up for much sleepless time. Suddenly the horse stopped and Nikita nearly fell forward onto his nose.

'You know we're off the track again!' said Vasili Andreevich.

'How's that?'

'Why, there are no way-marks to be seen. We must have got off the road again.'

'Well, if we've lost the road we must find it,' said Nikita curtly, and getting out and stepping lightly on his pigeon-toed feet he started once more going about on the snow.

He walked about for a long time, now disappearing and now reappearing, and finally he came back.

'There is no road here. There may be farther on,' he said, getting into the sledge.

It was already growing dark. The snow-storm had not increased but had also not subsided.

'If we could only hear those peasants!' said Vasili Andreevich.

'Well they haven't caught us up. We must have gone far astray. Or maybe they have lost their way too.'

'Where are we to go then?' asked Vasili Andreevich.

'Why, we must let the horse take its own way,' said Nikita. 'He will take us right. Let me have the reins.'

Vasili Andreevich gave him the reins, the more willingly because his hands were beginning to feel frozen in his thick gloves.

Nikita took the reins, but only held them, trying not to shake them and rejoicing at his favourite's sagacity. And indeed the clever horse, turning first one ear and then the other now to one side and then to the other, began to wheel round.

'The one thing he can't do is to talk,' Nikita kept saying. 'See what he is doing! Go on, go on! You know best. That's it, that's it!'

The wind was now blowing from behind and it felt warmer.

'Yes, he's clever,' Nikita continued, admiring the horse. 'A Kirgiz horse is strong but stupid. But this one, just see what he's doing with his ears! He doesn't need any telegraph. He can scent a mile off.'

Before another half-hour had passed they saw something dark ahead of them, a wood or a village, and stakes again appeared to the right. They had evidently come out onto the road.

'Why, that's Grishkino again!' Nikita suddenly exclaimed.

And indeed, there on their left was that same barn with the snow flying from it, and farther on the same line with the frozen washing, shirts and trousers, which still fluttered desperately in the wind.

Again they drove into the street and again it grew quiet, warm, and cheerful, and again they could see the manure-stained street and hear voices and songs and the barking of a dog. It was already so dark that there were lights in some of the windows.

Half-way through the village Vasili Andreevich turned the horse towards a large double-fronted brick house and stopped at the porch.

Nikita went to the lighted snow-covered window, in the rays of which flying snow-flakes glittered, and knocked at it with his whip.

'Who is there?' a voice replied to his knock.

'From Kresty, the Brekhunovs, dear fellow.' answered Nikita. 'Just come out for a minute.'

Someone moved from the window, and a minute or two later there was the sound of the passage door as it came unstuck, then the latch of the outside door clicked and a tall white-bearded peasant, with a sheepskin coat thrown over his white holiday shirt, pushed his way out holding the door firmly against the wind, followed by a lad in a red shirt and high leather boots.

'Is that you, Andreevich?' asked the old man.

'Yes, friend, we've gone astray,' said Vasili Andreevich. 'We wanted to get to Goryachkin but found ourselves here. We went a second time but lost our way again.'

'Just see how you have gone astray!' said the old man. 'Petrushka, go and open the gate!' he added, turning to the lad in the red shirt.

'All right,' said the lad in a cheerful voice, and ran back into the passage.

'But we're not staying the night,' said Vasili Andreevich.

'Where will you go in the night? You'd better stay!'

'I'd be glad to, but I must go on. It's business, and it can't be helped.'

'Well, warm yourself at least. The samovar is just ready.'

'Warm myself? Yes, I'll do that,' said Vasili Andreevich. 'It won't get darker. The moon will rise and it will be lighter. Let's go in and warm ourselves, Nikita.'

'Well, why not? Let us warm ourselves,' replied Nikita, who was stiff with cold and anxious to warm his frozen limbs.

Vasili Andreevich went into the room with the old man, and Nikita drove through the gate opened for him by Petrushka, by whose advice he backed the horse under the penthouse. The ground was covered with manure and the tall bow over the horse's head caught against the beam. The hens and the cock had already settled to roost there, and clucked peevishly, clinging to the beam with their claws. The disturbed sheep shied and rushed aside trampling the frozen manure with their hooves. The dog yelped desperately with fright and anger and then burst out barking like a puppy at the stranger.

Nikita talked to them all, excused himself to the fowls and assured them that he would not disturb them again, rebuked the sheep for being frightened without knowing why, and kept soothing the dog, while he tied up the horse.

'Now that will be all right,' he said, knocking the snow off his clothes. 'Just hear how he barks!' he added, turning to the dog. 'Be quiet, stupid! Be quiet. You are only troubling yourself for nothing. We're not thieves, we're friends. . . .'

'And these are, it's said, the three domestic counsellors,' remarked the lad, and with his strong arms he pushed under the pent-roof the sledge that had remained outside.

'Why counsellors?' asked Nikita.

'That's what is printed in Paulson. A thief creeps to a house, the dog barks, that means "Be on your guard!" The cock crows, that means, "Get up!" The cat licks herself, that means, "A welcome guest is coming. Get ready to receive him!"' said the lad with a smile.

Petrushka could read and write and knew Paulson's primer, his only book, almost by heart, and he was fond of quoting sayings from it that he thought suited the occasion, especially when he had had something to drink, as to-day.

'That's so,' said Nikita.

'You must be chilled through and through,' said Petrushka.

'Yes, I am rather,' said Nikita, and they went across the yard and the passage into the house.

IV

The household to which Vasili Andreevich had come was one of the richest in the village. The family had five allotments, besides renting other land. They had six horses, three cows, two calves, and some twenty sheep. There were twenty-two members belonging to the homestead: four married sons, six grandchildren (one of whom, Petrushka, was married), two great-grandchildren, three orphans, and four daughters-in-law with their babies. It was one of the few homesteads that remained still undivided, but even here the dull internal work of disintegration which would inevitably lead to separation had already begun, starting as usual among the women. Two sons were living in Moscow as water-carriers, and one was in the army. At home now were the old man and his wife, their second son who managed the homestead, the eldest who had come from Moscow for the holiday, and all the women and children. Besides these members of the family there was a visitor, a neighbour who was godfather to one of the children.

Over the table in the room hung a lamp with a shade, which brightly lit up the tea-things, a bottle of vodka, and some refreshments, besides illuminating the brick walls, which in the far corner were hung with icons on both sides of which were pictures. At the head of the table sat Vasili Andreevich in a black sheepskin coat, sucking his frozen moustache and observing the room and the people around him with his prominent hawk-like eyes. With him sat the old, bald, white-bearded master of the house in a white homespun shirt, and next him the son home from Moscow for the holiday, a man with a sturdy back and powerful shoulders and clad in a thin print shirt, then the second son, also broad-shouldered, who acted as head of the house, and then a lean red-haired peasant, the neighbour.

Having had a drink of vodka and something to eat, they were about to take tea, and the samovar standing on the floor beside the brick oven was already humming. The children could be seen in the top bunks and on the top of the oven. A woman sat on a lower bunk with a cradle beside her. The old housewife, her face covered with wrinkles which wrinkled even her lips, was waiting on Vasili Andreevich.

As Nikita entered the house she was offering her guest a small tumbler of thick glass which she had just filled with vodka.

'Don't refuse, Vasili Andreevich, you mustn't! Wish us a merry feast. Drink it, dear!' she said.

The sight and smell of vodka, especially now when he was chilled through and tired out, much disturbed Nikita's mind. He frowned, and having shaken the snow off his cap and coat, stopped in front of the icons as if not seeing anyone, crossed himself three times, and bowed to the icons. Then, turning to the old master of the house and bowing first to him, then to all those at table, then to the women who stood by the oven, and muttering: 'A merry holiday!' he began taking off his outer things without looking at the table.

'Why, you're all covered with hoar-frost, old fellow!' said the eldest brother, looking at Nikita's snow-covered face, eyes, and beard.

Nikita took off his coat, shook it again, hung it up beside the oven, and came up to the table. He too was offered vodka. He went through a moment of painful hesitation and nearly took up the glass and emptied the clear fragrant liquid down his throat, but he glanced at Vasili Andreevich, remembered his oath and the boots that he had sold for drink, recalled the cooper, remembered his son for whom he had promised to buy a horse by spring, sighed, and declined it.

'I don't drink, thank you kindly,' he said frowning, and sat down on a bench near the second window.

'How's that?' asked the eldest brother.

'I just don't drink,' replied Nikita without lifting his eyes but looking askance at his scanty beard and moustache and getting the icicles out of them.

'It's not good for him,' said Vasili Andreevich, munching a cracknel after emptying his glass.

'Well, then, have some tea,' said the kindly old hostess. 'You must be chilled through, good soul. Why are you women dawdling so with the samovar?'

'It is ready,' said one of the young women, and after flicking with her apron the top of the samovar which was now boiling over, she carried it with an effort to the table, raised it, and set it down with a thud.

Meanwhile Vasili Andreevich was telling how he had lost his way, how they had come back twice to this same village, and how they had gone astray and had met some drunken peasants. Their hosts were surprised, explained where and why they had missed their way, said who the tipsy people they had met were, and told them how they ought to go.

'A little child could find the way to Molchanovka from here. All you have to do is to take the right turning from the high road. There's a bush you can see just there. But you didn't even get that far!' said the neighbour.

'You'd better stay the night. The women will make up beds for you,' said the old woman persuasively.

'You could go on in the morning and it would be pleasanter,' said the old man, confirming what his wife had said.

'I can't, friend. Business!' said Vasili Andreevich. 'Lose an hour and you can't catch it up in a year,' he added, remembering the grove and the dealers who might snatch that deal from him. 'We shall get there, shan't we?' he said, turning to Nikita.

Nikita did not answer for some time, apparently still intent on thawing out his beard and moustache.

'If only we don't go astray again,' he replied gloomily. He was gloomy because he passionately longed for some vodka, and the only thing that could assuage that longing was tea and he had not yet been offered any.

'But we have only to reach the turning and then we shan't go wrong. The road will be through the forest the whole way,' said Vasili Andreevich.

'It's just as you please, Vasili Andreevich. If we're to go, let us go,' said Nikita, taking the glass of tea he was offered.

'We'll drink our tea and be off.'

Nikita said nothing but only shook his head, and carefully pouring some tea into his saucer began warming his hands, the fingers of which were always swollen with hard work, over the steam. Then, biting off a tiny bit of sugar, he bowed to his hosts, said, 'Your health!' and drew in the steaming liquid.

'If somebody would see us as far as the turning,' said Vasili Andreevich.

'Well, we can do that,' said the eldest son. 'Petrushka will harness and go that far with you.'

'Well, then, put in the horse, lad, and I shall be thankful to you for it.'

'Oh, what for, dear man?' said the kindly old woman. 'We are heartily glad to do it.'

'Petrushka, go and put in the mare,' said the eldest brother.

'All right,' replied Petrushka with a smile, and promptly snatching his cap down from a nail he ran away to harness.

While the horse was being harnessed the talk returned to the point at which it had stopped when Vasili Andreevich drove up to the window. The old man had been complaining to his neighbour, the village elder, about his third son who had not sent him anything for the holiday though he had sent a French shawl to his wife.

'The young people are getting out of hand,' said the old man.

'And how they do!' said the neighbour. 'There's no managing them! They know too much. There s Demochkin now, who broke his father's arm. It's all from being too clever, it seems.'

Nikita listened, watched their faces, and evidently would have liked to share in the conversation, but he was too busy drinking his tea and only nodded his head approvingly. He emptied one tumbler after another and grew warmer and warmer and more and more comfortable. The talk continued on the same subject for a long time, the harmfulness of a household dividing up, and it was clearly not an abstract discussion but concerned the question of a separation in that house; a separation demanded by the second son who sat there morosely silent.

It was evidently a sore subject and absorbed them all, but out of propriety they did not discuss their private affairs before strangers. At last, however, the old man could not restrain himself, and with tears in his eyes declared that he would not consent to a break-up of the family during his lifetime, that his house was prospering, thank God, but that if they separated they would all have to go begging.

'Just like the Matveevs,' said the neighbour. 'They used to have a proper house, but now they've split up none of them has anything.'

'And that is what you want to happen to us,' said the old man, turning to his son.

The son made no reply and there was an awkward pause. The silence was broken by Petrushka, who having harnessed the horse had returned to the hut a few minutes before this and had been listening all the time with a smile.

'There's a fable about that in Paulson,' he said. 'A father gave his sons a broom to break. At first they could not break it, but when they took it twig by twig they broke it easily. And it's the same here,' and he gave a broad smile. 'I'm ready!' he added.

'If you're ready, let's go,' said Vasili Andreevich. 'And as to separating, don't you allow it, Grandfather. You got everything together and you're the master. Go to the Justice of the Peace. He'll say how things should be done.'

'He carries on so, carries on so,' the old man continued in a whining tone. 'There's no doing anything with him. It's as if the devil possessed him.'

Nikita having meanwhile finished his fifth tumbler of tea laid it on its side instead of turning it upside down, hoping to be offered a sixth glass. But there was no more water in the samovar, so the hostess did not fill it up for him. Besides, Vasili Andreevich was putting his things on, so there was nothing for it but for Nikita to get up too, put back into the sugar-basin the lump of sugar he had nibbled all round, wipe his perspiring face with the skirt of his sheepskin, and go to put on his overcoat.

Having put it on he sighed deeply, thanked his hosts, said good-bye, and went out of the warm bright room into the cold dark passage, through which the wind was howling and where snow was blowing through the cracks of the shaking door, and from there into the yard.

Petrushka stood in his sheepskin in the middle of the yard by his horse, repeating some lines from Paulson's primer. He said with a smile:

'Storms with mist the sky conceal,
Snowy circles wheeling wild.
Now like savage beast 'twill howl,
And now 'tis wailing like a child.'

Nikita nodded approvingly as he arranged the reins.

The old man, seeing Vasili Andreevich off, brought a lantern into the passage to show him a light, but it was blown out at once. And even in the yard it was evident that the snowstorm had become more violent.

'Well, this is weather!' thought Vasili Andreevich. 'Perhaps we may not get there after all. But there is nothing to be done. Business! Besides, we have got ready, our host's horse has been harnessed, and we'll get there with God's help!'

Their aged host also thought they ought not to go, but he had already tried to persuade them to stay and had not been listened to.

'It's no use asking them again. Maybe my age makes me timid. They'll get there all right, and at least we shall get to bed in good time and without any fuss,' he thought.

Petrushka did not think of danger. He knew the road and the whole district so well, and the lines about 'snowy circles wheeling wild' described what was happening outside so aptly that it cheered him up. Nikita did not wish to go at all, but he had been accustomed not to have his own way and to serve others for so long that there was no one to hinder the departing travellers.

V

Vasili Andreevich went over to his sledge, found it with difficulty in the darkness, climbed in and took the reins.

'Go on in front!' he cried.

Petrushka kneeling in his low sledge started his horse. Mukhorty, who had been neighing for some time past, now scenting a mare ahead of him started after her, and they drove out into the street. They drove again through the outskirts of the village and along the same road, past the yard where the frozen linen had hung (which, however, was no longer to be seen), past the same barn, which was now snowed up almost to the roof and from which the snow was still endlessly pouring past the same dismally moaning, whistling, and swaying willows, and again entered into the sea of blustering snow raging from above and below. The wind was so strong that when it blew from the side and the travellers steered against it, it tilted the sledges and turned the horses to one side. Petrushka drove his good mare in front at a brisk trot and kept shouting lustily. Mukhorty pressed after her.

After travelling so for about ten minutes, Petrushka turned round and shouted something. Neither Vasili Andreevich nor Nikita could hear anything because of the wind, but they guessed that they had arrived at the turning. In fact Petrushka had turned to the right, and now the wind that had blown from the side blew straight in their faces, and through the snow they saw something dark on their right. It was the bush at the turning.

'Well now, God speed you!'

'Thank you, Petrushka!'

'Storms with mist the sky conceal!' shouted Petrushka as he disappeared.

'There's a poet for you!' muttered Vasili Andreevich, pulling at the reins.

'Yes, a fine lad, a true peasant,' said Nikita.

They drove on.

Nikita, wrapping his coat closely about him and pressing his head down so close to his shoulders that his short beard covered his throat, sat silently, trying not to lose the warmth he had obtained while drinking tea in the house. Before him he saw the straight lines of the shafts which constantly deceived him into thinking they were on a well-travelled road, and the horse's swaying crupper with his knotted tail blown to one side, and farther ahead the high shaft-bow and the swaying head and neck of the horse with its waving mane. Now and then he caught sight of a way-sign, so that he knew they were still on a road and that there was nothing for him to be concerned about.

Vasili Andreevich drove on, leaving it to the horse to keep to the road. But Mukhorty, though he had had a breathing-space in the village, ran reluctantly, and seemed now and then to get off the road, so that Vasili Andreevich had repeatedly to correct him.

'Here's a stake to the right, and another, and here's a third,' Vasili Andreevich counted, 'and here in front is the forest,' thought he, as he looked at something dark in front of him. But what had seemed to him a forest was only a bush. They passed the bush and drove on for another hundred yards but there was no fourth way-mark nor any forest.

'We must reach the forest soon,' thought Vasili Andreevich, and animated by the vodka and the tea he did not stop but shook the reins, and the good obedient horse responded, now ambling, now slowly trotting in the direction in which he was sent, though he knew that he was not going the right way. Ten minutes went by, but there was still no forest.

'There now, we must be astray again,' said Vasili Andreevich, pulling up.

Nikita silently got out of the sledge and holding his coat, which the wind now wrapped closely about him and now almost tore off, started to feel about in the snow, going first to one side and then to the other. Three or four times he was completely lost to sight. At last he returned and took the reins from Vasili Andreevich's hand.

'We must go to the right,' he said sternly and peremptorily, as he turned the horse.

'Well, if it's to the right, go to the right,' said Vasili Andreevich, yielding up the reins to Nikita and thrusting his freezing hands into his sleeves.

Nikita did not reply.

'Now then, friend, stir yourself!' he shouted to the horse, but in spite of the shake of the reins Mukhorty moved only at a walk.

The snow in places was up to his knees, and the sledge moved by fits and starts with his every movement.

Nikita took the whip that hung over the front of the sledge and struck him once. The good horse, unused to the whip, sprang forward and moved at a trot, but immediately fell back into an amble and then to a walk. So they went on for five minutes. It was dark and the snow whirled from above and rose from below, so that sometimes the shaft-bow could not be seen. At times the sledge seemed to stand still and the field to run backwards. Suddenly the horse stopped abruptly, evidently aware of something close in front of him. Nikita again sprang lightly out, throwing down the reins, and went ahead to see what had brought him to a standstill, but hardly had he made a step in front of the horse before his feet slipped and he went rolling down an incline.

'Whoa, whoa, whoa!' he said to himself as he fell, and he tried to stop his fall but could not, and only stopped when his feet plunged into a thick layer of snow that had drifted to the bottom of the hollow.

The fringe of a drift of snow that hung on the edge of the hollow, disturbed by Nikita's fall, showered down on him and got inside his collar.

'What a thing to do!' said Nikita reproachfully, addressing the drift and the hollow and shaking the snow from under his collar.

'Nikita! Hey, Nikita!' shouted Vasili Andreevich from above.

But Nikita did not reply. He was too occupied in shaking out the snow and searching for the whip he had dropped when rolling down the incline. Having found the whip he tried to climb straight up the bank where he had rolled down, but it was impossible to do so: he kept rolling down again, and so he had to go along at the foot of the hollow to find a way up. About seven yards farther on he managed with difficulty to crawl up the incline on all fours, then he followed the edge of the hollow back to the place where the horse should have been. He could not see either horse or sledge, but as he walked against the wind he heard Vasili Andreevich's shouts and Mukhorty's neighing, calling him.

'I'm coming! I'm coming! What are you cackling for?' he muttered.

Only when he had come up to the sledge could he make out the horse, and Vasili Andreevich standing beside it and looking gigantic.

'Where the devil did you vanish to? We must go back, if only to Grishkino,' he began reproaching Nikita.

'I'd be glad to get back, Vasili Andreevich, but which way are we to go? There is such a ravine here that if we once get in it we shan't get out again. I got stuck so fast there myself that I could hardly get out.'

'What shall we do, then? We can't stay here! We must go somewhere!' said Vasili Andreevich.

Nikita said nothing. He seated himself in the sledge with his back to the wind, took off his boots, shook out the snow that had got into them, and taking some straw from the bottom of the sledge, carefully plugged with it a hole in his left boot.

Vasili Andreevich remained silent, as though now leaving everything to Nikita. Having put his boots on again, Nikita drew his feet into the sledge, put on his mittens and took up the reins, and directed the horse along the side of the ravine. But they had not gone a hundred yards before the horse again stopped short. The ravine was in front of him again.

Nikita again climbed out and again trudged about in the snow. He did this for a considerable time and at last appeared from the opposite side to that from which he had started.

'Vasili Andreevich, are you alive?' he called out.

'Here!' replied Vasili Andreevich. 'Well, what now?'

'I can't make anything out. It's too dark. There's nothing but ravines. We must drive against the wind again.'

They set off once more. Again Nikita went stumbling through the snow, again he fell in, again climbed out and trudged about, and at last quite out of breath he sat down beside the sledge.

'Well, how now?' asked Vasili Andreevich.

'Why, I am quite worn out and the horse won't go.'

'Then what's to be done?'

'Why, wait a minute.'

Nikita went away again but soon returned.

'Follow me!' he said, going in front of the horse.

Vasili Andreevich no longer gave orders but implicitly did what Nikita told him.

'Here, follow me!' Nikita shouted, stepping quickly to the right, and seizing the rein he led Mukhorty down towards a snow-drift.

At first the horse held back, then he jerked forward, hoping to leap the drift, but he had not the strength and sank into it up to his collar.

'Get out!' Nikita called to Vasili Andreevich who still sat in the sledge, and taking hold of one shaft he moved the sledge closer to the horse. 'It's hard, brother!' he said to Mukhorty, 'but it can't be helped. Make an effort! Now, now, just a little one!' he shouted.

The horse gave a tug, then another, but failed to clear himself and settled down again as if considering something.

'Now, brother, this won't do!' Nikita admonished him. 'Now once more!'

Again Nikita tugged at the shaft on his side, and Vasili Andreevich did the same on the other.

Mukhorty lifted his head and then gave a sudden jerk.

'That's it! That's it!' cried Nikita. 'Don't be afraid, you won't sink!'

One plunge, another, and a third, and at last Mukhorty was out of the snow-drift, and stood still, breathing heavily and shaking the snow off himself. Nikita wished to lead him farther, but Vasili Andreevich, in his two fur coats, was so out of breath that he could not walk farther and dropped into the sledge.

'Let me get my breath!' he said, unfastening the kerchief with which he had tied the collar of his fur coat at the village.

'It's all right here. You lie there,' said Nikita. 'I will lead him along.' And with Vasili Andreevich in the sledge he led the horse by the bridle about ten paces down and then up a slight rise, and stopped.

The place where Nikita had stopped was not completely in the hollow where the snow sweeping down from the hillocks might have buried them altogether, but still it was partly sheltered from the wind by the side of the ravine. There were moments when the wind seemed to abate a little, but that did not last long and as if to make up for that respite the storm swept down with tenfold vigour and tore and whirled the more fiercely. Such a gust struck them at the moment when Vasili Andreevich, having recovered his breath, got out of the sledge and went up to Nikita to consult him as to what they should do. They both bent down involuntarily and waited till the violence of the squall should have passed. Mukhorty too laid back his ears and shook his head discontentedly. As soon as the violence of the blast had abated a little, Nikita took off his mittens, stuck them into his belt, breathed onto his hands, and began to undo the straps of the shaft-bow.

'What's that you are doing there?' asked Vasili Andreevich.

'Unharnessing. What else is there to do? I have no strength left,' said Nikita as though excusing himself.

'Can't we drive somewhere?'

'No, we can't. We shall only kill the horse. Why, the poor beast is not himself now,' said Nikita, pointing to the horse, which was standing submissively waiting for what might come, with his steep wet sides heaving heavily. 'We shall have to stay the night here,' he said, as if preparing to spend the night at an inn, and he proceeded to unfasten the collar-straps. The buckles came undone.

'But shan't we be frozen?' remarked Vasili Andreevich.

'Well, if we are we can't help it,' said Nikita.

VI

Although Vasili Andreevich felt quite warm in his two fur coats, especially after struggling in the snow-drift, a cold shiver ran down his back on realizing that he must really spend the night where they were. To calm himself he sat down in the sledge and got out his cigarettes and matches.

Nikita meanwhile unharnessed Mukhorty. He unstrapped the belly-band and the back-band, took away the reins, loosened the collar-strap, and removed the shaft-bow, talking to him all the time to encourage him.

'Now come out! come out!' he said, leading him clear of the shafts. 'Now we'll tie you up here and I'll put down some straw and take off your bridle. When you've had a bite you'll feel more cheerful.'

But Mukhorty was restless and evidently not comforted by Nikita's remarks. He stepped now on one foot and now on another, and pressed close against the sledge, turning his back to the wind and rubbing his head on Nikita's sleeve. Then, as if not to pain Nikita by refusing his offer of the straw he put before him, he hurriedly snatched a wisp out of the sledge, but immediately decided that it was now no time to think of straw and threw it down, and the wind instantly scattered it, carried it away, and covered it with snow.

'Now we will set up a signal,' said Nikita, and turning the front of the sledge to the wind he tied the shafts together with a strap and set them up on end in front of the sledge. 'There now, when the snow covers us up, good folk will see the shafts and dig us out,' he said, slapping his mittens together and putting them on. 'That's what the old folk taught us!'

Vasili Andreevich meanwhile had unfastened his coat, and holding its skirts up for shelter, struck one sulphur match after another on the steel box. But his hands trembled, and one match after another either did not kindle or was blown out by the wind just as he was lifting it to the cigarette. At last a match did burn up, and its flame lit up for a moment the fur of his coat, his hand with the gold ring on the bent forefinger, and the snow-sprinkled oat-straw that stuck out from under the drugget. The cigarette lighted, he eagerly took a whiff or two, inhaled the smoke, let it out through his moustache, and would have inhaled again, but the wind tore off the burning tobacco and whirled it away as it had done the straw.

But even these few puffs had cheered him.

'If we must spend the night here, we must!' he said with decision. 'Wait a bit, I'll arrange a flag as well,' he added, picking up the kerchief which he had thrown down in the sledge after taking it from round his collar, and drawing off his gloves and standing up on the front of the sledge and stretching himself to reach the strap, he tied the handkerchief to it with a tight knot.

The kerchief immediately began to flutter wildly, now clinging round the shaft, now suddenly streaming out, stretching and flapping.

'Just see what a fine flag!' said Vasili Andreevich, admiring his handiwork and letting himself down into the sledge. 'We should be warmer together, but there's not room enough for two,' he added.

'I'll find a place,' said Nikita. 'But I must cover up the horse first, he sweated so, poor thing. Let go!' he added, drawing the drugget from under Vasili Andreevich.

Having got the drugget he folded it in two, and after taking off the breechband and pad, covered Mukhorty with it.

'Anyhow it will be warmer, silly!' he said, putting back the breechband and the pad on the horse over the drugget. Then having finished that business he returned to the sledge, and addressing Vasili Andreevich, said: 'You won't need the sackcloth, will you? And let me have some straw.'

And having taken these things from under Vasili Andreevich, Nikita went behind the sledge, dug out a hole for himself in the snow, put straw into it, wrapped his coat well round him, covered himself with the sackcloth, and pulling his cap well down seated himself on the straw he had spread, and leant against the wooden back of the sledge to shelter himself from the wind and the snow.

Vasili Andreevich shook his head disapprovingly at what Nikita was doing, as in general he disapproved of the peasant's stupidity and lack of education, and he began to settle himself down for the night.

He smoothed the remaining straw over the bottom of the sledge, putting more of it under his side. Then he thrust his hands into his sleeves and settled down, sheltering his head in the corner of the sledge from the wind in front.

He did not wish to sleep. He lay and thought: thought ever of the one thing that constituted the sole aim, meaning, pleasure, and pride of his life, of how much money he had made and might still make, of how much other people he knew had made and possessed, and of how those others had made and were making it, and how he, like them, might still make much more. The purchase of the Goryachkin grove was a matter of immense importance to him. By that one deal he hoped to make perhaps ten thousand rubles. He began mentally to reckon the value of the wood he had inspected in autumn, and on five acres of which he had counted all the trees.

'The oaks will go for sledge-runners. The undergrowth will take care of itself, and there'll still be some thirty sazheens of fire-wood left on each desyatin,' said he to himself. 'That means there will be at least two hundred and twenty-five rubles' worth left on each desyatin. Fifty-six desyatiins means fifty-six hundreds, and fifty-six hundreds, and fifty-six tens, and another fifty-six tens, and then fifty-six fives. . . .' He saw that it came out to more than twelve thousand rubles, but could not reckon it up exactly without a counting-frame. 'But I won't give ten thousand, anyhow. I'll give about eight thousand with a deduction on account of the glades. I'll grease the surveyor's palm, give him a hundred rubles, or a hundred and fifty, and he'll reckon that there are some five desyatins of glade to be deducted. And he'll let it go for eight thousand. Three thousand cash down. That'll move him, no fear!' he thought, and he pressed his pocket-book with his forearm.

'God only knows how we missed the turning. The forest ought to be there, and a watchman's hut, and dogs barking. But the damned things don't bark when they're wanted.' He turned his collar down from his ear and listened, but as before only the whistling of the wind could be heard, the flapping and fluttering of the kerchief tied to the shafts, and the pelting of the snow against the woodwork of the sledge. He again covered up his ear.

'If I had known I would have stayed the night. Well, no matter, we'll get there to-morrow. It's only one day lost. And the others won't travel in such weather.' Then he remembered that on the 9th he had to receive payment from the butcher for his oxen. 'He meant to come himself, but he won't find me, and my wife won't know how to receive the money. She doesn't know the right way of doing things,' he thought, recalling how at their party the day before she had not known how to treat the police-officer who was their guest. 'Of course she's only a woman! Where could she have seen anything? In my father's time what was our house like? Just a rich peasant's house: just an oatmll and an inn, that was the whole property. But what have I done in these fifteen years? A shop, two taverns, a flour-mill, a grain-store, two farms leased out, and a house with an iron-roofed barn,' he thought proudly. 'Not as it was in Father's time! Who is talked of in the whole district now? Brekhunov! And why? Because I stick to business. I take trouble, not like others who lie abed or waste their time on foolishness while I don't sleep of nights. Blizzard or no blizzard I start out. So business gets done. They think money-making is a joke. No, take pains and rack your brains! You get overtaken out of doors at night, like this, or keep awake night after night till the thoughts whirling in your head make the pillow turn,' he meditated with pride. 'They think people get on through luck. After all, the Mironovs are now millionaires. And why? Take pains and God gives. If only He grants me health!'

The thought that he might himself be a millionaire like Mironov, who began with nothing, so excited Vasili Andreevich that he felt the need of talking to somebody. But there was no one to talk to. . . . If only he could have reached Goryachkin he would have talked to the landlord and shown him a thing or two.

'Just see how it blows! It will snow us up so deep that we shan't be able to get out in the morning!' he thought, listening to a gust of wind that blew against the front of the sledge, bending it and lashing the snow against it. He raised himself and looked round. All he could see through the whirling darkness was Mukhorty's dark head, his back covered by the fluttering drugget, and his thick knotted tail; while all round, in front and behind, was the same fluctuating whity darkness, sometimes seeming to get a little lighter and sometimes growing denser still.

'A pity I listened to Nikita,' he thought. 'We ought to have driven on. We should have come out somewhere, if only back to Grishkino and stayed the night at Taras's. As it is we must sit here all night. But what was I thinking about? Yes, that God gives to those who take trouble, but not to loafers, lie-abeds, or fools. I must have a smoke!'

He sat down again, got out his cigarette-case, and stretched himself flat on his stomach, screening the matches with the skirt of his coat. But the wind found its way in and put out match after match. At last he got one to burn and lit a cigarette. He was very glad that he had managed to do what he wanted, and though the wind smoked more of the cigarette than he did, he still got two or three puffs and felt more cheerful. He again leant back, wrapped himself up, started reflecting and remembering, and suddenly and quite unexpectedly lost consciousness and fell asleep.

Suddenly something seemed to give him a push and awoke him. Whether it was Mukhorty who had pulled some straw from under him, or whether something within him had startled him, at all events it woke him, and his heart began to beat faster and faster so that the sledge seemed to tremble under him. He opened his eyes. Everything around him was just as before. 'It looks lighter,' he thought. 'I expect it won't be long before dawn.' But he at once remembered that it was lighter because the moon had risen. He sat up and looked first at the horse. Mukhorty still stood with his back to the wind, shivering all over. One side of the drugget, which was completely covered with snow, had been blown back, the breeching had slipped down and the snow-covered head with its waving forelock and mane were now more visible. Vasili Andreevich leant over the back of the sledge and looked behind. Nikita still sat in the same position in which he had settled himself. The sacking with which he was covered, and his legs, were thickly covered with snow.

'If only that peasant doesn't freeze to death! His clothes are so wretched. I may be held responsible for him. What shiftless people they are, such a want of education,' thought Vasili Andreevich, and he felt like taking the drugget off the horse and putting it over Nikita, but it would be very cold to get out and move about and, moreover, the horse might freeze to death. 'Why did I bring him with me? It was all her stupidity!' he thought, recalling his unloved wife, and he rolled over into his old place at the front part of the sledge. 'My uncle once spent a whole night like this,' he reflected, 'and was all right.' But another case came at once to his mind. 'But when they dug Sebastian out he was dead, stiff like a frozen carcass. If I'd only stopped the night in Grishkino all this would not have happened!'

And wrapping his coat carefully round him so that none of the warmth of the fur should be wasted but should warm him all over, neck, knees, and feet, he shut his eyes and tried to sleep again. But try as he would he could not get drowsy, on the contrary he felt wide awake and animated. Again he began counting his gains and the debts due to him, again he began bragging to himself and feeling pleased with himself and his position, but all this was continually disturbed by a stealthily approaching fear and by the unpleasant regret that he had not remained in Grishkino.

'How different it would be to be lying warm on a bench!'

He turned over several times in his attempts to get into a more comfortable position more sheltered from the wind, he wrapped up his legs closer, shut his eyes, and lay still. But either his legs in their strong felt boots began to ache from being bent in one position, or the wind blew in somewhere, and after lying still for a short time he again began to recall the disturbing fact that he might now have been lying quietly in the warm hut at Grishkino. He again sat up, turned about, muffled himself up, and settled down once more.

Once he fancied that he heard a distant cock-crow. He felt glad, turned down his coat-collar and listened with strained attention, but in spite of all his efforts nothing could be heard but the wind whistling between the shafts, the flapping of the kerchief, and the snow pelting against the frame of the sledge.

Nikita sat just as he had done all the time, not moving and not even answering Vasili Andreevich who had addressed him a couple of times. 'He doesn't care a bit, he's probably asleep!' thought Vasili Andreevich with vexation, looking behind the sledge at Nikita who was covered with a thick layer of snow.

Vasili Andreevich got up and lay down again some twenty times. It seemed to him that the night would never end. 'It must be getting near morning,' he thought, getting up and looking around. 'Let's have a look at my watch. It will be cold to unbutton, but if I only know that it's getting near morning I shall at any rate feel more cheerful. We could begin harnessing.'

In the depth of his heart Vasili Andreevich knew that it could not yet be near morning, but he was growing more and more afraid, and wished both to get to know and yet to deceive himself. He carefully undid the fastening of his sheepskin, pushed in his hand, and felt about for a long time before he got to his waistcoat. With great difficulty he managed to draw out his silver watch with its enamelled flower design, and tried to make out the time. He could not see anything without a light. Again he went down on his knees and elbows as he had done when he lighted a cigarette, got out his matches, and proceeded to strike one. This time he went to work more carefully, and feeling with his fingers for a match with the largest head and the greatest amount of phosphorus, lit it at the first try. Bringing the face of the watch under the light he could hardly believe his eyes. . . . It was only ten minutes past twelve. Almost the whole night was still before him.

'Oh, how long the night is!' he thought, feeling a cold shudder run down his back, and having fastened his fur coats again and wrapped himself up, he snuggled into a corner of the sledge intending to wait patiently. Suddenly, above the monotonous roar of the wind, he clearly distinguished another new and living sound. It steadily strengthened, and having become quite clear diminished just as gradually. Beyond all doubt it was a wolf, and he was so near that the movement of his jaws as he changed his cry was brought down the wind. Vasili Andreevich turned back the collar of his coat and listened attentively. Mukhorty too strained to listen, moving his ears, and when the wolf had ceased its howling he shifted from foot to foot and gave a warning snort. After this Vasili Andreevich could not fall asleep again or even calm himself. The more he tried to think of his accounts, his business, his reputation, his worth and his wealth, the more and more was he mastered by fear, and regrets that he had not stayed the night at Grishkino dominated and mingled in all his thoughts.

'Devil take the forest! Things were all right without it, thank God. Ah, if we had only put up for the night!' he said to himself. 'They say it's drunkards that freeze,' he thought, 'and I have had some drink.' And observing his sensations he noticed that he was beginning to shiver, without knowing whether it was from cold or from fear. He tried to wrap himself up and lie down as before, but could no longer do so. He could not stay in one position. He wanted to get up, to do something to master the gathering fear that was rising in him and against which he felt himself powerless. He again got out his cigarettes and matches, but only three matches were left and they were bad ones. The phosphorus rubbed off them all without lighting.

'The devil take you! Damned thing! Curse you!' he muttered, not knowing whom or what he was cursing, and he flung away the crushed cigarette. He was about to throw away the matchbox too, but checked the movement of his hand and put the box in his pocket instead. He was seized with such unrest that he could no longer remain in one spot. He climbed out of the sledge and standing with his back to the wind began to shift his belt again, fastening it lower down in the waist and tightening it.

'What's the use of lying and waiting for death? Better mount the horse and get away!' The thought suddenly occurred to him. 'The horse will move when he has someone on his back. As for him,' he thought of Nikita, 'it's all the same to him whether he lives or dies. What is his life worth? He won't grudge his life, but I have something to live for, thank God.'

He untied the horse, threw the reins over his neck and tried to mount, but his coats and boots were so heavy that he failed. Then he clambered up in the sledge and tried to mount from there, but the sledge tilted under his weight, and he failed again. At last he drew Mukhorty nearer to the sledge, cautiously balanced on one side of it, and managed to lie on his stomach across the horse's back. After lying like that for a while he shifted forward once and again, threw a leg over, and finally seated himself, supporting his feet on the loose breeching-straps. The shaking of the sledge awoke Nikita. He raised himself, and it seemed to Vasili Andreevich that he said something.

'Listen to such fools as you! Am I to die like this for nothing?' exclaimed Vasili Andreevich. And tucking the loose skirts of his fur coat in under his knees, he turned the horse and rode away from the sledge in the direction in which he thought the forest and the forester's hut must be.

VII

From the time he had covered himself with the sackcloth and seated himself behind the sledge, Nikita had not stirred. Like all those who live in touch with nature and have known want, he was patient and could wait for hours, even days, without growing restless or irritable. He heard his master call him, but did not answer because he did not want to move or talk. Though he still felt some warmth from the tea he had drunk and from his energetic struggle when clambering about in the snowdrift, he knew that this warmth would not last long and that he had no strength left to warm himself again by moving about, for he felt as tired as a horse when it stops and refuses to go further in spite of the whip, and its master sees that it must be fed before it can work again. The foot in the boot with a hole in it had already grown numb, and he could no longer feel his big toe. Besides that, his whole body began to feel colder and colder.

The thought that he might, and very probably would, die that night occurred to him, but did not seem particularly unpleasant or dreadful. It did not seem particularly unpleasant, because his whole life had been not a continual holiday, but on the contrary an unceasing round of toil of which he was beginning to feel weary. And it did not seem particularly dreadful, because besides the masters he had served here, like Vasili Andreevich, he always felt himself dependent on the Chief Master, who had sent him into this life, and he knew that when dying he would still be in that Master's power and would not be ill-used by Him. 'It seems a pity to give up what one is used to and accustomed to. But there's nothing to be done, I shall get used to the new things.'

'Sins?' he thought, and remembered his drunkenness, the money that had gone on drink, how he had offended his wife, his cursing, his neglect of church and of the fasts, and all the things the priest blamed him for at confession. 'Of course they are sins. But then, did I take them on of myself? That's evidently how God made me. Well, and the sins? Where am I to escape to?'

So at first he thought of what might happen to him that night, and then did not return to such thoughts but gave himself up to whatever recollections came into his head of themselves. Now he thought of Martha's arrival, of the drunkenness among the workers and his own renunciation of drink, then of their present journey and of Taras's house and the talk about the breaking-up of the family, then of his own lad, and of Mukhorty now sheltered under the drugget, and then of his master who made the sledge creak as he tossed about in it. 'I expect you're sorry yourself that you started out, dear man,' he thought. 'It would seem hard to leave a life such as his! It's not like the likes of us.'

Then all these recollections began to grow confused and got mixed in his head, and he fell asleep.

But when Vasili Andreevich, getting on the horse, jerked the sledge, against the back of which Nikita was leaning, and it shifted away and hit him in the back with one of its runners, he awoke and had to change his position whether he liked it or not. Straightening his legs with difficulty and shaking the snow off them he got up, and an agonizing cold immediately penetrated his whole body. On making out what was happening he called to Vasili Andreevich to leave him the drugget which the horse no longer needed, so that he might wrap himself in it.

But Vasili Andreevich did not stop, but disappeared amid the powdery snow.

Left alone Nikita considered for a moment what he should do. He felt that he had not the strength to go off in search of a house. It was no longer possible to sit down in his old place, it was by now all filled with snow. He felt that he could not get warmer in the sledge either, for there was nothing to cover himself with, and his coat and sheepskin no longer warmed him at all. He felt as cold as though he had nothing on but a shirt. He became frightened. 'Lord, heavenly Father!' he muttered, and was comforted by the consciousness that he was not alone but that there was One who heard him and would not abandon him. He gave a deep sigh, and keeping the sackcloth over his head he got inside the sledge and lay down in the place where his master had been.

But he could not get warm in the sledge either. At first he shivered all over, then the shivering ceased and little by little he began to lose consciousness. He did not know whether he was dying or falling asleep, but felt equally prepared for the one as for the other.

VIII

Meanwhile Vasili Andreevich, with his feet and the ends of the reins, urged the horse on in the direction in which for some reason he expected the forest and forester's hut to be. The snow covered his eyes and the wind seemed intent on stopping him, but bending forward and constantly lapping his coat over and pushing it between himself and the cold harness pad which prevented him from sitting properly, he kept urging the horse on. Mukhorty ambled on obediently though with difficulty, in the direction in which he was driven.

Vasili Andreevich rode for about five minutes straight ahead, as he thought, seeing nothing but the horse's head and the white waste, and hearing only the whistle of the wind about the horse's ears and his coat collar.

Suddenly a dark patch showed up in front of him. His heart beat with joy, and he rode towards the object, already seeing in imagination the walls of village houses. But the dark patch was not stationary, it kept moving; and it was not a village but some tall stalks of wormwood sticking up through the snow on the boundary between two fields, and desperately tossing about under the pressure of the wind which beat it all to one side and whistled through it. The sight of that wormwood tormented by the pitiless wind made Vasili Andreevich shudder, he knew not why, and he hurriedly began urging the horse on, not noticing that when riding up to the wormwood he had quite changed his direction and was now heading the opposite way, though still imagining that he was riding towards where the hut should be. But the horse kept making towards the right, and Vasili Andreevich kept guiding it to the left.

Again something dark appeared in front of him. Again he rejoiced, convinced that now it was certainly a village. But once more it was the same boundary line overgrown with wormwood, once more the same wormwood desperately tossed by the wind and carrying unreasoning terror to his heart. But its being the same wormwood was not all, for beside it there was a horse's track partly snowed over. Vasili Andreevich stopped, stooped down and looked carefully. It was a horse-track only partially covered with snow, and could be none but his own horse's hoofprints. He had evidently gone round in a small circle. 'I shall perish like that!' he thought, and not to give way to his terror he urged on the horse still more, peering into the snowy darkness in which he saw only flitting and fitful points of light. Once he thought he heard the barking of dogs or the howling of wolves, but the sounds were so faint and indistinct that he did not know whether he heard them or merely imagined them, and he stopped and began to listen intently.

Suddenly some terrible, deafening cry resounded near his ears, and everything shivered and shook under him. He seized Mukhorty's neck, but that too was shaking all over and the terrible cry grew still more frightful. For some seconds Vasili Andreevich could not collect himself or understand what was happening. It was only that Mukhorty, whether to encourage himself or to call for help, had neighed loudly and resonantly. 'Ugh, you wretch! How you frightened me, damn you!' thought Vasili Andreevich. But even when he understood the cause of his terror he could not shake it off.

'I must calm myself and think things over,' he said to himself, but yet he could not stop, and continued to urge the horse on, without noticing that he was now going with the wind instead of against it. His body, especially between his legs where it touched the pad of the harness and was not covered by his overcoats, was getting painfully cold, especially when the horse walked slowly. His legs and arms trembled and his breathing came fast. He saw himself perishing amid this dreadful snowy waste, and could see no means of escape.

Suddenly the horse under him tumbled into something and, sinking into a snow-drift, began to plunge and fell on his side. Vasili Andreevich jumped off, and in so doing dragged to one side the breechband on which his foot was resting, and twisted round the pad to which he held as he dismounted. As soon as he had jumped off, the horse struggled to his feet, plunged forward, gave one leap and another, neighed again, and dragging the drugget and the breechband after him, disappeared, leaving Vasili Andreevich alone on the snow-drift.

The latter pressed on after the horse, but the snow lay so deep and his coats were so heavy that, sinking above his knees at each step, he stopped breathless after taking not more than twenty steps. 'The copse, the oxen, the lease-hold, the shop, the tavern, the house with the iron-roofed barn, and my heir,' thought he. 'How can I leave all that? What does this mean? It cannot be!' These thoughts flashed through his mind. Then he thought of the wormwood tossed by the wind, which he had twice ridden past, and he was seized with such terror that he did not believe in the reality of what was happening to him. 'Can this be a dream?' he thought, and tried to wake up but could not. It was real snow that lashed his face and covered him and chilled his right hand from which he had lost the glove, and this was a real desert in which he was now left alone like that wormwood, awaiting an inevitable, speedy, and meaningless death.

'Queen of Heaven! Holy Father Nicholas, teacher of temperance!' he thought, recalling the service of the day before and the holy icon with its black face and gilt frame, and the tapers which he sold to be set before that icon and which were almost immediately brought back to him scarcely burnt at all, and which he put away in the store-chest. He began to pray to that same Nicholas the Wonder-Worker to save him, promising him a thanksgiving service and some candles. But he clearly and indubitably realized that the icon, its frame, the candles, the priest, and the thanksgiving service, though very important and necessary in church, could do nothing for him here, and that there was and could be no connexion between those candles and services and his present disastrous plight. 'I must not despair,' he thought. 'I must follow the horse's track before it is snowed under. He will lead me out, or I may even catch him. Only I must not hurry, or I shall stick fast and be more lost than ever.'

But in spite of his resolution to go quietly, he rushed forward and even ran, continually falling, getting up and falling again. The horse's track was already hardly visible in places where the snow did not lie deep. 'I am lost!' thought Vasili Andreevich. 'I shall lose the track and not catch the horse.' But at that moment he saw something black. It was Mukhorty, and not only Mukhorty, but the sledge with the shafts and the kerchief. Mukhorty, with the sacking and the breechband twisted round to one side, was standing not in his former place but nearer to the shafts, shaking his head which the reins he was stepping on drew downwards. It turned out that Vasili Andreevich had sunk in the same ravine Nikita had previously fallen into, and that Mukhorty had been bringing him back to the sledge and he had got off his back no more than fifty paces from where the sledge was.

Having stumbled back to the s edge Vasili Andreevich caught hold of it and for a long time stood motionless, trying to calm himself and recover his breath. Nikita was not in his former place, but something, already covered w th snow, was lying in the sledge and Vasili Andreevich concluded that this was Nikita. His terror had now quite left him, and if he felt any fear it was lest the dreadful terror should return that he had experienced when on the horse and especially when he was left alone in the snow-drift. At any cost he had to avoid that terror, and to keep it away he must do something, occupy himself with something. And the first thing he did was to turn his back to the wind and open his fur coat. Then, as soon as he recovered his breath a little, he shook the snow out of his boots and out of his left-hand glove (the right-hand glove was hopelessly lost and by this time probably lying somewhere under a dozen inches of snow); then as was his custom when going out of his shop to buy grain from the peasants, he pulled his girdle low down and tightened it and prepared for action. The first thing that occurred to him was to free Mukhorty's leg from the rein. Having done that, and tethered him to the iron cramp at the front of the sledge where he had been before, he was going round the horse's quarters to put the breechband and pad straight and cover him with the cloth but at that moment he noticed that something was moving in the sledge and Nikita's head rose up out of the snow that covered it. Nikita, who was half frozen, rose with great difficulty and sat up, moving his hand before his nose in a strange manner just as if he were driving away flies. He waved his hand and said something, and seemed to Vasili Andreevich to be calling him. Vasili Andreevich left the cloth unadjusted and went up to the sledge.

'What is it?' he asked. 'What are you saying?'

'I'm dy . . . ing, that's what,' said Nikita brokenly and with difficulty. 'Give what is owing to me to my lad, or to my wife, no matter.'

'Why, are you really frozen?' asked Vasili Andreevich.

'I feel it's my death. Forgive me for Christ's sake . . .' said Nikita in a tearful voice, continuing to wave his hand before his face as if driving away flies.

Vasili Andreevich stood silent and motionless for half a minute. Then suddenly, with the same resolution with which he used to strike hands when making a good purchase, he took a step back and turning up his sleeves began raking the snow off Nikita and out of the sledge. Having done this he hurriedly undid his girdle, opened out his fur coat, and having pushed Nikita down, lay down on top of him, covering him not only with his fur coat but with the whole of his body, which glowed with warmth. After pushing the skirts of his coat between Nikita and the sides of the sledge, and holding down its hem with his knees, Vasili Andreevich lay like that face down, with his head pressed against the front of the sledge. Here he no longer heard the horse's movements or the whistling of the wind, but only Nikita's breathing. At first and for a long time Nikita lay motionless, then he sighed deeply and moved.

'There, and you say you are dying! Lie still and get warm, that's our way . . .' began Vasili Andreevich.

But to his great surprise he could say no more, for tears came to his eyes and his lower jaw began to quiver rapidly. He stopped speaking and only gulped down the risings in his throat. 'Seems I was badly frightened and have gone quite weak,' he thought. But this weakness was not only unpleasant, but gave him a peculiar joy such as he had never felt before.

'That's our way!' he said to himself, experiencing a strange and solemn tenderness. He lay like that for a long time, wiping his eyes on the fur of his coat and tucking under his knee the right skirt, which the wind kept turning up.

But he longed so passionately to tell somebody of his joyful condition that he said: 'Nikita!'

'It's comfortable, warm!' came a voice from beneath.

'There, you see, friend, I was going to perish. And you would have been frozen, and I should have . . .'

But again his jaws began to quiver and his eyes to fill with tears, and he could say no more.

'Well, never mind,' he thought. 'I know about myself what I know.'

He remained silent and lay like that for a long time.

Nikita kept him warm from below and his fur coats from above. Only his hands, with which he kept his coat-skirts down round Nikita's sides, and his legs which the wind kept uncovering, began to freeze, especially his right hand which had no glove. But he did not think of his legs or of his hands but only of how to warm the peasant who was lying under him. He looked out several times at Mukhorty and could see that his back was uncovered and the drugget and breeching lying on the snow, and that he ought to get up and cover him, but he could not bring himself to leave Nikita and disturb even for a moment the joyous condition he was in. He no longer felt any kind of terror.

'No fear, we shan't lose him this time!' he said to himself, referring to his getting the peasant warm with the same boastfulness with which he spoke of his buying and selling.

Vasili Andreevich lay in that way for one hour, another, and a third, but he was unconscious of the passage of time. At first impressions of the snow-storm, the sledge-shafts, and the horse with the shaft-bow shaking before his eyes, kept passing through his mind, then he remembered Nikita lying under him, then recollections of the festival, his wife, the police-officer, and the box of candles, began to mingle with these; then again Nikita, this time lying under that box, then the peasants, customers and traders, and the white walls of his house with its iron roof with Nikita lying underneath, presented themselves to his imagination. Afterwards all these impressions blended into one nothingness. As the colours of the rainbow unite into one white light, so all these different impressions mingled into one, and he fell asleep.

For a long time he slept without dreaming, but just before dawn the visions recommenced. It seemed to him that he was standing by the box of tapers and that Tikhon's wife was asking for a five kopek taper for the Church fete. He wished to take one out and give it to her, but his hands would not life, being held tight in his pockets. He wanted to walk round the box but his feet would not move and his new clean goloshes had grown to the stone floor, and he could neither lift them nor get his feet out of the goloshes. Then the taper-box was no longer a box but a bed, and suddenly Vasili Andreevich saw himself lying in his bed at home. He was lying in his bed and could not get up. Yet it was necessary for him to get up because Ivan Matveich, the police-officer, would soon call for him and he had to go with him, either to bargain for the forest or to put Mukhorty's breeching straight.

He asked his wife: 'Nikolaevna, hasn't he come yet?' 'No, he hasn't,' she replied. He heard someone drive up to the front steps. 'It must be him.' 'No, he's gone past.' 'Nikolaevna! I say, Nikolaevna, isn't he here yet?' 'No.' He was still lying on his bed and could not get up, but was always waiting. And this waiting was uncanny and yet joyful. Then suddenly his joy was completed. He whom he was expecting came; not Ivan Matveich the police-officer, but someone else, yet it was he whom he had been waiting for. He came and called him; and it was he who had called him and told him to lie down on Nikita. And Vasili Andreevich was glad that that one had come for him.

'I'm coming!' he cried joyfully, and that cry awoke him, but woke him up not at all the same person he had been when he fell asleep. He tried to get up but could not, tried to move his arm and could not, to move his leg and also could not, to turn his head and could not. He was surprised but not at all disturbed by this. He understood that this was death, and was not at all disturbed by that either.

He remembered that Nikita was lying under him and that he had got warm and was alive, and it seemed to him that he was Nikita and Nikita was he, and that his life was not in himself but in Nikita. He strained his ears and heard Nikita breathing and even slightly snoring. 'Nikita is alive, so I too am alive!' he said to himself triumphantly.

And he remembered his money, his shop, his house, the buying and selling, and Mironov's millions, and it was hard for him to understand why that man, called Vasili Brekhunov, had troubled himself with all those things with which he had been troubled.

'Well, it was because he did not know what the real thing was,' he thought, concerning that Vasili Brekhunov. 'He did not know, but now I know and know for sure. Now I know!' And again he heard the voice of the one who had called him before. 'I'm coming! Coming!' he responded gladly, and his whole being was filled with joyful emotion. He felt himself free and that nothing could hold him back any longer.

After that Vasili Andreevich neither saw, heard, nor felt anything more in this world.

All around the snow still eddied. The same whirlwinds of snow circled about, covering the dead Vasili Andreevich's fur coat, the shivering Mukhorty, the sledge, now scarcely to be seen, and Nikita lying at the bottom of it, kept warm beneath his dead master.

X

Nikita awoke before daybreak. He was aroused by the cold that had begun to creep down his back. He had dreamt that he was coming from the mill with a load of his master's flour and when crossing the stream had missed the bridge and let the cart get stuck. And he saw that he had crawled under the cart and was trying to lift it by arching his back. But strange to say the cart did not move, it stuck to his back and he could neither lift it nor get out from under it. It was crushing the whole of his loins. And how cold it felt! Evidently he must crawl out. 'Have done!' he exclaimed to whoever was pressing the cart down on him. 'Take out the sacks!' But the cart pressed down colder and colder, and then he heard a strange knocking, awoke completely, and remembered everything. The cold cart was his dead and frozen master lying upon him. And the knock was produced by Mukhorty, who had twice struck the sledge with his hoof.

'Andreevich! Eh, Andreevich!' Nikita called cautiously, beginning to realize the truth, and straightening his back. But Vasili Andreevich did not answer and his stomach and legs were stiff and cold and heavy like iron weights.

'He must have died! May the Kingdom of Heaven be his!' thought Nikita.

He turned his head, dug with his hand through the snow about him and opened his eyes. It was daylight; the wind was whistling as before between the shafts, and the snow was falling in the same way, except that it was no longer driving against the frame of the sledge but silently covered both sledge and horse deeper and deeper, and neither the horse's movements nor his breathing were any longer to be heard.

'He must have frozen too,' thought Nikita of Mukhorty, and indeed those hoof knocks against the sledge, which had awakened Nikita, were the last efforts the already numbed Mukhorty had made to keep on his feet before dying.

'O Lord God, it seems Thou art calling me too!' said Nikita. 'Thy Holy Will be done. But it's uncanny. . . . Still, a man can't die twice and must die once. If only it would come soon!'

And he again drew in his head, closed his eyes, and became unconscious, fully convinced that now he was certainly and finally dying.

It was not till noon that day that peasants dug Vasili Andreevich and Nikita out of the snow with their shovels, not more than seventy yards from the road and less than half a mile from the village.

The snow had hidden the sledge, but the shafts and the kerchief tied to them were still visible. Mukhorty, buried up to his belly in snow, with the breeching and drugget hanging down, stood all white, his dead head pressed against his frozen throat: icicles hung from his nostrils, his eyes were covered with hoar-frost as though filled with tears, and he had grown so thin in that one night that he was nothing but skin and bone.

Vasili Andreevich was stiff as a frozen carcass, and when they rolled him off Nikita his legs remained apart and his arms stretched out as they had been. His bulging hawk eyes were frozen, and his open mouth under his clipped moustache was full of snow. But Nikita though chilled through was still alive. When he had been brought to, he felt sure that he was already dead and that what was taking place with him was no longer happening in this world but in the next. When he heard the peasants shouting as they dug him out and rolled the frozen body of Vasili Andreevich from off him, he was at first surprised that in the other world peasants should be shouting in the same old way and had the same kind of body, and then when he realized that he was still in this world he was sorry rather than glad, especially when he found that the toes on both his feet were frozen.

Nikita lay in hospital for two months. They cut off three of his toes, but the others recovered so that he was still able to work and went on living for another twenty years, first as a farm-labourer, then in his old age as a watchman. He died at home as he had wished, only this year, under the icons with a lighted taper in his hands. Before he died he asked his wife's forgiveness and forgave her for the cooper. He also took leave of his son and grandchildren, and died sincerely glad that he was relieving his son and daughter-in-law of the burden of having to feed him, and that he was now really passing from this life of which he was weary into that other life which every year and every hour grew clearer and more desirable to him. Whether he is better or worse off there where he awoke after his death, whether he was disappointed or found there what he expected, we shall all soon learn.

My Dream

"As a daughter she no longer exists for me. Can't you understand? She simply doesn't exist. Still, I cannot possibly leave her to the charity of strangers. I will arrange things so that she can live as she pleases, but I do not wish to hear of her. Who would ever have thought . . . the horror of it, the horror of it."

He shrugged his shoulders, shook his head, and raised his eyes. These words were spoken by Prince Michael Ivanovich to his brother Peter, who was governor of a province in Central Russia. Prince Peter was a man of fifty, Michael's junior by ten years.

On discovering that his daughter, who had left his house a year before, had settled here with her child, the elder brother had come from St. Petersburg to the provincial town, where the above conversation took place.

Prince Michael Ivanovich was a tall, handsome, white-haired, fresh coloured man, proud and attractive in appearance and bearing. His family consisted of a vulgar, irritable wife, who wrangled with him continually over every petty detail, a son, a ne'er-do-well, spendthrift and roué, yet a "gentleman," according to his father's code, two daughters, of whom the elder had married well, and was living in St. Petersburg; and the younger, Lisa, his favourite, who had disappeared from home a year before. Only a short while ago he had found her with her child in this provincial town.

Prince Peter wanted to ask his brother how, and under what circumstances, Lisa had left home, and who could possibly be the father of her child. But he could not make up his mind to inquire.

That very morning, when his wife had attempted to condole with her brother-in-law, Prince Peter had observed a look of pain on his brother's face. The look had at once been masked by an expression of unapproachable pride, and he had begun to question her about their flat, and the price she paid. At luncheon, before the family and guests, he had been witty and sarcastic as usual. Towards every one, excepting the children, whom he treated with almost reverent tenderness, he adopted an attitude of distant hauteur. And yet it was so natural to him that every one somehow acknowledged his right to be haughty.

In the evening his brother arranged a game of whist. When he retired to the room which had been made ready for him, and was just beginning to take out his artificial teeth, some one tapped lightly on the door with two fingers.

"Who is that?"

"C'est moi, Michael."

Prince Michael Ivanovich recognised the voice of his sister-in-law, frowned, replaced his teeth, and said to himself, "What does she want?" Aloud he said, "Entrez."

His sister-in-law was a quiet, gentle creature, who bowed in submission to her husband's will. But to many she seemed a crank, and some did not hesitate to call her a fool. She was pretty, but her hair was always carelessly dressed, and she herself was untidy and absent-minded. She had, also, the strangest, most unaristocratic ideas, by no means fitting in the wife of a high official. These ideas she would express most unexpectedly, to everybody's astonishment, her husband's no less than her friends'.

"Fous pouvez me renvoyer, ma s je ne m'en irai pas, je vous le dis d'avance," she began, in her characteristic, indifferent way.

"Dieu preserve," answered her brother-in-law, with his usual somewhat exaggerated politeness, and brought forward a chair for her.

"Ca ne vous derange pas?" she asked, taking out a cigarette. "I'm not going to say anything unpleasant, Michael. I only wanted to say something about Lisochka."

Michael Ivanovich sighed, the word pained him; but mastering himself at once, he answered with a tired smile. "Our conversation can only be on one subject, and that is the subject you wish to discuss." He spoke without looking at her, and avoided even naming the subject. But his plump, pretty little sister-in-law was unabashed. She continued to regard him with the same gentle, imploring look in her blue eyes, sighing even more deeply.

"Michael, mon bon ami, have pity on her. She is only human."

"I never doubted that," said Michael Ivanovich with a bitter smile.

"She is your daughter."

"She was but my dear Aline, why talk about this?"

"Michael, dear, won't you see her? I only wanted to say, that the one who is to blame"

Prince Michael Ivanovich flushed; his face became cruel.

"For heaven's sake, let us stop. I have suffered enough. I have now but one desire, and that is to put her in such a position that she will be independent of others, and that she shall have no further need of communicating with me. Then she can live her own life, and my family and I need know nothing more about her. That is all I can do."

"Michael, you say nothing but 'I'! She, too, is 'I.'"

"No doubt; but, dear Aline, please let us drop the matter. I feel it too deeply."

Alexandra Dmitrievna remained silent for a few moments, shaking her head. "And Masha, your wife, thinks as you do?"

"Yes, quite."

Alexandra Dmitrievna made an inarticulate sound.

"Brisons la dessus et bonne nuit," said he. But she did not go. She stood silent a moment. Then, "Peter tells me you intend to leave the money with the woman where she lives. Have you the address?"

"I have."

"Don't leave it with the woman, Michael! Go yourself. Just see how she lives. If you don't want to see her, you need not. HE isn't there; there is no one there."

Michael Ivanovich shuddered violently.

"Why do you torture me so? It's a sin against hospitality!"

Alexandra Dmitrievna rose, and almost in tears, being touched by her own pleading, said, "She is so miserable, but she is such a dear."

He got up, and stood waiting for her to finish. She held out her hand.

"Michael, you do wrong," said she, and left him.

For a long while after she had gone Michael Ivanovich walked to and fro on the square of carpet. He frowned and shivered, and exclaimed, "Oh, oh!" And then the sound of his own voice frightened him, and he was silent.

His wounded pride tortured him. His daughter, his, brought up in the house of her mother, the famous Avdotia Borisovna, whom the Empress honoured with her visits, and acquaintance with whom was an honour for all the world! His daughter; and he had lived his life as a knight of old, knowing neither fear nor blame. The fact that he had a natural son born of a Frenchwoman, whom he had settled abroad, did not lower his own self-esteem. And now this daughter, for whom he had not only done everything that a father could and should do; this daughter to whom he had given a splendid education and every opportunity to make a match in the best Russian society, this daughter to whom he had not only given all that a girl could desire, but whom he had really LOVED; whom he had admired, been proud of this daughter had repaid him with such disgrace, that he was ashamed and could not face the eyes of men!

He recalled the time when she was not merely his child, and a member of his family, but his darling, his joy and his pride. He saw her again, a little thing of eight or nine, bright, intelligent, lively, impetuous, graceful, with brilliant black eyes and flowing auburn hair. He remembered how she used to jump up on his knees and hug him, and tickle his neck; and how she would laugh, regardless of his protests, and continue to tickle him, and kiss his lips, his eyes, and his cheeks. He was naturally opposed to all demonstration, but this impetuous love moved him, and he often submitted to her petting. He remembered also how sweet it was to caress her. To remember all this, when that sweet child had become what she now was, a creature of whom he could not think without loathing.

He also recalled the time when she was growing into womanhood, and the curious feeling of fear and anger that he experienced when he became aware that men regarded her as a woman. He thought of his jealous love when she came coquettishly to him dressed for a ball, and knowing that she was pretty. He dreaded the passionate glances which fell upon her, that she not only did not understand but rejoiced in. "Yes," thought he, "that superstition of woman's purity! Quite the contrary, they do not know shame, they lack this sense." He remembered how, quite inexplicably to him, she had refused two very good suitors. She had become more and more fascinated by her own success in the round of gaieties she lived in.

But this success could not last long. A year passed, then two, then three. She was a familiar figure, beautiful but her first youth had passed, and she had become somehow part of the ball-room furniture. Michael Ivanovich remembered how he had realised that she was on the road to spinsterhood, and desired but one thing for her. He must get her married off as quickly as possible, perhaps not quite so well as might have been arranged earlier, but still a respectable match.

But it seemed to him she had behaved with a pride that bordered on insolence. Remembering this, his anger rose more and more fiercely against her. To think of her refusing so many decent men, only to end in this disgrace. "Oh, oh!" he groaned again.

Then stopping, he lit a cigarette, and tried to think of other things. He would send her money, without ever letting her see him. But memories came again. He remembered, it was not so very long ago, for she was more than twenty then, her beginning a flirtation with a boy of fourteen, a cadet of the Corps of Pages who had been staying with them in the country. She had driven the boy half crazy; he had wept in his distraction. Then how she had rebuked her father severely, coldly, and even rudely, when, to put an end to this stupid affair, he had sent the boy away. She seemed somehow to consider herself insulted. Since then father and daughter had drifted into undisguised hostility.

"I was right," he said to himself. "She is a wicked and shameless woman."

And then, as a last ghastly memory, there was the letter from Moscow, in which she wrote that she could not return home; that she was a miserable, abandoned woman, asking only to be forgiven and forgotten. Then the horrid recollection of the scene with his wife came to him; their surmises and their suspicions, which became a certainty. The calamity had happened in Finland, where they had let her visit her aunt; and the culprit was an insignificant Swede, a student, an empty-headed, worthless creature and married.

All this came back to him now as he paced backwards and forwards on the bedroom carpet, recollecting his former love for her, his pride in her. He recoiled with terror before the incomprehensible fact of her downfall, and he hated her for the agony she was causing him. He remembered the conversation with his sister-in-law, and tried to imagine how he might forgive her. But as soon as the thought of "him" arose, there surged up in his heart horror, disgust, and wounded pride. He groaned aloud, and tried to think of something else.

"No, it is impossible; I will hand over the money to Peter to give her monthly. And as for me, I have no longer a daughter."

And again a curious feeling overpowered him: a mixture of self-pity at the recollection of his love for her, and of fury against her for causing him this anguish.

II

During the last year Lisa had without doubt lived through more than in all the preceding twenty-five. Suddenly she had realised the emptiness of her whole life. It rose before her, base and sordid, this life at home and among the rich set in St. Petersburg, this animal existence that never sounded the depths, but only touched the shallows of life.

It was well enough for a year or two, or perhaps even three. But when it went on for seven or eight years, with its parties, balls, concerts, and suppers; with its costumes and coiffures to display the charms of the body; with its adorers old and young, all alike seemingly possessed of some unaccountable right to have everything, to laugh at everything; and with its summer months spent in the same way, everything yielding but a superficial pleasure, even music and reading merely touching upon life's problems, but never solving them, all this holding out no promise of change, and losing its charm more and more, she began to despair. She had desperate moods when she longed to die.

Her friends directed her thoughts to charity. On the one hand, she saw poverty which was real and repulsive, and a sham poverty even more repulsive and pitiable; on the other, she saw the terrible indifference of the lady patronesses who came in carriages and gowns worth thousands. Life became to her more and more unbearable. She yearned for something real, for life itself, not this playing at living, not this skimming life of its cream. Of real life there was none. The best of her memories was her love for the little cadet Koko. That had been a good, honest, straight-forward impulse, and now there was nothing like it. There could not be. She grew more and more depressed, and in this gloomy mood she went to visit an aunt in Finland. The fresh scenery and surroundings, the people strangely different to her own, appealed to her at any rate as a new experience.

How and when it all began she could not clearly remember. Her aunt had another guest, a Swede. He talked of his work, his people, the latest Swedish novel. Somehow, she herself did not know how that terrible fascination of glances and smiles began, the meaning of which cannot be put into words.

These smiles and glances seemed to reveal to each, not only the soul of the other, but some vital and universal mystery. Every word they spoke was invested by these smiles with a profound and wonderful significance. Music, too, when they were listening together, or when they sang duets, became full of the same deep meaning. So, also, the words in the books they read aloud. Sometimes they would argue, but the moment their eyes met, or a smile flashed between them, the discussion remained far behind. They soared beyond it to some higher plane consecrated to themselves.

How it had come about, how and when the devil, who had seized hold of them both, first appeared behind these smiles and glances, she could not say. But, when terror first seized her, the invisible threads that bound them were already so interwoven that she had no power to tear herself free. She could only count on him and on his honour. She hoped that he would not make use of his power; yet all the while she vaguely desired it.

Her weakness was the greater, because she had nothing to support her in the struggle. She was weary of society life and she had no affection for her mother. Her father, so she thought, had cast her away from him, and she longed passionately to live and to have done with play. Love, the perfect love of a woman for a man, he d the promise of life for her. Her strong, passionate nature, too, was dragging her thither. In the tall, strong figure of this man, with his fair hair and light upturned moustache, under which shone a smile attractive and compelling, she saw the promise of that life for which she longed. And then the smiles and glances, the hope of something so incredibly beautiful, led, as they were bound to lead, to that which she feared but unconsciously awaited.

Suddenly all that was beautiful, joyous, spiritual, and full of promise for the future, became animal and sordid, sad and despairing.

She looked into his eyes and tried to smile, pretending that she feared nothing, that everything was as it should be; but deep down in her soul she knew it was all over. She understood that she had not found in him what she had sought; that which she had once known in herself and in Koko. She told him that he must write to her father asking her hand in marriage. This he promised to do; but when she met him next he said it was impossible for him to write just then. She saw something vague and furtive in his eyes, and her distrust of him grew. The following day he wrote to her, telling her that he was already married, though his wife had left him long since; that he knew she would despise him for the wrong he had done her, and implored her forgiveness. She made him come to see her. She said she loved him; that she felt herself bound to him for ever whether he was married or not, and would never leave him. The next time they met he told her that he and his parents were so poor that he could only offer her the meanest existence. She answered that she needed nothing, and was ready to go with him at once wherever he wished. He endeavoured to dissuade her, advising her to wait; and so she waited. But to live on with this secret, with occasional meetings, and merely corresponding with him, all hidden from her family, was agonising, and she insisted again that he must take her away. At first, when she returned to St. Petersburg, be wrote promising to come, and then letters ceased and she knew no more of him.

She tried to lead her old life, but it was impossible. She fell ill, and the efforts of the doctors were unavailing; in her hopelessness she resolved to kill herself. But how was she to do this, so that her death might seem natural? She really desired to take her life, and imagined that she had irrevocably decided on the step. So, obtaining some poison, she poured it into a glass, and in another instant would have drunk it, had not her sister's little son of five at that very moment run in to show her a toy his grandmother had given him. She caressed the child, and, suddenly stopping short, burst into tears.

The thought overpowered her that she, too, might have been a mother had he not been married, and this vision of motherhood made her look into her own soul for the first time. She began to think not of what others would say of her, but of her own life. To kill oneself because of what the world might say was easy; but the moment she saw her own life dissociated from the world, to take that life was out of the question. She threw away the poison, and ceased to think of suicide.

Then her life within began. It was real life, and despite the torture of it, had the possibility been given her, she would not have turned back from it. She began to pray, but there was no comfort in prayer; and her suffering was less for herself than for her father, whose grief she foresaw and understood.

Thus months dragged along, and then something happened which entirely transformed her life. One day, when she was at work upon a quilt, she suddenly experienced a strange sensation. No, it seemed impossible. Motionless she sat with her work in hand. Was it possible that this was IT. Forgetting everything, his baseness and deceit, her mother's querulousness, and her father's sorrow, she smiled. She shuddered at the recollection that she was on the point of killing it, together with herself.

She now directed all her thoughts to getting away, somewhere where she could bear her child and become a miserable, pitiful mother, but a mother withal. Somehow she planned and arranged it all, leaving her home and settling in a distant provincial town, where no one could find her, and where she thought she would be far from her people. But, unfortunately, her father's brother received an appointment there, a thing she could not possibly foresee. For four months she had been living in the house of a midwife, one Maria Ivanovna; and, on learning that her uncle had come to the town, she was preparing to fly to a still remoter hiding-place.

III

Michael Ivanovich awoke early next morning. He entered his brother's study, and handed him the cheque, filled in for a sum which he asked him to pay in monthly instalments to his daughter. He inquired when the express left for St. Petersburg. The train left at seven in the evening, giving him time for an early dinner before leaving. He breakfasted with his sister-in-law, who refrained from mentioning the subject which was so painful to him, but only looked at him timidly; and after breakfast he went out for his regular morning walk.

Alexandra Dmitrievna followed him into the hall.

"Go into the public gardens, Michael, it is very charming there, and quite near to Everything," said she, meeting his sombre looks with a pathetic glance.

Michael Ivanovich followed her advice and went to the public gardens, which were so near to Everything, and meditated with annoyance on the stupidity, the obstinacy, and heartlessness of women.

"She is not in the very least sorry for me," he thought of his sister-in-law. "She cannot even understand my sorrow. And what of her?" He was thinking of his daughter. "She knows what all this means to me, the torture. What a blow in one's old age! My days will be shortened by it! But I'd rather have it over than endure this agony. And all that 'pour les beaux yeux d'un chenapan', oh!" he moaned; and a wave of hatred and fury arose in him as he thought of what would be said in the town when every one knew. (And no doubt every one knew already.) Such a feeling of rage possessed him that he would have liked to beat it into her head, and make her understand what she had done. These women never understand. "It is quite near Everything," suddenly came to his mind, and getting out his notebook, he found her address. Vera Ivanovna Silvestrova, Kukonskaya Street, Abromov's house. She was living under this name. He left the gardens and called a cab.

"Whom do you wish to see, sir?" asked the midwife, Maria Ivanovna, when he stepped on the narrow landing of the steep, stuffy staircase.

"Does Madame Silvestrova live here?"

"Vera Ivanovna? Yes; please come in. She has gone out; she's gone to the shop round the corner. But she'll be back in a minute."

Michael Ivanovich followed the stout figure of Maria Ivanovna into a tiny parlour, and from the next room came the screams of a baby, sounding cross and peevish, which filled him with disgust. They cut him like a knife.

Maria Ivanovna apologised, and went into the room, and he could hear her soothing the child. The child became quiet, and she returned.

"That is her baby; she'll be back in a minute. You are a friend of hers, I suppose?"

"Yes, a friend, but I think I had better come back later on," said Michael Ivanovich, preparing to go. It was too unbearable, this preparation to meet her, and any explanation seemed impossible.

He had just turned to leave, when he heard quick, light steps on the stairs, and he recognised Lisa's voice.

"Maria Ivanovna has he been crying while I've been gone, I was"

Then she saw her father. The parcel she was carrying fell from her hands.

"Father!" she cried, and stopped in the doorway, white and trembling.

He remained motionless, staring at her. She had grown so thin. Her eyes were larger, her nose sharper, her hands worn and bony. He neither knew what to do, nor what to say. He forgot all his grief about his dishonour. He only felt sorrow, infinite sorrow for her; sorrow for her thinness, and for her miserable rough clothing; and most of all, for her pitiful face and imploring eyes.

"Father, forgive," she said, moving towards him.

"Forgive, forgive me," he murmured; and he began to sob like a child, kissing her face and hands, and wetting them with his tears.

In his pity for her he understood himself. And when he saw himself as he was, he realised how he had wronged her, how guilty he had been in his pride, in his coldness, even in his anger towards her. He was glad that it was he who was guilty, and that he had nothing to forgive, but that he himself needed forgiveness. She took him to her tiny room, and told him how she lived; but she did not show him the child, nor did she mention the past, knowing how painful it would be to him.

He told her that she must live differently.

"Yes; if I could only live in the country," said she.

"We will talk it over," he said. Suddenly the child began to wail and to scream. She opened her eyes very wide; and, not taking them from her father's face, remained hesitating and motionless.

"Well, I suppose you must feed him," said Michael Ivanovich, and frowned with the obvious effort.

She got up, and suddenly the wild idea seized her to show him whom she loved so deeply the thing she now loved best of all in the world. But first she looked at her father's face. Would he be angry or not? His face revealed no anger, only suffering.

"Yes, go, go," said he; "God bless you. Yes. I'll come again to-morrow, and we will decide. Good-bye, my darling, good-bye." Again he found it hard to swallow the lump in his throat.

When Michael Ivanovich returned to his brother's house, Alexandra Dmitrievna immediately rushed to him.

"Well?"

"Well? Nothing."

"Have you seen?" she asked, guessing from his expression that something had happened.

"Yes," he answered shortly, and began to cry. "I'm getting old and stupid," said he, mastering his emotion.

"No; you are growing wise, very wise."

An Old Acquaintance
(Prince Nekhiludof Relates how, during an Expedition in the Caucasus, he met an Acquaintance from Moscow)

Our division had been out in the field. The work in hand was accomplished: we had cut a way through the forest, and each day we were expecting from headquarters orders for our return to the fort. Our division of fieldpieces was stationed at the top of a steep mountain- crest which was terminated by the swift mountain-river Mechik, and had to command the plain that stretched before us. Here and there on this picturesque plain, out of the reach of gunshot, now and then, especially at evening, groups of mounted mountaineers showed themselves, attracted by curiosity to ride up and view the Russian camp.

The evening was clear, mild, and fresh, as it is apt to be in December in the Caucasus; the sun was setting behind the steep chain of the mountains at the left, and threw rosy rays upon the tents scattered over the slope, upon the soldiers moving about, and upon our two guns, which seemed to crane their necks as they rested motionless on the earthwork two paces from us. The infantry picket, stationed on the knoll at the left, stood in perfect silhouette against the light of the sunset; no less distinct were the stacks of muskets, the form of the sentry, the groups of soldiers, and the smoke of the smouldering camp-fire.

At the right and left of the slope, on the b ack, sodden earth, the tents gleamed white; and behind the tents, black, stood the bare trunks of the platane forest, which rang with the incessant sound of axes, the crackling of the bonfires, and the crashing of the trees as they fell under the axes. The bluish smoke arose from tobacco-pipes on all sides, and vanished in the transparent blue of the frosty sky. By the tents and on the lower ground around the arms rushed the Cossacks, dragoons, and artillerists, with great galloping and snorting of horses as they returned from getting water. t began to freeze; all sounds were heard with extraordinary distinctness, and one could see an immense distance across the plain through the clear, rare atmosphere. The groups of the enemy, their curiosity at seeing the soldiers satisfied, quietly galloped off across the fields, still yellow with the golden corn- stubble, toward their auls, or villages, which were visible beyond the forest, with the tall posts of the cemeteries and the smoke rising in the air.

Our tent was pitched not far from the guns on a place high and dry, from which we had a remarkably extended view. Near the tent, on a cleared space, around the battery itself, we had our games of skittles, or chushki. The obliging soldiers had made for us rustic benches and tables. On account of all these amusements, the artillery officers, our comrades, and a few infantry men liked to gather of an evening around our battery, and the place came to be called the club.

As the evening was fine, the best players had come, and we were amusing ourselves with skittles [Footnote: Gorodki]. Ensign D., Lieutenant O., and myself had played two games in succession; and to the common satisfaction and amusement of all the spectators, officers, soldiers, and servants [Footnote: Denshchiki] who were watching us from their tents, we had twice carried the winning party on our backs from one end of the ground to the other. Especially droll was the situation of the huge fat Captain S., who, puffing and smiling good-naturedly, with legs dragging on the ground, rode pickaback on the feeble little Lieutenant O.

When it grew somewhat later, the servants brought three glasses of tea for the six men of us, and not a spoon; and we who had finished our game came to the plaited settees.

There was standing near them a small bow-legged man, a stranger to us, in a sheepskin jacket, and a papakha, or Circassian cap, with a long overhanging white crown. As soon as we came near where he stood, he took a few irresolute steps, and put on his cap; and several times he seemed to make up his mind to come to meet us, and then stopped again. But after deciding, probably, that it was impossible to remain irresolute, the stranger took off his cap, and, going in a circuit around us, approached Captain S.

"Ah, Guskantinli, how is it, old man?" [Footnote: Nu chto, batenka,] said S., still smiling good-naturedly, under the influence of his ride.

Guskantni, as S. called him, instantly replaced his cap, and made a motion as though to thrust his hands into the pockets of his jacket; [Footnote: Polushubok, little half shuba, or fur cloak.] but on the side toward me there was no pocket in the jacket, and his small red hand fell into an awkward position. I felt a strong desire to make out who this man was (was he a yunker, or a degraded officer?), and, not realizing that my gaze (that is, the gaze of a strange officer) disconcerted him, I continued to stare at his dress and appearance.

I judged that he was about thirty. His small, round, gray eyes had a sleepy expression, and at the same time gazed calmly out from under the dirty white lambskin of his cap, which hung down over his face. His thick, irregular nose, standing out between his sunken cheeks, gave evidence of emaciation that was the result of illness, and not natural. His restless lips, barely covered by a sparse, soft, whitish moustache, were constantly changing their shape as though they were trying to assume now one expression, now another. But all these expressions seemed to be endless, and his face retained one predominating expression of timidity and fright. Around his thin neck, where the veins stood out, was tied a green woollen scarf tucked into his jacket, his fur jacket, or polushubok, was worn bare, short, and had dog-fur sewed on the collar and on the false pockets. The trousers were checkered, of ash-gray color, and his sapogi had short, unblacked military bootlegs.

"I beg of you, do not disturb yourself," said I when he for the second time, timidly glancing at me, had taken off his cap.

He bowed to me with an expression of gratitude, replaced his hat, and, drawing from his pocket a dirty chintz tobacco-pouch with lacings, began to roll a cigarette.

I myself had not been long a yunker, an elderly yunker; and as I was incapable, as yet, of being good-naturedly serviceable to my younger comrades, and without means, I well knew all the moral difficulties of this situation for a proud man no longer young, and I sympathized with all men who found themselves in such a situation, and I endeavored to make clear to myself their character and rank, and the tendencies of their intellectual peculiarities, in order to judge of the degree of their moral sufferings. This yunker or degraded officer, judging by his restless eyes and that intentionally constant variation of expression which I noticed in him, was a man very far from stupid, and extremely egotistical, and therefore much to be pitied.

Captain S. invited us to play another game of skittles, with the stakes to consist, not only of the usual pickaback ride of the winning party, but also of a few bottles of red wine, rum, sugar, cinnamon, and cloves for the mulled wine which that winter, on account of the cold, was greatly popular in our division.

Guskantini, as S. again called him, was also invited to take part; but before the game began, the man, struggling between gratification because he had been invited and a certain timidity, drew Captain S. aside, and began to say something in a whisper. The good-natured captain punched him in the ribs with his big, fat hand, and replied, loud enough to be heard:

"Not at all, old fellow [Footnote: Batenka, Malo-Russian diminutive, little father], I assure you."

When the game was over, and that side in which the stranger whose rank was so low had taken part, had come out winners, and it fell to his lot to ride on one of our officers, Ensign D., the ensign grew red in the face: he went to the little divan and offered the stranger a cigarette by way of a compromise.

While they were ordering the mulled wine, and in the steward's tent were heard assiduous preparations on the part of Nikita, who had sent an orderly for cinnamon and cloves, and the shadow of his back was alternately lengthening and shortening on the dingy sides of the tent, we men, seven in all, sat around on the benches; and while we took turns in drinking tea from the three glasses, and gazed out over the plain, which was now beginning to glow in the twilight, we talked and laughed over the various incidents of the game.

The stranger in the fur jacket took no share in the conversation, obstinately refused to drink the tea which I several times offered him, and as he sat there on the ground in Tartar fashion, occupied himself in making cigarettes of fine-cut tobacco, and smoking them one after another, evidently not so much for his own satisfaction as to give himself the appearance of a man with something to do. When it was remarked that the summons to return was expected on the morrow, and that there might be an engagement, he lifted himself on his knees, and, addressing Captain B. only, said that he had been at the adjutant's, and had himself written the order for the return on the next day. We all said nothing while he was speaking; and notwithstanding the fact that he was so bashful, we begged him to repeat this most interesting piece of news. He repeated what he had said, adding only that he had been staying at the adjutant's (since he made it his home there) when the order came.

"Look here, old fellow, if you are not telling us false, I shall have to go to my company and give some orders for to-morrow," said Captain S.

"No . . . why . . . it may be, I am sure," . . . stammered the stranger, but suddenly stopped, and, apparently feeling himself affronted, contracted his brows, and, muttering something between his teeth, again began to roll a cigarette. But the fine-cut tobacco in his chintz pouch began to show signs of giving out, and he asked S. to lend him a little cigarette. [Footnote: PAPIROSTCHKA, diminished diminutive of PAPIROSKA, from PAPIROS.]

We kept on for a considerable time with that monotonous military chatter which every one who has ever been on an expedition will appreciate; all of us, with one and the same expression, complaining of the dullness and length of the expedition, in one and the same fashion sitting in judgment on our superiors, and all of us likewise, as we had done many times before, praising one comrade, pitying another, wondering how much this one had gained, how much that one had lost, and so on, and so on.

"Here, fellows, this adjutant of ours is completely broken up," said Captain S. "At headquarters he was everlastingly on the winning side; no matter whom he sat down with, he'd rake in everything; but now for two months past he has been losing all the time. The present expedition hasn't been lucky for him. I think he has got away with two thousand silver rubles and five hundred rubles' worth of articles, the carpet that he won at Mukhin's, Nikitin's pistols, Sada's gold watch which Vorontsof gave him. He has lost it all."

"The truth of the matter in his case," said Lieutenant O., "was that he used to cheat everybody; it was impossible to play with him."

"He cheated every one, but now it's all gone up in his pipe;" and here Captain S. laughed good-naturedly. "Our friend Guskof here lives with him. He hasn't quite lost HIM yet: that's so, isn't it, old fellow?" [Footnote: Batenka] he asked, addressing Guskof.

Guskof tried to laugh. It was a melancholy, sickly laugh, which completely changed the expression of his countenance. Till this moment it had seemed to me that I had seen and known this man before;

and, besides the name Guskof, by which Captain S. called him, was familiar to me; but how and when I had seen and known him, I actually could not remember.

"Yes," said Guskof, incessantly putting his hand to his moustaches, but instantly dropping it again without touching them. "Pavel Dmitrievitch's luck has been against him in this expedition, such a veine de malheur" he added in a careful but pure French pronunciation, again giving me to think that I had seen him, and seen him often, somewhere. "I know Pavel Dmitrievitch very well. He has great confidence in me," he proceeded to say; "he and I are old friends; that is, he is fond of me," he explained, evidently fearing that it might be taken as presumption for him to claim old friendship with the adjutant. "Pavel Dmitrievitch plays admirably; but now, strange as it may seem, it's all up with him, he is just about perfectly ruined; la chance a tourne," he added, addressing himself particularly to me.

At first we had listened to Guskof with condescending attention; but as soon as he made use of that second French phrase, we all involuntarily turned from him.

"I have played with him a thousand times, and we agreed then that it was strange," said Lieutenant O., with peculiar emphasis on the word STRANGE [Footnote: Stranno]. "I never once won a ruble from him. Why was it, when I used to win of others?"

"Pavel Dmitrievitch plays admirably: I have known him for a long time," said I. In fact, I had known the adjutant for several years; more than once I had seen him in the full swing of a game, surrounded by officers, and I had remarked his handsome, rather gloomy and always passionless calm face, his deliberate Malo-Russian pronunciation, his handsome belongings and horses, his bold, manly figure, and above all his skill and self-restraint in carrying on the game accurately and agreeably. More than once, I am sorry to say, as I looked at his plump white hands with a diamond ring on the index-finger, passing out one card after another, I grew angry with that ring, with his white hands, with the whole of the adjutant's person, and evil thoughts on his account arose in my mind. But as I afterwards reconsidered the matter coolly, I persuaded myself that he played more skilfully than all with whom he happened to play: the more so, because as I heard his general observations concerning the game, how one ought not to back out when one had laid the smallest stake, how one ought not to leave off in certain cases as the first rule for honest men, and so forth, and so forth, it was evident that he was always on the winning side merely from the fact that he played more sagaciously and coolly than the rest of us. And now it seemed that this self-reliant, careful player had been stripped not only of his money but of his effects, which marks the lowest depths of loss for an officer.

"He always had devilish good luck with me," said Lieutenant O. "I made a vow never to play with him again."

"What a marvel you are, old fellow!" said S., nodding at me, and addressing O. "You lost three hundred silver rubles, that's what you lost to him."

"More than that," said the lieutenant savagely.

"And now you have come to your senses; it is rather late in the day, old man, for the rest of us have known for a long time that he was the cheat of the regiment," said S., with difficulty restraining his laughter, and feeling very well satisfied with his fabrication. "Here is Guskof right here, he FIXES his cards for him. That's the reason of the friendship between them, old man" [Footnote: BATENKA MOI] . . . and Captain S., shaking all over, burst out into such a hearty "ha, ha, ha!" that he spilt the glass of mulled wine which he was holding in his hand. On Guskof's pale emaciated face there showed something like a color; he opened his mouth several times, raised his hands to his moustaches, and once more dropped them to his side where the pockets should have been, stood up, and then sat down again, and finally in an unnatural voice said to S.:

"It's no joke, Nikolai Ivanovitch, for you to say such things before people who don't know me and who see me in this unlined jacket . . . because" His voice failed him, and again his small red hands with their dirty nails went from his jacket to his face, touching his moustache, his hair, his nose, rubbing his eyes, or needlessly scratching his cheek.

"As to saying that, everybody knows it, old fellow," continued S., thoroughly satisfied with his jest, and not heeding Guskof's complaint. Guskof was still trying to say something; and placing the palm of his right hand on his left knee in a most unnatural position, and gazing at S., he had an appearance of smiling contemptuously.

"No," said I to myself, as I noticed that smile of his, "I have not only seen him, but have spoken with him somewhere."

"You and I have met somewhere," said I to him when, under the influence of the common silence, S.'s laughter began to calm down. Guskof's mobile face suddenly lighted up, and his eyes, for the first time with a truly joyous expression, rested upon me.

"Why, I recognized you immediately," he replied in French. "In '48 I had the pleasure of meeting you quite frequently in Moscow at my sister's."

I had to apologize for not recognizing him at first in that costume and in that new garb. He arose, came to me, and with his moist hand irresolutely and weakly seized my hand, and sat down by me. Instead of looking at me, though he apparently seemed so glad to see me, he gazed with an expression of unfriendly bravado at the officers.

Either because I recognized in him a man whom I had met a few years before in a dresscoat in a parlor, or because he was suddenly raised in his own opinion by the fact of being recognized, at all events it seemed to me that his face and even his motions completely changed: they now expressed lively intelligence, a childish self-satisfaction in the consciousness of such intelligence, and a certain contemptuous indifference; so that I confess, notwithstanding the pitiable position in which he found himself, my old acquaintance did not so much excite sympathy in me as it did a sort of unfavorable sentiment.

I now vividly remembered our first meeting. In 1848, while I was staying at Moscow, I frequently went to the house of Ivashin, who from childhood had been an old friend of mine. His wife was an agreeable hostess, a charming woman, as everybody said; but she never pleased me. . . . The winter that I knew her, she often spoke with hardly concealed pride of her brother, who had shortly before completed his course, and promised to be one of the most fashionable and popular young men in the best society of Petersburg. As I knew by reputation the father of the Guskofs, who was very rich and had a distinguished position, and as I knew also the sister's ways, I felt some prejudice against meeting the young man. One evening when I was at Ivashin's, I saw a short, thoroughly pleasant-looking young man, in a black coat, white vest and necktie. My host hastened to make me acquainted with him. The young man, evidently dressed for a ball, with his cap in his hand, was standing before Ivashin, and was eagerly but politely arguing with him about a common friend of ours, who had distinguished himself at the time of the Hungarian campaign. He said that this acquaintance was not at all a hero or a man born for war, as was said of him, but was simply a clever and cultivated man. I recollect, I took part in the argument against Guskof, and went to the extreme of declaring also that intellect and cultivation always bore an inverse relation to bravery; and I recollect how Guskof pleasantly and cleverly pointed out to me that bravery was necessarily the result of intellect and a decided degree of development, a statement which I, who considered myself an intellectual and cultivated man, could not in my heart of hearts agree with.

I recollect that towards the close of our conversation Madame Ivashina introduced me to her brother; and he, with a condescending smile, offered me his little hand on which he had not yet had time to draw his kid gloves, and weakly and irresolutely pressed my hand as he did now. Though I had been prejudiced against Guskof, I could not help granting that he was in the right, and agreeing with his sister that he was really a clever and agreeable young man, who ought to have great success in society. He was extraordinarily neat, beautifully dressed, and fresh, and had affectedly modest manners, and a thoroughly youthful, almost childish appearance, on account of which you could not help excusing his expression of self-sufficiency, though it modified the impression of his high-mightiness caused by his intellectual face and especially his smile. It is said that he had great success that winter with the high- born ladies of Moscow. As I saw him at his sister's I could only infer how far this was true by the feeling of pleasure and contentment constantly excited in me by his youthful appearance and by his sometimes indiscreet anecdotes. He and I met half a dozen times, and talked a good deal; or, rather, he talked a good deal, and I listened. He spoke for the most part in French, always with a good accent, very fluently and ornately; and he had the skill of drawing others gently and politely into the conversation. As a general thing, he behaved toward all, and toward me, in a somewhat supercilious manner, and I felt that he was perfectly right in this way of treating people. I always feel that way in regard to men who are firmly convinced that they ought to treat me superciliously, and who are comparative strangers to me.

Now, as he sat with me, and gave me his hand, I keenly recalled in him that same old haughtiness of expression; and it seemed to me that he did not properly appreciate his position of official inferiority, as, in the presence of the officers, he asked me what I had been doing in all that time, and how I happened to be there. In spite of the fact that I invariably made my replies in Russian, he kept putting his questions in French, expressing himself as before in remarkably correct language. About himself he said fluently that after his unhappy, wretched story (what the story was, I did not know, and he had not yet told me), he had been three months under arrest, and then had been sent to the Caucasus to the N. regiment, and now had been serving three years as a soldier in that regiment.

"You would not believe," said he to me in French, "how much I have to suffer in these regiments from the society of the officers. Still it is a pleasure to me, that I used to know the adjutant of whom we were just speaking: he is a good man, it's a fact," he remarked condescendingly. "I live with him, and that's something of a relief for me. Yes, my dear, the days fly by, but they aren't all alike," [Footnote: OUI, MON CHER, LES JOURS SE SUIVENT, MAIS NE SE RESSEMBLENT PAS: in French in the original.] he added; and suddenly hesitated, reddened, and stood up, as he caught sight of the adjutant himself coming toward us.

"It is such a pleasure to meet such a man as you," said Guskof to me in a whisper as he turned from me. "I should like very, very much, to have a long talk with you."

I said that I should be very happy to talk with him, but in reality I confess that Guskof excited in me a sort of dull pity that was not akin to sympathy.

I had a presentiment that I should feel a constraint in a private conversation with him; but still I was anxious to learn from him several things, and, above all, why it was, when his father had been so rich, that he was in poverty, as was evident by his dress and appearance.

The adjutant greeted us all, including Guskof, and sat down by me in the seat which the cashiered officer had just vacated. Pavel Dmitrievitch, who had always been calm and leisurely, a genuine gambler, and a man of means, was now very different from what he had been in the flowery days of his success; he seemed to be in haste to go somewhere, kept constantly glancing at everybody, and it was not five minutes before he proposed to Lieutenant O., who had sworn off from playing, to set up a small faro-bank. Lieutenant O. refused, under the pretext of having to attend to his duties, but in reality because, as he knew that the adjutant had few possessions and little money left, he did not feel himself justified in risking his three hundred rubles against a hundred or even less which the adjutant might stake.

"Well, Pavel Dmitrievitch," said the lieutenant, anxious to avoid a repetition of the invitation, "is it true, what they tell us, that we return to-morrow?"

"I don't know," replied the adjutant. "Orders came to be in readiness; but if it's true, then you'd better play a game. I would wager my Kabarda cloak."

"No, to-day already" . . .

"It's a gray one, never been worn; but if you prefer, play for money. How is that?"

"Yes, but . . . I should be willing, pray don't think that" . . . said Lieutenant O., answering the implied suspicion; "but as there may be a raid or some movement, I must go to bed early."

The adjutant stood up, and, thrusting his hands into his pockets, started to go across the grounds. His face assumed its ordinary expression of coldness and pride, which I admired in him.

"Won't you have a glass of mulled wine?" I asked him.

"That might be acceptable," and he came back to me; but Guskof politely took the glass from me, and handed it to the adjutant, striving at the same time not to look at him. But as he did not notice the tent-rope, he stumbled over it, and fell on his hand, dropping the glass.

"What a bungler!" exclaimed the adjutant, still holding out his hand for the glass. Everybody burst out laughing, not excepting Guskof, who was rubbing his hand on his sore knee, which he had somehow struck as he fell. "That's the way the bear waited on the hermit," continued the adjutant. "It's the way he waits on me every day. He has pulled up all the tent-pins; he's always tripping up."

Guskof, not hearing him, apologized to us, and glanced toward me with a smile of almost noticeable melancholy, as though saying that I alone could understand him. He was pitiable to see; but the adjutant, his protector, seemed, on that very account, to be severe on his messmate, and did not try to put him at his ease.

"Well, you're a graceful lad! Where did you think you were going?"

"Well, who can help tripping over these pins, Pavel Dmitrievitch?" said Guskof. "You tripped over them yourself the other day."

"I, old man, [Footnote: batiushka] I am not of the rank and file, and such gracefulness is not expected of me."

"He can be lazy," said Captain S., keeping the ball rolling, "but low- rank men have to make their legs fly."

"Ill-timed jest," said Guskof, almost in a whisper, and casting down his eyes. The adjutant was evidently vexed with his messmate; he listened with inquisitive attention to every word that he said.

"He'll have to be sent out into ambuscade again," said he, addressing S., and pointing to the cashiered officer.

"Well, there'll be some more tears," said S., laughing. Guskof no longer looked at me, but acted as though he were going to take some tobacco from his pouch, though there had been none there for some time.

"Get ready for the ambuscade, old man," said S., addressing him with shouts of laughter. "To-day the scouts have brought the news, there'll be an attack on the camp to-night, so it's necessary to designate the trusty lads." Guskof's face showed a fleeting smile as though he were preparing to make some reply, but several times he cast a supplicating look at S.

"Well, you know I have been, and I'm ready to go again if I am sent," he said hastily.

"Then you'll be sent."

"Well, I'll go. Isn't that all right?"

"Yes, as at Arguna, you deserted the ambuscade and threw away your gun," said the adjutant; and turning from him he began to tell us the orders for the next day.

As a matter of fact, we expected from the enemy a cannonade of the camp that night, and the next day some sort of diversion. While we were still chatting about various subjects of general interest, the adjutant, as though from a sudden and unexpected impulse, proposed to Lieutenant O. to have a little game. The lieutenant most unexpectedly consented; and, together with S. and the ensign, they went off to the adjutant's tent, where there was a folding green table with cards on it. The captain, the commander of our division, went to our tent to sleep; the other gentlemen also separated, and Guskof and I were left alone. I was not mistaken, it was really very uncomfortable for me to have a tete-a-tete with him; I arose involuntarily, and began to promenade up and down on the battery. Guskof walked in silence by my side, hastily and awkwardly wheeling around so as not to delay or incommode me.

"I do not annoy you?" he asked in a soft, mournful voice. So far as I could see his face in the dim light, it seemed to me deeply thoughtful and melancholy.

"Not at all," I replied; but as he did not immediately begin to speak, and as I did not know what to say to him, we walked in silence a considerably long time.

The twilight had now absolutely changed into dark night; over the black profile of the mountains gleamed the bright evening heat-lightning; over our heads in the light-blue frosty sky twinkled the little stars; on all sides gleamed the ruddy flames of the smoking watch-fires; near us, the white tents stood out in contrast to the frowning blackness of our earth-works. The light from the nearest watch-fire, around which our servants, engaged in quiet conversation, were warming themselves, occasionally flashed on the brass of our heavy guns, and fell on the form of the sentry, who, wrapped in his cloak, paced with measured tread along the battery.

"You cannot imagine what a delight it is for me to talk with such a man as you are," said Guskof, although as yet he had not spoken a word to me. "Only one who had been in my position could appreciate it."

I did not know how to reply to him, and we again relapsed into silence, although it was evident that he was anxious to talk and have me listen to him.

"Why were you . . . why did you suffer this?" I inquired at last, not being able to invent any better way of breaking the ice.

"Why, didn't you hear about this wretched business from Metenin?"

"Yes, a duel, I believe; I did not hear much about it," I replied. "You see, I have been for some time in the Caucasus."

"No, it wasn't a duel, but it was a stupid and horrid story. I will tell you all about it, if you don't know. It happened that the same year that I met you at my sister's I was living at Petersburg. I must tell you I had then what they call une position dans le monde, a position good enough if it was not brilliant. Mon pere me donnait ten thousand par an. In '49 I was promised a place in the embassy at Turin; my uncle on my mother's side had influence, and was always ready to do a great deal for me. That sort of thing is all past now. J'etais recu dans la meilleure societe de Petersburg; I might have aspired to any girl in the city. I was well educated, as we all are who come from the school, but was not especially cultivated; to be sure, I read a good deal afterwards, mais j'avais surtout, you know, ce jargon du monde, and, however it came about, I was looked upon as a leading light among the young men of Petersburg. What raised me more than all in common estimation, c'est cette liaison avec Madame D., about which a great deal was said in Petersburg; but I was frightfully young at that time, and did not prize these advantages very highly. I was simply young and stupid. What more did I need? Just then that Metenin had some notoriety"

And Guskof went on in the same fashion to relate to me the history of his misfortunes, which I will omit, as it would not be at all interesting.

"Two months I remained under arrest," he continued, "absolutely alone; and what thoughts did I not have during that time? But, you know, when it was all over, as though every tie had been broken with the past, then it became easier for me. Mon pere, you have heard tell of him, of course, a man of iron will and strong convictions, il m'a desherite, and broken off all intercourse with me. According to his convictions he had to do as he did, and I don't blame him at all. He was consistent. Consequently, I have not taken a step to induce him to change his mind. My sister was abroad. Madame D. is the only one who wrote to me when I was released, and she sent me assistance; but you understand that I could not accept it, so that I had none of those little things which make one's position a little easier, you know, books, linen, food, nothing at all. At this time I thought things over and over, and began to look at life with different eyes. For instance, this noise, this society gossip about me in Petersburg, did not interest me, did not flatter me; it all seemed to me ridiculous. I felt that I myself had been to blame; I was young and indiscreet; I had spoiled my career, and I only thought how I might get into the right track again. And I felt that I had strength and energy enough for it. After my arrest, as I told you, I was sent here to the Caucasus to the N. regiment.

"I thought," he went on to say, all the time becoming more and more animated, "I thought that here in the Caucasus, la vie de camp, the simple, honest men with whom I should associate, and war and danger, would all admirably agree with my mental state, so that I might begin a new life. They will see me under fire. [Footnote: On me verra au feu.] I shall make myself liked; I shall be respected for my real self, the cross non-commissioned officer; they will relieve me of my fine; and I shall get up again, et vous savez avec ce prestige du malheur! But, quel desenchantement! You can't imagine how I have been deceived! You know what sort of men the officers of our regiment are."

He did not speak for some little time, waiting, as it appeared, for me to tell him that I knew the society of our officers here was bad; but I made him no reply. It went against my grain that he should expect me, because I knew French, forsooth, to be obliged to take issue with the society of the officers, which, during my long residence in the Caucasus, I had had time enough to appreciate fully, and for which I had far higher respect than for the society from which Mr. Guskof had sprung. I wanted to tell him so, but his position constrained me.

"In the N. regiment the society of the officers is a thousand times worse than it is here," he continued. "I hope that it is saying a good deal; J'ESPERE QUE C'EST BEAUCOUP DIRE; that is, you cannot imagine what it is. I am not speaking of the yunkers and the soldiers. That is horrible, it is so bad. At first they received me very kindly, that is absolutely the truth; but when they saw that I could not help despising them, you know, in these inconceivably small circumstances, they saw that I was a man absolutely different, standing far above them, they got angry with me, and began to put various little humiliations on me. You haven't an idea what I had to suffer. [Footnote: CE QUE J'AI EUA SOUFFRIR VOUS NE FAITES PAS UNE IDEE.] Then this forced relationship with the yunkers, and especially with the small means that I had, I lacked everything; [Footnote: AVEC LES PETITS MOYENS QUE J'AVAIS, JE MANQUAIS DE TOUT] I had only what my sister used to send me. And here's a proof for you! As much as it made me suffer, I with my character, AVEC MA FIERTE J'AI ECRIS A MON PERE, begged him to send me something. I understand how living four years of such a life may make a man like our cashiered Dromof who drinks with soldiers, and writes notes to all the officers asking them to loan him three rubles, and signing it, TOUT A VOUS, DROMOF. One must have such a character as I have, not to be mired in the least by such a horrible position."

For some time he walked in silence by my side.

"Have you a cigarette?" [Footnote: "Avez-vous un papiros?"] he asked me.

"And so I stayed right where I was? Yes. I could not endure it physically, because, though we were wretched, cold, and ill-fed, I lived like a common soldier, but still the officers had some sort of consideration for me. I had still some prestige that they regarded. I wasn't sent out on guard nor for drill. I could not have stood that. But morally my sufferings were frightful; and especially because I didn't see any escape from my position. I wrote my uncle, begged him to get me transferred to my present regiment, which, at least, sees some service; and I thought that here Pavel Dmitrievitch, qui est le fils de l'intendant de mon pere, might be of some use to me. My uncle did this for me; I was transferred. After that regiment this one seemed to me a collection of chamberlains. Then Pavel Dmitrievitch was here; he knew who I was, and I was splendidly received. At my uncle's request, a Guskof, vous savez; but I forgot that with these men without cultivation and undeveloped, they can't appreciate a man, and show him marks of esteem, unless he has that aureole of wealth, of friends; and I noticed how, little by little, when they saw that I was poor, their behavior to me showed more and more indifference until they have come almost to despise me. It is horrible, but it is absolutely the truth.

"Here I have been in action, I have fought, they have seen me under fire," [Footnote: On m'a vu au feu.] he continued; "but when will it all end? I think, never. And my strength and energy have already begun to flag. Then I had imagined la guerre, la vie de camp; but it isn't at all what I see, in a sheepskin jacket, dirty linen, soldier's boots, and you go out in ambuscade, and the whole night long lie in the ditch with some Antonof reduced to the ranks for drunkenness, and any minute from behind the bush may come a rifle-shot and hit you or Antonof, it's all the same which. That is not bravery; it's horrible, c'est affreux, it's killing!" [Footnote: Ca tue]

"Well, you can be promoted a non-commissioned officer for this campaign, and next year an ensign," said I.

"Yes, it may be: they promised me that in two years, and it's not up yet. What would those two years amount to, if I knew any one! You can imagine this life with Pavel Dmitrievitch; cards, low jokes, drinking all the time; if you wish to tell anything that is weighing on your mind, you would not be understood, or you would be laughed at: they talk with you, not for the sake of sharing a thought, but to get something funny out of you. Yes, and so it has gone, in a brutal, beastly way, and you are always conscious that you belong to the rank and file; they always make you feel that. Hence you can't realize what an enjoyment it is to talk a coeur ouvert to such a man as you are."

I had never imagined what kind of a man I was, and consequently I did not know what answer to make him.

"Will you have your lunch now?" asked Nikita at this juncture, approaching me unseen in the darkness, and, as I could perceive, vexed at the presence of a guest. "Nothing but curd dumplings, there's none of the roast beef left."

"Has the captain had his lunch yet?"

"He went to bed long ago," replied Nikita, gruffly, "According to my directions, I was to bring you lunch here and your brandy." He muttered something else discontentedly, and sauntered off to his tent. After loitering a while longer, he brought us, nevertheless, a lunch-case; he placed a candle on the lunch-case, and shielded it from the wind with a sheet of paper. He brought a saucepan, some mustard in a jar, a tin dipper with a handle, and a bottle of absinthe. After arranging these things, Nikita lingered around us for some moments, and looked on as Guskof and I were drinking the liquor, and it was evidently very distasteful to him. By the feeble light shed by the candle through the paper, amid the encircling darkness, could be seen the seal-skin cover of the lunch-case, the supper arranged upon it, Guskof's sheepskin jacket, his face, and his small red hands which he used in lifting the patties from the pan. Everything around us was black; and only by straining the sight could be seen the dark battery, the dark form of the sentry moving along the breastwork, on all sides the watch-fires, and on high the ruddy stars.

Guskof wore a melancholy, almost guilty smile as though it were awkward for him to look into my face after his confession. He drank still another glass of liquor, and ate ravenously, emptying the saucepan.

"Yes; for you it must be a relief all the same," said I, for the sake of saying something, "your acquaintance with the adjutant. He is a very good man, I have heard."

"Yes," replied the cashiered officer, "he is a kind man; but he can't help being what he is, with his education, and it is useless to expect it."

A flush seemed suddenly to cross his face. "You remarked his coarse jest this evening about the ambuscade;" and Guskof, though I tried several times to interrupt him, began to justify himself before me, and to show that he had not run away from the ambuscade, and that he was not a coward as the adjutant and Capt. S. tried to make him out.

"As I was telling you," he went on to say, wiping his hands on his jacket, "such people can't show any delicacy toward a man, a common soldier, who hasn't much money either. That's beyond their strength. And here recently, while I haven't received anything at all from my sister, I have been conscious that they have changed toward me. This sheepskin jacket, which I bought of a soldier, and which hasn't any warmth in it, because it's all worn off" (and here he showed me where the wool was gone from the inside), "it doesn't arouse in him any sympathy or consideration for my unhappiness, but scorn, which he does not take pains to hide. Whatever my necessities may be, as now when I have nothing to eat except soldiers' gruel, and nothing to wear," he continued, casting down his eyes, and pouring out for himself still another glass of liquor, "he does not even offer to lend me some money, though he knows perfectly well that I would give it back to him; but he waits till I am obliged to ask him for it. But you appreciate how it is for me to go to him. In your case I should say, square and fair, vous etes audessus de cela, mon cher, je n'ai pas le sou. And you know," said he, looking straight into my eyes with an expression of desperation, "I am going to tell you, square and fair, I am in a terrible situation: pouvez-vous me preter dix rubles argent? My sister ought to send me some by the mail, et mon pere"

"Why, most willingly," said I, although, on the contrary, it was trying and unpleasant, especially because the evening before, having lost at cards, I had left only about five rubles in Nikita's care. "In a moment," said I, arising, "I will go and get it at the tent."

"No, by and by: ne vous derangez pas."

Nevertheless, not heeding him, I hastened to the closed tent, where stood my bed, and where the captain was sleeping.

"Aleksei Ivanuitch, let me have ten rubles, please, for rations," said I to the captain, shaking him.

"What! have you been losing again? But this very evening, you were not going to play any more," murmured the captain, still half asleep.

"No, I have not been playing; but I want the money; let me have it, please."

"Makatiuk!" shouted the captain to his servant, [Footnote: Denshchik.] "hand me my bag with the money."

"Hush, hush!" said I, hearing Guskof's measured steps near the tent.

"What? Why hush?"

"Because that cashiered fellow has asked to borrow it of me. He's right there."

"Well, if you knew him, you wouldn't let him have it," remarked the captain. "I have heard about him. He's a dirty, low-lived fellow."

Nevertheless, the captain gave me the money, ordered his man to put away the bag, pulled the flap of the tent neatly to, and, again saying, "If you only knew him, you wouldn't let him have it," drew his head down under the coverlet. "Now you owe me thirty-two, remember," he shouted after me.

When I came out of the tent, Guskof was walking near the settees; and his slight figure, with his crooked legs, his shapeless cap, his long white hair, kept appearing and disappearing in the darkness, as he passed in and out of the light of the candles. He made believe not to see me.

I handed him the money. He said "Merci," and, crumpling the bank-bill, thrust it into his trousers pocket.

"Now I suppose the game is in full swing at the adjutant's," he began immediately after this.

"Yes, I suppose so."

"He's a wonderful player, always bold, and never backs out. When he's in luck, it's fine; but when it does not go well with him, he can lose frightfully. He has given proof of that. During this expedition, if you reckon his valuables, he has lost more than fifteen hundred rubles. But, as he played discreetly before, that officer of yours seemed to have some doubts about his honor."

"Well, that's because he . . . Nikita, haven't we any of that red Kavkas wine [Footnote: Chikir] left?" I asked, very much enlivened by Guskof's conversational talent. Nikita still kept muttering; but he brought us the red wine, and again looked on angrily as Guskof drained his glass. In Guskof's behavior was noticeable his old freedom from constraint. I wished that he would go as soon as possible; it seemed as if his only reason for not going was because he did not wish to go immediately after receiving the money. I said nothing.

"How could you, who have means, and were under no necessity, simply de gaiete de coeur, make up your mind to come and serve in the Caucasus? That's what I don't understand," said he to me.

I endeavored to explain this act of renunciation, which seemed so strange to him.

"I can imagine how disagreeable the society of those officers, men without any comprehension of culture, must be for you. You could not understand each other. You see, you might live ten years, and not see anything, and not hear about anything, except cards, wine, and gossip about rewards and campaigns."

It was unpleasant for me, that he wished me to put myself on a par with him in his position; and with absolute honesty, I assured him that I was very fond of cards and wine, and gossip about campaigns, and that I did not care to have any better comrades than those with whom I was associated. But he would not believe me.

"Well, you may say so," he continued; "but the lack of women's society, I mean, of course, FEMMES COMME IL FAUT, is that not a terrible deprivation? I don't know what I would give now to go into a parlor, if only for a moment, and to have a look at a pretty woman, even though it were through a crack."

He said nothing for a little, and drank still another glass of the red wine.

"Oh, my God, my God! [Footnote: AKH, BOZHE MOI, BOZHE MOI.] If it only might be our fate to meet again, somewhere in Petersburg, to live and move among men, among ladies!"

He drank up the dregs of the wine still left in the bottle, and when he had finished it he said: "AKH! PARDON, maybe you wanted some more. It was horribly careless of me. However, I suppose I must have taken too much, and my head isn't very strong. [Footnote: ET JE N'AI PAS LA TETE FORTE.]

There was a time when I lived on Morskaia Street, AU REZ-DE- CHAUSSEE, and had marvellous apartments, furniture, you know, and I was able to arrange it all beautifully, not so very expensively though; my father, to be sure, gave me porcelains, flowers, and silver, a wonderful lot. Le matin je sortais, visits, 5 heures regulierement. I used to go and dine with her; often she was alone. Il faut avouer que c'etait une femme ravissante! You didn't know her at all, did you?"

"No."

"You see, there was such high degree of womanliness in her, and such tenderness, and what love! Lord! I did not know how to appreciate my happiness then. We would return after the theatre, and have a little supper together. It was never dull where she was, toujours gaie, toujours aimante. Yes, and I had never imagined what rare happiness it was. Et j'ai beaucoup a me reprocher in regard to her. Je l'ai fait souffrir et souvent. I was outrageous. AKH! What a marvellous time that was! Do I bore you?"

"No, not at all."

"Then I will tell you about our evenings. I used to go, that stairway, every flower-pot I knew, the door-handle, all was so lovely, so familiar; then the vestibule, her room. . . . No, it will never, never come back to me again! Even now she writes to me: if you will let me, I will show you her letters. But I am not what I was; I am ruined; I am no longer worthy of her. . . . Yes, I am ruined for ever. Je suis casse. There's no energy in me, no pride, nothing, nor even any rank. . . . [Footnote: Blagorodstva, noble birth, nobility.] Yes, I am ruined; and no one will ever appreciate my sufferings. Every one is indifferent. I am a lost man. Never any chance for me to rise, because I have fallen morally . . . into the mire, I have fallen. . . ."

At this moment there was evident in his words a genuine, deep despair: he did not look at me, but sat motionless.

"Why are you in such despair?" I asked.

"Because I am abominable. This life has degraded me, all that was in me, all is crushed out. It is not by pride that I hold out, but by abjectness: there's no dignite dans le malheur. I am humiliated every moment; I endure it all; I got myself into this abasement. This mire has soiled me. I myself have become coarse; I have forgotten what I used to know; I can't speak French any more; I am conscious that I am base and low. I cannot tear myself away from these surroundings, indeed I cannot. I might have been a hero: give me a regiment, gold epaulets, a trumpeter, but to march in the ranks with some wild Anton Bondarenko or the like, and feel that between me and him there was no difference at all, that he might be killed or I might be killed, all the same, that thought is maddening. You understand how horrible it is to think that some ragamuffin may kill me, a man who has thoughts and feelings, and that it would make no difference if alongside of me some Antonof were killed, a being not different from an animal and that it might easily happen that I and not this Antonof were killed, which is always UNE FATALITE for every lofty and good man. I know that they call me a coward: grant that I am a coward, I certainly am a coward, and can't be anything else. Not only am I a coward, but I am in my way a low and despicable man. Here I have just been borrowing money of you, and you have the right to despise me. No, take back your money." And he held out to me the crumpled bank-bill. "I want you to have a good opinion of me." He covered his face with his hands, and burst into tears. I really did not know what to say or do.

"Calm yourself," I said to him. "You are too sensitive; don't take everything so to heart; don't indulge in self-analysis, look at things more simply. You yourself say that you have character. Keep up good heart, you won't have long to wait," I said to him, but not very consistently, because I was much stirred both by a feeling of sympathy and a feeling of repentance, because I had allowed myself mentally to sin in my judgment of a man truly and deeply unhappy.

"Yes," he began, "if I had heard even once, at the time when I was in that hell, one single word of sympathy, of advice, of friendship, one humane word such as you have just spoken, perhaps I might have calmly endured all; perhaps I might have struggled, and been a soldier. But now this is horrible. . . . When I think soberly, I long for death. Why should I love my despicable life and my own self, now that I am ruined for all that is worth while in the world? And at the least danger, I suddenly, in spite of myself, begin to pray for my miserable life, and to watch over it as though it were precious, and I cannot, je ne puis pas, control myself. That is, I could," he continued again after a minute's silence, "but this is too hard work for me, a monstrous work, when I am alone. With others, under special circumstances, when you are going into action, I am brave, j'ai fait mes epreuves, because I am vain and proud: that is my failing, and in presence of others. . . . Do you know, let me spend the night with you: with us, they will play all night long; it makes no difference, anywhere, on the ground.'

While Nikita was making the bed, we got up, and once more began to walk up and down in the darkness on the battery. Certainly Guskof's head must have been very weak, because two glasses of liquor and two of wine made him dizzy. As we got up and moved away from the candles, I noticed that he again thrust the ten-ruble bill into his pocket, trying to do so without my seeing it. During all the foregoing conversation, he had held it in his hand. He continued to reiterate how he felt that he might regain his old station if he had a man such as I were to take some interest in him.

We were just going into the tent to go to bed when suddenly a cannon- ball whistled over us, and buried itself in the ground not far from us. So strange it was, that peacefully sleeping camp, our conversation, and suddenly the hostile cannon-ball which flew from God knows where, the midst of our tents, so strange that it was some time before I could realize what it was. Our sentinel, Andreief, walking up and down on the battery, moved toward me.

"Ha! he's crept up to us. It was the fire here that he aimed at," said he.

"We must rouse the captain," said I, and gazed at Guskof.

He stood cowering close to the ground, and stammered, trying to say, "Th-that's th-the ene-my's . . . f-f-fire-th-that's-hidi-." Further he could not say a word, and I did not see how and where he disappeared so instantaneously.

In the captain's tent a candle gleamed; his cough, which always troubled him when he was awake, was heard; and he himself soon appeared, asking for a linstock to light his little pipe.

"What does this mean, old man?" [Footnote: Batiushka] he asked with a smile. "Aren't they willing to give me a little sleep to-night? First it's you with your cashiered friend, and then it's Shamyl. What shall we do, answer him or not? There was nothing about this in the instructions, was there?"

"Nothing at all. There he goes again," said I. "Two of them!"

Indeed, in the darkness, directly in front of us, flashed two fires, like two eyes; and quickly over our heads flew one cannon-ball and one heavy shell. It must have been meant for us, coming with a loud and penetrating hum. From the neighboring tents the soldiers hastened. You could hear them hawking and talking and stretching themselves.

"Hist! the fuse sings like a nightingale," was the remark of the artillerist.

"Send for Nikita," said the captain with his perpetually benevolent smile. "Nikita, don't hide yourself, but listen to the mountain nightingales."

"Well, your honor," [Footnote: VASHE VUISOKOBLAGORODIE. German, HOCHWOHLGEBORENER, high, well-born; regulation title of officers from major to general] said Nikita, who was standing near the captain, "I have seen them, these nightingales. I am not afraid of 'em; but here was that stranger who was here, he was drinking up your red wine. When he heard how that shot dashed by our tents, and the shell rolled by, he cowered down like some wild beast."

"However, we must send to the commander of the artillery," said the captain to me, in a serious tone of authority, "and ask whether we shall reply to the fire or not. It will probably be nothing at all, but still it may. Have the goodness to go and ask him. Have a horse saddled. Do it as quickly as possible, even if you take my Polkan."

In five minutes they brought me a horse, and I galloped off to the commander of the artillery. "Look you, return on foot," whispered the punctilious captain, "else they won't let you through the lines."

It was half a verst to the artillery commander's, the whole road ran between the tents. As soon as I rode away from our fire, it became so black that I could not see even the horse's ears, but only the watch- fires, now seeming very near, now very far off, as they gleamed into my eyes. After I had ridden some distance, trusting to the intelligence of the horse whom I allowed free rein, I began to distinguish the white four-cornered tents and then the black tracks of the road. After a half- hour, having asked my way three times, and twice stumbled over the tent- stakes, causing each time a volley of curses from the tents, and twice been detained by the sentinels, I reached the artillery commander's. While I was on the way, I heard two more cannon shot in the direction of our camp; but the projectiles did not reach to the place where the headquarters were. The artillery commander ordered not to reply to the firing, the more as the enemy did not remain in the same place; and I went back, leading the horse by the bridle, making my way on foot between the infantry tents. More than once I delayed my steps, as I went by some soldier's tent where a light was shining, and some merry-andrew was telling a story; or I listened to some educated soldier reading from some book while the whole division overflowed the tent, or hung around it, sometimes interrupting the reading with various remarks; or I simply listened to the talk about the expedition, about the fatherland, or about their chiefs.

As I came around one of the tents of the third battalion, I heard Guskof's rough voice: he was speaking hilariously and rapidly. Young voices replied to him, not those of soldiers, but of gay gentlemen. It was evidently the tent of some yunker or sergeant-major. I stopped short.

"I've known him a long time," Guskof was saying. "When I lived in Petersburg, he used to come to my house often; and I went to his. He moved in the best society."

"Whom are you talking about?" asked the drunken voice.

"About the prince," said Guskof. "We were relatives, you see, but, more than all, we were old friends. It's a mighty good thing, you know, gentlemen, to have such an acquaintance. You see he's fearfully rich. To him a hundred silver rubles is a mere bagatelle. Here, I just got a little money out of him, enough to last me till my sister sends."

"Let's have some."

"Right away. Savelitch, my dear," said Guskof, coming to the door of the tent, "here's ten rubles for you: go to the sutler, get two bottles of Kakhetinski. Anything else, gentlemen? What do you say?" and Guskof, with unsteady gait, with dishevelled hair, without his hat, came out of the tent. Throwing open his jacket, and thrusting his hands into the pockets of his trousers, he stood at the door of the tent. Though he was in the light, and I in darkness; I trembled with fear lest he should see me, and I went on, trying to make no noise.

"Who goes there?" shouted Guskof after me in a thoroughly drunken voice. Apparently, the cold took hold of him. "Who the devil is going off with that horse?"

I made no answer, and silently went on my way.

Polikushka, or The Lot of a Wicked Court Servant

CHAPTER I.
Polikey was a court man, one of the staff of servants belonging to the court household of a boyarinia (lady of the nobility).

He held a very insignificant position on the estate, and lived in a rather poor, small house with his wife and children.

The house was built by the deceased nobleman whose widow he still continued to serve, and may be described as follows: The four walls surrounding the one izba (room) were built of stone, and the interior was ten yards square. A Russian stove stood in the centre, around which was a free passage. Each corner was fenced off as a separate enclosure to the extent of several feet, and the one nearest to the door (the smallest of all) was known as "Polikey's corner." Elsewhere in the room stood the bed (with quilt, sheet, and cotton pillows), the cradle (with a baby lying therein), and the three-legged table, on which the meals were prepared and the family washing was done. At the latter also Polikey was at work on the preparation of some materials for use in his profession, that of an amateur veterinary surgeon. A calf, some hens, the family clothes and household utensils, together with seven persons, filled the little home to the utmost of its capacity. It would indeed have been almost impossible for them to move around had it not been for the convenience of the stove, on which some of them slept at night, and which served as a table in the day-time.

It seemed hard to realize how so many persons managed to live in such close quarters.

Polikey's wife, Akulina, did the washing, spun and wove, bleached her linen, cooked and baked, and found time also to quarrel and gossip with her neighbors.

The monthly allowance of food which they received from the noblewoman's house was amply sufficient for the whole family, and there was always enough meal left to make mash for the cow. Their fuel they got free, and likewise the food for the cattle. In addition they were given a small piece of land on which to raise vegetables. They had a cow, a calf, and a number of chickens to care for.

Polikey was employed in the stables to take care of two stallions, and, when necessary, to bleed the horses and cattle and clean their hoofs.

In his treatment of the animals he used syringes, plasters, and various other remedies and appliances of his own invention. For these services he received whatever provisions were required by his family, and a certain sum of money, all of which would have been sufficient to enable them to live comfortably and even happily, if their hearts had not been filled with the shadow of a great sorrow.

This shadow darkened the lives of the entire family.

Polikey, while young, was employed in a horse-breeding establishment in a neighboring village. The head stableman was a notorious horse-thief, known far and wide as a great rogue, who, for his many misdeeds, was finally exiled to Siberia. Under his instruction Polikey underwent a course of training, and, being but a boy, was easily induced to perform many evil deeds. He became so expert in the various kinds of wickedness practiced by his teacher that, though he many times would gladly have abandoned his evil ways, he could not, owing to the great hold these early-formed habits had upon him. His father and mother died when he was but a child, and he had no one to point out to him the paths of virtue.

In addition to his other numerous shortcomings, Polikey was fond of strong drink. He also had a habit of appropriating other people's property, when the opportunity offered of his doing so without being seen. Collar-straps, padlocks, perch-bolts, and things even of greater value belonging to others found their way with remarkable rapidity and in great quantities to Polikey's home. He did not, however, keep such things for his own use, but sold them whenever he could find a purchaser. His payment consisted chiefly of whiskey, though sometimes he received cash.

This sort of employment, as his neighbors said, was both light and profitable; it required neither education nor labor. It had one drawback, however, which was calculated to reconcile his victims to their losses: Though he could for a time have all his needs supplied without expending either labor or money, there was always the possibility of his methods being discovered; and this result was sure to be followed by a long term of imprisonment. This impending danger made life a burden for Polikey and his family.

Such a setback indeed very nearly happened to Polikey early in his career. He married while still young, and God gave him much happiness. His wife, who was a shepherd's daughter, was a strong, intelligent, hard-working woman. She bore him many children, each of whom was said to be better than the preceding one.

Polikey still continued to steal, but once was caught with some small articles belonging to others in his possession. Among them was a pair of leather reins, the property of another peasant, who beat him severely and reported him to his mistress.

From that time on Polikey was an object of suspicion, and he was twice again detected in similar escapades. By this time the people began to abuse him, and the clerk of the court threatened to recruit him into the army as a soldier (which is regarded by the peasants as a great punishment and disgrace). His noble mistress severely reprimanded him; his wife wept from grief for his downfall, and everything went from bad to worse.

Polikey, notwithstanding his weakness, was a good-natured sort of man, but his love of strong drink had so overcome every moral instinct that at times he was scarcely responsible for his actions. This habit he vainly endeavored to overcome. It often happened that when he returned home intoxicated, his wife, losing all patience, roundly cursed him and cruelly beat him. At times he would cry like a child, and bemoan his fate, saying: "Unfortunate man that I am, what shall I do? LET MY EYES BURST INTO PIECES if I do not forever give up the vile habit! I will not again touch vodki."

In spite of all his promises of reform, but a short period (perhaps a month) would elapse when Polikey would again mysteriously disappear from his home and be lost for several days on a spree.

"From what source does he get the money he spends so freely?" the neighbors inquired of each other, as they sadly shook their heads.

One of his most unfortunate exploits in the matter of stealing was in connection with a clock which belonged to the estate of his mistress. The clock stood in the private office of the noblewoman, and was so old as to have outlived its usefulness, and was simply kept as an heirloom. It so happened that Polikey went into the office one day when no one was present but himself, and, seeing the old clock, it seemed to possess a peculiar fascination for him, and he speedily transferred it to his person. He carried it to a town not far from the village, where he very readily found a purchaser.

As if purposely to secure his punishment, it happened that the storekeeper to whom he sold it proved to be a relative of one of the court servants, and who, when he visited his friend on the next holiday, related all about his purchase of the clock.

An investigation was immediately instituted, and all the details of Polikey's transaction were brought to light and reported to his noble mistress. He was called into her presence, and, when confronted with the story of the theft, broke down and confessed all. He fell on his knees before the noblewoman and plead with her for mercy. The kind-hearted lady lectured him about God, the salvation of his soul, and his future life. She talked to him also about the misery and disgrace he brought upon his family, and altogether so worked upon his feelings that he cried like a child. In conclusion his kind mistress said: "I will forgive you this time on the condition that you promise faithfully to reform, and never again to take what does not belong to you."

Polikey, still weeping, replied: "I will never steal again in all my life, and if I break my promise may the earth open and swallow me up, and let my body be burned with red-hot irons!"

Polikey returned to his home, and throwing himself on the oven spent the entire day weeping and repeating the promise made to his mistress.

From that time on he was not again caught stealing, but his life became extremely sad, for he was regarded with suspicion by every one and pointed to as a thief.

When the time came round for securing recruits for the army, all the peasants singled out Polikey as the first to be taken. The superintendent was especially anxious to get rid of him, and went to his mistress to induce her to have him sent away. The kind-hearted and merciful woman, remembering the peasant's repentance, refused to grant the superintendent's request, and told him he must take some other man in his stead.

CHAPTER II.
One evening Polikey was sitting on his bed beside the table, preparing some medicine for the cattle, when suddenly the door was thrown wide open, and Aksiutka, a young girl from the court, rushed in. Almost out of breath, she said: "My mistress has ordered you, Polikey Illitch [son of Ilia], to come up to the court at once!"

The girl was standing and still breathing heavily from her late exertion as she continued: "Egor Mikhailovitch, the superintendent, has been to see our lady about having you drafted into the army, and, Polikey Illitch, your name was mentioned among others. Our lady has sent me to tell you to come up to the court immediately."

As soon as Aksiutka had delivered her message she left the room in the same abrupt manner in which she had entered.

Akulina, without saying a word, got up and brought her husband's boots to him. They were poor, worn-out things which some soldier had given him, and his wife did not glance at him as she handed them to him.

"Are you going to change your shirt, Illitch?" she asked, at last.

"No," replied Polikey.

Akulina did not once look at him all the time he was putting on his boots and preparing to go to the court. Perhaps, after all, it was better that she did not do so. His face was very pale and his lips trembled. He slowly combed his hair and was about to depart without saying a word, when his wife stopped him to arrange the ribbon on his shirt, and, after toying a little with his coat, she put his hat on for him and he left the little home.

Polikey's next-door neighbors were a joiner and his wife. A thin partition only separated the two families, and each could hear what the other said and did. Soon after Polikey's departure a woman was heard to say: "Well, Polikey Illitch, so your mistress has sent for you!"

The voice was that of the joiner's wife on the other side of the partition. Akulina and the woman had quarrelled that morning about some trifling thing done by one of Polikey's children, and it afforded her the greatest pleasure to learn that her neighbor had been summoned into the presence of his noble mistress. She looked upon such a circumstance as a bad omen. She continued talking to herself and said: "Perhaps she wants to send him to the town to make some purchases for her household. I did not suppose she would select such a faithful man as you are to perform such a service for her. If it should prove that she DOES want to send you to the next town, just buy me a quarter-pound of tea. Will you, Polikey Illitch?"

Poor Akulina, on hearing the joiner's wife talking so unkindly of her husband, could hardly suppress the tears, and, the tirade continuing, she at last became angry, and wished she could in some way punish her.

Forgetting her neighbor's unkindness, her thoughts soon turned in another direction, and glancing at her sleeping children she said to herself that they might soon be orphans and she herself a soldier's widow. This thought greatly distressed her, and burying her face in her hands she seated herself on the bed, where several of her progeny were fast asleep. Presently a little voice interrupted her meditations by crying out, "Mamushka [little mother], you are crushing me," and the child pulled her nightdress from under her mother's arms.

Akulina, with her head still resting on her hands, said: "Perhaps it would be better if we all should die. I only seem to have brought you into the world to suffer sorrow and misery."

Unable longer to control her grief, she burst into violent weeping, which served to increase the amusement of the joiner's wife, who had not forgotten the morning's squabble, and she laughed loudly at her neighbor's woe.

CHAPTER III.

About half an hour had passed when the youngest child began to cry and Akulina arose to feed it. She had by this time ceased to weep, and after feeding the infant she again fell into her old position, with her face buried in her hands. She was very pale, but this only increased her beauty. After a time she raised her head, and staring at the burning candle she began to question herself as to why she had married, and as to the reason that the Czar required so many soldiers.

Presently she heard steps outside, and knew that her husband was returning. She hurriedly wiped away the last traces of her tears as she arose to let him pass into the centre of the room.

Polikey made his appearance with a look of triumph on his face, threw his hat on the bed, and hastily removed his coat; but not a word did he utter.

Akulina, unable to restrain her impatience, asked, "Well, what did she want with you?"

"Pshaw!" he replied, "it is very well known that Polikushka is considered the worst man in the village; but when it comes to business of importance, who is selected then? Why, Polikushka, of course."

"What kind of business?" Akulina timidly inquired.

But Polikey was in no hurry to answer her question. He lighted his pipe with a very imposing air and spit several times on the floor before he replied.

Still retaining his pompous manner, he said, "She has ordered me to go to a certain merchant in the town and collect a considerable sum of money."

"You to collect money?" questioned Akulina.

Polikey only shook his head and smiled significantly, saying:

"'You,' the mistress said to me, 'are a man resting under a grave suspicion, a man who is considered unsafe to trust in any capacity; but I have faith in you, and will intrust you with this important business of mine in preference to any one else.'"

Polikey related all this in a loud voice, so that his neighbor might hear what he had to say.

"'You promised me to reform,' my noble mistress said to me, 'and I will be the first to show you how much faith I have in your promise. I want you to ride into town, and, going to the principal merchant there, collect a sum of money from him and bring it to me.' I said to my mistress: 'Everything you order shall be done. I will only too gladly obey your slightest wish.'

Then my mistress said: 'Do you understand, Polikey, that your future lot depends upon the faithful performance of this duty I impose upon you?' I replied: 'Yes, I understand everything, and feel that I will suceed in performing acceptably any task which you may impose upon me. I have been accused of every kind of evil deed that it is possible to charge a man with, but I have never done anything seriously wrong against you, your honor.' In this way I talked to our mistress until I succeeded in convincing her that my repentance was sincere, and she became greatly softened toward me, saying, 'If you are successful I will give you the first place at the court.'"

"And how much money are you to collect?" inquired Akulina.

"Fifteen hundred rubles," carelessly answered Polikey.

Akulina sadly shook her head as she asked, "When are you to start?"

"She ordered me to leave here to-morrow," Polikey replied. 'Take any horse you please,' she said. 'Come to the office, and I will see you there and wish you God-speed on your journey.'"

"Glory to Thee, O Lord!" said Akulina, as she arose and made the sign of the cross. "God, I am sure, will bless you, Illitch," she added, in a whisper, so that the people on the other side of the partition could not hear what she said, all the while holding on to his sleeve. "Illitch," she cried at last, excitedly, "for God's sake promise me that you will not touch a drop of vodki. Take an oath before God, and kiss the cross, so that I may be sure that you will not break your promise!"

Polikey replied in most contemptuous tones: "Do you think I will dare to touch vodki when I shall have such a large sum of money in my care?"

"Akulina, have a clean shirt ready for the morning," were his parting words for the night.

So Polikey and his wife went to sleep in a happy frame of mind and full of bright dreams for the future.

CHAPTER IV.

Very early the next morning, almost before the stars had hidden themselves from view, there was seen standing before Polikey's home a low wagon, the same in which the superintendent himself used to ride; and harnessed to it was a large-boned, dark-brown mare, called for some unknown reason by the name of Baraban (drum). Aniutka, Polikey's eldest daughter, in spite of the heavy rain and the cold wind which was blowing, stood outside barefooted and held (not without some fear) the reins in ore hand, while with the other she endeavored to keep her green and yellow overcoat wound around her body, and also to hold Polikey's sheepskin coat.

In the house there were the greatest noise and confusion. The morning was still so dark that the little daylight there was failed to penetrate through the broken panes of glass, the window being stuffed in many places with rags and paper to exclude the cold air.

Akulina ceased from her cooking for a while and helped to get Polikey ready for the journey. Most of the children were still in bed, very likely as a protection against the cold, for Akulina had taken away the big overcoat which usually covered them and had substituted a shawl of her own. Polikey's shirt was all ready, nice and clean, but his shoes badly needed repairing, and this fact caused his devoted wife much anxiety. She took from her own feet the thick woollen stockings she was wearing, and gave them to Polikey. She then began to repair his shoes, patching up the holes so as to protect his feet from dampness.

While this was going on he was sitting on the side of the bed with his feet dangling over the edge, and trying to turn the sash which confined his coat at the waist. He was anxious to look as clean as possible, and he declared his sash looked like a dirty rope.

One of his daughters, enveloped in a sheepskin coat, was sent to a neighbor's house to borrow a hat.

Within Polikey's home the greatest confusion reigned, for the court servants were constantly arriving with innumerable small orders which they wished Polikey to execute for them in town. One wanted needles, another tea, another tobacco, and last came the joiner's wife, who by this time had prepared her samovar, and, anxious to make up the quarrel of the previous day, brought the traveller a cup of tea.

Neighbor Nikita refused the loan of the hat, so the old one had to be patched up for the occasion. This occupied some time, as there were many holes in it.

Finally Polikey was all ready, and jumping on the wagon started on his journey, after first making the sign of the cross.

At the last moment his little boy, Mishka, ran to the door, begging to be given a short ride; and then his little daughter, Mashka, appeared on the scene and pleaded that she, too, might have a ride, declaring that she would be quite warm enough without furs.

Polikey stopped the horse on hearing the children, and Akulina placed them in the wagon, together with two others belonging to a neighbour, all anxious to have a short ride.

As Akulina helped the little ones into the wagon she took occasion to remind Polikey of the solemn promise he had made her not to touch a drop of vodki during the journey.

Polikey drove the children as far as the blacksmith's place, where he let them out of the wagon, telling them they must return home. He then arranged his clothing, and, setting his hat firmly on his head, started his horse on a trot.

The two children, Mishka and Mashka, both barefooted, started running at such a rapid pace that a strange dog from another village, seeing them flying over the road, dropped his tail between his legs and ran home squealing.

The weather was very cold, a sharp cutting wind blowing continuously; but this did not disturb Polikey, whose mind was engrossed with pleasant thoughts. As he rode through the wintry blasts he kept repeating to himself: "So I am the man they wanted to send to Siberia, and whom they threatened to enroll as a soldier, the same man whom every one abused, and said he was lazy, and who was pointed out as a thief and given the meanest work on the estate to do! Now I am going to receive a large sum of money, for which my mistress is sending me because she trusts me. I am also riding in the same wagon that the superintendent himself uses when he is riding as a representative of the court. I have the same harness, leather horse-collar, reins, and all the other gear."

Polikey, filled with pride at thought of the mission with which he had been intrusted, drew himself up with an air of pride, and, fixing his old hat more firmly on his head, buttoned his coat tightly about him and urged his horse to greater speed.

"Just to think," he continued; "I shall have in my possession three thousand half-rubles [the peasant manner of speaking of money so as to make it appear a larger sum than it really is], and will carry them in my bosom. If I wished to I might run away to Odessa instead of taking the money to my mistress. But no; I will not do that. I will surely carry the money straight to the one who has been kind enough to trust me."

When Polikey reached the first kabak (tavern) he found that from long habit the mare was naturally turning her head toward it; but he would not allow her to stop, though money had been given him to purchase both food and drink. Striking the animal a sharp blow with the whip, he passed by the tavern. The performance was repeated when he reached the next kabak, which looked very inviting; but he resolutely set his face against entering, and passed on.

About noon he arrived at his destination, and getting down from the wagon approached the gate of the merchant's house where the servants of the court always stopped. Opening it he led the mare through, and (after unharnessing her) fed her. This done, he next entered the house and had dinner with the merchant's workingman, and to them he related what an important mission he had been sent on, making himself very amusing by the pompous air which he assumed. Dinner over, he carried a letter to the merchant which the noblewoman had given him to deliver.

The merchant, knowing thoroughly the reputation which Polikey bore, felt doubtful of trusting him with so much money, and somewhat anxiously inquired if he really had received orders to carry so many rubles.

Polikey tried to appear offended at this question, but did not succeed, and he only smiled.

The merchant, after reading the letter a second time and being convinced that all was right, gave Polikey the money, which he put in his bosom for safe-keeping.

On his way to the house he did not once stop at any of the shops he passed. The clothing establishments possessed no attractions for him, and after he had safely passed them all he stood for a moment, feeling very pleased that he had been able to withstand temptation, and then went on his way.

"I have money enough to buy up everything," he said; "but I will not do so."

The numerous commissions which he had received compelled him to go to the bazaar. There he bought only what had been ordered, but he could not resist the temptation to ask the price of a very handsome sheep-skin coat which attracted his attention. The merchant to whom he spoke looked at Polikey and smiled, not believing that he had sufficient money to purchase such an expensive coat. But Polikey, pointing to his breast, said that he could buy out the whole shop if he wished to. He thereupon ordered the shop-keeper to take his measure. He tried the coat on and looked himself over carefully, testing the quality and blowing upon the hair to see that none of it came out. Finally, heaving a deep sigh, he took it off.

"The price is too high," he said. "If you could let me have it for fifteen rubles"

But the merchant cut him short by snatching the coat from him and throwing it angrily to one side.

Polikey left the bazaar and returned to the merchant's house in high spirits.

After supper he went out and fed the mare, and prepared everything for the night. Returning to the house he got up on the stove to rest, and while there he took out the envelope which contained the money and looked long and earnestly at it. He could not read, but asked one of those present to tell him what the writing on the envelope meant. It was simply the address and the announcement that it contained fifteen hundred rubles.

The envelope was made of common paper and was sealed with dark-brown sealing wax. There was one large seal in the centre and four smaller ones at the corners. Polikey continued to examine it carefully, even inserting his finger till he touched the crisp notes. He appeared to take a childish delight in having so much money in his possession.

Having finished his examination, he put the envelope inside the lining of his old battered hat, and placing both under his head he went to sleep; but during the night he frequently awoke and always felt to know if the money was safe. Each time that he found that it was safe he rejoiced at the thought that he, Polikey, abused and regarded by every one as a thief, was intrusted with the care of such a large sum of money, and also that he was about to return with it quite as safely as the superintendent himself could have done.

CHAPTER V.
Before dawn the next morning Polikey was up, and after harnessing the mare and looking in his hat to see that the money was all right, he started on his return journey.

Many times on the way Polikey took off his hat to see that the money was safe. Once he said to himself, "I think that perhaps it would be better if I should put it in my bosom." This would necessitate the untying of his sash, so he decided to keep it still in his hat, or until he should have made half the journey, when he would be compelled to stop to feed his horse and to rest.

He said to himself: "The lining is not sewn in very strongly and the envelope might fall out, so I think I had better not take off my hat until I reach home."

The money was safe, at least, so it seemed to him, and he began to think how grateful his mistress would be to him, and in his excited imagination he saw the five rubles he was so sure of receiving.

Once more he examined the hat to see that the money was safe, and finding everything all right he put on his hat and pulled it well down over his ears, smiling all the while at his own thoughts.

Akulina had carefully sewed all the holes in the hat, but it burst out in other places owing to Polikey's removing it so often.

In the darkness he did not notice the new rents, and tried to push the envelope further under the lining, and in doing so pushed one corner of it through the plush.

The sun was getting high in the heavens, and Polikey having slept but little the previous night and feeling its warm rays fell fast asleep, after first pressing his hat more firmly on his head. By this action he forced the envelope still further through the plush, and as he rode along his head bobbed up and down.

Polikey did not awake till he arrived near his own house, and his first act was to put his hand to his head to learn if his hat was all right. Finding that it was in its place, he did not think it necessary to examine it and see that the money was safe. Touching the mare gently with the whip she started into a trot, and as he rode along he arranged in his own mind how much he was to receive. With the air of a man already holding a high position at the court, he looked around him with an expression of lofty scorn on his face.

As he neared his house he could see before him the one room which constituted their humble home, and the joiner's wife next door carry- ing her rolls of linen. He saw also the office of the court and his mistress's house, where he hoped he would be able presently to prove that he was an honest, trustworthy man.

He reasoned with himself that any person can be abused by lying tongues, but when his mistress would see him she would say: "Well done, Polikey; you have shown that you can be honest. Here are three, it may be five, perhaps ten rubles for you;" and also she would order tea for him, and might treat him to vodki, who knows?

The latter thought gave him great pleasure, as he was feeling very cold.

Speaking aloud he said: "What a happy holy-day we can have with ten rubles! Having so much money, I could pay Nikita the four rubles fifty kopecks which I owe him, and yet have some left to buy shoes for the children."

When near the house Polikey began to arrange his clothes, smoothing down his fur collar, re-tying his sash, and stroking his hair. To do the latter he had to take off his hat, and when doing so felt in the lining for the envelope. Quicker and quicker he ran his hand around the lining, and not finding the money used both hands, first one and then the other. But the envelope was not to be found.

Polikey was by this time greatly distressed, and his face was white with fear as he passed his hand through the crown of his old hat. Polikey stopped the mare and began a diligent search through the wagon and its contents. Not finding the precious envelope, he felt in all his pockets BUT THE MONEY COULD NOT BE FOUND!

Wildly clutching at his hair, he exclaimed: "Batiushka! What will I do now? What will become of me?" At the same time he realized that he was near his neighbors' house and could be seen by them; so he turned the mare around, and, pulling his hat down securely upon his head, he rode quickly back in search of his lost treasure.

CHAPTER VI.

The whole day passed without any one in the village of Pokrovski having seen anything of Polikey. During the afternoon his mistress inquired many times as to his whereabouts, and sent Aksiutka frequently to Akulina, who each time sent back word that Polikey had not yet returned, saying also that perhaps the merchant had kept him, or that something had happened to the mare.

His poor wife felt a heavy load upon her heart, and was scarcely able to do her housework and put everything in order for the next day (which was to be a holy-day). The children also anxiously awaited their father's appearance, and, though for different reasons, could hardly restrain their impatience. The noblewoman and Akulina were concerned only in regard to Polikey himself, while the children were interested most in what he would bring them from the town.

The only news received by the villagers during the day concerning Polikey was to the effect that neighboring peasants had seen him running up and down the road and asking every one he met if he or she had found an envelope.

One of them had seen him also walking by the side of his tired-out horse. "I thought," said he, "that the man was drunk, and had not fed his horse for two days, the animal looked so exhausted."

Unable to sleep, and with her heart palpitating at every sound, Akulina lay awake all night vainly awaiting Polikey's return. When the cock crowed the third time she was obliged to get up to attend to the fire. Day was just dawning and the church-bells had begun to ring. Soon all the children were also up, but there was still no tidings of the missing husband and father.

In the morning the chill blasts of winter entered their humble home, and on looking out they saw that the houses, fields, and roads were thickly covered with snow. The day was clear and cold, as if befitting the holy-day they were about to celebrate. They were able to see a long distance from the house, but no one was in sight.

Akulina was busy baking cakes, and had it not been for the joyous shouts of the children she would not have known that Polikey was coming up the road, for a few minutes later he came in with a bundle in his hand and walked quietly to his corner. Akulina noticed that he was very pale and that his face bore an expression of suffering as if he would like to have cried but could not do so. But she did not stop to study it, but excitedly inquired: "What! Illitch, is everything all right with you?"

He slowly muttered something, but his wife could not understand what he said.

"What!" she cried out, "have you been to see our mistress?"

Polikey still sat on the bed in his corner, glaring wildly about him, and smiling bitterly. He did not reply for a long time, and Akulina again cried:

"Eh? Illitch! Why don't you answer me? Why don't you speak?"

Finally he said: "Akulina, I delivered the money to our mistress; and oh, how she thanked me!" Then he suddenly looked about him, with an anxious, startled air, and with a sad smile on his lips. Two things in the room seemed to engross the most of his attention: the baby in the cradle, and the rope which was attached to the ladder. Approaching the cradle, he began with his thin fingers quickly to untie the knot in the rope by which the two were connected. After untying it he stood for a few moments looking silently at the baby.

Akulina did not notice this proceeding, and with her cakes on the board went to place them in a corner.

Polikey quickly hid the rope beneath his coat, and again seated himself on the bed.

"What is it that troubles you, Illitch?" inquired Akulina. "You are not yourself."

"I have not slept," he answered.

Suddenly a dark shadow crossed the window, and a minute later the girl Aksiutka quickly entered the room, exclaiming:

"The boyarinia commands you, Polikey Illitch, to come to her this moment!"

Polikey looked first at Akulina and then at the girl.

"This moment!" he cried. "What more is wanted?"

He spoke the last sentence so softly that Akulina became quieted in her mind, thinking that perhaps their mistress intended to reward her husband.

"Say that I will come immediately," he said.

But Polikey failed to follow the girl, and went instead to another place.

From the porch of his house there was a ladder reaching to the attic. Arriving at the foot of the ladder Polikey looked around him, and seeing no one about, he quickly ascended to the garret.

* * * * * * *

Meanwhile the girl had reached her mistress's house.

"What does it mean that Polikey does not come?" said the noblewoman impatiently. "Where can he be? Why does he not come at once?"

Aksiutka flew again to his house and demanded to see Polikey.

"He went a long time ago," answered Akulina, and looking around with an expression of fear on her face, she added, "He may have fallen asleep somewhere on the way."

About this time the joiner's wife, with hair unkempt and clothes bedraggled, went up to the loft to gather the linen which she had previously put there to dry. Suddenly a cry of horror was heard, and the woman, with her eyes closed, and crazed by fear, ran down the ladder like a cat.

"Illitch," she cried, "has hanged himself!"

Poor Akulina ran up the ladder before any of the people, who had gathered from the surrounding houses, could prevent her. With a loud shriek she fell back as if dead, and would surely have been killed had not one of the spectators succeeded in catching her in his arms.

Before dark the same day a peasant of the village, while returning from the town, found the envelope containing Polikey's money on the roadside, and soon after delivered it to the boyarinia.

A Russian Christmas Party

Count Rostow's affairs were going from bad to worse. He was of a warm, generous nature, with unlimited faith in his servants, and hence was blind to the mismanagement and dishonesty which had sapped his fortune. The possessor of a handsome establishment at the Russian capital, Moscow, the owner of rich provincial estates, and the inheritor of a noble name and wealth, he was nevertheless on the verge of ruin. He had given up his appointment as Marechal de la Noblesse, which he had gone to his seat of Otradnoe to assume, because it entailed too many expenses; and yet there was no improvement in the state of his finances.

Nicolas and Natacha, his son and daughter, often found their father and mother in anxious consultation, talking in low tones of the sale of their Moscow house or of their property in the neighborhood. Having thus retired into private life, the count now gave neither fetes nor entertainments. Life at Otradnoe was much less gay than in past years; still, the house and domain were as full of servants as ever, and twenty persons or more sat down to dinner daily. These were dependants, friends, and intimates, who were regarded almost as part of the family, or at any rate seemed unable to tear themselves away from it: among them a musician named Dimmler and his wife, loghel the dancing-master and his family, and old Mlle. Below, former governess of Natacha and Sonia, the count's niece and adopted child, and now the tutor of Petia, his younger son; besides others who found it simpler to live at the count's expense than at their own. Thus, though there were no more festivities, life was carried on almost as expensively as of old, and neither the master nor the mistress ever imagined any change possible. Nicolas, again, had added to the hunting establishment; there were still fifty horses in the stables, still fifteen drivers; handsome presents were given on all birthdays and fete days, which invariably wound up as of old with a grand dinner to all the neighborhood; the count still played whist or boston, invariably letting his cards be seen by his friends, who were always ready to make up his table, and relieve him without hesitation of the few hundred roubles which constituted their principal income. The old man marched on blindfold through the tangle of his pecuniary difficulties, trying to conceal them, and only succeeding in augmenting them; having neither the courage nor the patience to untie the knots one by one.

The loving heart by his side foresaw their children's ruin, but she could not accuse her husband, who was, alas! too old for amendment; she could only seek some remedy for the disaster. From her woman's point of view there was but one: Nicolas's marriage, namely, with some rich heiress. She clung desperately to this last chance of salvation; but if her son should refuse the wife she should propose to him, every hope of reinstating their fortune would vanish. The young lady whom she had in view was the daughter of people of the highest respectability, whom the Rostows had known from her infancy: Julie Karaguine, who, by the death of her second brother, had suddenly come into great wealth.

The countess herself wrote to Mme. Karaguine to ask her whether she could regard the match with favor, and received a most flattering answer. Indeed, Mme. Karaguine invited Nicolas to her house at Moscow, to give her daughter an opportunity of deciding for herself.

Nicolas had often heard his mother say, with tears in her eyes, that her dearest wish was to see him married. The fulfilment of this wish would sweeten her remaining days, she would say, adding covert hints as to a charming girl who would exactly suit him. One day she took the opportunity of speaking plainly to him of Julie's charms and merits, and urged him to spend a short time in Moscow before Christmas. Nicolas, who had no difficulty in guessing what she was aiming at, persuaded her to be explicit on the matter, and she owned frankly that her hope was to see their sinking fortunes restored by his marriage with her dear Julie!

"Then, mother, if I loved a penniless girl, you would desire me to sacrifice my feelings and my honor, to marry solely for money?"

"Nay, nay; you have misunderstood me," she said, not knowing how to excuse her mercenary hopes. "I wish only for your happiness!" And then, conscious that this was not her sole aim, and that she was not perfectly honest, she burst into tears.

"Do not cry, mamma; you have only to say that you really and truly desire it, and you know I would give my life to see you happy; that I would sacrifice everything, even my feelings."

But this was not his mother's notion. She asked no sacrifice, she would have none; she would sooner have sacrificed herself, if it had been possible.

"Say no more about it; you do not understand," she said, drying away her tears.

"How could she think of such a marriage?" thought Nicolas. "Does she think that because Sonia is poor I do not love her? And yet I should be a thousand times happier with her than with a doll like Julie."

He stayed in the country, and his mother did not revert to the subject. Still, as she saw the growing intimacy between Nicolas and Sonia, she could not help worrying Sonia about every little thing, and speaking to her with colder formality. Sometimes she reproached herself for these continual pin-pricks of annoyance, and was quite vexed with the poor girl for submitting to them with such wonderful humility and sweetness, for taking every opportunity of showing her devoted gratitude, and for loving Nicolas with a faithful and disinterested affection which commanded her admiration.

Just about this time a letter came from Prince Andre, dated from Rome, whither he had gone to pass the year of probation demanded by his father as a condition to giving consent to his son's marriage with the Countess Natacha. It was the fourth the Prince had written since his departure. He ought long since to have been on his way home, he said, but the heat of the summer had caused the wound he had received at Austerlitz to reopen, and this compelled him to postpone his return till early in January.

Natacha, though she was so much in love that her very passion for Prince Andre had made her day-dreams happy, had hitherto been open to all the bright influences of her young life; but now, after nearly four months of parting, she fell into a state of extreme melancholy, and gave way to it completely. She bewailed her hard fate, she bewailed the time that was slipping away and lost to her, while her heart ached with the dull craving to love and be loved. Nicolas, too, had nearly spent his leave from his regiment, and the anticipation of his departure added gloom to the saddened household.

Christmas came; but, excepting the pompous high Mass and the other religious ceremonies, the endless string of neighbors and servants with the regular compliments of the season, and the new gowns which made their first appearance on the occasion, nothing more than usual happened on that day, or more extraordinary than twenty degrees of frost, with brilliant sunshine, a still atmosphere, and at night a glorious starry sky.

After dinner, on the third day of Christmas-tide, when every one had settled into his own corner once more, ennui reigned supreme throughout the house. Nicolas, who had been paying a round of visits in the neighborhood, was fast asleep in the drawing-room. The old count had followed his example in his room. Sonia, seated at a table in the sitting-room, was copying a drawing. The countess was playing out a "patience," and Nastacia Ivanovna, the old buffoon, with his peevish face, sitting in a window with two old women, did not say a word.

Natacha came into the room, and, after leaning over Sonia for a minute or two to examine her work, went over to her mother and stood still in front of her.

The countess looked up. "Why are you wandering about like a soul in torment? What do you want?" she said.

"Want! I want him!" replied Natacha, shortly, and her eyes glowed. "Now, here, at once!"

Her mother gazed at her anxiously.

"Do not look at me like that; you will make me cry."

"Sit down here."

"Mamma, I want him, I want him! Why must I die of weariness?" Her voice broke and tears started from her eyes. She hastily quitted the drawing-room and went to the housekeeper's room, where an old servant was scolding one of the girls who had just come in breathless from out-of-doors.

"There is a time for all things," growled the old woman. "You have had time enough for play."

"Oh, leave her in peace, Kondratievna," said Natacha. "Run away, Mavroucha, go."

Pursuing her wandering, Natacha went into the hall; an old man-servant was playing cards with two of the boys. Her entrance stopped their game and they rose. "And what am I to say to these?" thought she.

"Nikita, would you please go, what on earth can I ask for? go and find me a cock; and you, Micha, a handful of corn."

"A handful of corn?" said Micha, laughing.

"Go, go at once," said the old man.

"And you, Fedor, can you give me a piece of chalk?"

Then she went on to the servants' hall and ordered the samovar to be got ready, though it was not yet tea-time; she wanted to try her power over Foka, the old butler, the most morose and disobliging of all the servants. He could not believe his ears, and asked her if she really meant it. "What next will our young lady want?" muttered Foka, affecting to be very cross.

No one gave so many orders as Natacha, no one sent them on so many errands at once. As soon as a servant came in sight she seemed to invent some want or message; she could not help it. It seemed as though she wanted to try her power over them; to see whether, some fine day, one or another would not rebel against her tyranny; but, on the contrary, they always flew to obey her more readily than any one else.

"And now what shall I do, where can I go?' thought she, as she slowly went along the corridor, where she presently met the buffoon.

"Nastacia Ivanovna," said she, "if I ever have children, what will they be?"

"You! Fleas and grasshoppers, you may depend upon it!"

Natacha went on. "Good God! have mercy, have mercy!" she said to herself. "Wherever I go it is always, always the same. I am so weary; what shall I do?"

Skipping lightly from step to step, she went to the upper story and dropped in on the Ioghels. Two governesses were sitting chatting with M. and Mme. Ioghel; dessert, consisting of dried fruit, was on the table, and they were eagerly discussing the cost of living at Moscow and Odessa. Natacha took a seat for a moment, listened with pensive attention, and then jumped up again. "The island of Madagascar!" she murmured, "Ma-da-gas-car!" and she separated the syllables. Then she left the room without answering Mme. Schoss, who was utterly mystified by her strange exclamation.

She next met Petia and a companion, both very full of some fireworks which were to be let off that evening. "Petia!" she exclaimed, "carry me down-stairs!" And she sprang upon his back, throwing her arms round his neck; and, laughing and galloping, they thus scrambled along to the head of the stairs.

"Thank you, that will do. Madagascar!" she repeated; and, jumping down, she ran down the flight.

After thus inspecting her dominions, testing her power, and convincing herself that her subjects were docile, and that there was no novelty to be got out of them, Natacha settled herself in the darkest corner of the music-room with her guitar, striking the bass strings, and trying to make an accompaniment to an air from an opera that she and Prince Andre had once heard together at St. Petersburg. The uncertain chords which her unpractised fingers sketched out would have struck the least experienced ear as wanting in harmony and musical accuracy, while to her excited imagination they brought a whole train of memories. Leaning against the wall and half hidden by a cabinet, with her eyes fixed on a thread of light that came under the door from the rooms beyond, she listened in ecstasy and dreamed of the past.

Sonia crossed the room with a glass in her hand. Natacha glanced round at her and again fixed her eyes on the streak of light. She had the strange feeling of having once before gone through the same experience, sat in the same place, surrounded by the same details, and watching Sonia pass carrying a tumbler. "Yes, it was exactly the same," she thought.

"Sonia, what is this tune?" she said, playing a few notes.

"What, are you there?" said Sonia, startled. "I do not know," she said, coming closer to listen, "unless it is from 'La Tempete';" but she spoke doubtfully.

"It was exactly so," thought Natacha. "She started as she came forward, smiling so gently; and I thought then, as I think now, that there is something in her which is quite lacking in me. No," she said aloud, "you are quite out; it is the chorus from the 'Porteur d'Eau' listen," and she hummed the air. "Where are you going?"

"For some fresh water to finish my drawing."

"You are always busy and I never. Where is Nicolas?"

"Asleep, I think."

"Go and wake him, Sonia. Tell him to come and sing."

Sonia went, and Natacha relapsed into dreaming and wondering how it had all happened. Not being able to solve the puzzle, she drifted into reminiscence once more. She could see him, him, and feel his impassioned eyes fixed on her face. "Oh, make haste back! I am so afraid he will not come yet! Besides, it is all very well, but I am growing old; I shall be quite different from what I am now! Who knows? Perhaps he will come to-day! Perhaps he is here already! Here in the drawing-room. Perhaps he came yesterday and I have forgotten."

She rose, laid down the guitar, and went into the next room. All the household party were seated round the tea-table, the professors, the governesses, the guests; the servants were waiting on one and another but there was no Prince Andre.

"Ah, here she is," said her father. "Come and sit down here." But Natacha stopped by her mother without heeding his bidding.

"Oh, mamma, bring him to me, give him to me soon, very soon," she murmured, swallowing down a sob. Then she sat down and listened to the others. "Good God! always the same people! always the same thing! Papa holds his cup as he always does, and blows his tea to cool it as he did yesterday, and as he will to-morrow."

She felt a sort of dull rebellion against them all; she hated them for always being the same.

After tea Sonia, Natacha, and Nicolas huddled together in their favorite, snug corner of the drawing-room; that was where they talked freely to each other.

"Do you ever feel," Natacha asked her brother, "as if there was nothing left to look forward to; as if you had had all your share of happiness, and were not so much weary as utterly dull?"

"Of course I have. Very often I have seen my friends and fellow-officers in the highest spirits and been just as jolly myself, and suddenly have been struck so dull and dismal, have so hated life, that I have wondered whether we were not all to die at once. I remember one day, for instance, when I was with the regiment; the band was playing, and I had such a fit of melancholy that I never even thought of going to the promenade."

"How well I understand that! I recollect once," Natacha went on, "once when I was a little girl, I was punished for having eaten some plums, I think. I had not done it, and you were all dancing, and I was left alone in the school-room. How I cried! cried because I was so sorry for myself, and so vexed with you all for making me so unhappy."

"I remember; and I went to comfort you and did not know how; we were funny children then; I had a toy with bells that jingled, and I made you a present of it."

"Do you remember," said Natacha, "long before that, when we were no bigger than my hand, my uncle called us into his room, where it was quite dark, and suddenly we saw -"

"A negro!" interrupted Nicolas, smiling at her recollection. "To be sure. I can see him now; and to this day I wonder whether it was a dream or a reality, or mere fancy invented afterwards."

"He had white teeth and stared at us with his black eyes."

"Do you remember him, Sonia?"

"Yes, yes, but very dimly."

"But papa and mamma have always declared that no negro ever came to the house. And the eggs; do you remember the eggs we used to roll up at Easter; and one day how two little grinning old women came up through the floor and began to spin round the table?"

"Of course. And how papa used to put on his fur coat and fire off his gun from the balcony. And don't you remember?" And so they went on recalling, one after the other, not the bitter memories of old age, but the bright pictures of early childhood, which float and fade on a distant horizon of poetic vagueness, midway between reality and dreams. Sonia remembered being frightened once at the sight of Nicolas in his braided jacket, and her nurse promising her that she should some day have a frock trimmed from top to bottom.

"And they told me you had been found in the garden under a cabbage," said Natacha. "I dared not say it was not true, but it puzzled me tremendously."

A door opened, and a woman put in her head, exclaiming, "Mademoiselle, mademoiselle, they have fetched the cock!"

"I do not want it now; send it away again, Polia." said Natacha.

Dimmler, who had meanwhile come into the room, went up to the harp, which stood in a corner, and in taking off the cover made the strings ring discordantly.

"Edward Karlovitch, play my favorite nocturne. Field's," cried the countess, from the adjoining room.

Dimmler struck a chord. "How quiet you young people are," he said, addressing them.

"Yes, we are studying philosophy," said Natacha, and they went on talking of their dreams.

Dimmler had no sooner begun his nocturne than Natacha, crossing the room on tiptoe, seized the wax-light that was burning on the table and carried it into the next room; then she stole back to her seat, it was now quite dark in the larger room, especially in their corner, but the silvery moonbeams came in at the wide windows and lay in broad sheets on the floor.

"Do you know," whispered Natacha, while Dimmler, after playing the nocturne, let his fingers wander over the strings, uncertain what to play next, "when I go on remembering one thing beyond another, I go back so far, so far, that at last I remember things that happened before I was born, and"

"That is metempsychosis," interrupted Sonia, with a reminiscence of her early lessons. "The Egyptians believed that our souls had once inhabited the bodies of animals, and would return to animals again after our death."

"I do not believe that," said Natacha, still in a low voice, though the music had ceased. "But I am quite sure that we were angels once, somewhere there beyond, or, perhaps, even here; and that is the reason we remember a previous existence."

"May I join the party?" asked Dimmler, coming towards them.

"If we were once angels, how is it that we have fallen lower?"

"Lower? Who says that it is lower? Who knows what I was?" Natacha retorted with full conviction. "Since the soul is immortal, and I am to live forever in the future, I must have existed in the past, so I have eternity behind me, too."

"Yes; but it is very difficult to conceive of that eternity," said Dimmler, whose ironical smile had died away.

"Why?" asked Natacha. "After to-day comes to-morrow, and then the day after, and so on forever; yesterday has been, to-morrow will be"

"Natacha, now it is your turn; sing me something," said her mother. "What are you doing in that corner like a party of conspirators?"

"I am not at all in the humor, mamma," said she; nevertheless she rose. Nicolas sat down to the piano; and standing, as usual, in the middle of the room, where the voice sounded best, she sang her mother's favorite ballad.

Though she had said she was not in the humor, it was long since Natacha had sung so well as she did that evening, and long before she sang so well again. Her father, who was talking over business with Mitenka in his room, hurriedly gave him some final instructions as soon as he heard the first note, as a schoolboy scrambles through his tasks to get to his play; but as the steward did not go, he sat in silence, listening, while Mitenka, too, standing in his presence, listened with evident satisfaction. Nicolas did not take his eyes off his sister's face, and only breathed when she took breath. Sonia was under the spell of that exquisite voice and thinking of the gulf of difference that lay between her and her friend, full conscious that she could never exercise such fascination. The old countess had paused in her "patience," a sad, fond smile played on her lips, her eyes were full of tears, and she shook her head, remembering her own youth, looking forward to her daughter's future and reflecting on her strange prospects of marriage.

Dimmler, sitting by her side, listened with rapture, his eyes half closed.

"She really has a marvellous gift!" he exclaimed. "She has nothing to learn, such power, such sweetness, such roundness!"

"And how much I fear for her happiness!" replied the countess, who in her mother's heart could feel the flame that must some day be fatal to her child's peace.

Natacha was still singing when Petia dashed noisily into the room to announce, in triumphant tones, that a party of mummers had come.

"Idiot!" exclaimed Natacha, stopping short, and, dropping into a chair, she began to sob so violently that it was some time before she could recover herself. "It is nothing, mamma, really nothing at all," she declared, trying to smile. "Only Petia frightened me; nothing more." And her tears flowed afresh.

All the servants had dressed up, some as bears, Turks, tavern-keepers, or fine ladies; others as mongrel monsters. Bringing with them the chill of the night outside, they did not at first venture any farther than the hall; by degrees, however, they took courage; pushing each other forward for self-protection, they all soon came into the music-room. Once there, their shyness thawed; they became expansively merry, and singing, dancing, and sports were soon the order of the day. The countess, after looking at them and identifying them all, went back into the sitting-room, leaving her husband, whose jovial face encouraged them to enjoy themselves.

The young people had all vanished; but half an hour later an old marquise with patches appeared on the scene, none other than Nicolas; Petia as a Turk; a clown, Dimmler; a hussar, Natacha; and a Circassian, Sonia. Both the girls had blackened their eyebrows and given themselves mustaches with burned cork.

After being received with well-feigned surprise, and recognized more or less quickly, the children, who were very proud of their costumes, unanimously declared that they must go and display them elsewhere. Nicolas, who was dying to take them all for a long drive en troika,[C] proposed that, as the roads were in splendid order, they should go, a party of ten, to the Little Uncle's.

[C] A team of three horses harnessed abreast.

"You will disturb the old man, and that will be all," said the countess. "Why, he has not even room for you all to get into the house! If you must go out, you had better go to the Melukows'."

Mme. Melukow was a widow living in the neighborhood; her house, full of children of all ages, with tutors and governesses, was distant only four versts from Otradnoe.

"A capital idea, my dear," cried the count, enchanted. "I will dress up in costume and go, too. I will wake them up, I warrant you!"

But this did not at all meet his wife's views. Perfect madness! For him to go out with his gouty feet in such cold weather was sheer folly! The count gave way, and Mme. Schoss volunteered to chaperon the girls. Sonia's was by far the most successful disguise; her fierce eyebrows and mustache were wonderfully becoming, her pretty features gained expression, and she wore the dress of a man with unexpected swagger and smartness. Something in her inmost soul told her that this evening would seal her fate.

In a few minutes four sleighs with three horses abreast to each, their harness jingling with bells, drew up in a line before the steps, the runners creaking and crunching over the frozen snow. Natacha was the foremost, and the first to tune her spirits to the pitch of this carnival freak. This mirth, in fact, proved highly infectious, and reached its height of tumult and excitement when the party went down the steps and packed themselves into the sleighs, laughing and shouting to each other at the top of their voices. Two of the sleighs were drawn by light cart-horses, to the third the count's carriage horses were harnessed, and one of these was reputed a famous trotter from Orlow's stable; the fourth sleigh, with its rough-coated, black shaft-horse, was Nicolas's private property. In his marquise costume, over which he had thrown his hussar's cloak, fastened with a belt round the waist, he stood gathering up the reins. The moon was shining brightly, reflected in the plating of the harness and in the horses' anxious eyes as they turned their heads in uneasy amazement at the noisy group that clustered under the dark porch. Natacha, Sonia, and Mme. Schoss, with two women servants, got into Nicolas's sleigh; Dimmler and his wife, with Petia, into the count's; the rest of the mummers packed into the other sleighs.

"Lead the way, Zakhare!" cried Nicolas, to his father's coachman, promising himself the pleasure of outstripping him presently; the count's sleigh swayed and strained, the runners, which the frost had already glued to the ground, creaked, the bells rang out, the horses closed up for a pull, and off they went over the glittering, hard snow, flinging it up right and left like spray of powdered sugar. Nicolas started next, and the others followed along the narrow way, with no less jingling and creaking. While they drove under the wall of the park the shadows of the tall, skeleton trees lay on the road, checkering the broad moonlight; but as soon as they had left it behind them, the wide and spotless plain spread on all sides, its whiteness broken by myriads of flashing sparks and spangles of reflected light. Suddenly a rut caused the foremost sleigh to jolt violently, and then the others in succession; they fell away a little, their intrusive clatter breaking the supreme and solemn silence of the night.

"A hare's tracks!" exclaimed Natacha, and her voice pierced the frozen air like an arrow.

"How light it is, Nicolas," said Sonia. Nicolas turned round to look at the pretty face with its black mustache, under the sable hood, looking at once so far away and so close in the moonshine. "It is not Sonia at all," he said, smiling.

"Why, what is the matter?"

"Nothing," said he, returning to his former position.

When they got out on the high-road, beaten and ploughed by horses' hoofs and polished with the tracks of sleighs, his steeds began to pull and go at a great pace. The near horse, turning away his head, was galloping rather wildly, while the horse in the shafts pricked his ears and still seemed to doubt whether the moment for a dash had come. Zakhare's sleigh, lost in the distance, was no more than a black spot on the white snow, and as he drew farther away the ringing of the bells was fainter and fainter; only the shouts and songs of the maskers rang through the calm, clear night.

"On you go, my beauties!" cried Nicolas, shaking the reins and raising his whip. The sleigh seemed to leap forward, but the sharp air that cut their faces and the flying pace of the two outer horses alone gave them any idea of the speed they were making. Nicolas glanced back at the other two drivers; they were shouting and urging their shaft-horses with cries and cracking of whips, so as not to be quite left behind; Nicolas's middle horse, swinging steadily along under the shaft-bow, kept up his regular pace, quite ready to go twice as fast the moment he should be called upon.

They soon overtook the first troika, and after going down a slope they came upon a wide cross-road running by the side of a meadow.

"Where are we, I wonder," thought Nicolas; "this must be the field and slope by the river. No, I do not know where we are! This is all new and unfamiliar to me! God only knows where we are! But no matter!" And smacking his whip with a will, he went straight ahead. Zakhare held in his beasts for an instant, and turned his face, all fringed with frost, to look at Nicolas, who came flying onward.

"Steady there, sir!" cried the coachman, and leaning forward, with a click of his tongue he urged his horses in their turn to their utmost speed. For a few minutes the sleighs ran equal, but before long, in spite of all Zakhare could do, Nicolas gained on him and at last flew past him like a lightning flash; a cloud of fine snow, kicked up by the horses, came showering down on the rival sleigh; the women squeaked, and the two teams had a struggle for the precedence, their shadows crossing and mingling on the snow.

Then Nicolas, moderating his speed, looked about him; before, behind, and on each side of him stretched the fairy scene; a plain strewn with stars and flooded with light.

"To the left, Zakhare says. Why to the left?" thought he. "We were going to the Melukows'. But we are going where fate directs or as Heaven may guide us. It is all very strange and most delightful, is it not?" he said, turning to the others.

"Oh! look at his eyelashes and beard; they are quite white!" exclaimed one of the sweet young men, with pencilled mustache and arched eyebrows.

"That I believe is Natacha?" said Nicolas. "And that little Circassian, who is he? I do not know him, but I like his looks uncommonly! Are you not frozen?" Their answer was a shout of laughter.

Dimmler was talking himself hoarse, and he must be saying very funny things, for the party in his sleigh were in fits of laughing.

"Better and better," said Nicolas to himself; "now we are in an enchanted forest, the black shadows lie across a flooring of diamonds and mix with the sparkling of gems. That might be a fairy palace out there, built of large blocks of marble and jewelled tiles? Did I not hear the howl of wild beasts in the distance? Supposing it were only Melukovka that I am coming to after all! On my word, it would be no less miraculous to have reached port after steering so completely at random!"

It was, in fact, Melukovka, for he could see the house servants coming out on the balcony with lights, and then down to meet them, only too glad of this unexpected diversion.

"Who is there?" a voice asked within.

"The mummers from Count Rostow's; they are his teams," replied the servants.

* * * * *

Pelagueia Danilovna Melukow, a stout and commanding personality, in spectacles and a flowing dressing-gown, was sitting in her drawing-room surrounded by her children, whom she was doing her best to amuse by modelling heads in wax and tracing the shadows they cast on the wall, when steps and voices were heard in the ante-room. Hussars, witches, clowns, and bears were rubbing their faces, which were scorched by the cold and covered with rime, or shaking the snow off their clothes. As soon as they had cast off their furs they rushed into the large drawing-room, which was hastily lighted up. Dimmler, the clown, and Nicolas, the marquise, performed a dance, while the others stood close along the wall, the children shouting and jumping about them with glee.

"It is impossible to know who is who, can that really be Natacha? Look at her; does not she remind you of some one? Edward, before Karlovitch, how fine you are! and how beautifully you dance! Oh! and that splendid Circassian, why, it is Sonia! What a kind and delightful surprise; we were so desperately dull. Ha, ha! what a beautiful hussar! A real hussar, or a real monkey of a boy, which is he, I wonder? I cannot look at you without laughing." They all shouted and laughed and talked at once, at the top of their voices.

Natacha, to whom the Melukows were devoted, soon vanished with them to their own room, where corks and various articles of men's clothing were brought to them, and clutched by bare arms through a half-open door. Ten minutes later all the young people of the house rejoined the company, equally unrecognizable. Pelagueia Danilovna, going and coming among them all, with her spectacles on her nose and a quiet smile, had seats arranged and a supper laid out for the visitors, masters and servants alike. She looked straight in the face of each in turn, recognizing no one of the motley crew, neither the Rostows, nor Dimmler, nor even her own children, nor any of the clothes they figured in.

"That one, who is she?" she asked the governess, stopping a Kazan Tartar, who was, in fact, her own daughter. "One of the Rostows, is it not? And you, gallant hussar, what regiment do you belong to?" she went on, addressing Natacha. "Give some pastila to this Turkish lady," she cried to the butler; "it is not forbidden by her religion, I believe."

At the sight of some of the reckless dancing which the mummers performed under the shelter of their disguise, Pelagueia Danilovna could not help hiding her face in her handkerchief, while her huge person shook with uncontrollable laughter, the laugh of a kindly matron, frankly jovial and gay.

When they had danced all the national dances, ending with the Horovody, she placed every one, both masters and servants, in a large circle, holding a cord with a ring and a rouble, and for a while they played games. An hour after, when the finery was the worse for wear and heat and laughter had removed much of the charcoal, Pelagueia Danilovna could recognize them, compliment the girls on the success of their disguise, and thank the whole party for the amusement they had given her.

Supper was served for the company in the drawing-room, and for the servants in the large dining-room.

"You should try your fortune in the bathroom over there; that is enough to frighten you!" said an old maid who lived with the Melukows.

"Why?" said the eldest girl.

"Oh! you would never dare to do it; you must be very brave."

"Well, I will go," said Sonia.

"Tell us what happened to that young girl, you know," said the youngest Melukow.

"Once a young girl went to the bath, taking with her a cock and two plates with knives and forks, which is what you must do; and she waited. Suddenly she heard horses' bells, some one was coming; he stopped, came up-stairs, and she saw an officer walk into the room; a real live officer, at least so he seemed, who sat down opposite to her where the second cover was laid."

"Oh! how horrible!" exclaimed Natacha, wide-eyed. "And he spoke to her, really spoke?"

"Yes, just as if he had really been a man. He begged and prayed her to listen to him, and all she had to do was to refuse him and hold out till the cock crowed; but she was too much frightened. She covered her face with her hands, and he clasped her in his arms; luckily some girls who were on the watch rushed in when she screamed."

"Why do you terrify them with such nonsense?" said Pelagueia Danilovna.

"But, mamma, you know you wanted to try your fortune too."

"And if you try your fortune in a barn, what do you do?" asked Sonia.

"That is quite simple. You must go to the barn, now, for instance, and listen. If you hear thrashing, it is for ill-luck; if you hear grain dropping, that is good."

"Tell us, mother, what happened to you in the barn."

"It is so long ago," said the mother, with a smile, "that I have quite forgotten; besides, not one of you is brave enough to try it."

"Yes, I will go," said Sonia. "Let me go."

"Go by all means if you are not afraid."

"May I, Madame Schoss?" said Sonia to the governess.

Now, whether playing games or sitting quietly and chatting, Nicolas had not left Sonia's side the whole evening; he felt as if he had seen her for the first time, and only just now appreciated all her merits. Bright, bewitchingly pretty in her quaint costume, and excited as she very rarely was, she had completely fascinated him.

"What a simpleton I must have been!" thought he, responding in thought to those sparkling eyes and that triumphant smile which had revealed to him a little dimple at the tip of her mustache that he had never observed before.

"I am afraid of nothing," she declared. She rose, asked her way, precisely, to the barn, and every detail as to what she was to expect, waiting there in total silence; then she threw a fur cloak over her shoulders, glanced at Nicolas, and went on.

She went along the corridor and down the back-stairs; while Nicolas, saying that the heat of the room was too much for him, slipped out by the front entrance. It was as cold as ever, and the moon seemed to be shining even more brightly than before. The snow at her feet was strewn with stars, while their sisters overhead twinkled in the deep gloom of the sky, and she soon looked away from them, back to the gleaming earth in its radiant mantle of ermine.

Nicolas hurried across the hall, turned the corner of the house, and went past the side door where Sonia was to come out. Half-way to the barn stacks of wood, in the full moonlight, threw their shadows on the path, and beyond, an alley of lime-trees traced a tangled pattern on the snow with the fine crossed lines of their leafless twigs. The beams of the house and its snow-laden roof looked as if they had been hewn out of a block of opal, with iridescent lights where the facets caught the silvery moonlight. Suddenly a bough fell crashing off a tree in the garden; then all was still again. Sonia's heart beat high with gladness; as if she were drinking in not common air, but some life-giving elixir of eternal youth and joy.

"Straight on, if you please, miss, and on no account look behind you."

"I am not afraid," said Sonia, her little shoes tapping the stone steps and then crunching the carpet of snow as she ran to meet Nicolas, who was within a couple of yards of her. And yet not the Nicolas of every-day life. What had transfigured him so completely? Was it his woman's costume with frizzed-out hair, or was it that radiant smile which he so rarely wore, and which at this moment illumined his face?

"But Sonia is quite unlike herself, and yet she is herself," thought Nicolas on his side, looking down at the sweet little face in the moonlight. He slipped his arms under the fur cloak that wrapped her, and drew her to him, and he kissed her lips, which still tasted of the burned cork that had blackened her mustache.

"Nicolas, Sonia," they whispered; and Sonia put her little hands round his face. Then, hand in hand, they ran to the barn and back, and each went in by the different doors they had come out of.

Natacha, who had noted everything, managed so that she, Mme. Schoss, and Dimmler should return in one sleigh, while the maids went with Nicolas and Sonia in another. Nicolas was in no hurry to get home; he could not help looking at Sonia and trying to find under her disguise the true Sonia, his Sonia, from whom nothing now could ever part him. The magical effects of moonlight, the remembrance of that kiss on her sweet lips, the dizzy flight of the snow-clad ground under the horses' hoofs, the black sky, studded with diamonds, that bent over their heads, the icy air that seemed to give vigor to his lungs, all was enough to make him fancy that they were transported to a land of magic.

"Sonia, are you not cold?"

"No; and you?"

Nicolas pulled up, and giving the reins to a man to drive, he ran back to the sleigh in which Natacha was sitting.

"Listen," he said, in a whisper and in French; "I have made up my mind to tell Sonia."

"And you have spoken to her?" exclaimed Natacha, radiant with joy.

"Oh, Natacha, how queer that mustache makes you look! Are you glad?"

"Glad! I am delighted. I did not say anything, you know, but I have been so vexed with you. She is a jewel, a heart of gold. I-I am often naughty, and I have no right to have all the happiness to myself now. Go, go back to her."

"No. Wait one minute. Mercy, how funny you look!" he repeated, examining her closely and discovering in her face, too, an unwonted tenderness and emotion that struck him deeply. "Natacha, is there not some magic at the bottom of it all, heh?"

"You have acted very wisely. Go."

"If I had ever seen Natacha look as she does at this moment I should have asked her advice and have obeyed her, whatever she had bid me do; and all would have gone well. So you are glad?" he said, aloud. "I have done right?"

"Yes, yes, of course you have! I was quite angry with mamma the other day about you two. Mamma would have it that Sonia was running after you. I will not allow any one to say, no, nor even to think, any evil of her, for she is sweetness and truth itself."

"So much the better." Nicolas jumped down and in a few long strides overtook his own sleigh, where the little Circassian received him with a smile from under the fur hood; and the Circassian was Sonia, and Sonia beyond a doubt would be his beloved little wife!

When they got home the two girls went into the countess's room and gave her an account of their expedition; then they went to bed. Without stopping to wipe off their mustaches they stood chattering as they undressed; they had so much to say of their happiness, their future prospects, the friendship between their husbands:

"But, oh! when will it all be? I am so afraid it will never come to pass," said Natacha, as she went toward a table on which two looking-glasses stood.

"Sit down," said Sonia, "and look in the glass; perhaps you will see something about it." Natacha lighted two pairs of candles and seated herself. "I certainly see a pair of mustaches," she said, laughing.

"You should not laugh," said the maid, very gravely.

Natacha settled herself to gaze without blinking into the mirror; she put on a solemn face and sat in silence for some time, wondering what she should see. Would a coffin rise before her, or would Prince Andre presently stand revealed against the confused background in the shining glass? Her eyes were weary and could hardly distinguish even the flickering light of the candles. But with the best will in the world she could see nothing; not a spot to suggest the image either of a coffin or of a human form. She rose.

"Why do other people see things and I never see anything at all? Take my place, Sonia; you must look for yourself and for me, too. I am so frightened; if I could but know!"

Sonia sat down and fixed her eyes on the mirror.

"Sofia Alexandrovna will be sure to see something," whispered Douniacha; "but you always are laughing at such things." Sonia heard the remark and Natacha's whispered reply: "Yes, she is sure to see something; she did last year." Three minutes they waited in total silence. "She is sure to see something," Natacha repeated, trembling.

Sonia started back, covered her face with one hand, and cried out:

"Natacha!"

"You saw something? What did you see?" And Natacha rushed forward to hold up the glass.

But Sonia had seen nothing; her eyes were getting dim, and she was on the point of giving it up when Natacha's exclamation had stopped her; she did not want to disappoint them; but there is nothing so tiring as sitting motionless. She did not know why she had called out and hidden her face.

"Did you see him?" asked Natacha.

"Yes; stop a minute. I saw him," said Sonia, not quite sure whether "him" was to mean Nicolas or Prince Andre. "Why not make them believe that I saw something?" she thought. "A great many people have done so before, and no one can prove the contrary. Yes, I saw him," she repeated.

"How? standing up or lying down?"

"I saw him at first there was nothing; then suddenly I saw him lying down."

"Andre, lying down? Then he is ill!" And Natacha gazed horror-stricken at her companion.

"Not at all; he seemed quite cheerful, on the contrary," said she, beginning to believe in her own inventions.

"And then, Sonia, what then?"

"Then I saw only confusion, red and blue."

"And when will he come back, Sonia? When shall I see him again? O God! I am afraid for him, afraid of everything."

And, without listening to Sonia's attempts at comfort, Natacha slipped into bed, and, long after the lights were out, she lay motionless but awake, her eyes fixed on the moonshine that came dimly through the frost-embroidered windows.

There Are No Guilty People

I

Mine is a strange and wonderful lot! The chances are that there is not a single wretched beggar suffering under the luxury and oppression of the rich who feels anything like as keenly as I do either the injustice, the cruelty, and the horror of their oppression of and contempt for the poor; or the grinding humiliation and misery which befall the great majority of the workers, the real producers of all that makes life possible. I have felt this for a long time, and as the years have passed by the feeling has grown and grown, until recently it reached its climax. Although I feel all this so vividly, I still live on amid the depravity and sins of rich society; and I cannot leave it, because I have neither the knowledge nor the strength to do so. I cannot. I do not know how to change my life so that my physical needs, food, sleep, clothing, my going to and fro, may be satisfied without a sense of shame and wrongdoing in the position which I fill.

There was a time when I tried to change my position, which was not in harmony with my conscience; but the conditions created by the past, by my family and its claims upon me, were so complicated that they would not let me out of their grasp, or rather, I did not know how to free myself. I had not the strength. Now that I am over eighty and have become feeble, I have given up trying to free myself; and, strange to say, as my feebleness increases I realise more and more strongly the wrongfulness of my position, and it grows more and more intolerable to me.

It has occurred to me that I do not occupy this position for nothing: that Providence intended that I should lay bare the truth of my feelings, so that I might atone for all that causes my suffering, and might perhaps open the eyes of those, or at least of some of those, who are still blind to what I see so clearly, and thus might lighten the burden of that vast majority who, under existing conditions, are subjected to bodily and spiritual suffering by those who deceive them and also deceive themselves. Indeed, it may be that the position which I occupy gives me special facilities for revealing the artificial and criminal relations which exist between men, for telling the whole truth in regard to that position without confusing the issue by attempting to vindicate myself, and without rousing the envy of the rich and feelings of oppression in the hearts of the poor and downtrodden. I am so placed that I not only have no desire to vindicate myself; but, on the contrary, I find it necessary to make an effort lest I should exaggerate the wickedness of the great among whom I live, of whose society I am ashamed, whose attitude towards their fellow-men I detest with my whole soul, though I find it impossible to separate my lot from theirs. But I must also avoid the error of those democrats and others who, in defending the oppressed and the enslaved, do not see their failings and mistakes, and who do not make sufficient allowance for the difficulties created, the mistakes inherited from the past, which in a degree lessens the responsibility of the upper classes.

Free from desire for self-vindication, free from fear of an emancipated people, free from that envy and hatred which the oppressed feel for their oppressors, I am in the best possible position to see the truth and to tell it. Perhaps that is why Providence placed me in such a position. I will do my best to turn it to account.

II

Alexander Ivanovich Volgin, a bachelor and a clerk in a Moscow bank at a salary of eight thousand roubles a year, a man much respected in his own set, was staying in a country-house. His host was a wealthy landowner, owning some twenty-five hundred acres, and had married his guest's cousin. Volgin, tired after an evening spent in playing vint* for small stakes with [* A game of cards similar to auction bridge.] members of the family, went to his room and placed his watch, silver cigarette-case, pocket-book, big leather purse, and pocket-brush and comb on a small table covered with a white cloth, and then, taking off his coat, waistcoat, shirt, trousers, and underclothes, his silk socks and English boots, put on his nightshirt and dressing-gown. His watch pointed to midnight. Volgin smoked a cigarette, lay on his face for about five minutes reviewing the day's impressions; then, blowing out his candle, he turned over on his side and fell asleep about one o'clock, in spite of a good deal of restlessness. Awaking next morning at eight he put on his slippers and dressing-gown, and rang the bell.

The old butler, Stephen, the father of a family and the grandfather of six grandchildren, who had served in that house for thirty years, entered the room hurriedly, with bent legs, carrying in the newly blackened boots which Volgin had taken off the night before, a well-brushed suit, and a clean shirt. The guest thanked him, and then asked what the weather was like (the blinds were drawn so that the sun should not prevent any one from sleeping till eleven o'clock if he were so inclined), and whether his hosts had slept well. He glanced at his watch, it was still early, and began to wash and dress. His water was ready, and everything on the washing-stand and dressing-table was ready for use and properly laid out, his soap, his tooth and hair brushes, his nail scissors and files. He washed his hands and face in a leisurely fashion, cleaned and manicured his nails, pushed back the skin with the towel, and sponged his stout white body from head to foot. Then he began to brush his hair. Standing in front of the mirror, he first brushed his curly beard, which was beginning to turn grey, with two English brushes, parting it down the middle. Then he combed his hair, which was already showing signs of getting thin, with a large tortoise-shell comb. Putting on his underlinen, his socks, his boots, his trousers which were held up by elegant braces and his waistcoat, he sat down coatless in an easy chair to rest after dressing, lit a cigarette, and began to think where he should go for a walk that morning, to the park or to Littleports (what a funny name for a wood!). He thought he would go to Littleports. Then he must answer Simon Nicholaevich's letter; but there was time enough for that. Getting up with an air of resolution, he took out his watch. It was already five minutes to nine. He put his watch into his waistcoat pocket, and his purse with all that was left of the hundred and eighty roubles he had taken for his journey, and for the incidental expenses of his fortnight's stay with his cousin and then he placed into his trouser pocket his cigarette-case and electric cigarette-lighter, and two clean handkerchiefs into his coat pockets, and went out of the room, leaving as usual the mess and confusion which he had made to be cleared up by Stephen, an old man of over fifty. Stephen expected Volgin to "remunerate" him, as he said, being so accustomed to the work that he did not feel the slightest repugnance for it. Glancing at a mirror, and feeling satisfied with his appearance, Volgin went into the dining-room.

There, thanks to the efforts of the housekeeper, the footman, and under-butler, the latter had risen at dawn in order to run home to sharpen his son's scythe, breakfast was ready. On a spotless white cloth stood a boiling, shiny, silver samovar (at least it looked like silver), a coffee-pot, hot milk, cream, butter, and all sorts of fancy white bread and biscuits. The only persons at table were the second son of the house, his tutor (a student), and the secretary. The host, who was an active member of the Zemstvo and a great farmer, had already left the house, having gone at eight o'clock to attend to his work. Volgin, while drinking his coffee, talked to the student and the secretary about the weather, and yesterday's vint, and discussed Theodorite's peculiar behaviour the night before, as he had been very rude to his father without the slightest cause. Theodorite was the grown-up son of the house, and a ne'er-do-well. His name was Theodore, but some one had once called him Theodorite either as a joke or to tease him; and, as it seemed funny, the name stuck to him, although his doings were no longer in the least amusing. So it was now. He had been to the university, but left it in his second year, and joined a regiment of horse guards; but he gave that up also, and was now living in the country, doing nothing, finding fault, and feeling discontented with everything. Theodorite was still in bed: so were the other members of the household, Anna Mikhailovna, its mistress; her sister, the widow of a general; and a landscape painter who lived with the family.

Volgin took his panama hat from the hall table (it had cost twenty roubles) and his cane with its carved ivory handle, and went out. Crossing the veranda, gay with flowers, he walked through the flower garden, in the centre of which was a raised round bed, with rings of red, white, and blue flowers, and the initials of the mistress of the house done in carpet bedding in the centre. Leaving the flower garden Volgin entered the avenue of lime trees, hundreds of years old, which peasant girls were tidying and sweeping with spades and brooms. The gardener was busy measuring, and a boy was bringing something in a cart. Passing these Volgin went into the park of at least a hundred and twenty-five acres, filled with fine old trees, and intersected by a network of well-kept walks. Smoking as he strolled Volgin took his favourite path past the summer-house into the fields beyond. It was pleasant in the park, but it was still nicer in the fields. On the right some women who were digging potatoes formed a mass of bright red and white colour; on the left were wheat fields, meadows, and grazing cattle; and in the foreground, slightly to the right, were the dark, dark oaks of Littleports. Volgin took a deep breath, and felt glad that he was alive, especially here in his cousin's home, where he was so thoroughly enjoying the rest from his work at the bank.

"Lucky people to live in the country," he thought. "True, what with his farming and his Zemstvo, the owner of the estate has very little peace even in the country, but that is his own lookout." Volgin shook his head, lit another cigarette, and, stepping out firmly with his powerful feet clad in his thick English boots, began to think of the heavy winter's work in the bank that was in front of him. "I shall be there every day from ten to two, sometimes even till five. And the board meetings . . . And private interviews with clients. . . . Then the Duma. Whereas here. . . . It is delightful. It may be a little dull, but it is not for long." He smiled. After a stroll in Littleports he turned back, going straight across a fallow field which was being ploughed. A herd of cows, calves, sheep, and pigs, which belonged to the village community, was grazing there. The shortest way to the park was to pass through the herd. He frightened the sheep, which ran away one after another, and were followed by the pigs, of which two little ones stared solemnly at him. The shepherd boy called to the sheep and cracked his whip. "How far behind Europe we are," thought Volgin, recalling his frequent holidays abroad. "You would not find a single cow like that anywhere in Europe." Then, wanting to find out where the path which branched off from the one he was on led to and who was the owner of the herd, he called to the boy.

"Whose herd is it?"

The boy was so filled with wonder, verging on terror, when he gazed at the hat, the well-brushed beard, and above all the gold-rimmed eyeglasses, that he could not reply at once. When Volgin repeated his question the boy pulled himself together, and said, "Ours." "But whose is 'ours'?" said Volgin, shaking his head and smiling. The boy was wearing shoes of plaited birch bark, bands of linen round his legs, a dirty, unbleached shirt ragged at the shoulder, and a cap the peak of which had been torn.

"Whose is 'ours'?"

"The Pirogov village herd."

"How old are you?

"I don't know."

"Can you read?"

"No, I can't."

"Didn't you go to school?"

"Yes, I did."

"Couldn't you learn to read?"

"No."

"Where does that path lead?"

The boy told him, and Volgin went on towards the house, thinking how he would chaff Nicholas Petrovich about the deplorable condition of the village schools in spite of all his efforts.

On approaching the house Volgin looked at his watch, and saw that it was already past eleven. He remembered that Nicholas Petrovich was going to drive to the nearest town, and that he had meant to give him a letter to post to Moscow; but the letter was not written. The letter was a very important one to a friend, asking him to bid for him for a picture of the Madonna which was to be offered for sale at an auction. As he reached the house he saw at the door four big, well-fed, well-groomed, thoroughbred horses harnessed to a carriage, the black lacquer of which glistened in the sun. The coachman was seated on the box in a kaftan, with a silver belt, and the horses were jingling their silver bells from time to time.

A bare-headed, barefooted peasant in a ragged kaftan stood at the front door. He bowed. Volgin asked what he wanted.

"I have come to see Nicholas Petrovich."

"What about?"

"Because I am in distress, my horse has died."

Volgin began to question him. The peasant told him how he was situated. He had five children, and this had been his only horse. Now it was gone. He wept.

"What are you going to do?"

"To beg." And he knelt down, and remained kneeling in spite of Volgin's expostulations.

"What is your name?"

"Mitri Sudarikov," answered the peasant, still kneeling.

Volgin took three roubles from his purse and gave them to the peasant, who showed his gratitude by touching the ground with his forehead, and then went into the house. His host was standing in the hall.

"Where is your letter?" he asked, approaching Volgin; "I am just off."

"I'm awfully sorry, I'll write it this minute, if you will let me. I forgot all about it. It's so pleasant here that one can forget anything."

"All right, but do be quick. The horses have already been standing a quarter of an hour, and the f ies are biting viciously. Can you wait, Arsenty?" he asked the coachman.

"Why not?" said the coachman, thinking to himself, "why do they order the horses when they aren't ready? The rush the grooms and I had just to stand here and feed the flies."

"Directly, directly," Volgin went towards his room, but turned back to ask Nicholas Petrovich about the begging peasant.

"Did you see him? He's a drunkard, but still he is to be pitied. Do be quick!"

Volgin got out his case, with all the requisites for writing, wrote the letter, made out a cheque for a hundred and eighty roubles, and, sealing down the envelope, took it to Nicholas Petrovich.

"Good-bye."

Volgin read the newspapers till luncheon. He only read the Liberal papers: The Russian Gazette, Speech, sometimes The Russian Word but he would not touch The New Times, to which his host subscribed.

While he was scanning at his ease the political news, the Tsar's doings, the doings of President, and ministers and decisions in the Duma, and was just about to pass on to the general news, theatres, science, murders and cholera, he heard the luncheon bell ring.

Thanks to the efforts of upwards of ten human beings, counting laundresses, gardeners, cooks, kitchen-maids, butlers and footmen, the table was sumptuously laid for eight, with silver waterjugs, decanters, kvass, wine, mineral waters, cut glass, and fine table linen, while two men-servants were continually hurrying to and fro, bringing in and serving, and then clearing away the hors d'oeuvre and the various hot and cold courses.

The hostess talked incessantly about everything that she had been doing, thinking, and saying; ard she evidently considered that everything that she thought, said, or did was perfect, and that it would please every one except those who were fools. Volgin felt and knew that everything she said was stupid, but it would never do to let it be seen, and so he kept up the conversation. Theodorite was glum and silent; the student occasionally exchanged a few words with the widow. Now and again there was a pause in the conversation, and then Theodorite interposed, and every one became miserably depressed. At such moments the hostess ordered some dish that had not been served, and the footman hurried off to the kitchen, or to the housekeeper, and hurried back again. Nobody felt inclined either to talk or to eat. But they all forced themselves to eat and to talk, and so luncheon went on.

The peasant who had been begging because his horse had died was named Mitri Sudarikov. He had spent the whole day before he went to the squire over his dead horse. First of all he went to the knacker, Sanin, who lived in a village near. The knacker was out, but he waited for him, and it was dinner-time when he had finished bargaining over the price of the skin. Then he borrowed a neighbour's horse to take his own to a field to be buried, as it is forbidden to bury dead animals rear a village. Adrian would not lend his horse because he was getting in his potatoes, but Stephen took pity on Mitri and gave way to his persuasion. He even lent a hand in lifting the dead horse into the cart. Mitri tore off the shoes from the fore egs and gave them to his wife. One was broken, but the other one was whole. While he was digging the grave with a spade which was very blunt, the knacker appeared and took off the skin; and the carcass was then thrown into the hole and covered up. Mitri felt tired, and went into Matrena's hut, where he drank half a bottle of vodka with Sanin to console himself. Then he went home, quarrelled with his wife, and lay down to sleep on the hay. He did not undress, but slept just as he was, with a ragged coat for a coverlet. His wife was in the hut with the girls, there were four of them, and the youngest was only five weeks old. Mitri woke up before dawn as usual. He groaned as the memory of the day before broke in upon him, how the horse had struggled and struggled, and then fallen down. Now there was no horse, and all he had was the price of the skin, four roubles and eighty kopeks. Getting up he arranged the linen bands on his legs, and went through the yard into the hut. His wife was putting straw into the stove with one hand, with the other she was holding a baby girl to her breast, which was hanging out of her dirty chemise.

Mitri crossed himself three times, turning towards the corner in which the ikons hung, and repeated some utterly meaningless words, which he called prayers, to the Trinity and the Virgin, the Creed and our Father.

"Isn't there any water?"

"The girl's gone for it. I've got some tea. Will you go up to the squire?"

"Yes, I'd better." The smoke from the stove made him cough. He took a rag off the wooden bench and went into the porch. The girl had just come back with the water. Mitri filled his mouth with water from the pail and squirted it out on his hands, took some more in his mouth to wash his face, dried himself with the rag, then parted and smoothed his curly hair with his fingers and went out. A little girl of about ten, with nothing on but a dirty shirt, came towards him. "Good-morning, Uncle Mitri," she said; "you are to come and thrash." "All right, I'll come," replied Mitri. He understood that he was expected to return the help given the week before by Kumushkir, a man as poor as he was himself, when he was thrashing his own corn with a horse-driven machine.

"Tell them I'll come, I'll come at lunch time. I've got to go to Ugrumi." Mitri went back to the hut, and changing his birch-bark shoes and the linen bands on his legs, started off to see the squire. After he had got three roubles from Volgin, and the same sum from Nicholas Petrovich, he returned to his house, gave the money to his wife, and went to his neighbour's. The thrashing machine was humming, and the driver was shouting. The lean horses were going slowly round him, straining at their traces. The driver was shouting to them in a monotone, "Now, there, my dears." Some women were unbinding sheaves, others were raking up the scattered straw and ears, and others again were gathering great armfuls of corn and handing them to the men to feed the machine. The work was in full swing. In the kitchen garden, which Mitri had to pass, a girl, clad only in a long shirt, was digging potatoes which she put into a basket.

"Where's your grandfather?" asked Mitri. "He's in the barn "Mitri went to the barn and set to work at once. The old man of eighty knew of Mitri's trouble. After greeting him, he gave him his place to feed the machine.

Mitri took off his ragged coat, laid it out of the way near the fence, and then began to work vigorously, raking the corn together and throwing it into the machine. The work went on without interruption until the dinner-hour. The cocks had crowed two or three times, but no one paid any attention to them; not because the workers did not believe them, but because they were scarcely heard for the noise of the work and the talk about it. At last the whistle of the squire's steam thrasher sounded three miles away, and then the owner came into the barn. He was a straight old man of eighty. "It's time to stop," he said; "it's dinner-time." Those at work seemed to redouble their efforts. In a moment the straw was cleared away; the grain that had been thrashed was separated from the chaff and brought in, and then the workers went into the hut.

The hut was smoke-begrimed, as its stove had no chimney, but it had been tidied up, and benches stood round the table, making room for all those who had been working, of whom there were nine, not counting the owners. Bread, soup, boiled potatoes, and kvass were placed on the table.

An old one-armed beggar, with a bag slung over his shoulder, came in with a crutch during the meal.

"Peace be to this house. A good appetite to you. For Christ's sake give me something."

"God will give it to you," said the mistress, already an old woman, and the daughter-in-law of the master. "Don't be angry with us." An old man, who was still standing near the door, said, "Give him some bread, Martha. How can you?"

"I am only wondering whether we shall have enough." "Oh, it is wrong, Martha. God tells us to help the poor. Cut him a slice."

Martha obeyed. The beggar went away. The man in charge of the thrashing-machine got up, said grace, thanked his hosts, and went away to rest.

Mitri did not lie down, but ran to the shop to buy some tobacco. He was longing for a smoke. While he smoked he chatted to a man from Demensk, asking the price of cattle, as he saw that he would not be able to manage without selling a cow. When he returned to the others, they were already back at work again; and so it went on till the evening.

Among these downtrodden, duped, and defrauded men, who are becoming demoralised by overwork, and being gradually done to death by underfeeding, there are men living who consider themselves Christians; and others so enlightened that they feel no further need for Christianity or for any religion, so superior do they appear in their own esteem. And yet their hideous, lazy lives are supported by the degrading, excessive labour of these slaves, not to mention the labour of millions of other slaves, toiling in factories to produce samovars, silver, carriages, machines, and the like for their use. They live among these horrors, seeing them and yet not seeing them, although often kind at heart, old men and women, young men and maidens, mothers and children, poor children who are being vitiated and trained into moral blindness.

Here is a bachelor grown old, the owner of thousands of acres, who has lived a life of idleness, greed, and over-indulgence, who reads The New Times, and is astonished that the government can be so unwise as to permit Jews to enter the university. There is his guest, formerly the governor of a province, now a senator with a big salary, who reads with satisfaction that a congress of lawyers has passed a resolution in favor of capital punishment. Their political enemy, N. P., reads a liberal paper, and cannot understand the blindness of the government in allowing the union of Russian men to exist.

Here is a kind, gentle mother of a little girl reading a story to her about Fox, a dog that lamed some rabbits. And here is this little girl. During her walks she sees other children, barefooted, hungry, hunting for green apples that have fallen from the trees; and, so accustomed is she to the sight, that these children do not seem to her to be children such as she is, but only part of the usual surroundings, the familiar landscape.

Why is this?

Three Questions

It once occurred to a certain king, that if he always knew the right time to begin everything; if he knew who were the right people to listen to, and whom to avoid; and, above all, if he always knew what was the most important thing to do, he would never fail in anything he might undertake.

And this thought having occurred to him, he had it proclaimed throughout his kingdom that he would give a great reward to any one who would teach him what was the right time for every action, and who were the most necessary people, and how he might know what was the most important thing to do.

And learned men came to the King, but they all answered his questions differently.

In reply to the first question, some said that to know the right time for every action, one must draw up in advance, a table of days, months and years, and must live strictly according to it. Only thus, said they, could everything be done at its proper time. Others declared that it was impossible to decide beforehand the right time for every action; but that, not letting oneself be absorbed in idle pastimes, one should always attend to all that was going on, and then do what was most needful. Others, again, said that however attentive the King might be to what was going on, it was impossible for one man to decide correctly the right time for every action, but that he should have a Council of wise men, who would help him to fix the proper time for everything.

But then again others said there were some things which could not wait to be laid before a Council, but about which one had at once to decide whether to undertake them or not. But in order to decide that, one must know beforehand what was going to happen. It is only magicians who know that; and, therefore, in order to know the right time for every action, one must consult magicians.

Equally various were the answers to the second question. Some said, the people the King most needed were his councillors; others, the priests; others, the doctors; while some said the warriors were the most necessary.

To the third question, as to what was the most important occupation: some replied that the most important thing in the world was science. Others said it was skill in warfare; and others, again, that it was religious worship.

All the answers being different, the King agreed with none of them, and gave the reward to none. But still wishing to find the right answers to his questions, he decided to consult a hermit, widely renowned for his wisdom.

The hermit lived in a wood which he never quitted, and he received none but common folk. So the King put on simple clothes, and before reaching the hermit's cell dismounted from his horse, and, leaving his body-guard behind, went on alone.

When the King approached, the hermit was digging the ground in front of his hut. Seeing the King, he greeted him and went on digging. The hermit was frail and weak, and each time he stuck his spade into the ground and turned a little earth, he breathed heavily.

The King went up to him and said: "I have come to you, wise hermit, to ask you to answer three questions: How can I learn to do the right thing at the right time? Who are the people I most need, and to whom should I, therefore, pay more attention than to the rest? And, what affairs are the most important, and need my first attention?"

The hermit listened to the King, but answered nothing. He just spat on his hand and recommenced digging.

"You are tired," said the King, "let me take the spade and work awhile for you."

"Thanks!" said the hermit, and, giving the spade to the King, he sat down on the ground.

When he had dug two beds, the King stopped and repeated his questions. The hermit again gave no answer, but rose, stretched out his hand for the spade, and said:

"Now rest awhile-and let me work a bit."

But the King did not give him the spade, and continued to dig. One hour passed, and another. The sun began to sink behind the trees, and the King at last stuck the spade into the ground, and said:

"I came to you, wise man, for an answer to my questions. If you can give me none, tell me so, and I will return home."

"Here comes some one running," said the hermit, "let us see who it is."

The King turned round, and saw a bearded man come running out of the wood. The man held his hands pressed against his stomach, and blood was flowing from under them. When he reached the King, he fell fainting on the ground moaning feebly. The King and the hermit unfastened the man's clothing. There was a large wound in his stomach. The King washed it as best he could, and bandaged it with his handkerchief and with a towel the hermit had. But the blood would not stop flowing, and the King again and again removed the bandage soaked with warm blood, and washed and rebandaged the wound. When at last the blood ceased flowing, the man revived and asked for something to drink. The King brought fresh water and gave it to him. Meanwhile the sun had set, and it had become cool. So the King, with the hermit's help, carried the wounded man into the hut and laid him on the bed. Lying on the bed the man closed his eyes and was quiet; but the King was so tired with his walk and with the work he had done, that he crouched down on the threshold, and also fell asleep so soundly that he slept all through the short summer night. When he awoke in the morning, it was long before he could remember where he was, or who was the strange bearded man lying on the bed and gazing intently at him with shining eyes.

"Forgive me!" said the bearded man in a weak voice, when he saw that the King was awake and was looking at him.

"I do not know you, and have nothing to forgive you for," said the King.

"You do not know me, but I know you. I am that enemy of yours who swore to revenge himself on you, because you executed his brother and seized his property. I knew you had gone alone to see the hermit, and I resolved to kill you on your way back. But the day passed and you did not return. So I came out from my ambush to find you, and I came upon your bodyguard, and they recognized me, and wounded me. I escaped from them, but should have bled to death had you not dressed my wound. I wished to kill you, and you have saved my life. Now, if I live, and if you wish it, I will serve you as your most faithful slave, and will bid my sons do the same. Forgive me!"

The King was very glad to have made peace with his enemy so easily, and to have gained him for a friend, and he not only forgave him, but said he would send his servants and his own physician to attend him, and promised to restore his property.

Having taken leave of the wounded man, the King went out into the porch and looked around for the hermit. Before going away he wished once more to beg an answer to the questions he had put. The hermit was outside, on his knees, sowing seeds in the beds that had been dug the day before.

The King approached him, and said:

"For the last time, I pray you to answer my questions, wise man."

"You have already been answered!" said the hermit, still crouching on his thin legs, and looking up at the King, who stood before him.

"How answered? What do you mean?" asked the King.

"Do you not see," replied the hermit. "If you had not pitied my weakness yesterday, and had not dug those beds for me, but had gone your way, that man would have attacked you, and you would have repented of not having stayed with me. So the most important time was when you were digging the beds; and I was the most important man; and to do me good was your most important business. Afterwards when that man ran to us, the most important time was when you were attending to him, for if you had not bound up his wounds he would have died without having made peace with you. So he was the most important man, and what you did for him was your most important business. Remember then: there is only one time that is important. Now! It is the most important time because it is the only time when we have any power. The most necessary man is he with whom you are, for no man knows whether he will ever have dealings with any one else: and the most important affair is, to do him good, because for that purpose alone was man sent into this life!"

What Men Live By

"We know that we have passed out of death into life, because we love the brethren. He that loveth not abideth in death." "Epistle St. John" iii. 14.

"Whoso hath the world's goods, and beholdeth his brother in need, and shutteth up his compassion from him, how doth the love of God abide in him? My little children, let us not love in word, neither with the tongue; but in deed and truth." iii. 17-18.

"Love is of God; and every one that loveth is begotten of God, and knoweth God. He that loveth not knoweth not God; for God is love." iv. 7-8.

"No man hath beheld God at any time; if we love one another, God abideth in us." iv. 12.

"God is love; and he that abideth in love abideth in God, and God abideth in him." iv. 16.

"If a man say, I love God, and hateth his brother, he is a liar; for he that loveth not his brother whom he hath seen, how can he love God whom he hath not seen?" iv. 20.

A shoemaker named Simon, who had neither house nor land of his own, lived with his wife and children in a peasant's hut, and earned his living by his work. Work was cheap, but bread was dear, and what he earned he spent for food. The man and his wife had but one sheepskin coat between them for winter wear, and even that was torn to tatters, and this was the second year he had been wanting to buy sheep-skins for a new coat. Before winter Simon saved up a little money: a three-rouble note lay hidden in his wife's box, and five roubles and twenty kopeks were owed him by customers in the village.

So one morning he prepared to go to the village to buy the sheep- skins. He put on over his shirt his wife's wadded nankeen jacket, and over that he put his own cloth coat. He took the three-rouble note in his pocket, cut himself a stick to serve as a staff, and started off after breakfast. "I'll collect the five roubles that are due to me," thought he, "add the three I have got, and that will be enough to buy sheep-skins for the winter coat."

He came to the village and called at a peasant's hut, but the man was not at home. The peasant's wife promised that the money should be paid next week, but she would not pay it herself. Then Simon called on another peasant, but this one swore he had no money, and would only pay twenty kopeks which he owed for a pair of boots Simon had mended. Simon then tried to buy the sheep-skins on credit, but the dealer would not trust him.

"Bring your money," said he, "then you may have your pick of the skins. We know what debt-collecting is like." So all the business the shoemaker did was to get the twenty kopeks for boots he had mended, and to take a pair of felt boots a peasant gave him to sole with leather.

Simon felt downhearted. He spent the twenty kopeks on vodka, and started homewards without having bought any skins. In the morning he had felt the frost; but now, after drinking the vodka, he felt warm, even without a sheep-skin coat. He trudged along, striking his stick on the frozen earth with one hand, swinging the felt boots with the other, and talking to himself.

I
"I'm quite warm," said he, "though I have no sheep-skin coat. I've had a drop, and it runs through all my veins. I need no sheep- skins. I go along and don't worry about anything. That's the sort of man I am! What do I care? I can live without sheep-skins. I don't need them. My wife will fret, to be sure. And, true enough, it is a shame; one works all day long, and then does not get paid. Stop a bit! If you don't bring that money along, sure enough I'll skin you, blessed if I don't. How's that? He pays twenty kopeks at a time! What can I do with twenty kopeks? Drink it-that's all one can do! Hard up, he says he is! So he may be but what about me? You have a house, and cattle, and everything; I've only what I stand up in! You have corn of your own growing; I have to buy every grain. Do what I will, I must spend three roubles every week for bread alone. I come home and find the bread all used up, and I have to fork out another rouble and a half. So just pay up what you owe, and no nonsense about it!"

By this time he had nearly reached the shrine at the bend of the road. Looking up, he saw something whitish behind the shrine. The daylight was fading, and the shoemaker peered at the thing without being able to make out what it was. "There was no white stone here before. Can it be an ox? It's not like an ox. It has a head like a man, but it's too white; and what could a man be doing there?"

He came closer, so that it was clearly visible. To his surprise it really was a man, alive or dead, sitting naked, leaning motionless against the shrine. Terror seized the shoemaker, and he thought, "Some one has killed him, stripped him, and left him there. If I meddle I shall surely get into trouble."

So the shoemaker went on. He passed in front of the shrine so that he could not see the man. When he had gone some way, he looked back, and saw that the man was no longer leaning against the shrine, but was moving as if looking towards him. The shoemaker felt more frightened than before, and thought, "Shall I go back to him, or shall I go on? If I go near him something dreadful may happen. Who knows who the fellow is? He has not come here for any good. If I go near him he may jump up and throttle me, and there will be no getting away. Or if not, he'd still be a burden on one's hands. What could I do with a naked man? I couldn't give him my last clothes. Heaven only help me to get away!"

So the shoemaker hurried on, leaving the shrine behind him-when suddenly his conscience smote him, and he stopped in the road.

"What are you doing, Simon?" said he to himself. "The man may be dying of want, and you slip past afraid. Have you grown so rich as to be afraid of robbers? Ah, Simon, shame on you!"

So he turned back and went up to the man.

II

Simon approached the stranger, looked at him, and saw that he was a young man, fit, with no bruises on his body, only evidently freezing and frightened, and he sat there leaning back without looking up at Simon, as if too faint to lift his eyes. Simon went close to him, and then the man seemed to wake up. Turning his head, he opened his eyes and looked into Simon's face. That one look was enough to make Simon fond of the man. He threw the felt boots on the ground, undid his sash, laid it on the boots, and took off his cloth coat.

"It's not a time for talking," said he. "Come, put this coat on at once!" And Simon took the man by the elbows and helped him to rise. As he stood there, Simon saw that his body was clean and in good condition, his hands and feet shapely, and his face good and kind. He threw his coat over the man's shoulders, but the latter could not find the sleeves. Simon guided his arms into them, and drawing the coat well on, wrapped it closely about him, tying the sash round the man's waist.

Simon even took off his torn cap to put it on the man's head, but then his own head felt cold, and he thought: "I'm quite bald, while he has long curly hair." So he put his cap on his own head again. "It will be better to give him something for his feet," thought he; and he made the man sit down, and helped him to put on the felt boots, saying, "There, friend, now move about and warm yourself. Other matters can be settled later on. Can you walk?"

The man stood up and looked kindly at Simon, but could not say a word.

"Why don't you speak?" said Simon. "It's too cold to stay here, we must be getting home. There now, take my stick, and if you're feeling weak, lean on that. Now step out!"

The man started walking, and moved easily, not lagging behind.

As they went along, Simon asked him, "And where do you belong to?" "I'm not from these parts."

"I thought as much. I know the folks hereabouts. But, how did you come to be there by the shrine ?"

"I cannot tell."

"Has some one been ill-treating you?"

"No one has ill-treated me. God has punished me."

"Of course God rules all. Still, you'll have to find food and shelter somewhere. Where do you want to go to?"

"It is all the same to me."

Simon was amazed. The man did not look like a rogue, and he spoke gently, but yet he gave no account of himself. Still Simon thought, "Who knows what may have happened?" And he said to the stranger: "Well then, come home with me, and at least warm yourself awhile."

So Simon walked towards his home, and the stranger kept up with him, walking at his side. The wind had risen and Simon felt it cold under his shirt. He was getting over his tipsiness by now, and began to feel the frost. He went along sniffling and wrapping his wife's coat round him, and he thought to himself: "There now, talk about sheep-skins! I went out for sheep-skins and come home without even a coat to my back, and what is more, I'm bringing a naked man along with me. Matryona won't be pleased!" And when he thought of his wife he felt sad; but when he looked at the stranger and remembered how he had looked up at him at the shrine, his heart was glad.

III

Simon's wife had everything ready early that day. She had cut wood, brought water, fed the children, eaten her own meal, and now she sat thinking. She wondered when she ought to make bread: now or tomorrow? There was still a large piece left.

"If Simon has had some dinner in town," thought she, "and does not eat much for supper, the bread will last out another day."

She weighed the piece of bread in her hand again and again, and thought: "I won't make any more today. We have only enough flour left to bake one batch; We can manage to make this last out till Friday."

So Matryona put away the bread, and sat down at the table to patch her husband's shirt. While she worked she thought how her husband was buying skins for a winter coat.

"If only the dealer does not cheat him. My good man is much too simple; he cheats nobody, but any child can take him in. Eight roubles is a lot of money, he should get a good coat at that price. Not tanned skins, but still a proper winter coat. How difficult it was last winter to get on without a warm coat. I could neither get down to the river, nor go out anywhere. When he went out he put on all we had, and there was nothing left for me. He did not start very early today, but still it's time he was back. I only hope he has not gone on the spree!"

Hardly had Matryona thought this, when steps were heard on the threshold, and some one entered. Matryona stuck her needle into her work and went out into the passage. There she saw two men Simon, and with him a man without a hat, and wearing felt boots.

Matryona noticed at once that her husband smelt of spirits. "There now, he has been drinking," thought she. And when she saw that he was coatless, had only her jacket on, brought no parcel, stood there silent, and seemed ashamed, her heart was ready to break with disappointment. "He has drunk the money," thought she, "and has been on the spree with some good-for-nothing fellow whom he has brought home with him."

Matryona let them pass into the hut, followed them in, and saw that the stranger was a young, slight man, wearing her husband's coat. There was no shirt to be seen under it, and he had no hat. Having entered, he stood, neither moving, nor raising his eyes, and Matryona thought: "He must be a bad man, he's afraid."

Matryona frowned, and stood beside the oven looking to see what they would do.

Simon took off his cap and sat down on the bench as if things were all right.

"Come, Matryona; if supper is ready, let us have some."

Matryona muttered something to herself and did not move, but stayed where she was, by the oven. She looked first at the one and then at the other of them, and only shook her head. Simon saw that his wife was annoyed, but tried to pass it off. Pretending not to notice anything, he took the stranger by the arm.

"Sit down, friend," said he, "and let us have some supper."

The stranger sat down on the bench.

"Haven't you cooked anything for us?" said Simon.

Matryona's anger boiled over. "I've cooked, but not for you. It seems to me you have drunk your wits away. You went to buy a sheep- skin coat, but come home without so much as the coat you had on, and bring a naked vagabond home with you. I have no supper for drunkards like you."

"That's enough, Matryona. Don't wag your tongue without reason. You had better ask what sort of man"

"And you tell me what you've done with the money?"

Simon found the pocket of the jacket, drew out the three-rouble note, and unfolded it.

"Here is the money. Trifonof did not pay, but promises to pay soon."

Matryona got still more angry; he had bought no sheep-skins, but had put his only coat on some naked fellow and had even brought him to their house.

She snatched up the note from the table, took it to put away in safety, and said: "I have no supper for you. We can't feed all the naked drunkards in the world."

"There now, Matryona, hold your tongue a bit. First hear what a man has to say-"

"Much wisdom I shall hear from a drunken fool. I was right in not wanting to marry you-a drunkard. The linen my mother gave me you drank; and now you've been to buy a coat-and have drunk it, too!"

Simon tried to explain to his wife that he had only spent twenty kopeks; tried to tell how he had found the man but Matryona would not let him get a word in. She talked nineteen to the dozen, and dragged in things that had happened ten years before.

Matryona talked and talked, and at last she flew at Simon and seized him by the sleeve.

"Give me my jacket. It is the only one I have, and you must needs take it from me and wear it yourself. Give it here, you mangy dog, and may the devil take you."

Simon began to pull off the jacket, and turned a sleeve of it inside out; Matryona seized the jacket and it burst its seams, She snatched it up, threw it over her head and went to the door. She meant to go out, but stopped undecided she wanted to work off her anger, but she also wanted to learn what sort of a man the stranger was.

IV

Matryona stopped and said: "If he were a good man he would not be naked. Why, he hasn't even a shirt on him. If he were all right, you would say where you came across the fellow."

"That's just what I am trying to tell you," said Simon. "As I came to the shrine I saw him sitting all naked and frozen. It isn't quite the weather to sit about naked! God sent me to him, or he would have perished. What was I to do? How do we know what may have happened to him? So I took him, clothed him, and brought him along. Don't be so angry, Matryona. It is a sin. Remember, we all must die one day."

Angry words rose to Matryona's lips, but she looked at the stranger and was silent. He sat on the edge of the bench, motionless, his hands folded on his knees, his head drooping on his breast, his eyes closed, and his brows knit as if in pain. Matryona was silent: and Simon said: "Matryona, have you no love of God?"

Matryona heard these words, and as she looked at the stranger, suddenly her heart softened towards him. She came back from the door, and going to the oven she got out the supper. Setting a cup on the table, she poured out some kvas. Then she brought out the last piece of bread, and set out a knife and spoons.

"Eat, if you want to," said she.

Simon drew the stranger to the table.

"Take your place, young man," said he.

Simon cut the bread, crumbled it into the broth, and they began to eat. Matryona sat at the corner of the table resting her head on her hand and looking at the stranger.

And Matryona was touched with pity for the stranger, and began to feel fond of him. And at once the stranger's face lit up; his brows were no longer bent, he raised his eyes and smiled at Matryona.

When they had finished supper, the woman cleared away the things and began questioning the stranger. "Where are you from?" said she.

"I am not from these parts."

"But how did you come to be on the road?"

"I may not tell."

"Did some one rob you?"

"God punished me."

"And you were lying there naked?"

"Yes, naked and freezing. Simon saw me and had pity on me. He took off his coat, put it on me and brought me here. And you have fed me, given me drink, and shown pity on me. God will reward you!"

Matryona rose, took from the window Simon's old shirt she had been patching, and gave it to the stranger. She also brought out a pair of trousers for him.

"There," said she, "I see you have no shirt. Put this on, and lie down where you please, in the loft or on the oven ."

The stranger took off the coat, put on the shirt, and lay down in the loft. Matryona put out the candle, took the coat, and climbed to where her husband lay.

Matryona drew the skirts of the coat over her and lay down, but could not sleep; she could not get the stranger out of her mind.

When she remembered that he had eaten their last piece of bread and that there was none for tomorrow, and thought of the shirt and trousers she had given away, she felt grieved; but when she remembered how he had smiled, her heart was glad.

Long did Matryona lie awake, and she noticed that Simon also was awake, he drew the coat towards him.

"Simon!"

"Well?"

"You have had the last of the bread, and I have not put any to rise. I don't know what we shall do tomorrow. Perhaps I can borrow some of neighbor Martha."

"If we're alive we shall find something to eat."

The woman lay still awhile, and then said, "He seems a good man, but why does he not tell us who he is?"

"I suppose he has his reasons."

"Simon!"

"Well?"

"We give; but why does nobody give us anything?"

Simon did not know what to say; so he only said, "Let us stop talking," and turned over and went to sleep.

V

In the morning Simon awoke. The children were still asleep; his wife had gone to the neighbor's to borrow some bread. The stranger alone was sitting on the bench, dressed in the old shirt and trousers, and looking upwards. His face was brighter than it had been the day before.

Simon said to him, "Well, friend; the belly wants bread, and the naked body clothes. One has to work for a living What work do you know?"

"I do not know any."

This surprised Simon, but he said, "Men who want to learn can learn anything."

"Men work, and I will work also."

"What is your name?"

"Michael."

"Well, Michael, if you don't wish to talk about yourself, that is your own affair; but you'll have to earn a living for yourself. If you will work as I tell you, I will give you food and shelter."

"May God reward you! I will learn. Show me what to do."

Simon took yarn, put it round his thumb and began to twist it.

"It is easy enough, see!"

Michael watched him, put some yarn round his own thumb in the same way, caught the knack, and twisted the yarn also.

Then Simon showed him how to wax the thread. This also Michael mastered. Next Simon showed him how to twist the bristle in, and how to sew, and this, too, Michael learned at once.

Whatever Simon showed him he understood at once, and after three days he worked as if he had sewn boots all his life. He worked without stopping, and ate little. When work was over he sat silently, looking upwards. He hardly went into the street, spoke only when necessary, and neither joked nor laughed. They never saw him smile, except that first evening when Matryona gave them supper.

VI

Day by day and week by week the year went round. Michael lived and worked with Simon. His fame spread till people said that no one sewed boots so neatly and strongly as Simon's workman, Michael; and from all the district round people came to Simon for their boots, and he began to be well off.

One winter day, as Simon and Michael sat working, a carriage on sledge-runners, with three horses and with bells, drove up to the hut. They looked out of the window; the carriage stopped at their door, a fine servant jumped down from the box and opened the door. A gentleman in a fur coat got out and walked up to Simon's hut. Up jumped Matryona and opened the door wide. The gentleman stooped to enter the hut, and when he drew himself up again his head nearly reached the ceiling, and he seemed quite to fill his end of the room.

Simon rose, bowed, and looked at the gentleman with astonishment. He had never seen any one like him. Simon himself was lean, Michael was thin, and Matryona was dry as a bone, but this man was like some one from another world: red-faced, burly, with a neck like a bull's, and looking altogether as if he were cast in iron.

The gentleman puffed, threw off his fur coat, sat down on the bench, and said, "Which of you is the master bootmaker?"

"I am, your Excellency," said Simon, coming forward.

Then the gentleman shouted to his lad, "Hey, Fedka, bring the leather!"

The servant ran in, bringing a parcel. The gentleman took the parcel and put it on the table.

"Untie it," said he. The lad untied it.

The gentleman pointed to the leather.

"Look here, shoemaker," said he, "do you see this leather?"

"Yes, your honor."

"But do you know what sort of leather it is?"

Simon felt the leather and said, "It is good leather."

"Good, indeed! Why, you fool, you never saw such leather before in your life. It's German, and cost twenty roubles."

Simon was frightened, and said, "Where should I ever see leather like that?"

"Just so! Now, can you make it into boots for me?"

"Yes, your Excellency, I can."

Then the gentleman shouted at him: "You can, can you? Well, remember whom you are to make them for, and what the leather is. You must make me boots that will wear for a year, neither losing shape nor coming unsown. If you can do it, take the leather and cut it up; but if you can't, say so. I warn you now if your boots become unsewn or lose shape within a year, I will have you put in prison. If they don't burst or lose shape for a year I will pay you ten roubles for your work."

Simon was frightened, and did not know what to say. He glanced at Michael and nudging him with his elbow, whispered: "Shall I take the work?"

Michael nodded his head as if to say, "Yes, take it."

Simon did as Michael advised, and undertook to make boots that would not lose shape or split for a whole year.

Calling his servant, the gentleman told him to pull the boot off his left leg, which he stretched out.

"Take my measure!" said he.

Simon stitched a paper measure seventeen inches long, smoothed it out, knelt down, wiped his hand well on his apron so as not to soil the gentleman's sock, and began to measure. He measured the sole, and round the instep, and began to measure the calf of the leg, but the paper was too short. The calf of the leg was as thick as a beam.

"Mind you don't make it too tight in the leg."

Simon stitched on another strip of paper. The gentleman twitched his toes about in his sock, looking round at those in the hut, and as he did so he noticed Michael.

"Whom have you there?" asked he.

"That is my workman. He will sew the boots."

"Mind," said the gentleman to Michael, "remember to make them so that they will last me a year."

Simon also looked at Michael, and saw that Michael was not looking at the gentleman, but was gazing into the corner behind the gentleman, as if he saw some one there. Michael looked and looked, and suddenly he smiled, and his face became brighter.

"What are you grinning at, you fool?" thundered the gentleman. "You had better look to it that the boots are ready in time."

"They shall be ready in good time," said Michael.

"Mind it is so," said the gentleman, and he put on his boots and his fur coat, wrapped the latter round him, and went to the door. But he forgot to stoop, and struck his head against the lintel.

He swore and rubbed his head. Then he took his seat in the carriage and drove away.

When he had gone, Simon said: "There's a figure of a man for you! You could not kill him with a mallet. He almost knocked out the lintel, but little harm it did him."

And Matryona said: "Living as he does, how should he not grow strong? Death itself can't touch such a rock as that."

VII

Then Simon said to Michael: "Well, we have taken the work, but we must see we don't get into trouble over it. The leather is dear, and the gentleman hot-tempered. We must make no mistakes. Come, your eye is truer and your hands have become nimbler than mine, so you take this measure and cut out the boots. I will finish off the sewing of the vamps."

Michael did as he was told. He took the leather, spread it out on the table, folded it in two, took a knife and began to cut out.

Matryona came and watched him cutting, and was surprised to see how he was doing it. Matryona was accustomed to seeing boots made, and she looked and saw that Michael was not cutting the leather for boots, but was cutting it round.

She wished to say something, but she thought to herself: "Perhaps I do not understand how gentleman's boots should be made. I suppose Michael knows more about it and I won't interfere."

When Michael had cut up the leather, he took a thread and began to sew not with two ends, as boots are sewn, but with a single end, as for soft slippers.

Again Matryona wondered, but again she did not interfere. Michael sewed on steadily till noon. Then Simon rose for dinner, looked around, and saw that Michael had made slippers out of the gentleman's leather.

"Ah," groaned Simon, and he thought, "How is it that Michael, who has been with me a whole year and never made a mistake before, should do such a dreadful thing? The gentleman ordered high boots, welted, with whole fronts, and Michael has made soft slippers with single soles, and has wasted the leather. What am I to say to the gentleman? I can never replace leather such as this."

And he said to Michael, "What are you doing, friend? You have ruined me! You know the gentleman ordered high boots, but see what you have made!"

Hardly had he begun to rebuke Michael, when "rat-tat" went the iron ring that hung at the door. Some one was knocking. They looked out of the window; a man had come on horseback, and was fastening his horse. They opened the door, and the servant who had been with the gentleman came in.

"Good day," said he.

Good day," replied Simon. "What can we do for you?"

"My mistress has sent me about the boots."

"What about the boots?"

"Why, my master no longer needs them. He is dead."

"Is it possible?"

"He did not live to get home after leaving you, but died in the carriage. When we reached home and the servants came to help him alight, he rolled over like a sack. He was dead already, and so stiff that he could hardly be got out of the carriage. My mistress sent me here, saying: 'Tell the bootmaker that the gentleman who ordered boots of him and left the leather for them no longer needs the boots, but that he must quickly make soft slippers for the corpse. Wait till they are ready, and bring them back with you.' That is why I have come."

Michael gathered up the remnants of the leather; rolled them up, took the soft slippers he had made, slapped them together, wiped them down with his apron, and handed them and the roll of leather to the servant, who took them and said: "Good-bye, masters, and good day to you!"

VIII

Another year passed, and another, and Michael was now living his sixth year with Simon. He lived as before. He went nowhere, only spoke when necessary, and had only smiled twice in all those years, once when Matryona gave him food, and a second time when the gentleman was in their hut. Simon was more than pleased with his workman. He never now asked him where he came from, and only feared lest Michael should go away.

They were all at home one day. Matryona was putting iron pots in the oven; the children were running along the benches and looking out of the window; Simon was sewing at one window, and Michael was fastening on a heel at the other.

One of the boys ran along the bench to Michael, leant on his shoulder, and looked out of the window.

"Look, Uncle Michael! There is a lady with little girls! She seems to be coming here. And one of the girls is lame."

When the boy said that, Michael dropped his work, turned to the window, and looked out into the street.

Simon was surprised. Michael never used to look out into the street, but now he pressed against the window, staring at something. Simon also looked out, and saw that a well-dressed woman was really coming to his hut, leading by the hand two little girls in fur coats and woolen shawls. The girls could hardly be told one from the other, except that one of them was crippled in her left leg and walked with a limp.

The woman stepped into the porch and entered the passage. Feeling about for the entrance she found the latch, which she lifted, and opened the door. She let the two girls go in first, and followed them into the hut.

"Good day, good folk!"

"Pray come in," said Simon. "What can we do for you?"

The woman sat down by the table. The two little girls pressed close to her knees, afraid of the people in the hut.

"I want leather shoes made for these two little girls for spring."

"We can do that. We never have made such small shoes, but we can make them; either welted or turnover shoes, linen lined. My man, Michael, is a master at the work."

Simon glanced at Michael and saw that he had left his work and was sitting with his eyes fixed on the little girls. Simon was surprised. It was true the girls were pretty, with black eyes, plump, and rosy-cheeked, and they wore nice kerchiefs and fur coats, but still Simon could not understand why Michael should look at them like that, just as if he had known them before. He was puzzled, but went on talking with the woman, and arranging the price. Having fixed it, he prepared the measure. The woman lifted the lame girl on to her lap and said: "Take two measures from this little girl. Make one shoe for the lame foot and three for the sound one. They both have the same size feet. They are twins."

Simon took the measure and, speaking of the lame girl, said: "How did it happen to her? She is such a pretty girl. Was she born so?"

"No, her mother crushed her leg."

Then Matryona joined in. She wondered who this woman was, and whose the children were, so she said: "Are not you their mother then?"

"No, my good woman; I am neither their mother nor any relation to them. They were quite strangers to me, but I adopted them."

"They are not your children and yet you are so fond of them?"

"How can I help being fond of them? I fed them both at my own breasts. I had a child of my own, but God took him. I was not so fond of him as I now am of them."

"Then whose children are they?"

IX

The woman, having begun talking, told them the whole story.

"It is about six years since their parents died, both in one week: their father was buried on the Tuesday, and their mother died on the Friday. These orphans were born three days after their father's death, and their mother did not live another day. My husband and I were then living as peasants in the village. We were neighbors of theirs, our yard being next to theirs. Their father was a lonely man; a wood-cutter in the forest. When felling trees one day, they let one fall on him. It fell across his body and crushed his bowels out. They hardly got him home before his soul went to God; and that same week his wife gave birth to twins, these little girls. She was poor and alone; she had no one, young or old, with her. Alone she gave them birth, and alone she met her death."

"The next morning I went to see her, but when I entered the hut, she, poor thing, was already stark and cold. In dying she had rolled on to this child and crushed her leg. The village folk came to the hut, washed the body, laid her out, made a coffin, and buried her. They were good folk. The babies were left alone. What was to be done with them? I was the only woman there who had a baby at the time. I was nursing my first-born, eight weeks old. So I took them for a time. The peasants came together, and thought and thought what to do with them; and at last they said to me: "For the present, Mary, you had better keep the girls, and later on we will arrange what to do for them." So I nursed the sound one at my breast, but at first I did not feed this crippled one. I did not suppose she would live. But then I thought to myself, why should the poor innocent suffer? I pitied her, and began to feed her. And so I fed my own boy and these two, the three of them, at my own breast. I was young and strong, and had good food, and God gave me so much milk that at times it even overflowed. I used sometimes to feed two at a time, while the third was waiting. When one had enough I nursed the third. And God so ordered it that these grew up, while my own was buried before he was two years old. And I had no more children, though we prospered. Now my husband is working for the corn merchant at the mill. The pay is good, and we are well off. But I have no children of my own, and how lonely I should be without these little girls! How can I help loving them! They are the joy of my life!"

She pressed the lame little girl to her with one hand, while with the other she wiped the tears from her cheeks.

And Matryona sighed, and said: "The proverb is true that says, 'One may live without father or mother, but one cannot live without God.'"

So they talked together, when suddenly the whole hut was lighted up as though by summer lightning from the corner where Michael sat. They all looked towards him and saw him sitting, his hands folded on his knees, gazing upwards and smiling.

X

The woman went away with the girls. Michael rose from the bench, put down his work, and took off his apron. Then, bowing low to Simon and his wife, he said: "Farewell, masters. God has forgiven me. I ask your forgiveness, too, for anything done amiss."

And they saw that a light shone from Michael. And Simon rose, bowed down to Michael, and said: "I see, Michael, that you are no common man, and I can neither keep you nor question you. Only tell me this: how is it that when I found you and brought you home, you were gloomy, and when my wife gave you food you smiled at her and became brighter? Then when the gentleman came to order the boots, you smiled again and became brighter still? And now, when this woman brought the little girls, you smiled a third time, and have become as bright as day? Tell me, Michael, why does your face shine so, and why did you smile those three times?"

And Michael answered: "Light shines from me because I have been punished, but now God has pardoned me. And I smiled three times, because God sent me to learn three truths, and I have learnt them. One I learnt when your wife pitied me, and that is why I smiled the first time. The second I learnt when the rich man ordered the boots, and then I smiled again. And now, when I saw those little girls, I learn the third and last truth, and I smiled the third time."

And Simon said, "Tell me, Michael, what did God punish you for? and what were the three truths? that I, too, may know them."

And Michael answered: "God punished me for disobeying Him. I was an angel in heaven and disobeyed God. God sent me to fetch a woman's soul. I flew to earth, and saw a sick woman lying alone, who had just given birth to twin girls. They moved feebly at their mother's side, but she could not lift them to her breast. When she saw me, she understood that God had sent me for her soul, and she wept and said: 'Angel of God! My husband has just been buried, killed by a falling tree. I have neither sister, nor aunt, nor mother: no one to care for my orphans. Do not take my soul! Let me nurse my babes, feed them, and set them on their feet before I die. Children cannot live without father or mother.' And I hearkened to her. I placed one child at her breast and gave the other into her arms, and returned to the Lord in heaven. I flew to the Lord, and said: 'I could not take the soul of the mother. Her husband was killed by a tree; the woman has twins, and prays that her soul may not be taken. She says: "Let me nurse and feed my children, and set them on their feet. Children cannot live without father or mother." I have not taken her soul.' And God said: 'Go-take the mother's soul, and learn three truths: Learn What dwells in man, What is not given to man, and What men live by. When thou has learnt these things, thou shalt return to heaven.' So I flew again to earth and took the mother's soul. The babes dropped from her breasts. Her body rolled over on the bed and crushed one babe, twisting its leg. I rose above the village, wishing to take her soul to God; but a wind seized me, and my wings drooped and dropped off. Her soul rose alone to God, while I fell to earth by the roadside."

XI

And Simon and Matryona understood who it was that had lived with them, and whom they had clothed and fed. And they wept with awe and with joy. And the angel said: "I was alone in the field, naked. I had never known human needs, cold and hunger, till I became a man. I was famished, frozen, and did not know what to do. I saw, near the field I was in, a shrine built for God, and I went to it hoping to find shelter. But the shrine was locked, and I could not enter. So I sat down behind the shrine to shelter myself at least from the wind. Evening drew on. I was hungry, frozen, and in pain. Suddenly I heard a man coming along the road. He carried a pair of boots, and was talking to himself. For the first time since I became a man I saw the mortal face of a man, and his face seemed terrible to me and I turned from it. And I heard the man talking to himself of how to cover his body from the cold in winter, and how to feed wife and children. And I thought: "I am perishing of cold and hunger, and here is a man thinking only of how to clothe himself and his wife, and how to get bread for themselves. He cannot help me. When the man saw me he frowned and became still more terrible, and passed me by on the other side. I despaired; but suddenly I heard him coming back. I looked up, and did not recognize the same man; before, I had seen death in his face; but now he was alive, and I recognized in him the presence of God. He came up to me, clothed me, took me with him, and brought me to his home. I entered the house; a woman came to meet us and began to speak. The woman was still more terrible than the man had been; the spirit of death came from her mouth; I could not breathe for the stench of death that spread around her. She wished to drive me out into the cold, and I knew that if she did so she would die. Suddenly her husband spoke to her of God, and the woman changed at once. And when she brought me food and looked at me, I glanced at her and saw that death no longer dwelt in her; she had become alive, and in her, too, I saw God.

"Then I remembered the first lesson God had set me: 'Learn what dwells in man.' And I understood that in man dwells Love! I was glad that God had already begun to show me what He had promised, and I smiled for the first time. But I had not yet learnt all. I did not yet know What is not given to man, and What men live by.

"I lived with you, and a year passed. A man came to order boots that should wear for a year without losing shape or cracking. I looked at him, and suddenly, behind his shoulder, I saw my comrade, the angel of death. None but me saw that angel; but I knew him, and knew that before the sun set he would take that rich man's soul. And I thought to myself, 'The man is making preparations for a year, and does not know that he will die before evening.' And I remembered God's second saying, 'Learn what is not given to man.'

"What dwells in man I already knew. Now I learnt what is not given him. It is not given to man to know his own needs. And I smiled for the second time. I was glad to have seen my comrade angel, glad also that God had revealed to me the second saying.

"But I still did not know all. I did not know What men live by. And I lived on, waiting till God should reveal to me the last lesson. In the sixth year came the girl-twins with the woman; and I recognized the girls, and heard how they had been kept alive. Having heard the story, I thought, 'Their mother besought me for the children's sake, and I believed her when she said that children cannot live without father or mother; but a stranger has nursed them, and has brought them up.' And when the woman showed her love for the children that were not her own, and wept over them, I saw in her the living God and understood What men live by. And I knew that God had revealed to me the last lesson, and had forgiven my sin. And then I smiled for the third time."

XII

And the angel's body was bared, and he was clothed in light so that eye could not look on him; and his voice grew louder, as though it came not from him but from heaven above. And the angel said:

"I have learnt that all men live not by care for themselves but by love.

"It was not given to the mother to know what her children needed for their life. Nor was it given to the rich man to know what he himself needed. Nor is it given to any man to know whether, when evening comes, he will need boots for his body or slippers for his corpse.

"I remained alive when I was a man, not by care of myself, but because love was present in a passer-by, and because he and his wife pitied and loved me. The orphans remained alive not because of their mother's care, but because there was love in the heart of a woman, a stranger to them, who pitied and loved them. And all men live not by the thought they spend on their own welfare, but because love exists in man.

"I knew before that God gave life to men and desires that they should live; now I understood more than that.

"I understood that God does not wish men to live apart, and therefore he does not reveal to them what each one needs for himself; but he wishes them to live united, and therefore reveals to each of them what is necessary for all.

"I have now understood that though it seems to men that they live by care for themselves, in truth it is love alone by which they live. He who has love, is in God, and God is in him, for God is love."

And the angel sang praise to God, so that the hut trembled at his voice. The roof opened, and a column of fire rose from earth to heaven. Simon and his wife and children fell to the ground. Wings appeared upon the angel's shoulders, and he rose into the heavens.

And when Simon came to himself the hut stood as before, and there was no one in it but his own family.

The Young Tsar

The young Tsar had just ascended the throne. For five weeks he had worked without ceasing, in the way that Tsars are accustomed to work. He had been attending to reports, signing papers, receiving ambassadors and high officials who came to be presented to him, and reviewing troops. He was tired, and as a traveller exhausted by heat and thirst longs for a draught of water and for rest, so he longed for a respite of just one day at least from receptions, from speeches, from parades, a few free hours to spend like an ordinary human being with his young, clever, and beautiful wife, to whom he had been married only a month before.

It was Christmas Eve. The young Tsar had arranged to have a complete rest that evening. The night before he had worked till very late at documents which his ministers of state had left for him to examine. In the morning he was present at the Te Deum, and then at a military service. In the afternoon he received official visitors; and later he had been obliged to listen to the reports of three ministers of state, and had given his assent to many important matters. In his conference with the Minister of Finance he had agreed to an increase of duties on imported goods, which should in the future add many millions to the State revenues. Then he sanctioned the sale of brandy by the Crown in various parts of the country, and signed a decree permitting the sale of alcohol in villages having markets. This was also calculated to increase the principal revenue to the State, which was derived from the sale of spirits. He had also approved of the issuing of a new gold loan required for a financial negotiation. The Minister of justice having reported on the complicated case of the succession of the Baron Snyders, the young Tsar confirmed the decision by his signature; and also approved the new rules relating to the application of Article 1830 of the penal code, providing for the punishment of tramps. In his conference with the Minister of the Interior he ratified the order concerning the collection of taxes in arrears, signed the order settling what measures should be taken in regard to the persecution of religious dissenters, and also one providing for the continuance of martial law in those provinces where it had already been established. With the Minister of War he arranged for the nomination of a new Corps Commander for the raising of recruits, and for punishment of breach of discipline. These things kept him occupied till dinner-time, and even then his freedom was not complete. A number of high officials had been invited to dinner, and he was obliged to talk to them: not in the way he felt disposed to do, but according to what he was expected to say. At last the tiresome dinner was over, and the guests departed.

The young Tsar heaved a sigh of relief, stretched himself and retired to his apartments to take off his uniform with the decorations on it, and to don the jacket he used to wear before his accession to the throne. His young wife had also retired to take off her dinner-dress, remarking that she would join him presently.

When he had passed the row of footmen who were standing erect before him, and reached his room; when he had thrown off his heavy uniform and put on his jacket, the young Tsar felt glad to be free from work; and his heart was filled with a tender emotion which sprang from the consciousness of his freedom, of his joyous, robust young life, and of his love. He threw himself on the sofa, stretched out his legs upon it, leaned his head on his hand, fixed his gaze on the dull glass shade of the lamp, and then a sensation which he had not experienced since his childhood, the pleasure of going to sleep, and a drowsiness that was irresistible, suddenly came over him.

"My wife will be here presently and will find me asleep. No, I must not go to sleep," he thought. He let his elbow drop down, laid his cheek in the palm of his hand, made himself comfortable, and was so utterly happy that he only felt a desire not to be aroused from this delightful state.

And then what happens to all of us every day happened to him, he fell asleep without knowing himself when or how. He passed from one state into another without his will having any share in it, without even desiring it, and without regretting the state out of which he had passed. He fell into a heavy sleep which was like death. How long he had slept he did not know, but he was suddenly aroused by the soft touch of a hand upon his shoulder.

"It is my darling, it is she," he thought. "What a shame to have dozed off!"

But it was not she. Before his eyes, which were wide open and blinking at the light, she, that charming and beautiful creature whom he was expecting, did not stand, but HE stood. Who HE was the young Tsar did not know, but somehow it did not strike him that he was a stranger whom he had never seen before. It seemed as if he had known him for a long time and was fond of him, and as if he trusted him as he would trust himself. He had expected his beloved wife, but in her stead that man whom he had never seen before had come. Yet to the young Tsar, who was far from feeling regret or astonishment, it seemed not only a most natural, but also a necessary thing to happen.

"Come!" said the stranger.

"Yes, let us go," said the young Tsar, not knowing where he was to go, but quite aware that he could not help submitting to the command of the stranger. "But how shall we go?" he asked.

"In this way."

The stranger laid his hand on the Tsar's head, and the Tsar for a moment lost consciousness. He could not tell whether he had been unconscious a long or a short time, but when he recovered his senses he found himself in a strange place. The first thing he was aware of was a strong and stifling smell of sewage. The place in which he stood was a broad passage lit by the red glow of two dim lamps. Running along one side of the passage was a thick wall with windows protected by iron gratings. On the other side were doors secured with locks. In the passage stood a soldier, leaning up against the wall, asleep. Through the doors the young Tsar heard the muffled sound of living human beings: not of one alone, but of many. HE was standing at the side of the young Tsar, and pressing his shoulder slightly with his soft hand, pushed him to the first door, unmindful of the sentry. The young Tsar felt he could not do otherwise than yield, and approached the door. To his amazement the sentry looked straight at him, evidently without seeing him, as he neither straightened himself up nor saluted, but yawned loudly and, lifting his hand, scratched the back of his neck. The door had a small hole, and in obedience to the pressure of the hand that pushed him, the young Tsar approached a step nearer and put his eye to the small opening. Close to the door, the foul smell that stifled him was stronger, and the young Tsar hesitated to go nearer, but the hand pushed him on. He leaned forward, put his eye close to the opening, and suddenly ceased to perceive the odour. The sight he saw deadened his sense of smell. In a large room, about ten yards long and six yards wide, there walked unceasingly from one end to the other, six men in long grey coats, some in felt boots, some barefoot. There were over twenty men in all in the room, but in that first moment the young Tsar only saw those who were walking with quick, even, silent steps. It was a horrid sight to watch the continual, quick, aimless movements of the men who passed and overtook each other, turning sharply when they reached the wall, never looking at one another, and evidently concentrated each on his own thoughts. The young Tsar had observed a similar sight one day when he was watching a tiger in a menagerie pacing rapidly with noiseless tread from one end of his cage to the other, waving its tail, silently turning when it reached the bars, and looking at nobody. Of these men one, apparently a young peasant, with curly hair, would have been handsome were it not for the unnatural pallor of his face, and the concentrated, wicked, scarcely human, look in his eyes. Another was a Jew, hairy and gloomy. The third was a lean old man, bald, with a beard that had been shaven and had since grown like bristles. The fourth was extraordinarily heavily built, with well-developed muscles, a low receding forehead and a flat nose. The fifth was hardly more than a boy, long, thin, obviously consumptive. The sixth was small and dark, with nervous, convulsive movements. He walked as if he were skipping, and muttered continuously to himself. They were all walking rapidly backwards and forwards past the hole through which the young Tsar was looking. He watched their faces and their gait with keen interest. Having examined them closely, he presently became aware of a number of other men at the back of the room, standing round, or lying on the shelf that served as a bed. Standing close to the door he also saw the pail which caused such an unbearable stench. On the shelf about ten men, entirely covered with their cloaks, were sleeping. A red-haired man with a huge beard was sitting sideways on the shelf, with his shirt off. He was examining it, lifting it up to the light, and evidently catching the vermin on it. Another man, aged and white as snow, stood with his profile turned towards the door. He was praying, crossing himself, and bowing low, apparently so absorbed in his devotions as to be oblivious of all around him.

"I see, this is a prison," thought the young Tsar. "They certainly deserve pity. It is a dreadful life. But it cannot be helped. It is their own fault."

But this thought had hardly come into his head before HE, who was his guide, replied to it.

"They are all here under lock and key by your order. They have all been sentenced in your name. But far from meriting their present condition which is due to your human judgment, the greater part of them are far better than you or those who were their judges and who keep them here. This one" he pointed to the handsome, curly-headed fellow "is a murderer. I do not consider him more guilty than those who kill in war or in duelling, and are rewarded for their deeds. He had neither education nor moral guidance, and his life had been cast among thieves and drunkards. This lessens his guilt, but he has done wrong, nevertheless, in being a murderer. He killed a merchant, to rob him. The other man, the Jew, is a thief, one of a gang of thieves. That uncommonly strong fellow is a horse-stealer, and guilty also, but compared with others not as culpable. Look!" and suddenly the young Tsar found himself in an open field on a vast frontier. On the right were potato fields; the plants had been rooted out, and were lying in heaps, blackened by the frost; in alternate streaks were rows of winter corn. In the distance a little village with its tiled roofs was visible; on the left were fields of winter corn, and fields of stubble. No one was to be seen on any side, save a black human figure in front at the border-line, a gun slung on his back, and at his feet a dog. On the spot where the young Tsar stood, sitting beside him, almost at his feet, was a young Russian soldier with a green band on his cap, and with his rifle slung over his shoulders, who was rolling up a paper to make a cigarette. The soldier was obviously unaware of the presence of the young Tsar and his companion, and had not heard them. He did now turn round when the Tsar, who was standing directly over the soldier, asked, "Where are we?" "On the Prussian frontier," his guide answered. Suddenly, far away in front of them, a shot was fired. The soldier jumped to his feet, and seeing two men running, bent low to the ground, hastily put his tobacco into his pocket, and ran after one of them. "Stop, or I'll shoot!" cried the soldier. The fugitive, without stopping, turned his head and called out something evidently abusive or blasphemous.

"Damn you!" shouted the soldier, who put one foot a little forward and stopped, after which, bending his head over his rifle, and raising his right hand, he rapidly adjusted something, took aim, and, pointing the gun in the direction of the fugitive, probably fired, although no sound was heard. "Smokeless powder, no doubt," thought the young Tsar, and looking after the fleeing man saw him take a few hurried steps, and bending lower and lower, fall to the ground and crawl on his hands and knees. At last he remained lying and did not move. The other fugitive, who was ahead of him, turned round and ran back to the man who was lying on the ground. He did something for him and then resumed his flight.

"What does all this mean?" asked the Tsar.

"These are the guards on the frontier, enforcing the revenue laws. That man was killed to protect the revenues of the State."

"Has he actually been killed?"

The guide again laid his hand upon the head of the young Tsar, and again the Tsar lost consciousness. When he had recovered his senses he found himself in a small room, the customs office. The dead body of a man, with a thin grizzled beard, an aquiline nose, and big eyes with the eyelids closed, was lying on the floor. His arms were thrown asunder, his feet bare, and his thick, dirty toes were turned up at right angles and stuck out straight. He had a wound in his side, and on his ragged cloth jacket, as well as on his blue shirt, were stains of clotted blood, which had turned black save for a few red spots here and there. A woman stood close to the wall, so wrapped up in shawls that her face could scarcely be seen. Motionless she gazed at the aquiline nose, the upturned feet, and the protruding eyeballs; sobbing and sighing, and drying her tears at long, regular intervals. A pretty girl of thirteen was standing at her mother's side, with her eyes and mouth wide open. A boy of eight clung to his mother's skirt, and looked intensely at his dead father without blinking.

From a door near them an official, an officer, a doctor, and a clerk with documents, entered. After them came a soldier, the one who had shot the man. He stepped briskly along behind his superiors, but the instant he saw the corpse he went suddenly pale, and quivered; and dropping his head stood still. When the official asked him whether that was the man who was escaping across the frontier, and at whom he had fired, he was unable to answer. His lips trembled, and his face twitched. "The s-s-s-" he began, but could not get out the words which he wanted to say. "The same, your excellency." The officials looked at each other and wrote something down.

"You see the beneficial results of that same system!"

In a room of sumptuous vulgarity two men sat drinking wine. One of them was old and grey, the other a young Jew. The young Jew was holding a roll of bank-notes in his hand, and was bargaining with the old man. He was buying smuggled goods.

"You've got 'em cheap," he said, smiling.

"Yes, but the risk"

"This is indeed terrible," said the young Tsar; but it cannot be avoided. Such proceedings are necessary."

His companion made no response, saying merely, "Let us move on," and laid his hand again on the head of the Tsar. When the Tsar recovered consciousness, he was standing in a small room lit by a shaded lamp. A woman was sitting at the table sewing. A boy of eight was bending over the table, drawing, with his feet doubled up under him in the armchair. A student was reading aloud. The father and daughter of the family entered the room noisily.

"You signed the order concerning the sale of spirits," said the guide to the Tsar.

"Well?" said the woman.

"He's not likely to live."

"What's the matter with him?"

"They've kept him drunk all the time."

"It's not possible!" exclaimed the wife.

"It's true. And the boy's only nine years old, that Vania Moroshkine."

"What did you do to try to save him?" asked the wife.

"I tried everything that could be done. I gave him an emetic and put a mustard-plaster on him. He has every symptom of delirium tremens."

"It's no wonder, the whole family are drunkards. Annisia is only a little better than the rest, and even she is generally more or less drunk," said the daughter.

"And what about your temperance society?" the student asked his sister.

"What can we do when they are given every opportunity of drinking? Father tried to have the public-house shut up, but the law is against him. And, besides, when I was trying to convince Vasily Ermiline that it was disgraceful to keep a public-house and ruin the people with drink, he answered very haughtily, and indeed got the better of me before the crowd: 'But I have a license with the Imperial eagle on it. If there was anything wrong in my business, the Tsar wouldn't have issued a decree authorising it.' Isn't it terrible? The whole village has been drunk for the last three days. And as for feast-days, it is simply horrible to think of! It has been proved conclusively that alcohol does no good in any case, but invariably does harm, and it has been demonstrated to be an absolute poison. Then, ninety-nine per cent. of the crimes in the world are committed through its influence. We all know how the standard of morality and the general welfare improved at once in all the countries where drinking has been suppressed, like Sweden and Finland, and we know that it can be suppressed by exercising a moral influence over the masses. But in our country the class which could exert that influence, the Government, the Tsar and his officials, simply encourage drink. Their main revenues are drawn from the continual drunkenness of the people. They drink themselves, they are always drinking the health of somebody: 'Gentlemen, the Regiment!' The preachers drink, the bishops drink"

Again the guide touched the head of the young Tsar, who again lost consciousness. This time he found himself in a peasant's cottage. The peasant, a man of forty, with red face and blood-shot eyes, was furiously striking the face of an old man, who tried in vain to protect himself from the blows. The younger peasant seized the beard of the old man and held it fast.

"For shame! To strike your father!"

"I don't care, I'll kill him! Let them send me to Siberia, I don't care!"

The women were screaming. Drunken officials rushed into the cottage and separated father and son. The father had an arm broken and the son's beard was torn out. In the doorway a drunken girl was making violent love to an old besotted peasant.

"They are beasts!" said the young Tsar.

Another touch of his guide's hand and the young Tsar awoke in a new place. It was the office of the justice of the peace. A fat, bald-headed man, with a double chin and a chain round his neck, had just risen from his seat, and was reading the sentence in a loud voice, while a crowd of peasants stood behind the grating. There was a woman in rags in the crowd who did not rise. The guard gave her a push.

"Asleep! I tell you to stand up!" The woman rose.

"According to the decree of his Imperial Majesty" the judge began reading the sentence. The case concerned that very woman. She had taken away half a bundle of oats as she was passing the thrashing-floor of a landowner. The justice of the peace sentenced her to two months' imprisonment. The landowner whose oats had been stolen was among the audience. When the judge adjourned the court the landowner approached, and shook hands, and the judge entered into conversation with him. The next case was about a stolen samovar. Then there was a trial about some timber which had been cut, to the detriment of the landowner. Some peasants were being tried for having assaulted the constable of the district.

When the young Tsar again lost consciousness, he awoke to find himself in the middle of a village, where he saw hungry, half-frozen children and the wife of the man who had assaulted the constable broken down from overwork.

Then came a new scene. In Siberia, a tramp is being flogged with the lash, the direct result of an order issued by the Minister of justice. Again oblivion, and another scene. The family of a Jewish watchmaker is evicted for being too poor. The children are crying, and the Jew, Isaaks, is greatly distressed. At last they come to an arrangement, and he is allowed to stay on in the lodgings.

The chief of police takes a bribe. The governor of the province also secretly accepts a bribe. Taxes are being collected. In the village, while a cow is sold for payment, the police inspector is bribed by a factory owner, who thus escapes taxes altogether. And again a village court scene, and a sentence carried into execution - the lash!

"Ilia Vasilievich, could you not spare me that?"

"No."

The peasant burst into tears. "Well, of course, Christ suffered, and He bids us suffer too."

Then other scenes. The Stundists, a sect, being broken up and dispersed; the clergy refusing first to marry, then to bury a Protestant. Orders given concerning the passage of the Imperial railway train. Soldiers kept sitting in the mud, cold, hungry, and cursing. Decrees issued relating to the educational institutions of the Empress Mary Department. Corruption rampant in the foundling homes. An undeserved monument. Thieving among the clergy. The reinforcement of the political police. A woman being searched. A prison for convicts who are sentenced to be deported. A man being hanged for murdering a shop assistant.

Then the result of military discipline: soldiers wearing uniform and scoffing at it. A gipsy encampment. The son of a millionaire exempted from military duty, while the only support of a large family is forced to serve. The university: a teacher relieved of military service, while the most gifted musicians are compelled to perform it. Soldiers and their debauchery and the spreading of disease.

Then a soldier who has made an attempt to desert. He is being tried. Another is on trial for striking an officer who has insulted his mother. He is put to death. Others, again, are tried for having refused to shoot. The runaway soldier sent to a disciplinary battalion and flogged to death. Another, who is guiltless, flogged, and his wounds sprinkled with salt till he dies. One of the superior officers stealing money belonging to the soldiers. Nothing but drunkenness, debauchery, gambling, and arrogance on the part of the authorities.

What is the general condition of the people: the children are half-starving and degenerate; the houses are full of vermin; an everlasting dull round of labour, of submission, and of sadness. On the other hand: ministers, governors of provinces, covetous, ambitious, full of vanity, and anxious to inspire fear.

"But where are men with human feelings?"

"I will show you where they are."

Here is the cell of a woman in solitary confinement at Schlusselburg. She is going mad. Here is another woman, a girl, indisposed, violated by soldiers. A man in exile, alone, embittered, half-dead. A prison for convicts condemned to hard labour, and women flogged. They are many.

Tens of thousands of the best people. Some shut up in prisons, others ruined by false education, by the vain desire to bring them up as we wish. But not succeeding in this, whatever might have been is ruined as well, for it is made impossible. It is as if we were trying to make buckwheat out of corn sprouts by splitting the ears. One may spoil the corn, but one could never change it to buckwheat. Thus all the youth of the world, the entire younger generation, is being ruined.

But woe to those who destroy one of these little ones, woe to you if you destroy even one of them. On your soul, however, are hosts of them, who have been ruined in your name, all of those over whom your power extends.

"But what can I do?" exclaimed the Tsar in despair. "I do not wish to torture, to flog, to corrupt, to kill any one! I only want the welfare of all. Just as I yearn for happiness myself, so I want the world to be happy as well. Am I actually responsible for everything that is done in my name? What can I do? What am I to do to rid myself of such a responsibility? What can I do? I do not admit that the responsibility for all this is mine. If I felt myself responsible for one-hundredth part of it, I would shoot myself on the spot. It would not be possible to live if that were true. But how can I put an end, to all this evil? It is bound up with the very existence of the State. I am the head of the State! What am I to do? Kill myself? Or abdicate? But that would mean renouncing my duty. O God, O God, God, help me!" He burst into tears and awoke.

"How glad I am that it was only a dream," was his first thought. But when he began to recollect what he had seen in his dream, and to compare it with actuality, he realised that the problem propounded to him in dream remained just as important and as insoluble now that he was awake. For the first time the young Tsar became aware of the heavy responsibility weighing on him, and was aghast. His thoughts no longer turned to the young Queen and to the happiness he had anticipated for that evening, but became centred on the unanswerable question which hung over him: "What was to be done?"

In a state of great agitation he arose and went into the next room. An old courtier, a co-worker and friend of his father's, was standing there in the middle of the room in conversation with the young Queen, who was on her way to join her husband. The young Tsar approached them, and addressing his conversation principally to the old courtier, told him what he had seen in his dream and what doubts the dream had left in his mind.

"That is a noble idea. It proves the rare nobility of your spirit," said the old man. "But forgive me for speaking frankly, you are too kind to be an emperor, and you exaggerate your responsibility. In the first place, the state of things is not as you imagine it to be. The people are not poor. They are well-to-do. Those who are poor are poor through their own fault. Only the guilty are punished, and if an unavoidable mistake does sometimes occur, it is like a thunderbolt, an accident, or the will of God. You have but one responsibility: to fulfil your task courageously and to retain the power that is given to you. You wish the best for your people and God sees that. As for the errors which you have committed unwittingly, you can pray for forgiveness, and God will guide you and pardon you. All the more because you have done nothing that demands forgiveness, and there never have been and never will be men possessed of such extraordinary qualities as you and your father. Therefore all we implore you to do is to live, and to reward our endless devotion and love with your favour, and every one, save scoundrels who deserve no happiness, will be happy."

"What do you think about that?" the young Tsar asked his wife.

"I have a different opinion," said the clever young woman, who had been brought up in a free country. "I am glad you had that dream, and I agree with you that there are grave responsibilities resting upon you. I have often thought about it with great anxiety, and I think there is a simple means of casting off a part of the responsibility you are unable to bear, if not all of it. A large proportion of the power which is too heavy for you, you should delegate to the people, to its representatives, reserving for yourself only the supreme control, that is, the general direction of the affairs of State."

The Queen had hardly ceased to expound her views, when the old courtier began eagerly to refute her arguments, and they started a polite but very heated discussion.

For a time the young Tsar followed their arguments, but presently he ceased to be aware of what they said, listening only to the voice of him who had been his guide in the dream, and who was now speaking audibly in his heart.

"You are not only the Tsar," said the voice. "but more. You are a human being, who only yesterday came into this world, and will perchance to-morrow depart out of it. Apart from your duties as a Tsar, of which that old man is now speaking, you have more immediate duties not by any means to be disregarded; human duties, not the duties of a Tsar towards his subjects, which are only accidental, but an eternal duty, the duty of a man in his relation to God, the duty toward your own soul, which is to save it, and also, to serve God in establishing his kingdom on earth. You are not to be guarded in your actions either by what has been or what will be, but only by what it is your own duty to do.

He opened his eyes, his wife was awakening him. Which of the three courses the young Tsar chose, will be told in fifty years.

Leo Tolstoy (1828-1910) – A Short Biography

Along with Feodor Dostoyevsky, Ivan Turgenev and Vladimir Nabokov, Leo Tolstoy is one of the most important pillars of Russian literature. He is mainly remembered for what is considered by many readers and critics as the greatest novel of all times, *War and Peace*. He is also the author of other successful novels such as *Anna Karenina* and *The Death of Ivan Ilyich*. His texts display his unique narratorial style and the strength of his descriptive techniques.

Tolstoy was born in 1828 in the Russian province of Tula to a noble family with considerable wealth. His Tula family estate, named Yasnaya Polyana, was transformed into The Tolstoy National Museum after his death. He was a brother to four other boys in the family. Their mother soon died to be followed by their father just a few years later and the children were confined to members of their father's family near the city of Kazan. As a young child, Tolstoy had home tutorials by private tutors who introduced him to the basics of reading and writing. He was not any brilliant, though. He rather showed early disinterest in formal education. When he was sent to the University of Kazan in 1843 to study oriental languages and then law, his lack of seriousness made him leave the university before receiving any degree. By that time, Tolstoy decided to go back home and manage his family's farm.

As a farmer, Tolstoy was very enthusiastic in his work. He treated his serfs as friends and even started teaching them before he built schools for them at a later stage. However, despite his great enthusiasm and vivacity, Tolstoy was not serious in farming either. He was a regular absentee. In fact, he was so fond of partying and socializing, a habit that suited his literary evasions more than it suited the labors of a true farmer. He started writing a diary during his farming years when one of his older brothers suggested that he joins him in the army. In the 1850s, Tolstoy had to take part in the Crimean War between Russia and an alliance of France, Britain and Ottoman Turkey. During his free time, he used to carry on with his diary. He eventually finished his first autobiographical book that he entitled *Childhood*. The publication of the latter in 1852 was an immediate success and was encouraged by publishers. It was then followed by a second part and a third part respectively entitled *Boyhood* (1854) and *Youth* (1857).

Apart from this autobiographical trilogy, Tolstoy also wrote about his experience in the army and the horrors and futility of wars. This was in *The Cossacks* that he finished later and published in 1862 and also in another trilogy entitled *Sevastopol Tales*. On Tolstoy's return home after the end of the Crimean war, he realized that he had already made himself a name that even the Tsar himself had heard about and appreciated. Yet, Tolstoy stubbornly refused to settle in Petersburg and join the Russian literary élite of the time. He rather chose to travel around Europe, visiting London and Paris and meeting with figures like Victor Hugo and Charles Darwin. He is even said to have attended some of the latter's historical lectures. Tolstoy's instability soon pushed him to return to Russia, though.

It was in the 1860s that Tolstoy started working on his masterpiece, *War and Peace*. An important part of it was first published in the famous periodical *The Russian Messenger* before it was finished in 1869. *War and Peace*, which was equally an immediate and everlasting success, was characterized by a large cast of characters representing real people that Tolstoy had actually met. Written in a rather epic style, the novel mainly described the horrors of war in concrete details from somebody who had a first-hand experience with killing and bloodshed. Though the story as well as the characters were fictional, the narrative developed in a very realistic way by recounting events from the Napoleonic Wars that took place in the very beginning of the 19th century. The novel was not only a seminal war fiction that would influence many a writer of the nineteenth and twentieth centuries, it also contained philosophical contemplation of universal issues related to the meaning and use of human conflicts.

After the phenomenal success of *War and Peace*, Tolstoy started working on his second most popular novel, *Anna Karenina*. A realistic novel too, the latter was first published in a series of installments in *The Russian Messenger* (1873-1877). The eponymous protagonist was a married woman belonging to aristocracy who had an affair with another man than her husband. The novel was hailed as a refined work of fiction by such important literary men as Nabokov, Dostoevsky and William Faulkner.

Such a huge success of his novels quickly made of Tolstoy a very rich man. His great wealth helped him realize many of his own dreams as well as the dreams of his young wife and his many children. However, money also became a source of trouble in his household. After the publication of *Anna Karenina*, Tolstoy was very concerned about his existential quest, trying to find a meaning and an objective for his life, something that he did not find in the Russian Orthodox Church. In a number of publications that followed, he explained his own personalized vision of the Christian faith. These works were "Confession" (1879), *The Mediator* (1883), *What I Believe* (1885) and "The Kingdom of God is Within You" (1894). Tolstoy's revolutionary views about faith and existence soon became popular and had followers not only in Russia, but also in other parts of the world. This influence made Russian authorities keep him under surveillance, mainly because he was critical of Russia's war policies as well as of the Orthodox Church and of the Tsar's religious role. Indeed, Tolstoy was among the advocates of the separation between Church and State.

One of the most remarkable characteristics of Tolstoy's reformed faith, if so to call it, was austerity and charity. He led a life of asceticism and vegetarianism and put his socialist ideals into practice by establishing numerous schools for the poor and funding public meals. He also believed that he had to give most of his fortunes away, which was strongly objected by his young wife. Generally, the latter did not appreciate her husband's new ideals and lifestyle, which caused serious misunderstandings between the couple towards Tolstoy's twilight years. By the end, the couple grudgingly came to an agreement according to which part of the wealth went to the wife.

Due to the effect of his war experiences, Tolstoy was also among the pioneers of the non-violent resistance of injustice. He strongly believed in pacifist actions and strategies of struggle. This made him become a source of inspiration for numerous political leaders, including his contemporary Mohandas Gandhi and later Martin Luther King, Jr.

Most of Tolstoy's later novels bore the influence of his rather new life of a mystic. He held convictions on the universality of faith, believing that "God is love." He realized the resemblances between different world religious traditions and mysticisms, including Christianity's various denominations, Buddhism, Judaism, Islam and Hinduism. For him, a common feature united all human faiths which was based on universal divine love. In 1886, Tolstoy published another bestselling title, *The Death of Ivan Ilyich*, which also represented a philosophical journey into questions about life, death and faith. *Father Sergius*, another novel that equally delves into questions of belief, was published in 1898. It was followed by *Resurrection* in 1989 and by *The Living Corpse* in 1890.

The year 1901 witnessed Tolstoy's excommunication from the Church and also his deselection from the Nobel Prize for Literature for uncertain reasons while he was incontestably the most qualified. Despite his extraordinary fame and worldwide success, Tolstoy's twilight years were marked by numerous problems. He had serious problems with his wife who disapproved of his religious transformation. He was tightly controlled by Russian authorities which feared his growing influence. He was also pursued by journalists and fans who did not allow him to enjoy a peaceful and intimate life. In addition to all this, Tolstoy started to suffer from old age and serious health problems. In October 1910, Tolstoy decided to go on a pilgrimage, being accompanied by his daughter Aleksandra. Upon taking the train, the 82-year-old man did not stand the hardships of the trip and soon caught pneumonia. He resorted to the stationmaster's home in Astapovo which was not very far from Tolstoy's home itself. On November 9th, 1910, Leo Tolstoy passed away to be buried in his old estate Yasnaya Polyana.